Sunday Morning

JEWEL E. ANN

USA Today & Wall Street Journal
BESTSELLING AUTHOR

SUNDAY MORNING

SUNDAY MORNING SERIES

JEWEL E. ANN

Cover Design: Boja99designs

Photo: © Jaime Burrow Photography

Formatting: Jenn Beach

For all the girls who giggle in church, learn about sex from music, and fall for the bad boy

Chapter One

Terri Gibbs, "Somebody's Knockin'"

1985

IT WAS Easter morning when the devil sat in the back pew of my dad's church. I stood front and center in the choir, singing the last line of "Great is Thy Faithfulness." I barely recognized him until his gaze locked with mine, and he smirked.

Did he recognize me? I couldn't imagine.

Isaac Cory enlisted in the service six years earlier because his dad threatened to shoot him after a minor scuffle with police that arose from impregnating the football coach's daughter and driving her two hours north of Devil's Head, Missouri, to a Planned Parenthood.

Danielle Harvey got around. I was twelve then, but I remember overhearing Dad tell my mom that Danielle needed to close her knees. It took a couple of years before I made that connection. After all, my mom used to tell me to close my knees

1

when I wore a dress without tights. Mom later gossiped to Sandy, our neighbor, down the way, that Isaac was equally as guilty.

So after Coach Harvey called the police and threatened to kill Isaac, Wesley Cory grabbed his shotgun and led his oldest son to the barn for what he called a *coming to Jesus moment*. Right after graduation, Isaac enlisted.

"Praise the Lord," Dad said as the choir sat along the three rows of wood benches that cracked like the old wood flooring. "Let us pray."

The congregation all bowed their heads—except Isaac. He unwrapped a Cadbury Creme Egg and took a bite. The white fondant dripped down his chin.

I snorted, smacking a hand over my mouth. Keeping my chin tucked to my chest, I shifted my gaze to my dad, *Pastor Jacobson*. He scowled at me while thanking God for sacrificing His Son for our sins. I feared he might sacrifice me next, so I pinched my eyes shut and folded my hands in my lap, squeezing so tightly that my fingers felt numb.

By the time the congregation echoed my dad's "Amen," Isaac had finished the egg and wiped his chin clean.

"Is that Matt's brother?" my best friend Heather leaned over and whispered in my ear. Her breath smelled like the fruity jellybeans she'd been sneaking between songs.

It was a reprieve from the usual smell of musky hymnals and burning candles.

"I think so," I said through clenched teeth and a fake smile.

Isaac used to have long, black hair, a pack of cigarettes in his pocket, and an ear that he pierced himself. He and his friends formed a band in high school. My dad called their music an abomination to God.

2

And if I recall correctly, that might have been their official band name.

Isaac now had buzzed hair, no earrings, broad shoulders, and a chiseled jawline. He'd become a man in every sense of the word.

During the rest of the sermon, Heather nudged me with her elbow, then her knee, and sometimes she tapped my shoe with hers.

We became friends before we took our first steps, so she didn't have to say a word. I knew what every poke and jab meant— my boyfriend's older brother was *hot*.

"Have a blessed rest of your Easter," Dad said, looking like a Ken doll with his pearly smile and coiffed blond waves. He shifted his blue eyes toward the choir, our cue to stand and lead everyone with the closing hymn, "It Is Well with My Soul."

Minutes later, the choir hung their red robes in the back closet next to my dad's office, which smelled like instant coffee. I joined my parents and two younger sisters, Eve and Gabby, at the altar before we exited the church together as we did every Sunday. Matt and his family waited at the bottom of the church stairs. We were invited to their house for Easter dinner.

My boyfriend looked handsome in his Sunday best: a navy suit and Robin's egg blue tie. His dirty blond hair was coarse and wavy, like his mother's, whereas Isaac looked exactly like his dad Wesley—tan skin, dark hair, and deep brown eyes that could bring even the strongest person to shake in their boots.

"Happy Easter, Sarah," Matt's mom Violet hugged me. "You look so pretty." She released me, smoothing her hands down my long blond hair to my white cardigan over a pink sleeveless dress.

Dad insisted shoulders be covered in church, only making exceptions for brides in their wedding gowns. I assumed he figured they were on the verge of becoming women by losing their virginity because, in *my* father's eyes, all brides were pure.

"Thank you," I murmured to Violet as she combed her long nails through her feathered blond hair just as Matt took my hand.

"Isaac, you don't look like the same boy who left here," my dad said, shaking Isaac's hand and eyeing his ripped jeans, dirty cowboy boots, and wrinkled white button-down with the sleeves rolled up to show the world his tattoos, including a heart with a knife through it.

I was impressed to see a cross. However, I think my dad focused on the snake coiled around it, and he might have read into it as yet another abomination of God.

"I'll take that as a compliment, Pete."

Wesley cleared his throat, giving Isaac a raised eyebrow.

Isaac tried to hide his reaction, but I didn't miss the slight upturn of his full lips despite his apology. "Sorry, *Pastor Jacobson.*"

My dad's name was Peter. Most everyone called him Pastor Jacobson. My mom and grandparents called him Peter. But no one called him Pete.

I pressed my lips together to hide my amusement, and Matt narrowed his eyes at me like he didn't understand what had me fighting a grin. But Isaac knew, and the way he looked at me with a deviant twinkle in his eyes suggested he was doing it just for my reaction.

"Mom, can I go to Erin's house?" Eve asked, tugging on

the shoulder of my mom's canary yellow sundress with three-quarter sleeves and her grandma's double-string of pearls around her neck.

Mom brushed her bangs away from her face before stroking the back of her silky brown mullet. "No, Eve. We're having dinner with the Corys."

"But, Mom—"

"Eve," Dad said with his signature deep tone that kept every sheep in line, and that's all it took to end the conversation.

Eve couldn't help but roll her big brown eyes and sigh with a grumble. She was sixteen going on twenty. I was the oldest, but not nearly as rebellious as Eve, who was supposed to be the even-keeled middle child, according to my grandma Jacobson. My opposition to authority was more subtle because I had the people-pleaser gene.

Eve would spit out food if she didn't like it; I'd hide mine in a napkin and give it to the dog after dinner. Gabby, however, swallowed anything with a smile. She was fourteen, trying to be a pleaser child like me, or so she led everyone to believe. But I knew she was just biding her time before showing our parents that she could suck the patience from them and test their faith tenfold. Never mind that she scribbled poems inside her Bible during every Sunday service while our parents thought she was diligently following the sermon and making annotations.

"Matty, you didn't mention you were dating the preacher's daughter," Isaac murmured to Matt, ruffling his hair until he batted away Isaac's hand.

"Knock it off. It doesn't matter." Matt released my hand and retreated from our circle, joining some of his baseball buddies in the grass along the north side of the pristine white church with a gold steeple.

Matt was a pitcher, a basketball point guard, the homecoming king, and most likely to be valedictorian at our upcoming graduation.

My parents adored him because he never kept me out past curfew and always made it to church on time. He had no intention of doing more than kissing me or holding my hand, and he rarely used inappropriate language, even when adults were nowhere in earshot.

Matthew Cory was a true disciple and a real catch. I knew it, and so did everyone else.

While my parents were being pulled in the opposite direction to shake a few more hands, Gabby followed Eve to the car. Before I could move, Violet and Wesley stepped aside to visit with the Vanderleests, leaving me alone with Isaac and his wandering gaze.

"You grew up," he said while scratching his jaw.

I buttoned my cardigan with fumbling fingers. "You've been gone for six years; what did you expect?"

Wetting his lips, he slowly shook his head. "I don't know, but not this."

Embarrassment crawled up my neck in waves of stifling heat. "How was your Cadbury egg?" It wasn't much of a comeback, but it was all I had.

"Sweet, warm, and moist. Just how I like things," he said.

I couldn't decide if the Army failed to help Isaac grow up or if he grew up too much. Where did sexually suggestive language fall on the spectrum of maturity?

"Funny," I said, faking a confident grin.

"Are you and PC getting married? I bet our parents would love that."

"PC?" I narrowed my eyes.

"Perfect Child," Isaac replied with a wink.

I ignored his nickname for Matt, except for an eye roll before clearing my throat. "We're still in high school. I don't think anyone's talking about getting married."

That wasn't entirely true. Our parents had dropped plenty of hints.

"We could be family," Isaac said. "Wouldn't that be interesting?"

"Interesting" was an *interesting* word, especially given how Isaac smirked.

"Hey, Sarah, want to go to Joanna's house later? Her parents will be gone for the evening," Heather said, looping her arm around mine and pretending to ignore Isaac.

But she was far from ignoring him, and Heather knew I wasn't allowed to be at a friend's house if their parents weren't there. She also knew that we'd had matching crushes on Isaac Cory as preteens who didn't know better.

"Heather, do you remember Matt's brother Isaac?" I played along like neither one of us had written Isaac's name on the inside of a notebook between pages of pre-algebra problems.

She flipped her long, curly blond hair over her shoulder, igniting the surrounding air with the burning scent of ammonia from her new perm. Everyone had perms except me because my mom said the chemicals would damage my hair.

Like makeup clogged my pores.

Tight jeans made me look like a sinner.

And listening to "trashy" rock and roll disappointed my father *and* Thy Heavenly Father.

"Totally." Heather grinned, gripping my arm tightly.

"But you probably don't remember me." She scrunched her nose. "I would have been like twelve or thirteen when you were a senior."

"Sorry," Isaac shrugged. "No recollection. But I remember Sunday Morning because Matty talked about her nonstop. And I think I babysat her one or two times."

"Sunday Morning?" Heather eyed me as if I were Isaac's translator.

Pressing my lips together, I returned the slightest lift of my shoulders. I didn't want to look like an idiot in front of Isaac, but I had no clue what or who he was talking about. Since he was six years older, I figured he knew more slang than I did.

"So I heard you went into the Army," Heather said, brushing off Isaac's cryptic comment.

"Did you now? I might have heard that too." He was too cool. Too confident. Too everything.

Heather blushed as if Isaac were flirting with her, but when he glanced at me, I got a different, mocking vibe. It felt like he knew I'd had a crush on him before his brother became my first real boyfriend.

"Let's go, Sarah," Mom called, nodding toward the parking lot.

"I'm having dinner at Matt's house," I told Heather, punctuating it with a frown.

"Fine." She tried a pouty face but failed because she was enamored with Isaac. "Nice seeing you," she said, nervously rubbing her hands down the front of her dress.

Isaac returned a subtle "mm-hmm" while keeping his gaze on me.

As Heather moseyed in the opposite direction, I buttoned and unbuttoned the top of my cardigan at least three times. "I guess I'll see you at your house," I said, surveying the area. "If you see Matt, tell him I'm riding with my parents."

Isaac nodded with his lips twisted. And when I walked a few feet away from him, he said, "Sure thing, Sunday Morning."

I stopped and glanced over my shoulder. "*I'm* Sunday Morning?"

"Who else do you think Matty talked about?"

Matt and I started dating during our sophomore year, but I didn't know he'd had a crush on me since we were twelve. Then again, crushes were usually secrets.

"Sunday Morning Sarah." Isaac grinned. "Matty's first wet dream."

I choked on my gasp and a little saliva. Isaac Cory said *wet dream* just beyond the front doors to my father's church.

He put the Devil in Devil's Head.

Chapter Two

Michael Jackson, "P.Y.T. (Pretty Young Thing)"

THE CORYS WERE third-generation ranchers who owned most of the land in Devil's Head. While Matt was nearly perfect in everyone's eyes, he had no interest in taking over the ranch or farming the land as his legacy, like the men before him. That put Wesley Cory in a predicament since Isaac had proven to be a disappointment. The Army was the Cory family's last hope to salvage their eldest son's soul.

As we pulled down the long gravel road toward their white, two-story, twentieth-century farmhouse, a shadow caught my eye, followed by a puff of smoke. Isaac was leaning on an old cottonwood, one boot propped against the trunk and a cigarette in his hand. Thankfully, no one else noticed him. Had my sisters spotted him, they would have tattled immediately, and it could have sparked another "smoking will kill you" lecture from my parents.

I hated the smell of cigarette smoke, but Isaac made it look cool and *sexy,* like the Marlboro Man—every parent's worst nightmare.

Dad parked in our usual spot beside the detached two-car garage, and the five of us spilled out of our light-blue Ford Crown Victoria. He popped the trunk, and we loaded our arms with pies and dinner rolls that Mom contributed to Violet's Easter ham dinner.

As we trekked up the dirt path toward the screened-in porch, gravel crunched beneath the tires of Matt's red 1972 El Camino, stopping in front of the garage. The car was an early graduation present from his grandparents.

Matt jumped out and jogged toward us. "Let me get that," he said, taking the rhubarb pie from my mom just in time to open the screen door for us.

Matt grinned when I stepped past him, bringing up the rear with the basket of dinner rolls I helped form into knots. "You look pretty, Sarah," he said with a generous smile.

"She really does," Isaac chimed.

"Shut up," Matt mumbled.

"What?" Isaac held open the door while Matt led me into the house. "P.Y.T.," he murmured behind me so only I could hear him.

Pretty Young Thing.

My father disapproved of Michael Jackson's music, but I loved every song, including P.Y.T.'s sultry lyrics and catchy tempo.

Did I like Isaac breathing those three letters behind me like a dirty secret? Let's just say I didn't hate it.

"Janet, you baked up a storm," Violet gushed over my mom's pies and rolls as we set them on the antique buffet in the dining room, which was adjacent to the living room with a wood-burning stove. The staircase to the second floor separated the spacious kitchen from the living and dining room.

"My girls helped me," Mom said, giving us a proud nod of approval as we sat on the sofa like three life-sized dolls—two brunettes and a blonde with smiles on our makeup-less faces, hands folded in our laps.

"Sarah, do you want to help me with the deviled eggs?" Violet asked. She always asked me to help in the kitchen. "Matthew loves deviled eggs."

Violet seized every opportunity to teach me things she thought would please her youngest son. I wasn't stupid. I knew everyone was grooming me to be his wife—the next matron of the Cory Ranch. However, that didn't change the fact that Matt wanted to attend college and play baseball. He had no interest in ranching cattle, raising hogs, or growing corn and hay. And while I had been in 4-H as long as I can remember—sewing, canning, and showing livestock for the Corys—my heart belonged to Pat Benatar, Whitney Houston, and Laura Branigan more than it did to Matthew Cory.

Our families were too intertwined to see that Matt and I had no intention of starting the next chapters of our lives as each other's betrothed.

The problem was that Matt and I had been each other's security blankets, and we didn't know how to let go even when holding on felt too suffocating—at least, that was my perception. Matt was indifferent to everything. He seemed equally willing to marry me or break up, as long as it didn't affect his baseball plans. I had plans, too, but nobody cared about them.

"Janet, have you seen my newest quilt?" Violet nodded for my mom to follow her upstairs as I finished halving the peeled eggs and scooped the yolks into a bowl.

"Sarah, do you want a Coke?" Matt asked, retrieving a bottle opener to remove the cap from the sixteen-ounce glass bottle.

"No. I'm good. But thanks."

"I'll take the rest," Isaac said, filling a glass with ice before pouring the rest of the Coke into it.

"I'll be outside with our dads," Matt said before opening the squeaky screen door to the porch.

"The preacher's daughter making deviled eggs for Easter dinner." Isaac chuckled, shaking his head. "Why do you suppose they're called deviled eggs?"

I parted my lips to speak, but nothing came out because I was too distracted by the flask in Isaac's hand. He unscrewed the cap and poured a generous amount into his Coke.

When I lifted my gaze from the flask to his face, he smirked. "I like the way you look at me."

I swallowed hard and focused on the eggs, as Isaac stood uncomfortably close to me, his backside against the counter. "How do I look at you?"

"Like you're thirsty." He lifted his glass, offering it to me.

I smooshed the yolks with the back of the spoon. "I said no when Matt offered. What makes you think I'm suddenly thirsty?"

"Your cheeks are red."

I rolled my head between my shoulders, dismissing him without a verbal response. Isaac was goading me. He still thought of me as *Matty's* innocent twelve-year-old crush. And that irked me. "Smoking will kill you," I mumbled.

That was it—my best comeback.

He chuckled. "When?"

"When what?"

"When will it kill me?"

I shrugged. "Someday."

"Sunday Morning, something will kill all of us *someday*."

"Well," I nudged him aside to retrieve a spoon from the drawer for the mayonnaise, "God's not taking you to Heaven. I'm pretty sure there's no smoking in Heaven."

"What if smoking *is* Heaven? Have you tried it?" He took a swig of his drink.

"It's disgusting," I said, removing the lid from the mayonnaise jar.

"So you've tried it?"

He was so annoying.

"No. I haven't tried it." I scooped the mayonnaise into the measuring cup. "I also haven't licked a cow's butthole, but I bet it's a universally shared sentiment that doing so is *disgusting*."

He barked a laugh. "You can't speak for the universe. Ass-licking may be considered a sacred ritual in certain cultures."

"Do you think Mom would care if I had a Coke?" Eve asked, strolling into the kitchen. "Since it's Easter?"

My parents never let us have pop with a meal, just as a "special treat," which meant we snuck it whenever possible.

"Why don't you wait and ask her," I said.

"Here. Take mine. I won't tell anyone." Isaac held out his nearly full glass of Coke and whatever was in that flask.

Eve's brown eyes widened. "Thanks—"

"That's mine." I dropped the spoon and snatched the glass before Eve could blink. I didn't wait for the taste to register. It burned the entire way down, all eleven gulps.

I counted.

Eve frowned. "Fine. I'll ask Mom." She spun on her heels and stomped out of the kitchen.

I shoved the empty glass into Isaac's chest. "Don't be a butt nugget."

Isaac wrapped his fingers around the glass, lifting both eyebrows. His smile immediately curled into something more satanic than the stuffed eggs I was supposed to finish.

Instead of acknowledging that look on his face, I threw the rest of the ingredients into the bowl without measuring.

"Do you think that's enough salt?" Isaac asked before tipping the glass at his lips and sucking a piece of ice into his mouth.

"How's everything coming along?" Violet's melodic voice announced her and my mom's descent down the stairs.

I replied with a tight, "Fine," while stirring the ingredients.

"Well, look at you." Violet patted Isaac's back. "My boy became a man. A good man who helps in the kitchen." She gushed as her son screwed the lids onto the ingredients I haphazardly threw into the bowl.

Isaac was a man. All man. I had no dispute with that. But a *good* man?

No.

He was not a good man. Not even close.

"My pleasure," he said.

"Sarah, let's move everything to the kitchen table so I can get the ham and scalloped potatoes out of the oven," Violet said. "Maybe your sisters can help you fill the eggs."

I opened my mouth for an "okay," but the only thing that escaped was a loud belch. As my mom winced with a painfully sour face, I cupped a hand over my mouth. What did I expect after chugging that much soda all at once?

"Sarah," my mom said in a harsh whisper as Isaac snickered with his fist over his mouth.

"Excuse me," I murmured, tucking my chin and carrying the bowl to the kitchen table.

"Eve, Gabby, come help your sister fill the eggs," Mom called.

"Isaac, go find the rest of the men and tell them dinner will be served in about ten minutes." Violet nodded toward the door.

He eyed me while passing the table on his way out. I kept a neutral expression as if nothing had happened, as if I didn't have approximately two to three shots of hard liquor in my system.

I felt a little warmer and cared a little less. And that wasn't good.

Ten minutes later, everyone sat at the dining room table —the dads at opposite ends, our moms and my sisters on one side, and me sandwiched between Matt and Isaac on the other side.

My dad cleared his throat. "Shall we say grace?" Dad held out his hands, and everyone followed suit.

Then the darndest thing happened: that liquid poison messed with my memory. I forgot Matt was on my left, so with my *right* hand, I put his hand (only not his hand) on my inner thigh.

There were two things worth noting:

1.) Under sober conditions, I would not have done that.

2.) Isaac was on my right.

Okay, there were three things worth noting.

3.) Matt's hand (which was actually Isaac's) squeezed my leg, and it felt good, so I said as much.

Out. Loud.

"That feels so good." Once I heard my voice, I opened my eyes. For the record, I was praying even if my dad had stopped, which he had. I was praying I didn't say those words outside my head.

From the confused gazes on me, I knew the answer. So I looked at Matt for help. Why did he do that? His hand was no longer on my leg. Still, it was pretty disrespectful for him to put me in that position, even if it felt good. And even if I did sort of instigate it. But Matt looked as confused as everyone else.

Everyone except Isaac, who was on my right.

Oh, no. It was his hand!

He smirked.

"Praise the Lord," I said. "It feels so good to Praise God."

Dad scowled, but Mom smoothed things over. "Praise God, indeed," she said, unfolding her napkin and draping it on her lap while flashing Violet an angelic smile. "Everything looks and smells amazing, Vi. May it all nourish and bless our bodies."

"Amen," everyone mumbled before passing the food around the table.

I was too buzzed to hit my plate with the food, so after my slice of ham landed on the table beside the plate (which nearly no one saw), Isaac served me the rest of the food. Thankfully, his assistance went unnoticed.

Throughout the meal, I spontaneously giggled and immediately covered my mouth with a fist, disguising it as a cough. My parents talked about my sisters working at the church to help run Vacation Bible School, which I had done in previous summers.

"What about you, Sarah?" Violet asked. "Have you decided what you're doing this summer? We'd love to have you help on the ranch."

I was eighteen, so I got to choose my summer job for the first time.

"It's nothing personal," Matt said politely. "But Sarah doesn't want to work on the ranch." He smiled at me as if he'd just done me a huge favor.

"We're trying to talk her into a mission trip," Dad said, giving me a nod of encouragement.

I felt like my eyes were bouncing around in my head, unable to concentrate on anyone or anything for more than a few seconds. A tiny voice told my eyes and brain to get it together and focus, but the buzz demanded all my attention —that and the memory of Isaac squeezing my leg.

"Sarah, are you feeling okay?" Mom asked in a concerned tone.

I choked on another giggle and shook my head. "I, uh, need to use the restroom. I just feel a little off." I scooted back in my chair and stood. The room spun.

"Is it a headache?" Mom questioned.

"It," I returned a jerky nod like my head was on a spring, "could be the start of one."

All I had to do was make it a few feet to turn the corner into the kitchen. A few normal steps. But it was *so* hard.

"Sarah?" Violet called my name.

I cringed. Had she noticed my inability to walk a straight line? Everything was ready to unravel. I knew I'd have to rat out Isaac because there was no way anyone would've believed I had a flask with alcohol stashed in my purse.

"Hmm?" I stopped, pressing my hand to the wall while praying for a new excuse. Did I think God would answer my prayers with a well-thought-out lie for me to use?

With that amount of hard liquor in my blood, anything felt possible.

"The toilet off the kitchen hasn't been flushing right. Use the one upstairs," she said.

Upstairs?

Fun fact: I had never been upstairs. Preacher's daughters weren't allowed anywhere near the bedrooms of nonfamily members. I felt like I was being rewarded for my bad behavior.

Was that possible?

At the top of the creaky stairs covered in a faded blue carpet runner, there was a bedroom to the right. It had an unmade single bed in the corner and shelves with baseball trophies and ribbons—Matt's room. On the opposite side, there was another room with a bed made so neatly that you could bounce a quarter off the top. Rock band posters, everything from Tom Petty to Aerosmith and ZZ Top, covered the walls. An electric guitar sat on a stand beside the window overlooking the garage.

The buzz led me into Isaac's room, where I sat on the edge of his bed and flopped backward, making everything spin even more. That made me giggle, so I snatched his pillow and covered my face to muffle my laughter.

It smelled like Drakkar Noir with hints of rosemary, cardamom, and cedar. When it registered that I was sniffing my boyfriend's brother's pillow, I tossed it aside and stood, wobbling a bit before tiptoeing to the guitar. Since it wasn't plugged in, I plucked a few strings. I'd dreamed of playing the guitar, but my parents insisted I stick to the piano. It was kinder to my delicate fingers.

"If you touch something of mine, I get to touch something of yours, but I guess you tried to get me to feel you up during prayer, so that counts."

I jumped out of my skin, slapping a hand over my mouth

while staring at Isaac through wide, unblinking eyes. "What are you doing in here?" I mumbled, then giggled behind my hand.

"It's my room. The question is, what are you doing here?" Isaac was pure sin; everything my dad had warned me about all wrapped up into one *hot* man with a cherry on top.

"I think you got me drunk." I nibbled on my thumbnail, failing to suppress another snort.

He smirked. "I never would have guessed." His gaze averted to my side. "What were you doing on my bed?"

"Huh?" I followed his gaze. "Nothing. I wasn't."

"My blanket is wrinkled, and my pillow is ruffled." He took pleasure in calling me out like Goldilocks.

I sighed. "Why does your pillow smell so good? You *smoke*," I slurred the word with an extra long O. "Smokers are stinky. I'm tipsy." My eyes rolled with a heavy blink. "I've never been tipsy. I like it. And I re-e-ealy like how your pillow smells."

He held a finger to his lips, shooshing me while glancing over his shoulder.

I cupped my hands around my mouth. "I can't believe they let you up here with me," I whispered. Well, it was a partial whisper. "I'm not allowed to be in boys' bedrooms. I could accidentally have sex."

Isaac rolled his lips between his teeth, but it did little to hide his amusement. "I have Tylenol." He grabbed the white bottle from his nightstand "My mom wanted Matt to get it for you, but I told her it was probably in my room. Do you need a Tylenol for your headache?" He held the bottle in my face between his thumb and his forefinger. Isaac had enormous hands, even larger than Matt's.

I didn't care. How much hand did one man need?

"You should teach me to play your guitar." I turned, lifting it from its stand.

"I don't think I'll be teaching you anything." Isaac stole the guitar from me and returned it to its spot.

When he faced me, I was in his space, or he was in mine. So, I tipped my head back and smiled while jabbing my pointer finger into his chest. "I bet you have a lot to teach because you," I tapped my finger like a woodpecker, "were in a band."

His chest was hard, and I wondered if he had tattoos on it too.

"Go slide into Matty's bed and sniff his pillow. I'll tell everyone you took two Tylenol and needed a nap. Maybe you can do a better job of not embarrassing yourself in an hour or two. My parents have the croquet set up in the backyard. I'd hate for you to do anything inappropriate with one of the mallets. So sleep it off, Sunday Morning."

I squinted, but it didn't help my vision issues. "You were going to get my sister drunk."

Isaac rolled his eyes. "You're so ignorant. I wasn't going to let her drink it. And even if she had taken it, after one sip, she would have spit it out or at least known that it wasn't just Coke."

I canted my head. "Your eyes are so dark. And the white part is really white."

"The sky is blue, and the grass is green. Are there any more brilliant observations you want to discuss before you take a nap?"

"Do you believe in God?"

Isaac returned a blank look. I was unsure if it was a stare-off, but if so, I lost.

"Fine," I grumbled, stiffly holding my arms out to the

side while attempting to walk an imaginary line between Isaac's room and Matt's, seeing if I could pass a field sobriety test. Heather's uncle failed one the previous year.

I failed too.

Collapsing onto Matt's bed, I curled onto my side with my folded hands tucked under my cheek and fell asleep.

Chapter Three

Huey Lewis & The News, "I Want a New Drug"

"MY BED's going to smell like you. Now, I'm never going to wash my sheets."

I snapped my eyes open. My mouth was dry, and my thoughts were sluggish.

Matt stood a few feet away from his bed, arms crossed, lower lip trapped between his teeth. I sat up and yawned. My vision was back to normal, and the numbing buzz had disappeared.

"My dad gave me three minutes to check on you." He looked at his silver watch with a black leather band. "I now have two minutes before he comes looking for me."

"Where is everyone?" I asked, running my hands through my hair.

"In the backyard. Your parents said they'll be leaving

soon. What happened during dinner? You were acting weird."

"If I tell you, can you promise to keep it a secret?"

"Of course." Matt rubbed the back of his neck.

"After you went outside with our dads, Isaac poured the rest of your Coke into a glass and added alcohol from a flask."

Matt shrugged. "So what? That can't surprise you. He's not exactly a rule-follower. And he's twenty-four. My parents know he drinks and smokes, but they don't say anything because they think he earned it after six years in the Army."

"You didn't let me finish. Eve wanted a drink, so he started to hand his to her. And I panicked and grabbed the glass, telling Eve it was mine. And then I gulped the whole thing down."

Matt raised a single brow as if he doubted me.

"By dinner, I was buzzed and numb and couldn't stop giggling." I scrunched my nose.

"Your parents will totally forbid you from ever coming over here if they find out."

"No duh."

"How do you feel now?" he asked.

"My stomach isn't great." I pressed a flat hand to it. "I didn't eat very much."

"Come on." He held out his hand. "Let's get a snack."

He pulled me to my feet and slid his hands around my waist. "Did you talk your dad into letting you go to prom this year?"

"Pfft. What do you think?"

"I think we should convince him to let you go. Maybe your mom could volunteer to chaperone?"

"And subject herself to sinful music?"

"Even my mom thinks it's unfair to keep you from experiencing a school dance," Matt said.

I twisted my lips. "Hmm, maybe your mom should say something to my mom."

Matt grinned. "Maybe." He dipped his head and kissed me.

"Hey, kids."

We jumped apart, turning toward Isaac like soldiers coming to attention. His broad shoulders and unmatched confidence engulfed the whole doorway.

"Matty, stop trying to pick the lock to Sarah's chastity belt. Her parents are ready to go home."

"Shut up." Matt pushed him, but Isaac didn't move until he was ready to step aside. He had too much size on his little brother. "I wasn't picking the lock to her chastity belt. Come on, Sarah," he said, jogging down the stairs without me.

"Are you sobered up?" Isaac gave me a slow once-over.

I adjusted my sweater. "Why do you think I have a chastity belt?"

"Where to begin ..." He scratched his chin. "You're wearing a cardigan. You're Matty's girlfriend. My parents think God sent you just for him. So, I don't want to think of you as a dumb blonde, but you're making it hard on me by asking that question."

I planted my fists on my hips. "We're all sinners. What makes you think I'm so innocent?"

I was innocent in action but impure in thought. Some of my favorite song lyrics were about sex, not God. Every day, I thought about sex. Whenever Matt kissed me, I imagined what it would feel like if he did more than just kiss me. Half of my friends had already had sex, and the other half had at least been felt up.

Not me.

Matt talked big, but that's where it ended. I don't know if it was *Pastor* Jacobson, his dad threatening Isaac's life after he impregnated a minor, or just his morality, but Matt always talked me out of anything more than French kissing. And honestly, we barely made it into France. We were more like a rock in the Swiss Alps that rolled just over the border into the French Alps.

"Sunday Morning, no matter how high you tip your chin and puff out your tiny chest, your boots are still too big for your feet, not the other way around. So you'd better button up your cardigan and skitter out of here before I call your sad attempt at a bluff."

I took two steps closer to Satan. "You know nothing about me."

He gazed down at me, and his face was alight with amusement. "Have you cheated on my brother?"

I squinted. "Of course not."

"Then your hymen is still intact. Now, run along." He turned to the side and made a shooing motion with his hand.

A wave of heat surged up my neck and pulsed in my cheeks. I was equal parts angry and embarrassed. But I wasn't angry at Isaac. I was angry at Matt for being too good.

Too cautious.

Too worried.

Too obedient.

We were eighteen: barely eighteen, but legal adults. In five weeks, we would have our diplomas.

Maybe that's why he wanted me to convince my dad to let us go to prom. He was ready to take the next step.

"Just because I haven't had an abortion doesn't mean Matt and I haven't done it."

Guys who didn't wear ties to Easter Sunday Service and ate Cadbury Creme Eggs during prayer should not have been on my list of people to impress. Yet, there I stood, lying to Satan because heaven forbid I let him think the preacher's oldest daughter was a virgin.

"*Done it?*" He wasted no time mocking me.

"Sarah, what are you doing? Are you coming?" Matt called up the stairs.

Isaac's grin nearly cracked his face in half. "That's a problem," he whispered. "Your boyfriend doesn't know if you're coming."

I swallowed hard.

Don't react.

"If you *did it*," Isaac scratched his chin before leaning closer to me, "you didn't do it right."

I turned sideways to slide past him without making physical contact.

"Sorry," I said to Matt as I lifted the skirt of my dress on my way down the stairs. "Isaac was asking me about Jesus and if I truly believe He loves sinners like your brother."

Matt chuckled. "Did he really?"

At that point, what was one more lie?

"Uh-huh." I lifted onto my toes and gave him a quick kiss. "Bye," I said before skipping past him, slipping my feet into my white flats, and heading outside.

"Sarah, how's your head?" Violet asked as she, my mom, and my sisters plucked the croquet hoops from the grass while my dad and Mr. Cory assembled the mallets and balls in the wooden storage stand.

"A lot better. Thanks," I said, using my hand to block the sun from my eyes.

"Honey, Violet has a job opportunity for you." Mom

rested her arm over my shoulders as we walked toward the car.

"I thought you were fine with letting me pick my job since I'm an adult," I mumbled under my breath.

"Just hear her out. I think you might like it better than working at Dixie's."

I shot Violet a fake smile when she approached me as my sisters piled into the back seat.

"Mary Lou Eddleton needs a hip replacement, so we don't have anyone to manage the farm stand. How would you feel about doing it? We'd pay you more than you'll make at Dixie's." Violet clasped her hands in front of her, rocking back and forth on the balls of her feet.

"Can you really pass up such a great offer?" Dad asked, opening the front passenger door for my mom.

The porch screen door creaked as Isaac and Matt stepped outside. Matt had changed out of his suit into cut-off sweatpants, a Devil's Head baseball T-shirt, and a matching hat.

"Matthew, should Sarah manage the farm stand this summer?" my mom called in his direction.

Matt said, "Yes," while Isaac said, "No."

But nobody asked for Isaac's opinion.

And I had no intention of saying yes *until* Isaac shared his unpopular opinion. He didn't want me around the ranch all summer.

The "farm stand" sounded simplistic, but it was a fully enclosed shed just off the road at the end of the Corys' long lane. It had windows, a bathroom in the corner, a register, a deep freezer with meat and raw dairy products, and shelves of farm goods: eggs, jams, honey, beeswax candles, and baked goods Violet made fresh every morning.

"It would be easier to make this decision if I weren't so distracted by my disappointment over missing my senior prom." I dropped my chin and folded my hands, twiddling my thumbs.

"Sarah," Dad said with a stern tone.

"Honey, let's talk about this at home," Mom suggested.

Was it okay for her to use Matt to guilt me into saying yes, but not okay for me to use my form of persuasion?

"Gabby and Eve are in the car, so we're all adults. Let's talk about it now." My buzz was gone, but there seemed to be some residual bravery dictating my words. "If you all raised us so well, then where is your trust in us, in yourselves, and in God that we can handle a school dance? Newsflash: we drive cars with radios. Don't you think we've heard all the sinful songs? And the dance will be chaperoned. No one's going to get pregnant on the dance floor. And I'm sure I still have a curfew despite being eighteen." I stopped short of rolling my eyes, but I wanted to.

Clap.

Clap.

Clap.

Our gazes shifted to the porch steps where Isaac sat, slowly clapping.

"Bravo. I think Sarah should go to law school instead of Matty. That was a brilliant case she made."

"Shut up." Matt smacked Isaac on the back of the head, and Isaac snickered.

"What if Mom volunteers to chaperone?" I added.

Mom squinted at me, but I kept a pleasant, unaffected smile.

"Janet," my dad said her name in a rare moment of deferring a decision to her.

"I'll volunteer too," Violet added.

I bit back my grin, and so did Matt.

"Okay," Mom murmured with a nervous smile.

"Okay," I said. "Since that's decided, I think I'll accept the job at the farm stand."

Everyone seemed happy with the state of affairs—except Satan.

Chapter Four

Madonna, "Like a Virgin"

"TOTALLY AWESOME!" Heather squealed as soon as I told her about prom.

I held the phone to my ear while doing sit-ups on my bedroom floor. "We have to go shopping next weekend for a dress. I bet there's nothing left since everyone else has picked the good ones. And don't you have weights? I need to do some butterflies to make my chest bigger."

Heather laughed. "Why do you need a bigger chest?"

"If I tell you, you can't tell anyone, and I mean anyone. Not even Joanna."

"I swear. Now, tell me."

I stopped exercising and untangled the phone cord from around my waist. "Earlier, when we were eating Easter dinner at Matt's house—oh my gosh, Heather, *so* much happened. I don't know where to start. First, Isaac still smokes."

"Well, duh. He's twenty-four, and he was in the Army. Of course, he still smokes."

I deflated at my naivety. "Also, he poured some sort of booze from a flask into his glass of Coke, and he offered it to Eve, so I freaked out and took it from him, guzzling it down all at once."

"Oh my gosh, are you totally being serious?"

"Yes." I proceeded to tell her everything, and when I finished, the line was silent. "Heather?"

"Isaac thinks you and Matt have had sex?"

I twirled the phone cord like a jump rope, every nerve in my body rapidly firing. "I don't know if he believed me, but yeah, he might."

"What did Matt say when you told him?"

I cringed. "I haven't told him yet."

"Sarah! What if Isaac says something to Matt? You'll look like a liar to both of them. You have to tell Matt."

"I can't tell Matt; he'll be mad that I was lying to his brother."

"Why *did* you lie to Isaac?"

I sighed, falling onto my back again. "Because Isaac is older and more experienced. And I'm eighteen, but I have the least experience of everyone. And it's embarrassing."

"Your dad's the preacher at the only church in Devil's Head. You know that even if you weren't a virgin, everyone would assume you were."

"What's it like?" I wrapped the cord around my finger.

"What's what like?"

"You know."

Heather laughed. "I've told you this so many times. It

was fine. Weird. But good. I feel like Travis came quickly, but what do I know?"

"Was it wet?" I asked with an unavoidable grin.

"The condom?"

"Was it wet before the condom?"

"I don't know. I didn't want to touch it."

I giggled.

"Why are you asking me about this again?"

"Because I need real-life details in case Isaac brings it up again this summer."

"This summer?"

I wrinkled my nose. "Yeah. I agreed to manage the Corys' farm stand, and Isaac is working on the ranch, so I'm sure I'll see him a lot."

That should not have made me feel so giddy, but it did because Isaac had a guitar in his room, and he'd been in a band. The only thing I felt truly passionate about was music. I wanted to play a guitar and sing songs—I wanted to sing *my* songs. I had pages of lyrics in a notebook. And when I really let myself dream big, I imagined crowds of adoring fans singing those lyrics back to me.

"Sarah," Heather said my name slowly. "You're going steady with Matt. Everyone knows you'll get married. Why are you planning sex talks with his brother? And why would he ask you if Matt's thingy was wet?" She laughed.

The line clicked.

"Sarah, I need to call Erin," Eve said, having picked up one of the other receivers in the house.

"Give me a minute," I said.

"Fine," Eve replied.

I waited for another click.

"Eve, I know you're still on the line. Hang up."

Click.

Heather laughed. "She's probably still listening. I bet she just muted the phone. Eve? Are you listening? Sarah wants to know how wet a guy's thingy is during sex."

"Stop!" I giggled. "We don't have any phones with mute buttons. She's not on the line. I heard the click. And I never said I wanted to marry Matt. We're eighteen. It's a little early to make the assumption."

"Tell that to your parents and his."

I groaned. "I know. Mr. Cory has been really generous to our family."

"*Because* he thinks you're his future daughter-in-law."

"That's the problem. We can't break up because my family is too indebted to his." I sighed. "Our families are practically married. If we break up, it will affect everyone. But I'm not ready to get married. What if we've been together for the wrong reasons? We have forty-two people in our graduating class. What if we're together for lack of a better choice or because our families have known each other forever and decided it's in their best interest?"

"You could do a lot worse than Matt."

I rubbed my forehead. "I'm aware. But it's not about him. You know I want to go to Nashville. He's going to be in Michigan. What if it's just not our time?"

"Just wait until the end of summer. If you're going to break up, do it when you're not working for his family."

I scraped my teeth along my bottom lip several times. "Break up sounds bad. I just want to go our separate ways. No big deal. Is that too much to ask?"

"I don't know. You'll have to ask Matt. Do you not love him anymore?"

"No. I mean ... I love him. We love each other. But he

34

loves baseball, and I love music. It doesn't feel like our love is what matters most to either one of us right now."

"What if the feeling is not mutual? Matt has loved you forever."

"He doesn't share my passion. I need someone who loves me enough to want to see me following my dreams, who supports me."

"Like you sit in the bleachers and watch him play baseball even though you're not a baseball fan."

"Which he doesn't know and ever will know," I said with emphasis.

"My lips are sealed."

"And don't tell Joanna or anyone that I'm having these thoughts about Matt, or else my parents will catch wind of it and ground me until I promise to marry him so we can breed little ranch helpers and missionaries."

"That's a little extreme." Heather laughed.

"It's not."

"Well, I have to finish my trig homework while you dream of both Cory boys."

"I am not dreaming of Isaac," I said.

"Sarah, we've *always* dreamed about Isaac."

I DIDN'T LIE to Heather. Matt loved baseball the way I loved the lyrics to Bonnie Tyler's "Total Eclipse of the Heart."

At eighteen, all we had was an abundance of aspiration. The only difference was everyone supported Matt's passion as a brave and admirable pursuit of happiness through his God-given talent.

No one cared that, if given the chance, I could make hearts bleed as much as Bonnie Tyler.

"Go Matt!" I yelled, flying to my feet when he hit a double his first time up to bat.

As I sat on the bleachers with Heather and Joanna, Violet and Isaac made their way toward me.

"We're late," Violet said, sliding on her sunglasses. "I thought I was going to get Wesley to come, but no such luck."

She hugged me before taking a seat behind us. "Oh, Isaac, there's bird poop." She pointed to the bench next to her.

"We'll scoot down," Heather offered while she and Joanna made me scooch to the left.

Isaac adjusted his cowboy hat and sat next to me. "Sunday Morning," he murmured.

"It's Sarah."

"I know," he smirked, gazing out at the baseball field.

His jean-clad leg pressed to mine, and I tried to scoot a little closer to Heather, but there wasn't wiggle room.

"Do you like baseball?" he asked.

Heather snorted, and I elbowed her.

"Duh, what do you think? I'm here, aren't I?"

"That's not an answer." He chuckled, and it felt like a condescending response. "I don't really care for it. I prefer football. Track. Basketball. Not baseball. It's pretty boring."

I glanced back at Violet to see if she was hearing him, but she was focused on Matt making it to home plate with the next batter.

"Then why are you here?" I asked.

"Same reason you are: to support Matty."

"Oh my gosh, you call him Matty?" Heather asked, leaning forward to see Isaac.

"Isaac has a problem with real names," I said.

"That's not true. I only have special names for special people," he said, playfully nudging my leg, which made Heather pinch my arm.

When I looked in her direction, she and Joanna were gawking at me and Isaac. I shot them a wide-eyed SOS signal before facing forward.

"Well, I'm calling you Isaac," I said.

"Because I'm not that special?"

"You're *something*," I murmured before lowering my voice to ensure Violet didn't hear me. "But special, is not it."

Isaac adjusted his body in a way that made his leg *and* arm press to mine.

"I'm going to the concession stand," I announced, quickly standing. "You coming?" I asked my friends.

"No, we'd better stay and save seats," Joanna said as Heather filled my space to sit close to Isaac.

She grinned at me.

"Since you're going," Isaac dug into his pocket and pulled out a ten-dollar bill, "mind getting me a Mountain Dew, Sweetarts, and popcorn?"

I stared at his money and then at him.

He smiled. It was a little lopsided, and it brought out a tiny dimple on his right cheek. "Thanks. You're the best." Sometimes he had a slight Southern accent, like he brought it out when he needed to sound convincing.

Heather and Joanna covered their mouths and snorted.

When I didn't take the money, Isaac pulled a five from his pocket and added it to the ten. "I'll get yours too." He grabbed my hand and shoved the bills into it.

"Isaac, what do you say?" Violet said.

I was dumbfounded. Isaac's mommy had to prompt her twenty-four-year-old son to use his manners.

He wet his lips, giving me a look that felt a little inappropriate. "Please."

I huffed before worming my way down the bleachers to the concession stand. It was a lot to carry, but I stuffed his roll of Sweetarts into one pocket and my peanut M&M's into the other. Then I hugged the bag of popcorn and held the two drinks in my hands. As I walked, I carried them filled to the brim with big ice cubes bobbing around.

Climbing the bleachers, I tried so hard not to spill on anyone, but as I handed the Mountain Dew to Isaac, my toe caught on the edge of the bleacher, and half of his drink sloshed onto his shirt and crotch.

"Oh my gosh!" I quickly sat next to him. "I'm so sorry."

"Sarah, don't worry about it. Isaac's used to getting dirty," Violet said.

Isaac shifted the drink from one hand to the other to wipe his arm on his jeans while scowling at me.

My nose wrinkled, and I handed him the popcorn. Then I retrieved his roll of Sweetarts and his change. He needed a third hand.

"Slide them in my front pocket," he said, leaning back a bit to give me access to his jeans front pocket.

My gaze flitted between his pocket and his eyes. "I'm not sure that's a good idea," I murmured, while shooting a glance at Violet, who was focused on the game because she actually liked baseball.

"Um ..." I handed my drink to Heather. "Hold this one second."

After she took my drink, I hooked one finger into Isaac's pocket to tug it open enough to slip one of the quarters into it, but I still had two dimes and three pennies to go, as well as four one-dollar bills and the Sweetarts.

Sweat gathered on my brow and upper lip.

He ducked his head and whispered in my ear. "As much as I love this slow seduction you're doing in front of my mom, maybe you should just hold my popcorn and let me do it."

Jerk!

Why didn't he just say that instead of asking me to do it? Why didn't *I* think of it?

Oh, that's right: Isaac made me lose my mind.

My face heated as I took his popcorn with one hand and wiped my brow with my other while looking at Heather and Joanna. "HELP. ME!" I mouthed.

They giggled.

I angled my body away from his for the rest of the game. When Matt pitched a perfect last inning, winning the game, I wasted no time standing to get out of there.

"We'll meet you in the parking lot. We're going to go say hi to Tyler's parents," Joanna said as she and Heather started down the bleachers before me.

"Sarah, tell Matt 'good game,' and we'll see him at home," Violet said, resting her hand on my shoulder and stepping in front of me before I could bolt.

"I will," I smiled, following her down the bleachers.

When she reached the bottom, one of the other moms started talking to her, and I stood off to the side to wait for Matt.

Isaac took my empty cup and added it to his trash, tossing everything in the bin a few feet from where I stood. When he turned back toward me, I slipped my hands into my back pockets, eyeing where I spilled the pop onto his shirt and the crotch of his jeans.

"I guess the only fair payback is for me to get you wet sometime."

"I'm really sorry," I said, lifting my gaze to his face and the weird smirk on it. That's when I realized his comment wasn't so innocent. "Gag me with a spoon," I grimaced and crossed my arms over my chest while turning my back to him and craning my neck over the crowd to look for Matt.

Isaac laughed. "I'm just playing with you, Sunday Morning."

"It's inappropriate."

"Don't be such a square."

"Don't be such a perv. I don't want to play with you."

"Why not? I'm infinitely more fun than Matty. More experienced too."

I scoffed.

Where are you, Matt?

I lifted onto my toes, but I still couldn't see him. Then I shrieked as my hands clawed Isaac's while he grabbed my waist and lifted me off my feet to see over the crowd.

"Put me down!"

Violet and her friends glanced in our direction. "Isaac, leave Sarah alone," she said with a grin and a headshake as if we were siblings goofing around.

When my feet touched the ground, I pivoted toward him. "Don't *ever* do that again."

He twisted his lips. "Touch you. Lift you off the ground? Or make you scream?"

Everything that fell from his lips sounded suggestive. Not that I was looking at his lips. Well, sometimes I looked at his lips because he was Satan. My dad told me to keep a close eye (and a safe distance) on anyone who reminded me of Satan. Isaac was sin in the flesh.

Sexy.

Smooth.

Tempting.

It was nearly impossible to stay pure of mind in his presence because I had a bad case of raging hormones, sexual curiosity, and an unstoppable need to feel like an adult making all of my own decisions, whether they were smart ones or not.

I wanted to be a rebel, but I didn't know how. While I acted offended and accused him of being a perv, I also imagined what it would be like to have sex with my boyfriend's older brother. Around Isaac, I became the heroine in all of my favorite movies that I wasn't supposed to watch, but did anyway.

I was Alex Owens' character in *Flashdance*—young with big dreams. And Isaac was Nick Hurley, the handsome older hero who caught her attention. This unrecognizable part of me wanted to be a woman seductively eating lobster while seducing the hot guy on the opposite side of the table.

So confident.

So bold.

So sinful.

I jumped when Matt came up behind me and slid his arms around my waist.

"Hey!" I turned. "Good game."

"Yes, bravo, Matty." Isaac clapped his hands behind me.

I ignored him.

Matt eyed Isaac and then me. He didn't look happy. "Walk me to my car?"

I cocked my head before nodding.

"Good game, sweetie. See you at home," Violet called as Matt hiked his bag onto his shoulder and took my hand.

"Mm-hmm," he hummed.

As we walked toward the parking lot, I quickly glanced back at Isaac.

Of course, he smirked. That wasn't a surprise. It was my grin, coming out of nowhere, that felt most inappropriate.

"We need to talk," Matt said.

Was he breaking up with me? Why did he sound so serious?

I had a metallic fuchsia prom dress with puffy sleeves and pumps dyed to match. We couldn't break up before prom or before the end of summer. My family was the Corys' favorite charity case.

We stopped at his El Camino, where he deposited his bag in the back and swapped his cleats for his dirty white Adidas high tops.

"Isaac asked me if we used a condom," Matt said, peering down at me through squinted eyes.

I nibbled the inside of my cheek. "What did you tell him?"

"Sarah!" He parked his hands on his waist and leaned toward my face. "So, you *did* tell him we had sex?"

"No," I said, shaking my head in frustration. "Isaac's just stirring up trouble. He likes to pester you. And you let him. If you didn't have this reaction to him, then he wouldn't do it to you. But you let him get under your skin, so he continues to do it. And he wanted to get a reaction from me on Easter, so I may have neither confirmed nor denied that we've had sex." I shifted my gaze to the influx of people in the parking lot, climbing into their cars.

"Why would you want him to think we've done it?"

I fidgeted with the hem of my T-shirt and shrugged. "Because sometimes I wish we'd do more than we do. I feel like everyone is doing it except me—*us*." I quickly corrected myself. "Except us." Of course, I meant *us*. Not me with some other guy. Definitely not me and Isaac.

Matt scoffed. "Your dad would kill me."

"I wouldn't tell my dad. Duh. Do you really think I'd casually mention it during dinner? 'Hey, Dad, what time is choir practice? And by the way, I'm having sex with Matt. Can you pass the butter'?"

Matt eyed me with an unreadable expression. "Do you want to do it? What if I go to college, and something happens, and we don't stay together? Will you regret—"

"No," I said a little too quickly. "Matt," I sighed, "I love you. You're my first love, and I couldn't ask for a better boyfriend. But I don't want to get married and pop out babies right now. Don't you want to go to college and have all those new experiences without feeling anchored to this place?"

Or me?

I shrugged. "We're comfortable with each other. Would it be so wrong to be each other's first without it meaning more? But it's up to you. I mean, do *you* want to?"

We discussed sex like going to a movie.

He did a terrible job at hiding his grin. "Maybe." He glanced to the side as Kevin got into his burgundy Ford Fairlane. "See ya," Matt said to him.

After Kevin backed out of his spot, Matt returned his attention to me. "But I know everyone who works at the store, the pharmacy, and the gas station. How am I supposed to buy protection?"

I couldn't believe we were having this conversation.

"Get one from Tyler or Andy."

Matt shook his head. "I can't tell anyone, and neither can

you. If this gets out, if even one person finds out, everyone will know."

"We're adults." I crossed my arms over my chest. That was my new favorite line.

"Adults who are still in school, living with our parents, and financially dependent on them."

I hated Matt's overabundance of common sense. There was no need to worry about him getting anyone pregnant and driving them two hours north to Planned Parenthood.

"Do your parents use them?" I asked.

He winced. "What? Gross. No, Sarah. I don't know what my parents use because I don't like to think about them doing that." He raked his fingers through his messy hair.

"Maybe I can snoop around in my parents' room for something."

"Sarah ..." Matt shook his head while squinting at the sky. "No. I can't do that."

"You just said—"

When he looked at me, he laughed. "I'm not wearing"—he glanced around again to see if anyone was listening before lowering his voice—"one of your dad's condoms to have premarital sex with his daughter."

"Dude!" I rubbed my face before tucking my hands into the back pockets of my pink cotton candy-colored shorts. "It's not like I'd steal a used one from the garbage."

"Yuck!" He fisted a hand at his mouth before turning his back to me. "Don't say that. Stop talking about it. I'll never be able to make eye contact with your dad again. I need to believe that your parents have done it three times. That's it."

"You're so weird." I hugged his back and giggled. "I'll figure something out. Maybe I'll drive to Runnells."

"No. Jeez. That's an hour away." He peeled my arms

from his waist and turned toward me again. "I can't have you taking care of it. That's my job. I'll figure it out."

I beamed because all of this meant that we were going to have sex.

"You won't feel guilty? Like God's judging you for sinning?" he asked.

"He's a loving God—a forgiving one. It's nothing a little prayer won't handle. And it's not like I'm killing anyone."

"Sarah," Matt rolled his eyes, "you're the worst preacher's daughter."

"Pfft ..." I smirked. "My sisters are worse. You just wait. Especially Gabby. She's quiet. Too quiet. Always writing in her Bible. Something's off about her. I promise you."

Matt chuckled. "I think you're wrong." He ducked his head and kissed me on the cheek.

I grabbed his neck with both hands to keep him close. "Kiss me like you mean it. Kiss me like we're going to have sex," I whispered.

Indecision loomed in his eyes. Matt was a good boy. Too good.

I didn't wait for him to overanalyze it; I kissed him. And when I opened my mouth, begging for him to stick his tongue in it, he pulled away.

"I'll call you after dinner," he said after clearing his throat.

"Fine." I returned a tight smile while he climbed into his car.

"Sarah!"

I turned toward Heather's shrill voice as she and Joanna shuffled their way toward me in the gravel parking lot, kicking up dust with their dirty Keds just as Matt pulled out of his spot.

Joanna smacked her gum, gathering her black permed hair in one hand while her other checked her voluminous mall bangs, which were held in place with so much hairspray that they could've survived a tornado.

"Did you tell Matt you were flirting with his brother?" Joanna eyed me.

"Shut up. I was not. Isaac is such a jerk."

"But a *hot* jerk," Heather said.

Yes. Isaac was very hot. Scorching hot. Burn-in-Hell level of hot.

"Oh, did you ask your parents about camping over the Fourth?" Heather asked.

"Mine said yes," Joanna said, absentmindedly twirling her hair around her finger.

I nodded. "They said as long as it's just girls and no guys."

"How would they know?" Heather waggled her eyebrows even though we weren't inviting guys.

"Who would you invite?" Joanna asked. "Matt or Isaac?"

Heather snorted, covering her mouth.

"Neither." I rolled my eyes. "It's just us girls."

Chapter Five

Foreigner, "I Want to Know What Love Is"

"ARE YOU WEARING A SHAWL?" Dad asked when I descended the stairs in my pink dress.

Matt's eyes sparkled as he watched me. He looked handsome in his black tux with a hot pink bowtie and matching cummerbund. And he looked older, a true adult who could have sex. I couldn't stop thinking about it.

It's *all* I'd been thinking about since we made the decision in the parking lot.

"Why would I wear a shawl?" I wrinkled my nose at my dad.

He frowned. "Because you're showing a lot of skin."

It was a floor-length dress with puffy sleeves that were off-the-shoulder. But I didn't have much of a chest (as Isaac had kindly pointed out), so it wasn't as if I had cleavage spilling over the bodice.

"I think she looks beautiful," Mom said with teary eyes.

"You do look beautiful," Matt added.

"Thank you. And you look very handsome." I rubbed my lightly glossed lips together to control my grin.

Despite the makeup restrictions, I felt beautiful. Mom let me wear a little blush, pink eyeshadow, mascara only on my upper lashes, and some lip gloss. No foundation or black eyeliner. She curled my hair, but instead of leaving the perfectly shaped ringlets, she brushed them out into waves. I looked like a flower child from a decade earlier.

"I got you a corsage." Matt removed it from the box and reached for the top of my dress, above my boob.

My dad cleared his throat.

"Here. Why don't you let me do it so you don't accidentally stick her." Mom smiled, taking it from Matt.

"Thanks." He seemed content letting her do it. I think his hands were shaking. He should have gotten me a wrist corsage.

After Mom pinned it to my dress and the boutonniere to his jacket, she used an entire roll of film for pictures on the front porch, mostly of us on the porch swing. "Matt, I told your mom I'd get plenty of pictures to share with her."

"Thanks," he said, opening the car door for me.

"Remember your curfew," Dad reminded us.

"Yes, Sir," Matt said.

"Be good examples for everyone else," he continued his sermon.

"Of course, Sir," Matt replied, tucking my dress into the car.

"I'll see you at post-prom." Mom waved.

I smiled and waved as Matt closed my door. How did we talk my parents into this?

We ate dinner with Heather and Tyler at the best steakhouse in Devil's Head, and then we arrived at the Holiday Inn, where they held the dance in the ballroom. It was the only ballroom in a fifty-mile radius, so all the wedding receptions took place there as well. You had to book it at least a year in advance.

Violet volunteered to chaperone at the dance. We were the only students with parents who ensured a concerned *representative* would keep an eye on us at both the dance and the post-prom party. For parents who wanted us to be together forever, they didn't trust us to be together alone.

"Did you get it?" I asked Matt while we were slow dancing to Foreigner's "I Want to Know What Love Is."

"Get what?"

"Protection," I whispered in his ear.

He nodded, and I tightened my grip around his neck. I couldn't believe I was hours from doing it for the first time. My pubes were trimmed (shaved on the sides, short on top), lotion, perfume, and sexy underwear that Heather bought for me because the preacher's daughter couldn't be seen buying lace and satin.

Of course, I couldn't tell Heather the truth since Matt didn't want us to tell anyone. So I told her I wanted to feel sexy even if I wasn't having it.

"Come on," Heather said, tugging my arm at the end of the song.

I released Matt. "Where are we going?"

"To change our clothes for post-prom. Do you want to come to my house?"

"I figured we were going to my house," Matt said. "I don't have clothes in the car."

"We'll meet you at the school," I told Heather while Matt took my hand and led me toward the exit.

"We have an hour," Matt said as we wormed our way through the parking lot. "Since your mom will be at post-prom, we won't be allowed to leave early. And you have a curfew, so this is our only chance."

"Where are we going?" I asked.

We had talked about *it*, but we didn't make plans beyond getting a condom.

"Doesn't matter." He opened my door. "The west side of Johnson's place?"

I nodded. There was a farm lane that no one used since Oren Johnson passed the previous year. His wife hadn't hired anyone to take care of the ranch, so everything was a neglected mess. My dad said it was only a matter of time before his dad bought the fifty acres from Mrs. Johnson.

Matt and I had parked there a handful of times to make out.

No heavy petting.

No removing clothes.

Not even a hickey.

We didn't speak a word on the ten-minute drive. I was nervous, but excited. I just wanted to get it over with. Honestly, I was looking forward to my second, third, or tenth time more than the first. Nerves sucked because we both had them. There was no one to soothe the tension—to be the teacher. We were two hormonally jacked-up teenagers eager to take the ultimate rite of passage into adulthood.

And we were clueless.

Matt parked and killed the engine. "I don't have a back seat."

I grinned with a nervous laugh. "Uh, yeah, I know."

"So," he scraped his teeth across his lower lip, "I'll sit in that seat and ..." He eyed me.

I nodded a half dozen times. "And I'll ..." I couldn't even say it.

I'll straddle your lap and ride you.

We used nods more than words to communicate. Matt stepped out of the car and walked around the front, nervously pumping his fists. He opened my door and helped me out before taking my place. Then he retrieved the condom from his wallet and set it on the dash while I reached for the zipper of my dress and scanned and listened for cars in the distance.

"Your dad's going to kill me," he mumbled when I kicked off my shoes and unzipped my dress.

"My dad is a strict Ten Commandment follower. He won't kill you. And why do you think he's going to find out?" I stepped out of my dress and draped it over the open door.

"Sarah," he whispered, his eyes the size of saucers as he wet his lips.

Matthew Cory was the coolest kid in school.

Smart.

Talented.

And every girl was beside herself with envy that he was my boyfriend. He bled confidence in everything he did.

But staring at me in nothing but a strapless bra and sexy underwear as I removed my pantyhose, he looked ready to crap his pants. I had no clue what I was doing. I just knew I wanted to do it.

"You've seen me in a swimsuit." I nervously laughed.

He slowly shook his head. "A one-piece."

"Are you going to do it with your clothes on?"

Matt glanced down as if he didn't know he still had them on. Then he wriggled out of his jacket and unbuttoned his bowtie. When he reached for the top button of his shirt, I ducked my head to climb inside, straddling his lap.

"Let me." I bit my lip, unbuttoning it.

Everything felt forced and robotic as he rested his hands at his sides.

"You can touch me," I said with heat crawling along my skin from my chest to my face, and my hands shook while unbuttoning his shirt. "Take off my bra," I whispered before kissing him. My voice trembled despite my efforts to feign confidence.

I wanted him to be the one taking charge or at least pretending to do it.

He fumbled my bra, failing to unhook it. A groan of frustration rumbled through his chest when he realized he couldn't kiss me and simultaneously remove my bra. Maybe that only happened in the movies.

"Just leave it on and lie down," he said in a clipped tone, running his hands through his hair with a long sigh. "In case we hear someone coming."

I nodded, reaching between us to unzip his pants. His breaths came fast and heavy over my face. When I saw his erection straining against his white briefs, I lifted my gaze to him.

I was *so* nervous.

He leaned forward, grabbing the condom. With hands as shaky as mine, he tried to rip it open.

"Want me to try?"

He shook his head. "I've got it." He pulled the round ring

from the foil packet and held it between his fingers while releasing his erection from his briefs.

I tried not to stare, but I failed.

When I flitted my gaze to him, we stared at each other for a brief moment, and vulnerability bled from his tense expression.

If he was embarrassed, he shouldn't have been. I had no one to compare him to, but his *part* looked big.

Big enough.

I wanted to touch it, but I didn't know how. Heather said a man's penis felt soft, warm, and smooth—especially the circumcised head.

Before I could make my move, he tried to roll on the condom. I don't know if he was attempting to put it on the wrong way or what, but it snapped out of his hold, and I jumped as if it was going to bite me before it landed on the floor by the accelerator.

"Dammit!" He hissed, stretching to the side to retrieve it.

We wrinkled our noses at the fuzz and dirt stuck to it.

"Did you bring more than one?" I asked.

Matt shook his head. "I'm an idiot." He tucked his shrinking erection into his briefs before closing his eyes and pinching the bridge of his nose.

"You could pull out."

"No way, Sarah. This is a sign that I'm not supposed to be taking the pastor's daughter's virginity out of wedlock."

"Are you mad?"

He continued to shake his head. "I'm just ... frustrated."

"At me?"

"At us." He opened his intense blue eyes. "This was a stupid idea. We've waited this long; what's a little longer?"

I laughed. "A little longer? Time's running out. Whatever. We don't have to be each other's firsts." As soon as I said the words, I regretted them. I was guilting him into having sex with me.

Father would be so proud.

He frowned. "You act like I did this on purpose. Besides. You know the second we do it, you'll have instant remorse because you act like you don't care what your dad thinks, but you do. You end up doing whatever he asks you to do."

I climbed out of the car and tried to balance on one foot while threading my other into my pantyhose with dirt stuck to the bottom of my feet. "Well, he didn't ask me to have sex with you, but here we are."

"*Not* having sex," Matt said, buttoning his shirt.

"Because you fumbled the stupid condom."

"You mean the condom that I had to figure out how to get? And then we weren't even in a bed. Instead, we're crammed into the front seat of my car, and you were crowding me when I was trying to roll it on. What did you expect to happen?"

"You're such a romantic." I hiked up my pantyhose and stepped into my dress while he slid across the bench seat.

"Whatever," he mumbled.

Not a peep was uttered on the way to his house to change our clothes for post-prom.

Matt didn't open my door or wait for me.

"You beat your mom home," Wesley said, glancing up from the newspaper when Matt stepped into the kitchen, letting the door to the porch nearly hit me in the face.

"We have to change our clothes. We won't be here long," he said on his way up the stairs.

"How was the dance?" Wesley asked me before I had a

chance to sneak around the corner to the main-level bathroom.

"It was good."

He gave me a quick glance before returning his attention to the paper.

I turned left.

"Remember to use the upstairs bathroom if you need a toilet," Wesley said.

With a sigh, I headed up the stairs with my bag over my shoulder. Just as I reached the bathroom, the door opened. Isaac stood in front of me wearing nothing but a faded pair of jeans and a smirk. He took the liberty of inspecting me without a hint of regret.

And I instinctively did the same to him. Earlier, I thought Matt looked like a man, but I was wrong. Isaac was *the* man—sculpted from hard muscles. He didn't have tattoos on his torso, so I had no excuse for staring for so long.

"I need to change my clothes," I murmured, checking my chin for drool.

"How'd it go?" he asked.

I forced my gaze to his scruffy face. "The dance was fine."

"Not the dance."

I narrowed my eyes.

"The other festivities," he said.

He was probably drunk. That seemed like the most logical explanation for his random babbling.

"What other festivities?"

"I made a donation. That makes me a vested interest. So I'm interested. How did it go?"

"What donation?"

Isaac leaned forward, bringing his lips to my ear, which

brought his bare chest so close I felt actual heat radiating from it.

He was *so* inappropriate, and yet, I allowed it.

"Sunday Morning," he whispered, "I donated the condom."

I wanted to die.

Matt asked *him* for a condom? I would have preferred anyone, literally anyone else. My face burned with embarrassment.

"It's none of your business." I tried to squeeze past him.

"It's a little of my business."

I turned and pushed the door shut. "Ask Matt." With warp speed, I changed into jeans, a pocket T-shirt, and checkered Vans. As I passed Isaac's closed bedroom door, I heard Madonna's "Like a Virgin" playing from his stereo.

"Jerk," I muttered to myself before descending the stairs where Matt waited by the door in jeans and a blue T-shirt.

"I'm sorry," he said with a frown which made me think he wasn't sorry at all. He just didn't want things to be awkward in front of my mom at post-prom.

I offered him an equally disingenuous smile, which only deepened his frown. Matt was my first love, but we fought often, and usually over his temper, which, according to Violet, he learned from Wesley.

And despite the hiccup with getting the football coach's daughter pregnant and being sent off to enlist, Isaac was supposedly like his mom—cool and even-keeled. However, I had only seen his obnoxious and slightly inappropriate side.

"I think it's weird that you're so desperate to do it," Matt said, breaking the silence a few miles from the school. "I've heard it can hurt for girls their first time."

"You know what I think is weird? I think it's weird that

you haven't been the one pushing for this to happen. Name one of your friends who hasn't done it or at least gone a lot further than we've gone?"

Matt ignored me.

"If my dad wasn't your pastor, would we have done more by now?"

He still didn't respond; he checked his mirrors like I didn't exist. Matt's silence always said more than his words.

I laughed, shaking my head. "Unbelievable. So if Melinda or Julie were your girlfriend, you'd walk into the pharmacy like a man, buy a box of condoms, and have sex with them. But I'm the preacher's daughter, so I have to beg for it, and by it, apparently, that means a condom, which you borrowed *from your brother,* that you fumbled and dropped onto the dirty floor."

Matt whipped his head in my direction as he pulled the car into the parking lot. "How did you know that?"

With my arms crossed over my chest, I stared out the window at the other students filing into the school. "He was coming out of the bathroom when I needed to change my clothes, and he asked me how it went."

"What did you say?" Matt put the car in *Park* and killed the engine.

"I told him to ask you."

"Great. What am I supposed to say now?"

"I don't know, Matt. But just make sure you tell him I was incredible." I climbed out of the car, locked the door, and shut it.

"Har har." He locked his door and jogged to catch up to me as a few raindrops fell.

As soon as we made it through the line and into the gym, my mom found us.

"How was the dance?"

I smiled. "Great."

"Did you go straight to Matt's house afterward?" Her question sounded like something my dad would have asked.

But I didn't give her the response I would have given my dad. With her, I occasionally showed my snarky side. "We parked on a gravel road and did it, then we went to Matt's house."

"Sarah!" Mom grabbed my shoulders and pressed her body into mine as if she were trying to smother me before I could say another word.

Matt held up his hands, eyes wide, while shaking his head. "I don't know what she's talking about, Mrs. Jacobson."

Mom's hands shifted from my shoulders to my face, and she squeezed my cheeks—hard.

"Ow!" I pulled away.

"Behave." She gave me the hairy eyeball.

I returned a toothy grin and blew her a kiss before following Matt toward a group of our friends playing games next to the snack and beverage table.

Matt eyed me the way I imagined my father would have had he heard what I said. "You're no fun." I stuck out my tongue.

Matt couldn't hold his scowl, so he grabbed me when his grin stole his expression. Pressing his chest to my back, he wrapped his arms around my shoulders and whispered in my ear, "You would have been incredible."

He had a way of talking big when we were somewhere he didn't have to prove himself, like fish stories, nowhere near a body of water.

Where was that level of confidence when we were half-naked in his car? Why did the fumbled condom ruin everything? Matt had ten fingers and a tongue. Where was his imagination?

It didn't matter. I would not lose sleep over the condom fiasco. Isaac playing "Like a Virgin" was the only memory that would stay permanently stamped into my brain for eternity. I couldn't get Madonna out of my head or Isaac's sculpted bare chest.

Chapter Six

Simple Minds, "Don't You Forget About Me"

HE WOULDN'T STOP STARING at me.

I'd come to love and hate Sunday morning service in equal parts because Isaac came with his family, but he sat in the back row and stared at me the whole time with an indiscernible expression that involved a wolfish grin.

"It's hot," I whispered to Heather while pulling at the neck of my choir robe.

"It's not. Your dad always has the AC set at fifty," she mumbled under her breath.

It was Satan. He brought the flames of Hell with him. And he loved watching me sweat and squirm through the whole service.

Matt never told me if they talked about the failed attempt at sex. And I didn't ask. It was history.

But every Sunday, Isaac taunted me.

When summer officially arrived, I had high hopes of making lots of money working at the farm stand so I could afford a trip to Nashville that didn't involve visiting Vanderbilt, where I hadn't gotten accepted. My parents thought a year or two at a community college and volunteering would increase my chances if I reapplied for the following year.

I wasn't a straight-A student like Matt. My interest in music and writing songs distracted me from academics, so I had silver honors cords around my neck at graduation instead of gold like Matt and many of my friends.

"Congratulations!" Violet hugged me as everyone congregated in front of the school after the ceremony, a sea of graduates adorned in blue with white tassels.

"Thanks." I unzipped my gown when she released me. Then I glanced up, getting a whiff of cigarette smoke.

Isaac stood across the street, puffing away in jeans and a KISS T-shirt. When he saw me looking at him, he flicked the cigarette butt and stepped on it with his boot before crossing the street. "Way to go, Sunday Morning," he said.

I searched for Matt, but he was nowhere in sight. My sisters were talking to some of their friends, and our parents were mingling with other graduates and parents. There was no one to save me from Satan.

"What's up with the loser cords?" He nodded toward me.

"Excuse me?" I wrinkled my nose.

"Silver cords. That's disappointing."

My jaw dropped. Was he implying that silver cords meant I was stupid? There were some students who didn't qualify for any cords.

"At least I have cords. I bet you barely got a gown and a hat with a tassel."

He pulled on my cords, removing them with a quick jerk. Then he used them to stretch over his head like Matt did with a baseball bat before his games.

"I was valedictorian like Matty."

"Pfft." I rolled my eyes.

Isaac grinned, and I couldn't tell if he was mocking me or gloating. "It's true. Hey, Mom?"

Violet turned toward us, narrowing her eyes at my cords stretched above Isaac's head as he twisted right and then left.

"Was I valedictorian of my class?"

"Give Sarah her cords back before you do something to them. Yes, you were valedictorian. Why?"

Had I wired it shut, I could not have prevented my jaw from dropping. The shock was too much.

Violet returned her attention to my friend Kennedy and her parents while Isaac's grin swelled to obnoxious proportions.

"I heard you didn't get into Vanderbilt. Maybe I could tutor you so you can retake your SATs and get a better score." Isaac lassoed my cords, catching my neck in the hole.

My eyes almost popped out of my head.

"What flavor of cake are you having at your party?" he asked.

I removed the cords, so I didn't look like a captured cow. "Chocolate and vanilla."

"Marble? Or separate?"

"Why?" I asked.

"Because I'm deciding which parties I'm going to hit based on the cake flavors being served."

"Who said you're invited to my party?"

His smirk returned. "Your parents invited my whole family. Are you having barbecued beef or those little turkey sandwiches on rolls with mayo and mustard? God, I love those. What about the mints? Are you serving the cream cheese kind? My mom and aunt made hundreds of them for Matty's party."

"He hates when you call him Matty. And I'm not a fan of Sunday Morning."

Isaac's eyebrows slid up his forehead. "I won't tell your dad that."

"You're an idiot."

He chuckled. "But I'm an idiot who loves little turkey sandwiches and cream cheese mints. So just give me the menu," he looked at his hefty military-grade watch, "so I can plan accordingly."

I pivoted, searching for Matt or anyone who I could talk to who wasn't Isaac Cory.

"Sarah! You didn't tell me Matt's going to play baseball at Michigan," Kristy snagged my arm. "He has a full ride? That's so cool. I'm going there too."

I fought for a non-catty smile. Kristy had a crush on Matt. She had ever since her family moved to Devil's Head our sophomore year. Despite knowing I was his girlfriend, she always talked about him in front of me like we were girls crushing on a movie star.

But *we* weren't.

He was my boyfriend, and Kristy was the psycho stalker.

"Sorry. I figured everyone knew," I said.

"Are you going to Michigan?"

I shook my head, and Kristy couldn't hide her excitement. "Well, I'll keep an eye on him for you. Do you think you'll stay together?"

"There you are," Matt said, hugging me from behind and burying his face into my neck.

Kristy deflated while I smirked, so she walked away.

"My mom said we'll go to your house for a while as long as we're home by four for my open house," he said.

I turned in his arms. "Kristy's going to Michigan. She said she'd keep an eye on you for me." I batted my eyelashes.

Matt rolled his eyes. "Please tell me you're not jealous."

"I'm not jealous. You can do whatever you want with Kristy."

He took a step back. "Don't do this. Nothing is set in stone."

"Stop. We know where this is headed." I shot him a toothy grin.

"I don't want to talk about it. And I don't want to do anything with anyone else. We have all summer. You act like I'm leaving tomorrow."

I grabbed his *gold* cords, pulled him back to me, and smiled. "Yes. We have the summer."

"Where we can do *things*?" He bit his lower lip.

Sex.

I lifted onto my toes to kiss him, but out of the corner of my eye, I caught my dad staring at us, so I pressed my lips to his cheek instead of his mouth for a quick peck.

Was it okay that we were using each other for sex? I knew God's answer, but mine was a little more flexible.

MATT'S FAMILY attended my open house for an hour before they had to get home for his. I planned on going there after mine ended at five.

Thirty minutes after they left, I ran inside to use the bathroom, only to find Isaac with his head in the fridge.

"The party is outside. And your family left. What are you still doing here?"

He turned, holding a jar of sliced dill pickles. "Beef burgers are a little disappointing, but I can deal with it as long as there are pickles." He set the jar on the counter next to his paper plate piled high with food. "I'm sure it was an oversight on your mom's part. No biggie." Isaac opened the jar and fished a slice out with his plastic fork.

"Didn't you ride with your parents?" I asked.

"Yes, but I wasn't done eating, so your mom said I can ride with you when you go to Matty's open house," he mumbled after shoving nearly half the sandwich into his mouth. "I carried a few heavy coolers to the back of the garage for her. I think she's starting to like me."

Before I could respond, my mom slid open the patio door.

"Did you really say Isaac could ride with me to their house?" I blurted.

"Well, yes. Why?" She tore off a trash bag from the roll under the sink.

"I figured I was riding with you guys."

Mom unfolded the bag and snapped it open. "I assumed you'd stay later than we will."

"Oh." That's it. I had no better response. Of course, I would stay longer and therefore drive. But I couldn't think in Isaac's proximity because he made me nervous and other things I hadn't yet defined.

Mom headed back out to the garage.

"You look pretty," Isaac said. "That dress makes the blue in your eyes pop. You have great eyes. Does Matty tell you that? They're really stunning."

I hated my body for blushing because Isaac wasn't serious. He said it in a mocking tone like he said *Matty*.

My pleated blue peasant dress that covered my knees and shoulders and had a thin vinyl belt wasn't sexy, and neither were my knee-high brown boots, but Isaac didn't say I looked sexy. He said I looked pretty.

Suddenly, I hated the word pretty.

Pretty meant sweet.

Sweet meant innocent.

Innocent meant a virgin.

Don't get me started on him calling my eyes stunning. No, "Matty" never said my eyes were stunning.

"I have to go to the bathroom," I mumbled, running up the stairs before the heat made my head pop like the valve on my mom's pressure cooker.

How was I going to be alone with him in my car?

Chapter Seven

Daryl Hall & John Oates, "Sara Smile"

"SARAH, you and Isaac go on ahead while we finish putting the food away," Mom said after the last person left our house.

I hiked my purse over my shoulder and fidgeted with my keys while Isaac stood by the door, eating his fourth piece of cake.

Yes, I'd been counting. I spent the entire afternoon keeping one eye on Satan.

"Okay," I said nervously.

Isaac finished the cake and tossed the plate into the trash before leading the way to my blue Plymouth Champ, where he opened my driver's side door.

"What are you doing?" I asked, freezing because it felt like a trap.

"Being a gentleman."

"You're not a gentleman," I said while tossing my purse behind the seat and stepping into the car.

"Sunday Morning, I'm a lot of things you know nothing about." He shut my door.

I fumbled my keys, looking for the right one.

"You know, my dad secretly hates that your family lives here," Isaac said as I shoved the key into the ignition.

"What?" I squinted at him while starting the car.

"He wants to demolish your house and use the land for crops. He said he'd make more money than your family's paying him for rent—he's mentioned your dad misses rent payments too often. And your house is the oldest house in Devil's Head. Its green paint is peeling, and there are potholes the size of your dinky car scattered along your circle drive. But my mom thinks evicting lifelong family friends (and her future daughter-in-law) is a bad idea. She also thinks my dad would go to Hell for kicking a man of God out of his house."

I popped the clutch and killed it.

"First time driving a stick?"

"No," I grumbled, peeling out of the gravel drive on my second attempt while avoiding the car-sized potholes.

The Corys owned our house and land, and apparently, they owned me—their future daughter-in-law. I was all too aware that those missed rent payments were overlooked because Wesley and Violet thought I was going to marry their son. But I didn't know they discussed it around Isaac.

"Mind if I smoke?" Isaac rolled down the window and lit a cigarette.

"Yes, I mind. My dad will kill me if he smells smoke in my car."

"That's why I have the window rolled down." He blew a cloud of poison out the window.

"Fasten your seat belt," I grumbled.

"Why? Are you going to crash?" He held his cancer stick between his thumb and pointer finger while the wind tangled my hair but did nothing to his short hair that had started to grow out of the military buzz cut.

"It's the law now," I said.

"And you're a rule follower, Sunday Morning?" He shot me a quick glance, but I kept my eyes on the road.

"I suppose people who smoke have a death wish, so never mind, don't fasten your seat belt. If we crash, maybe you'll go quickly."

"Jesus, Sunday Morning, you're such a drag."

"Because I don't want to die?"

"Because you're afraid of it," he said.

"What's the difference?"

He laughed. "God, your ignorance astounds me."

"Stop calling me that."

He smirked, puffing his cigarette. "If I wanted to die, I'd put a bullet in my head and be done. If I was afraid of dying, I'd give up smoking and fasten my seat belt. But I neither want to die nor am I afraid of it, so I get to be something you'll never be."

I didn't want to ask. I was mad at him as I gripped the steering wheel with one hand and the gearshift with my other. But Isaac had a way of making me do things I didn't want to do.

"What's that?" I asked, frustrated with myself for satisfying him by once again showing my *ignorance*.

"Fun," he chirped.

"I'm fun," I scoffed.

"You're fun to toy with, but you're not fun to be with. You're too uptight."

The car skidded on the gravel at the four-way stop, and Isaac shot me a knowing glance—I'd nearly run right through it.

I was fun, smart, and a bunch of other things he knew nothing about because he'd been in the service for six years.

As with so many things in my life, this moment had a worthwhile note too: the country roads in Devil's Head were mostly abandoned. Statistically, the chances of getting into a car accident if you ignored all of the stop signs were extremely low. *Thank God!*

As we stared at each other, he offered me the cigarette. "I promise it's better than a cow's butthole," he said.

I snorted. "Have you licked a cow's butthole?"

He shrugged. "It gets lonely on the ranch. Hours in the pasture, inhaling dirt and all that methane can lead to unfathomable boredom. The next thing you know, you're passing the backside of a cow, and a gentle stroke here and there leads to ..." He shrugged.

I tried to hate Isaac, but I liked him too much to be successful. *He* was fun, even if I had no plans of admitting it.

"Ew, I will never stick anything of yours in my mouth," I said.

I didn't mean it in that way. But when Isaac's expression morphed into something akin to surprise, as though I did mean it suggestively, I didn't want to convince him otherwise. It was the first time he looked at me like a worthy adversary.

So, I slowly raised my chin and smirked.

"Fuck me, Sunday Morning." Isaac shook his head. "I'm

taking that as a personal challenge." He pinched his lips around the cigarette.

After forgetting that I was at a four-way stop with no other cars, I slowly let up on the clutch and pulled through the intersection with my nerves frayed, heart racing, and mind reeling. Why was I goading him?

He turned on the radio and flipped through the stations.

"No!" I shook my head when he stopped on a station playing a song I *could not* listen to.

He laughed before belting out the lyrics to Daryl Hall and John Oates' "Sara Smile."

I reached to turn it off, but he grabbed my wrist, flicked his cigarette butt out the window, and wrapped his other hand around my forearm, using my hand as a microphone.

"Stop ..." I giggled.

Isaac beamed, hitting every note and nailing every word. It made my face hurt from smiling. He had a great voice, and I felt a pang of disappointment when the song ended and he released my arm.

Refusing to let my joy linger too long, knowing he'd eat it up and gloat for the rest of the day, I cleared my throat. "For the record, 'Sara Smile' is Sara without an H. I'm Sarah with an H."

"Oh, pardon me. So you're *Sarahhh*, like a really good orgasm."

How did I repeatedly hand him opportunities to embarrass me?

The radio station he picked played older songs. Other than Heather, none of my friends listened to anything before the 1980s. And it secretly thrilled me that Isaac did, too, because I had a soft spot for older songs.

Isaac jumped into The Spencer Davis Group's "Gimme

Some Lovin'," and I couldn't help but join in because I knew all the words, which seemed to surprise him. He peered over at me just as I shot him a quick glance while belting out the lyrics with the windows down and a cloud of gravel dust in the rearview mirror. I even slowed down a bit as we approached his drive because I wanted to finish singing the song with him.

As we turned right and the song faded into a commercial, I wiped the smile from my face. Suddenly, I felt ridiculous, like I couldn't let Isaac think I enjoyed singing with him or smiling in his presence.

"That was good, *Sarahhh* ..." He closed his eyes and tipped his head back like he was having—well, let's just say that it wasn't something my dad would have approved of.

I parked behind a long line of cars and jumped out.

"Are you running from me?" Isaac asked.

"No," I said without glancing back or slowing down.

"Then what's the hurry?" His boots crunched along the gravel behind me, getting closer despite my frantic pace.

I flew up the porch stairs and halted when I opened the door. A throng of people filled the space, but I didn't see Matt anywhere.

"Who knew Matty had so many friends," Isaac mumbled behind me as I tried to shoulder my way through the crowd to the front door, but it was nearly impossible. "You're being too nice," he said so close to my ear I could feel the warmth of his breath. "Just tell everyone to get the hell—or, in your case, *heck*—out of the way." His hands rested on my hips, guiding me.

I couldn't breathe.

"Sarah has to pee. Can everyone part the Red Sea?"

Isaac yelled, and the noise died to nothing more than a few whispers.

I wanted. To. Die! Why did he say that?

Flames of embarrassment engulfed my face as I tucked my chin and scurried into the house after everyone made room for me and my supposed urgent bladder.

"Hey, sweetie!" Violet spied me the second I opened the front door. She was busy refilling bowls of chips and plates of *little turkey sandwiches*. "Did the rest of your party go well?"

"It did." I smiled. "Thanks. Where's Matt?"

"He's out back. Wesley's starting a bonfire. You should have changed into something more casual." She eyed my dress and boots.

I shrugged. "It's fine."

"Did you get your fill?" Violet shifted her attention to Isaac as he stepped past me, but not before letting the back of his hand brush my ass.

My glutes tightened, and I pretended that it was an accident. But who was I kidding? Nothing he did was by accident.

Isaac snatched a plate and loaded it with food. "It was a start, but they didn't have my favorite turkey sandwiches."

"I'm surprised you stayed," Violet murmured without giving it much thought.

However, I couldn't think of anything else as I gawked at Isaac's mountain of food. When he glanced up at me, I scowled at him.

"Did you wet your pants?" he asked.

I rolled my eyes before heading toward the back door through the mudroom.

"Sarah!" Heather called. "Just in time." She ran toward me and threw her arms around my neck. "I'm so glad my party was last weekend. *Everyone* has theirs today." After a quick hug, she looped her arm with mine, and we walked down the hill toward the enormous pile of brush and tree limbs.

"I wondered when you'd get here." Matt smiled, and it was my favorite smile.

I felt complete adoration when he gave me that smile, and I would miss it when he left in the fall. There were some deep parts to our relationship, but it wasn't anywhere close to standing at an altar and promising forever.

"Did you have a lot of people? I bet it was packed with every single person from church."

"Of course," I said as Heather wandered toward some of the other kids. I wrapped an arm around Matt and stole his can of Coke even though I was a Pepsi girl. "Did you think it was weird that your brother stayed after you and your parents left?" I took a few sips and handed the can back to him.

"No. He knew Coach Harvey might show up here."

My eyebrows reached for my hairline. "You invited Coach Harvey?"

Matt smirked.

He did it just to upset his brother.

"Dude, let's go hit some targets," Tyler said to Matt.

The Corys had an area behind one of their barns with haystacks and empty can targets. Matt and his buddies liked to shoot BB guns.

"Coming?" Matt asked me.

I shook my head and hugged myself. "I'm cold. I'll hang out by the fire."

74

"There's a hoodie on my bed if you can sneak upstairs," Matt said before leading a few of the guys toward the barn.

I headed up the hill, staring at my feet to avoid making eye contact with Isaac sitting on the concrete steps at the back door. "Some of the guys are shooting BB guns behind the barn. You should go make friends."

"I have you, Sunday Morning. What other friends could I possibly need?"

"We're not friends. You're just my boyfriend's brother, who I tolerate." I squeezed past him.

"Where are you going?"

"None of your beeswax."

He chuckled. "Beeswax?"

I ignored him as the screen door shut behind me. Then I wormed my way through the people in the living room and dashed up the stairs when I didn't think anyone was looking. After I returned to the main level, Violet and some of the Corys' extended family pulled me aside to ask a million questions about my future plans. By the time I made it out back again, Isaac was nowhere in sight, and I relaxed while trekking toward the barn in Matt's sweatshirt that was too long in the arms.

Before I reached the back side of the barn, I heard something inside—a guitar. I paused my steps for a few seconds and listened to the melancholy chords. Falling prey to my curiosity, I eased open the creaky door and wandered toward the weathered ladder to the loft, where there was light coming from the corner. When I reached the top, the boards whined beneath my steps, and the music stopped.

"Are you lost?" Isaac said as I peeked around the corner of the stacked hay bales. He sat beneath a utility light with a soft yellow glow cast over him. With one knee bent and the other outstretched, he hugged an acoustic guitar.

"How many guitars do you have?" I asked, ignoring his question.

"A few." He strummed a new chord.

Through the old barn walls, I could hear the pinging of BBs hitting cans out back.

"So little turkey sandwiches are your favorite, yet you stayed at my house. Would it have anything to do with Coach Harvey?"

Isaac stopped strumming and eyed me with a serious expression. Then he rested the guitar beside him and picked up his half-eaten plate of food, resuming his feast. It was warm in the barn loft, so I pulled Matt's hoodie over my head and removed my clunky brown boots.

Isaac stopped chewing mid-bite, eyes wide. "Keep going," he said.

I wrinkled my nose at him while crossing my legs and sitting on the dirty planks of wood. When I picked up his guitar, he didn't stop me. I pressed my left fingers to the strings and strummed a chord with my right hand.

"Thought you didn't play," he said.

"I don't," I said, playing another chord. "But I've watched closely when other people have played, so I know like two chords."

"As long as you remember our deal," he mumbled over the food in his mouth.

"Deal?" I continued to pluck the strings while glancing up at him.

He smirked. "If you touch something that's mine, I get to touch something that's yours."

I began to care a little less that he made me blush, especially with a guitar in my hands. "What do you want to touch?" I don't know if it was the long day, the thick, musty air in the barn, the dim light, or holding something I loved, but I felt brave.

And curious.

Was Isaac messing with me the way he messed with Matt?

His grin swelled until it turned into a slight chuckle, and he rocked his head, but he didn't answer me. Matt thought Isaac was irritating; I found him amusing.

"What do you want to play?" he asked.

"Nothing," I murmured, staring at my hands. My parents weren't wrong; my fingers didn't have adequate callouses to play the guitar.

"Liar," Isaac said, setting his plate aside and standing.

I continued to strum my single chord while tracking him. My fingers slipped when he sat behind me, his legs sliding around me as his chest pressed to my back. He ghosted his arm along mine to my hand, cupping it; his fingers pressing mine to the strings. My shaky fingers cascaded down them.

It was intimate, and it made my tummy do weird flips that I told myself was just nerves.

"What should we play?" he asked so seductively that I stopped breathing.

"*Jesus Loves Me*," I whispered.

When he laughed, it vibrated my body too. "What else?"

"Bette Davis Eyes," I murmured with my heart in my throat.

Isaac moved my fingers, and we repeated the first part several times. The fourth time, I let my hands fall from the guitar onto his legs while he played it alone. Then, I sang the lyrics, softly at first, then stronger.

I closed my eyes and felt the words and every chord that accompanied them. But mostly, I felt Isaac's warm body pressed to mine and his face so close to me he must have memorized the scent of my shampoo.

When it ended, he didn't move, and neither did I for several seconds.

Then he cleared his throat. "We should get back to the party."

"Play it again," I said.

"I need a smoke." He lifted the guitar.

I scooted forward and turned to face him. Isaac's gaze dropped to where my dress rode up my leg, showing the skin along my inner thigh. I contemplated covering it, but I liked the way he looked at my leg. So I told myself that it was just a little skin.

"I want you to play it again so I can watch your hands," I said.

His gaze lingered on my leg until he wet his lips and brought his attention back to my face. "Do you think your desire to watch me play is more important than my desire to smoke?"

The problem with hanging out with Satan was it felt too easy to be a little naughty. I unbuttoned the top button of my dress, only because it was hot, and I leaned back on my hands, which made the opening of my dress slide down an inch. Isaac's eyes flitted between the tiny tease of my cleavage and my face.

I found too much pleasure in watching him try to figure me out. Was my fascination accidental and innocent or intentional and inappropriate?

I wasn't sure.

All I knew was it was the music that made me do it. The

love and desire I had for it helped me endure every obstacle, even if said obstacle was a twenty-four-year-old with a dangerous bout of sex appeal.

I sang the first line and waited.

Keeping his gaze locked on mine, he played the guitar. That moment was the most alive I had felt in years. My music-loving heart soared as I concentrated on every move his fingers made while the lyrics flowed effortlessly.

Isaac never focused on his hands; he only looked at me. It made me blush, and in a few areas, my voice trembled. That's when he nodded his head, encouraging me to keep going. Isaac Cory exuded enough confidence for both of us.

"Satisfied?" he asked after the last note.

My grin won. "Satisfied for now."

"Sunday Morning?"

"Huh?"

He jerked his head toward the front of the barn. "Get out of here."

I faked a frown and stood, pulling on my boots. Then I draped the hoodie over my arm. The words "thank you" were on my lips, but I swallowed them. "Girls don't like boys who smoke." I brushed past him to the ladder.

"And yet, here you are," he murmured.

"I don't like you." I climbed down the ladder.

"You're just using me?"

"Yep," I chirped with a huge grin on my face that he couldn't see as I strolled out of the barn.

"Sarah, what are you doing?" Matt asked as he, Heather, and a few other guys stepped around the corner from the back side of the barn.

"I heard something from inside the barn, so I checked it

out." I took his proffered hand. "Isaac was playing his guitar, so I asked him to show me a few chords."

"And he did?" Matt shot me a lifted eyebrow.

"Sort of." I downplayed it. "He humored me for two seconds before saying he needed a smoke." I was proud of myself for telling Matt the truth, or most of it.

"Is he still in the barn?" Heather breezily asked as if it didn't matter, as if Tyler wasn't standing right behind her. They weren't officially together, but I knew he liked her more than she liked him.

The second I nodded, she winked and made a U-turn, heading toward the barn and glancing back to stick her tongue out. It was a test. She wanted to see if I liked Isaac enough to stop her.

I was with Matt, at least for the rest of the summer, so I just rolled my eyes. I didn't care if Heather flirted with Isaac. He wasn't mine. As long as Tyler didn't care, who was I to object?

Besides, I didn't like guys who smoked. I loved Jesus, and I wanted to do the right thing (most of the time). So, it made no sense that I felt jealous when Heather headed back to the barn. It's not like she was going to be interested in his guitar.

"She's a big girl. Let her figure it out," Matt said to me, pulling me toward the chairs his dad had set around the bonfire.

"Dibs on the red chair!" Tyler jumped into the chair I was just about to take, leaving me nowhere to sit.

"You don't care that Heather's in the barn with Isaac?" I asked Tyler.

He popped the top to a Dr. Pepper. "We're not really together. She can do what she wants."

"Come here," Matt said, pulling me onto his lap. "I can't

wait for everyone to leave," he whispered in my ear as I stared at the flames. "I think we should take a drive. Are you in?"

My gaze shifted to the left, searching for Heather or Isaac.

"Sarah?"

"Hmm?" I turned my head toward Matt.

"Did you hear me?"

"Sorry. What?"

"Do you want to go for a drive when everyone leaves?" He cupped his hand over his mouth at my ear. "I have more condoms."

Sex. He was suggesting sex. A second attempt.

Yes. I wanted to have sex. And with him, of course. Who else would I have wanted to have sex with?

"Okay." I smiled, leaning the back of my head against his shoulder while returning my attention to the direction of the barn.

Ten minutes passed.

Twenty minutes passed.

My anxiety hit a boiling point. "I'm going to check on Heather," I said, resting my hands on Matt's thighs to stand.

He nodded without taking his attention off Tyler as they chatted about their next baseball game.

Isaac had already impregnated one girl; surely, he would not make the same mistake again. But there was a lot they could do that didn't involve actual sex. Or maybe he carried a condom on him at all times, having learned his lesson.

To my relief, they weren't in the barn. It was getting dark, but as I approached, I could see Isaac leaning against the side of it, puffing on a cigarette. He offered it to Heather, and she took it.

"Heather Renee Goeff!" I yelled like her mother.

She quickly handed it back to Isaac and took a step away from him. "Sarah, you scared me." Heather pressed her hand to her chest. "What are you doing?"

"What are *you* doing? Please tell me you weren't going to put that cancer stick in your mouth."

"Jeez, Sarah. I was going to take one puff. So what? I'm an adult."

It irritated me that she was using the adult card. That was my play.

"I'm going with Isaac to a late movie. If my parents ask, will you say I was with you?"

I coughed and waved my hand in front of my face when Isaac exhaled the smoke. "No. I'm not lying."

"Sarah, come on. I'd do it for you."

"Yeah, *Sarahhh*." Isaac smirked. "If you cover for Heather, I won't tell your parents that I bought Matty his own box of condoms."

Heather's eyes bugged out as she covered her mouth.

I didn't know who I was most upset with—Heather for her willingness to run off with a virtual stranger who was six years older than her, Matt for asking his brother to buy him condoms as if he wasn't old enough to do it himself, or Isaac for messing with everyone around me.

Never mind. With one glance in his direction, I knew the answer.

"Heather, why don't you meet me in my truck? It's the red one." He handed her the last third of his cigarette. "Don't get caught." He winked.

Heather took the cigarette like it was a million-dollar coin with endless possibilities. But I knew that she just wanted to wrap her lips around something that Isaac had wrapped his around.

"My parents won't ask, but *if* they do, you have my back. Right?" Heather eyed me.

I sighed and returned a slight nod. Of course, I had her back.

She smiled and mouthed, "Thank you."

After she was up the hill and out of sight, I shifted my attention to Isaac. "I'd appreciate you not trying to get my friend hooked on something that could kill her."

"Does she like butter on her popcorn?"

"Leave her alone." I planted my fists on my hips, stepped into his space, and tipped my chin up.

Isaac's lips twitched. "Careful. I might decide to touch something that's not mine."

I held my ground, narrowing my eyes—calling his bluff.

"I told him to make you come first," he said.

I couldn't have hid my reaction had my life depended on it. But instead of a blush, the blood drained from my face. Sex was still "doing it." The penis was a "thingy." And orgasms weren't part of any discussion I'd had with friends. Maybe nobody was having them.

"As for you, I'd say you should fake it. Make Matty feel like a god his first time. Not your god, of course. Unless that's what does it for you."

Why was Isaac the third wheel in my relationship with Matt? Why would Matt confide in the one person who belittled him for no good reason?

"Did you give Coach Harvey's daughter an ..." I couldn't say it.

Dang it!

"An orgasm?" He lifted an eyebrow.

I didn't answer or even blink.

"What do you think, Sunday Morning?"

"I don't think about you doing it or anything for that matter," I said.

He bent forward, mouth at my ear, eliciting an unwelcome chill along my skin. "Liar," he whispered just before trekking up the hill toward his truck and my friend, who had a crush on him and no issues about having sex out of wedlock.

Chapter Eight

Foreigner, "It Feels Like the First Time"

By nine thirty, everyone had left the party, and Matt and I were on our way to our usual spot to try *it* again.

He moved the bench seat back as far as it would go so we could lie across it with our heads on the driver's side.

"Let's just kiss for a while," I suggested as he shrugged off his shirt and unbuttoned his jeans before climbing on top of me.

"You don't want to—" he started to speak.

"No. I do. I just think we were in a hurry last time. And we're not as rushed now, so ..."

He grinned, and I was reminded of just how handsome my boyfriend was. There were many reasons I fell in love with Matt, but his sexy yet boyish smile was at the top of that list. "Okay," he whispered before kissing me.

It was nice. He had minty breath from the Tic Tacs we

shared on the way there. I let him settle between my spread legs, but my dress was still on. His erection pressed between my legs. It was a little uncomfortable because we still had on our underwear, and his zipper was scraping against my skin.

Still, I felt aroused.

Aroused because I'd been thinking about sex—a lot.

Aroused because I liked kissing Matt.

Aroused because I thought of Isaac's body pressed to mine while he helped me play the guitar.

Aroused from his compliment, even if he wasn't serious.

"You look pretty. That dress makes the blue in your eyes pop. You have great eyes. Does Matty tell you that? They're really stunning."

And I couldn't get the image out of my head of Isaac smirking after telling me he said Matt should give me an orgasm first.

"I love you," Matt murmured, kissing his way down my neck.

"I love you too," I whispered to the only boy I had ever loved.

It might not have been the way my father or God wanted me to lose my virginity, but it was love (of sorts), and that's all that mattered to me.

"Tell me if you want to stop," Matt said, palming my breast over my dress while he continued to pump his pelvis against mine.

"Don't stop," I whispered, closing my eyes and lifting my eager hips while my heels dug into the seat. I wanted to be a real woman more than anything.

I wanted to feel the desire and emotion conveyed in my favorite song lyrics.

He kneeled with one knee between my legs and the

other barely on the edge of the seat while pushing his pants and briefs midway down his legs and rolling on a condom.

This was it. I was on the verge of giving my virginity to Matt Cory. And while I wasn't sure any man "deserved" a woman's innocence, Matt was certainly worthy of it. Giving my virginity to my first love felt special, *wrong*, but special.

He slid off my underwear and set them on the dash while I gathered my dress in my hands. I wanted to watch the way I always gawked when a nurse took my blood, gave me a shot, or the time I got stitches in my knee after falling out of a tree at Heather's house.

Heather ...

Was she still with Isaac? What were they doing? Was he having sex with her?

Matt teased his finger between my spread legs.

I bit my bottom lip because it felt different, not what I expected.

"Do you like that?" he asked.

I nodded, but I wasn't sure if I did or didn't like it. I wanted him to touch me a little higher, where I liked to touch myself. But I couldn't bring myself to tell him or show him.

"Does that feel good?"

It hit me; he thought he was giving me an orgasm like Isaac had told him to do.

Again, I nodded, and I wanted to shift my hips so he'd hit the spot that might have actually led to an orgasm, but first-time jitters paralyzed me. So, instead, I closed my eyes and breathed heavier and faster like I did when I touched myself. But it was difficult because I wasn't feeling anything spectacular.

"Yes," I whispered.

Matt's hand disappeared, and my eyes opened just as he guided the head of his erection to my entrance. He pressed inside of me, and it felt like everything in my body tightened up to prevent the invasion, despite telling myself to relax.

In return, Matt's face twisted with intensity as he leaned forward with his hands on either side of my head and pushed into me a little more.

It hurt.

I knew that it would, but I thought he'd slide in a little easier, and the pain would be all mine. However, the look on his face resembled the grimace I got when I put on a new pair of pantyhose that hadn't been stretched out yet.

"Does it hurt?" Matt asked.

I shook my head, holding my breath.

He pushed a little more, and I hissed.

"Sarah"—he frowned—"I'll stop."

"No! Just ..." I swallowed hard. "Move a little."

"Are you sure?" Sweat beaded along his brow like it was killing him, but it might have been our body heat in close quarters.

I nodded quickly.

He moved in tiny increments. I'm not sure he had even half of his erection inside of me. But it was plenty.

"Yes," I said, and that seemed to make him move a little faster and a little deeper, but not too deep. "Yes, yes ..." I continued to chant because I was certain that's what women said in the throes of passion.

"Oh God, Sarah ..." Matt's harsh breaths quickened as the tiny motions of his hips became more erratic.

And then, it was over.

More than half the girls in our graduating class would

have killed to have Matt Cory's penis inside of them. But I was the lucky recipient, and I hated it.

I. Hated. Sex.

How was I supposed to write love songs, sexy love songs, if I hated sex?

Why was the clitoris so far away from the entrance for the penis?

Nothing made sense. There were nearly five billion people on the planet. That meant billions of couples did it. *But why?*

"I love you." He kissed me between breaths. "I'm never going to forget you." He deposited kisses all over my face.

It was sweet. I loved him too.

I loved holding his hand.

I loved kissing him.

I even loved the feel of his erection pressed between my legs with our underwear still on.

But I did not love sex.

However, I *needed* to hear him say that he would never forget me. That meant that he knew it was just sex. We were breaking up. He would go to Michigan (never forgetting me), and I would go to Nashville.

"This meant everything to me," he declared with urgency as he continued to kiss me while holding himself up on his forearms. His condom-covered, deflated penis brushed my inner thigh, and the end of it felt warm and squishy. "Maybe fate will bring us back together someday." He smirked as if his performance ruined me for any other man, so my only choice would be to marry him.

Marriage meant family.

Family meant sex.

Nope. I was not marrying him or anyone.

Matt opened the door and sat on the edge of the seat with his back to me while he removed the condom. I reached for my underwear and slipped them back on before hugging my knees to my chest.

I couldn't believe it. I knew the first time wouldn't be Disneyland, but I at least expected Six Flags. Instead, I got a cheap, small-town carnival where the ride broke, and I was stuck upside down for twenty minutes.

Matt lasted more like five, but who was I to point fingers?

Maybe it was God. What if wedding night sex was better? Perhaps God only allowed it to be good after marriage. But could I risk marrying Matt and it not be any better? Was I a sinner doomed to bad sex for eternity?

"I'm starving," Matt said, pulling his shirt over his head as he stood with the door open. "You don't have to be home for another hour. Do you want to go to McDonalds? I could use a burger and fries, but if you're not hungry, you could just get a Coke or an ice cream cone."

I sat up, fixed my dress, and pulled on my boots. "Uh, sure."

"Everything okay?"

"Fine. Great. Yeah." I smiled with a brave inhale.

Matt nodded before closing my door and jogging around the front of his car to hop into his seat. When he put it in *Reverse*, he reached for my leg, giving it a squeeze. "I can't believe we finally did it. We're ... having sex." He grinned triumphantly and shoved it into *Drive*. "It's going to make going our separate ways at the end of summer that much harder."

Agree to disagree.

As if my night couldn't get any worse, Isaac's truck was at McDonald's when we pulled into the parking lot.

"The movie must have been sold out," Matt said. After we parked, he ran around to open my door—post-coital chivalry. He looked so handsome and proud. At least one of us was glowing.

"Thanks." I played the part with a big smile.

We held hands on the way inside the restaurant, and Heather immediately saw us and waved. Isaac's back was to us, but he turned and eyed me quickly before smirking at Matt like they had a secret.

"Uh, I need to use the bathroom," I murmured just as Matt started to lead me toward the counter to order.

"What do you want me to order for you?"

"Ice cream is fine," I said, letting go of his hand and hurrying to the bathroom, where I sat on the toilet and peed. When I wiped, there was no blood and none on my underwear like Heather said she had after her first time.

As soon as I opened the stall door to wash my hands, Heather was in my face, grabbing my shoulders. "Did you do it? Tell me everything. Oh my god, I can't believe you didn't tell me you were thinking of doing it. Was it good? Did he go down on you? Tell me!"

I lowered my head to make sure there wasn't anyone in the other stall. Thankfully, there wasn't.

Pulling away from her hold on me, I washed my hands, feeling her gaze at my reflection in the mirror. "Can you keep a secret?"

"Of course," she said while I dried my hands and turned toward her.

I wrinkled my nose and whispered, "I hated it."

Heather's smile fell off her face, leaving a blank expression in its place. She blinked several times. "W-what do you mean? Like ... sure, it hurt a little. But hate is a strong word.

Did you ..." She widened her eyes and slanted her head in a game of charades.

Orgasm.

Maintaining my grimace, I slowly shook my head.

"I mean, did he try to ..." Again, she let me fill in the blank.

I kept shaking my head.

"Did you tell him?"

"No!" I whisper-yelled, running my hands through my hair. "I faked it, and he was so happy, telling me how much he loved me and that we could end up getting married after all. I didn't have the heart to tell him the truth."

Heather's face mirrored mine—totally cringed. "Dude, it couldn't have been *that* bad. I mean, how do you withstand wearing a tampon or Matt putting his finger in you?"

I averted my gaze and swallowed.

"Oh. My. God. Sarah, look at me!"

I forced myself to look at her.

"Matt hasn't fingered you?"

Biting my lower lip, I shook my head. Why did she ask me that? Had he ever fingered me, I would have told her. We told each other everything—almost everything.

"But you wear tampons, right?"

Again, I shook my head.

"Oh my god, are you totally serious?"

I nodded.

"You wear a pad? Yuck."

I shrugged. "My mom doesn't want me to get toxic shock syndrome."

Okay, I didn't tell her everything. Some things were too embarrassing—like TSS.

"No way." She laughed. "You have to leave it in for like

days. That's so gross. Wearing a pad is like wearing a diaper. How embarrassing. And how am I your best friend and just now finding out about this?"

I had no response. It wasn't just my pads that were embarrassing; my whole situation in the lower region was embarrassing.

"So, what has been inside of you *down there?*"

"Nothing."

Again, Heather responded with only a few blinks. "Sarah," she whispered with a sympathetic frown.

A woman and her young child came into the bathroom, so I tossed the paper towel and led the way out. "What did you do with Isaac?" I asked, walking as slowly as possible to the table.

"Not much. The movie stopped twenty minutes into it; there was some issue with the film, so we left."

"Were you really watching the movie?" I murmured with a smile as Matt glanced up from the table across from Isaac.

"I mean, we kissed. Or I kissed him. It was weird. I don't think he's interested in me," she said five feet from the table, so I couldn't ask any follow-up questions like why she would kiss someone who smoked and impregnated women only to have to drive them to Planned Parenthood.

Never mind that he tried to get a minor drunk on Easter Sunday.

Matt was all smiles, eating his burger and fries. I sat next to him and tried not to look at Isaac because I knew that while we were in the bathroom, Matt told him we had sex.

"What's going on here?" Isaac asked.

When no one else answered, I glanced up at him since

93

he was sitting across from me. He nodded to my vanilla ice cream cone that was upside down in a cup with a spoon.

"Her teeth are sensitive to cold, so she can't eat ice cream cones before they melt everywhere, so she gets them like this," Matt said because he knew me so well.

"Why not just get ice cream in a cup without the cone?" Isaac asked before bringing his straw to his lips.

"Because I like the cone," I said, spooning ice cream into my mouth while flipping the spoon over so it hit my tongue first. This gave me more control over keeping it away from my teeth until it warmed up a little.

"It's not a sugar cone. Those cake cones taste like cardboard." Isaac eyed me with disapproval.

"Are they as disgusting as smoking?" I rolled my eyes.

"More disgusting," he countered.

Matt and Heather chuckled.

Isaac scooted back in his chair, which made his leg slide between mine. I stiffened, but I couldn't move my leg without bumping Matt's leg, and that might have drawn his attention to his brother's leg unnecessarily invading my space. So I narrowed my eyes at Isaac instead.

He smirked as his lips wrapped around the straw for a quick sip. "So you're a licker. You can't get it past your teeth to let it slide down your throat."

Heather nearly spat out her drink as Matt tucked his chin and grinned. I had no choice but to act like I didn't hear him.

"So, what have you two been doing?" Heather asked, directing her gaze at Matt.

I wanted to kick her to shut her up, but *someone* had his leg wedged between mine, and I didn't want to move because moving would have felt like rubbing, and I wasn't going to rub any part of my body against Isaac. After all, I was a taken woman. Matt had claimed me with a third of his thingy and repeated declarations of love and the prospect of marriage.

"We went for a drive," Matt said, popping the last bite of his sandwich into his mouth.

Everyone at the table knew what we had done, so it was ridiculous to let Heather or Isaac tease and goad us.

"Was it a long drive or a short one?" Heather asked, tapping a french fry against her smirked lips.

"I'm sure it was a short one," Isaac said.

I shoveled ice cream into my mouth so quickly that each bite didn't have time to warm up before touching my sensitive teeth, but I welcomed the unnerving pain and what would be the subsequent brain freeze because it was preferable to the agony of the conversation.

"It wasn't that short," Matt added.

I whipped my gaze in his direction, and he, too, was wearing a cocky grin as he dipped a wad of fries into the ketchup on an empty burger wrapper.

"This is totally ridiculous," I mumbled while standing. "I'll be outside when you're done," I said, taking off toward the exit, wishing I had my own car so I could leave all of them behind.

"Sarah?" Matt chased me to his car.

I spun on my heels when I reached the passenger's door. "I don't want to *talk* about what happened in a stupid McDonald's in front of my best friend and your stupid brother."

He shrugged, holding his hands out to his sides. "What did you want me to say?"

"I wanted you to change the subject."

"Heather brought it up. You should be mad at her."

"I'm mad at all of you."

"Sarah," Matt said in a soft tone, taking my cup of ice cream and setting it on the roof of his car before cupping my face with his hands, "we had sex. We're adults. They're adults. Who cares if anyone makes a comment about what happened? No one's going to tell your parents. Are you embarrassed? Do you regret it?"

I wasn't embarrassed, and I didn't regret it. I simply hated sex and, therefore, didn't want to discuss it with anyone ever again.

With a sigh, I shook my head. "I think it's okay not to want to talk about it in a McDonald's with your brother and Heather without it meaning I regret it or I'm embarrassed."

Matt slowly nodded. "You're right. I'm sorry."

"No." I took a step back and retrieved my ice cream from the roof. "It was Heather who started it. It wasn't your fault."

He opened my door. "You must have told her in the bathroom."

"Or your brother mentioned it when he blurted out the fact that you asked him to buy you a box of condoms." I sat in his car without giving him a second glance. Of course, I told Heather, but Isaac wasn't exactly innocent.

Matt sighed. "I didn't know what else to do."

"It's fine. Just take me back so I can get my car and be home by curfew."

Chapter Nine

The Time, "Jungle Love"

THE NEXT DAY, I started my job at the farm stand. Matt had baseball practice most days, and he was working at a camp for younger kids. Violet showed me the ropes and told me to call the house if there were any issues. Wesley stopped by mid-morning to check on me, and over lunch, Satan delivered several dozen eggs for the stand.

"Hey," Isaac said, setting the crate of boxes on the counter and wiping his dirty brow with his sleeve before adjusting his cowboy hat.

I shot him a quick smile and arranged the boxes of eggs on the shelves by the coolers. "Listen, Heather is my friend, so aside from not getting her hooked on cigarettes, could you not impregnate her?"

"I don't know what you're talking about. I took her to a movie so Matty could get his dick wet with you."

97

I turned, crossing my arms. "You kissed."

He twisted his lips for a beat. "Is that what she said?"

I nodded.

"I see. Well, no babies were conceived. Happy?" He glanced at his watch. "How was Matty last night? Satisfying?"

I averted my gaze before turning my back to fiddle with the jars of honey that were already perfectly aligned.

"Will I need to get him another box of condoms by the end of the week?"

"He has three games this week plus camps, and your dad will keep him busy the rest of the time. So ..." I shrugged while contemplating if the infused honey needed to be alphabetized.

"That bad, huh?"

I turned, narrowing my eyes. "I didn't say that."

Isaac scratched his jaw. "You didn't have to. If it was good, you'd find time and space. You'd crave it like your next breath. He'd be on your mind twenty-four seven, and you'd risk everything to be with him. Your hands would itch to touch him the way they yearn to wrap around my guitar."

I slid the crate toward him. "I'm not sure anything will feel the way your guitar felt. So don't tell Matt that music is my first love." I winked, trying to play it off like a joke.

He took the crate. "I'll talk to him."

"No!" I rammed my hip into the counter, trying to get around it to stop him, but Katie Pedersen and her two young boys opened the door.

"Pardon me," Isaac said to them, holding the door.

I shot him a look, but he just smirked and strutted away with the crate dangling from his hand as the door swung shut.

FOUR HOURS LATER, I locked up the farm stand and carried the keys and the money down the lane to drop off at the house.

"Sarah," Matt said, startling me as he jogged up behind me, grabbing my hand and pulling me behind the garage.

"What are you—"

He kissed me, humming into my mouth as one hand cupped my breast like it did the previous night. Matt's eagerness felt like he couldn't get enough of me—like he craved me as much as his next breath.

And I wanted to feel that too, but I didn't. Sex ruined everything. I couldn't enjoy his touch out of fear that it would lead to more. And I didn't know how long I could fake it. Could I hold out for the summer? After all, hookers did it for a living. Surely, I could do it for the summer—without pay, of course.

"I have to clean out a few stalls, but then I'll shower, and we can go for a drive," he said breathlessly.

I found a fake smile just as Isaac rode his horse toward the gray barn. I couldn't see his expression under his cowboy hat, but I knew he was watching us.

Matt ducked his head and sucked the skin along my neck while guiding my hand to the bulge in his jeans—and Isaac watched everything.

"Why haven't I ever seen you ride a horse?" I asked.

Matt released my hand and lifted his head, confusion etched into his brow. "Because I don't ride horses that often. I'm more of a tractor person."

"Why does Isaac?"

"Because he likes horses, herding animals, and he ropes."

I thought of him lassoing me at graduation with my cords.

"Ropes?" I asked.

"At rodeos. He competes in calf roping for prize money," Matt replied. "He did it in high school, and he's practicing to compete again. Why?"

"No reason. Just curious."

"I'll pick you up after dinner around seven. Okay?"

"Call me first. I have to check with my mom. I might have to help prepare some arts and crafts kits for Vacation Bible School."

He frowned. "Okay. Even if it's later, I don't care. I just need to take a ride." He grinned.

"Take a ride" was our new sex code.

My smile felt fake, but Matt didn't seem to notice. He kissed me one last time and strutted toward the red sheep barn. I waited until he was out of sight, then jogged to the gray barn where Isaac took his horse.

I passed two stalls with ponies before reaching Isaac in the last stall, where he removed his horse's saddle.

"What is it, Sunday Morning?" he asked as if he had eyes in the back of his head.

"Please don't say anything to Matt. I was joking earlier."

"I don't think you were." He carried the saddle through a door to the tack room and rested it on a stand.

I followed him. "Can you just stay out of my business?"

"Says the girl who begged me to play her favorite song over and over." He turned, tucking his hands into his back pockets. "So what's it going to be? Are we going to be in each other's business this summer or not?"

Everything that escaped Isaac Cory's mouth sounded sexual.

"Are you saying you're going to let me play your guitar again?"

"Depends." He shrugged.

"On what?"

"What are you going to do for me?"

"I'll pray for you. Preachers' daughters' prayers carry more weight than the average person's. Should I pray for you to quit smoking or for your salvation?"

The corner of his mouth quirked into a half grin as amusement sparkled in his eyes. "Why do you want me to quit smoking so badly? Will your heart break if I die of cancer? Or do you secretly want to kiss me?"

I scoffed while surveying the area behind me, looking and listening for signs of Wesley, Matt, or anyone else. "I secretly want to kill you and steal your guitar, but you know the rules. Number six: Thou shalt not kill. And number eight: Thou shalt not steal. Or maybe you don't know the rules." I shrugged.

"I know the tenth commandment is Thou shalt not covet. And I've been breaking that one a lot lately," he said.

"How so?" I asked as Isaac physically brushed past me.

"Sunday Morning, I've been coveting the fuck out of you since Easter Sunday," he said, strolling out of the barn.

I died and went straight to Hell.

❧

I needed a best friend, but since Heather kissed Isaac, I wasn't sure I could tell her what he said in the barn, even though she said he didn't seem interested in her. And I couldn't tell any of my other friends because I didn't trust anyone like I trusted Heather.

But I was dying to tell someone.

Why did he say that? Maybe he didn't know what the word covet meant. But that made little sense. Isaac was a valedictorian.

It had to be part of his game. Isaac loved making people squirm and irritating them. He was an expert bear-poker.

"Sarah?" Eve yelled. "Matt's on the phone!"

I ran to my bedroom from the hall bathroom and picked it up. Then I composed myself, letting out a slow breath and finding my weakest voice. "Hello," I said as if I were on my last breath.

"Are you okay?" he asked.

"No. I started my period. And I have terrible cramps." I hadn't started my period, but I needed an excuse to stay home. I couldn't have sex *and* sort through the meaning of Isaac's statement on the same day. But mostly, I couldn't have sex again. How did all of those married women do it? *It* had to be a sacrifice as honorable as serving one's country—a physical invasion all in the name of procreation. Ensuring the survival of humanity. Women weren't simply loyal soldiers to a country; we were the Davids of the world, and sex was our Goliath.

"That sucks," Matt said. "I'm sorry. Is there anything I can do?"

"No," I faked a little groan at the end. "But you are sweet for asking."

"I love you," he said with disappointment in his words, like loving me was his consolation prize for the day.

I groaned, holding my stomach as if he could see me.

"Is it inconsiderate of me to ask how long it lasts?"

I flopped back onto my bed with my legs dangling over the side while I pinched the bridge of my nose. "You could never be inconsiderate. And it just depends. A week ... maybe two."

My periods were five days, but I was supposed to get my real period the following week, so I had to build in some extra time.

"I feel like in school, they said a week was the norm. If you're having it for two weeks, maybe you should get it checked out."

I rolled my eyes. Why did my boyfriend have to be so smart? He remembered how long a woman's menstrual cycle lasted, but he didn't remember the location of the clitoris?

"You're right. I hope nothing is wrong with me," I said, figuring I might buy even more time if he thought I was having serious female issues. "Maybe we should wait until I get things checked out."

"You should ask your mom."

"Maybe," I said, staring at the speckled texture on the ceiling that had a yellowish-brown stain from a roof leak. "Did you ask Isaac to take Heather to a movie so we could ... you know?"

"No. Why?"

"Well, when he dropped off eggs at the farm stand, he said that's why he took her to the movie. When's the last time he had a girlfriend?"

"I don't know. He's been in the Army. I suppose he might have met someone and had something short, but nothing we ever heard anything about. Why do you ask?"

"I just wondered if he's ever been serious about anyone or anything for that matter."

"He's loyal to the family and the ranch. There's nothing he wouldn't do for our parents," Matt said, and it made me pause for a moment. Was he *defending* his brother?

"Funny." I chuckled. "He calls you PC."

"PC?"

"Perfect child."

"Well, I'm not anymore," Matt said, and I didn't miss his suggestive tone.

I imagined him waggling his eyebrows.

"Sorry to disappoint you, but you weren't perfect before we did *it*."

"Duh. Yes, I know, Sarah."

"Listen, I'm going to bed early. Okay?"

"Hope you feel better soon. Love you."

"Thanks, bye." I hung up the phone and flopped back down onto my bed to stare at the ceiling. I said "thank you" as a reply to his "I love you." Was that bad of me? Or was I the mature one who stuck to our plans? I didn't have the focus to figure it out because I was too busy thinking about Isaac coveting me.

Chapter Ten

The Romantics, "Talking In Your Sleep"

THE FOLLOWING WEEK, Matt and his mom went to Michigan for a campus tour and to watch a baseball game while Wesley and Isaac manned the ranch, and I handled the farm stand. I arrived early Monday morning for inventory, per Violet's request.

As I made my way toward the house to get the key to the shed and the cash, I saw Isaac by the barn swinging a rope. I veered in his direction while he practiced on a stationary calf dummy. It was the first interaction I'd had with him since he made the coveting comment.

"Seems kind of lazy that you're roping something that's not moving," I said.

He grinned without glancing at me. "Sunday Morning, it seems like you think this is easier than it is."

I stepped onto the bottom fence plank and rested my

arms on the top one. "Why do you rope? Does your daddy not pay you enough?"

"Because I enjoy it." He threw the rope and snagged it on the horn of the dummy calf. "Don't you have work to do?"

"Don't you?"

He eyed me. "My mom left me in charge of keeping watch over you, so technically, I'm your boss this week. That means you do what I say."

"Then look at me and tell me what to do," I said before biting my lower lip.

"With that attitude, you're going to send your dad to his grave early. You and your sisters."

"I take offense on behalf of myself and my sisters. We're angels."

"Get to work before I find something else for you to do."

"I'm off at four. I want to play your guitar again."

"No."

I ignored his response. "Is it in the barn?"

The idea that Isaac liked me—coveted me—made me feel exhilarated.

Mature.

Irresistible.

Desired.

Basically, sin, sin, sin.

But also a little braver.

I should have kept my distance, especially with Matt out of town, but I was curious—to a fault.

"What if I let you touch something of mine?" As soon as I said the words, my heart raced with fear like I'd jumped out of a plane and didn't know if my parachute worked.

"You're in over your head, little girl."

I frowned because I wasn't a little girl.

Not a schoolgirl.

Not a minor.

Not a virgin.

"Why do you say that?"

He dropped the rope and scuffed his boots through the dirt toward me. "Do you love my little brother?"

I nodded. It was the truth. But just because I loved him, it didn't mean I wanted to marry him.

"Then why would you say that?" Isaac asked, leaning against the post and inspecting his fingernails.

"Because I want to play your guitar."

"At what cost?" he asked, keeping his head bowed.

"I don't know yet because you haven't made me an offer."

He trapped his lower lip between his teeth and shook his head. "It's in my closet. I have to pick up sheep from the Brady's later. Don't mess with anything else," he said, walking away.

"What do I have to do in return?" I called.

"I'll figure something out."

As soon as I closed the farm stand, I ran down the lane to return the key and cash and get Isaac's guitar. Lightning lit up the cloudy sky in the distance, so I didn't waste any time hanging up the key, discarding my dirty boots, and tiptoeing up the stairs, even though Isaac was gone. Wesley was most likely still in the machine shed working on equipment like he did most nights until dinner or later.

Heading into Isaac's room, I paused to hold still when I heard something. It came from their parents' bedroom.

For a second, I considered skipping the guitar and bolting out of the house. But I had already established my willingness to do just about anything to play the guitar, so I jumped over the threshold into Isaac's room like a dancer making a graceful leap, and I retrieved his acoustic guitar from the closet and took two steps toward the door when I heard a jarring curse in a man's voice.

"Jesus Christ," he said and then seethed.

I gulped.

"Slow down ..." It was Wesley's strained voice.

I couldn't tell if he was angry or injured. The tone held a mix of both. Hugging the guitar, I crept down the hallway. Before taking the last step, I stopped and craned my neck to peek into the room past the partially ajar door. As soon as my eyes focused, I reared my whole body in the opposite direction and covered my mouth to muffle my gasp. The floor squeaked, and I cringed, using both arms to hug the guitar again.

"Isaac?" Wesley called.

"Oh my god!" the woman whisper-yelled, making the bedroom floor squeak while she moved around the room.

I skittered back to Isaac's room and jumped into the closet, quietly shutting the bifold doors and praying Wesley didn't find me.

The squeaky hall floor sounded again, and I held my breath, heart racing.

"I thought you said he was gone," the woman said. She sounded familiar—and young— but she wasn't talking loud enough for me to place her.

"He is."

"Then what did you hear?"

They were right outside of the bedroom.

"I don't know. Probably nothing," Wesley said.

"Well, I have to get out of here. You need to drive me home before Isaac returns."

"It was nothing. Don't worry." His voice faded as they descended the stairs.

When I heard the door shut, I emerged from the closet.

Wesley Cory was cheating on Violet. I couldn't believe it. The previous day, he was at church with Vi before she and Matt left for St. Louis. They were holding hands, singing hymns, and praying along with everyone else.

It made no sense.

Why was he cheating? And what woman willingly had sex with a married man? Sex was awful.

I slithered down the stairs and checked the front windows. When I saw Wesley's truck turning out of their lane, I sprinted to my car, carefully slid the guitar in the back, and sped home. The secrets were piling up.

The woman straddling Wesley in bed had long black hair and a bikini tan line. And she sounded *so* familiar. What was I supposed to do with that disturbing revelation?

"Where did you get that?" Gabby asked when I walked into the house with Isaac's guitar.

"I'm borrowing it from Matt's brother," I said past my nerves.

"Borrowing it, or you stole it?" She grinned. "You look like you're freaking out."

"I'm not freaking out." I headed upstairs.

"How was work?" Dad called from the living room before I reached the top of the stairs.

"Uh, fine. It was a slow day. I think it was the on-and-off rain," I said in a breathless voice. Gabby was right—I was freaking out.

"Hey!" Mom chirped, scaring the bejesus out of me as she emerged from her bedroom.

"Hey," I rushed into my room.

"Whose guitar?"

"Isaac's. He's letting me borrow it."

Mom stood in my doorway. "That's nice of him. You've always wanted to play the guitar. But be careful; those strings will be unforgiving to your fingers, and you won't be able to play the piano."

I set the guitar on my bed and crossed my arms, then shoved my fingers into my jeans pockets for two seconds before I wrung them out in front of me, and finally, crossed my arms again.

Mom squinted. "What's wrong?"

"Nothing," I clipped too quickly to be believable.

She narrowed her eyes even more. "Sarah," she said slowly.

"If you saw something you weren't supposed to see, would you tell anyone?"

"What did you see?"

"Nothing. It's hypothetical."

"Sarah, is someone in trouble?"

"No. Well, not exactly."

"Just tell me."

I shook my head. "I can't. That's what I'm saying. If I thought I could tell you, I'd just tell you instead of asking you a hypothetical question. I may have seen something that's not any of my business. It's not like I witnessed a crime, well maybe a moral crime, but not like someone was breaking the law—robbing a bank or anything like that. And if I tell someone what I saw, really bad things could happen as a result. So I don't know what to do."

"You're being too cryptic. I can't help you if you don't give me more information."

I frowned. "I can't."

Mom shrugged. "Then I can't help you. But from the sounds of things, you need to pray about it and follow your heart. Do what you think God would want you to do."

That was just it. I had no clue what God wanted me to do. While Wesley broke one of the Ten Commandments, I didn't. Technically, I didn't know who it was, and I didn't see his actual thingy inside of her, so saying otherwise would have been bearing false witness. Right?

"I'll pray about it," I mumbled.

"Come help set the table. Dinner is almost done," Mom called, heading toward the stairs.

Two seconds later, Eve poked her head into my room. "Where did you get that guitar?"

I looked up, twisting my lips for a beat. "Shut my door," I whispered.

She frowned and spun on her heel shutting the door.

I hopped off the bed and quickly opened it. "I meant to stay in my room and shut the door."

Eve's lips parted into a silent "oh," and she slipped back into my room and shut the door. My sixteen-year-old sister wasn't my first choice when I had a secret, but in a pinch, she worked.

I folded my hands at my mouth and mumbled past them. "I need to tell you something."

"You're pregnant."

"What?" I winced, dropping my hands to my sides.

She shrugged. "Sorry. But Erin thinks you'll end up pregnant since you've been dating Matt for so long, and sex is forbidden, but everyone gravitates toward the forbidden."

"I'm not pregnant."

She widened her brown eyes. "But *are* you having sex? I won't tell anyone. I promise." Her nose wrinkled. "I want to have it." Eve didn't have a boyfriend, so I wasn't sure who she wanted to have sex with.

I shook my head. "Eve, just ... focus. I need to tell someone what I saw, but I can't tell Matt or Mom and Dad. And I don't know if I can tell Heather since she might have a crush on Matt's brother, but I'm losing my mind. I have to tell someone."

"What?" Eve whispered, leaning forward, eyes unblinking.

"The guitar," I nodded toward it, "is Isaac's. He let me borrow it. And when I went up to his room to get it from his closet, I heard something." I covered my face with my hands, feeling second-hand embarrassment. "Wesley Cory was having sex with another woman," I mumbled behind my hands.

"What?" Eve said, grabbing my wrists to pull my hands away from my face.

Pressing my lips together, I bobbed my head. "Matt's dad is cheating on his mom," I whispered.

Eve's eyes tried to pop out of their sockets while her jaw unhinged.

"I don't know what to do."

"You have to tell Matt," she said.

I shook my head. "I can't do that. It would ruin their family. And Wesley would find out it was me who ratted him out. We live on his land, in a house he owns, and there have been so many times that I know Mom and Dad haven't had the full amount of rent, but Wesley overlooks it because Dad is his pastor and I'm dating Matt."

"I don't know." She ran her hands through her hair. "I don't know what to tell you to do. This is awful. But you have to tell someone."

I chewed on my thumbnail. "What if I don't have to tell anyone? It's not my job to be the moral police. You know? Thou shalt not judge. I should leave that to God. We've all done things we wished we wouldn't have done. How would you like it if someone called you out every time you made a mistake? If Wesley feels guilty, then he'll confess. But it's not like he's breaking the law. Had I found a dead body in their house, I would say something."

"Sarah," Eve rolled her eyes. "You have to say something. If Matt finds out you knew and said nothing, he'll break up with you. And he may never forgive you."

"Well, I've only told you, so if he finds out I knew, I'll know who told him." I crossed my arms and eyed her with a hard gaze.

"If Matt knew Dad was cheating on Mom, would you want him to tell you?"

Had she asked me that a week earlier, I would have said yes. But I was no longer a doe-eyed virgin. "No." I tipped up my chin.

Eve scoffed. "You can't be serious."

"There are some things nobody should want to know. *Mom* should want to know if Dad is cheating on her, but I don't think she'd want *us* to know. I believe Violet would feel the same way. I think she'd be mortified if she found out I saw him in bed with another woman. So you can't say anything. I just had to tell someone. Can you be a grownup about this and keep it between us?"

"Duh." She rolled her eyes again. "Yes. I can keep your

secret. But it doesn't mean I agree with your decision. And if you tell anyone that you told me, I will deny it."

I sat on the end of my bed and picked up the guitar. "I'm not telling anyone." I plucked the strings. "It's sad when the feelings you have for someone change and you don't know why." I closed my eyes and envisioned Isaac's fingers, their placement, and their even-caressing of each string.

"You think Matt's dad doesn't love his mom anymore?"

I opened my eyes while my fingers kept playing. "No. I think he loves her. I just think he loves her differently."

"What if she never finds out? What if she wastes the rest of her life with him, thinking he's being loyal to her?"

I shrugged. "I don't know. Which is more important, honesty or kindness?"

"I think you should be both kind and honest."

I grinned. "Yes, in a perfect world. But we don't live in a perfect world, so is one always the right answer? If the kind answer to something is not the honest one, which do you want?"

"Which do you want?" she asked.

I thought of all the things Isaac said to me and how they made me feel, especially the things he said that made me feel good and I questioned his sincerity. I felt such a high that I didn't want to know if he was being honest with me. "Depends," I said. "But I can't ask Violet if she wants to know if Wesley is cheating on her. And nobody's going to ask me, so it's not like I'm lying. I didn't want to see that. I don't want this responsibility."

Eve grunted. "So you're sharing the burden with me?"

I smirked. "Exactly."

"Who taught you to play that?" She nodded to the guitar.

"Isaac."

"Dad said we should keep an eye on Isaac. He knows the Army probably helped him, but he thinks Isaac might not be the best influence. I heard him tell Mom that he's worried Isaac might rub off on Matt."

I didn't respond.

"But he's really cute." Eve bit her lip.

I stopped playing and shot my gaze to Eve and her flushed cheeks.

"Matt's cute too, but Isaac is manly." She sighed heavily. "Those tattoos. And he's a rebel."

I laughed. She wasn't wrong. But I knew Matt would be much different in six years. He would be *manly* too.

"I'm sad for Matt's family," Eve said just before opening the door.

My smile faded. "Me too."

Chapter Eleven

Lee Hazlewood, "These Boots Are Made For Walking"

"WHAT THE FUCK, SUNDAY MORNING?" The next afternoon, Isaac threw open the door to the farm stand.

There were no customers, but I don't know if he knew that before spewing his expletive.

Fuck was the crudest of all swear words. Not only did I not say it, I didn't think it.

Until Isaac ...

Everything he said to me was replayed on an endless loop.

"I've been coveting the fuck out of you since Easter Sunday."

He knew I knew about his dad and the mystery mistress. Wesley must have known it was me.

I gulped, grabbing a rag to wipe the counter that was already clean.

"You won't touch my guitar again."

My heart stopped.

Isaac rounded the corner of the counter and ate up every inch of my personal space while plucking a black permanent marker from the cup of pens by the register. He removed the cap with his teeth. I had never seen him so angry.

I gasped as he grabbed the neck of my T-shirt and stretched it down my chest.

Never—*ever*—in the history of my eighteen years on earth had I felt so shocked and utterly speechless as my boyfriend's older brother wrote *ISAAC'S* on the swell of my left breast. As quickly as he charged into the shed and vandalized my boob with a permanent marker, he capped it and stomped out the door while grumbling, "What the fuck is wrong with you?"

He didn't give me a chance to answer before slamming the door shut. It wasn't Wesley's affair.

Thank God.

Breathing heavily, I straightened my shirt and pressed a hand over the graffiti on my boob. Then I cupped my other hand over my mouth and released something between a laugh and a cry.

I wrote "Sarah's" in tiny letters on the inside of Isaac's guitar case, where it was nearly impossible to see unless you were actively looking for it. I did it because it made me feel like the guitar was mine. I was just a young woman with big dreams making a tiny mark in the music world.

It was stupid but also no big deal. How on earth did he see it?

I didn't use a permanent marker. The punishment didn't fit the crime.

"Oh my gosh!" I ran into the bathroom and grabbed a

wad of paper towels and soap to wash the marker from my boob. My skin burned and bloomed red and raw as I scrubbed it like a dirty Russet potato, but the ink didn't fade. Panic set in. It was summer. I went to the pool on the weekends, and Matt was counting down the days until the end of my imaginary period.

"Hello?"

I jumped, adjusted my shirt, and tossed the towels into the trash bin before opening the door. "Hi," I said in a high-pitched voice to Beverly Whitmore.

Her fingers caressed the floral scarf holding her long red and gray hair away from her face. "I preordered half a steer. Do I pick it up here?"

I knew there was not half a steer in the tiny deep freezer.

"Did you try the house?" I asked.

She nodded. "No one answered."

"Mrs. Cory is out of town this week," I said.

And her husband is cheating on her.

"Um, let me see if I can find Mr. Cory." I locked the register drawer, even though I didn't think Beverly was there to rob the place, and then I jogged down the lane. I was scared to check the house again. What if Wesley was in the bedroom with the mystery mistress again? Surely not at three in the afternoon on a Wednesday with Isaac on the farm.

"Hello?" I called, inching up the stairs.

Nothing.

I ran out to the machine shed. "Mr. Cory?" I called, opening the door.

"What is it?" Satan popped his head around the corner, wiping grease off his hands with a rag.

I scowled. "Not you."

"I'm Mr. Cory." He lifted his eyebrows.

"You're something, but not a Mister. Barely a human."

"I feel your anger. It's frustrating when someone does something so ruthless and unimaginable."

"What is your problem? How did you even see that? And it was *not* remotely close to what you did to me. And this won't come off, YOU BIG JERK!" I yelled, jabbing my boob.

"If revenge isn't memorable, then it's not really revenge. Is it? That will be on there for a while. It will be memorable," he said.

"Your brother is going to see it." I fisted my hands at my side. "What am I supposed to say?"

"Tell him the truth. You wrote your name on something that was mine, so I wrote my name on something that's yours. He'll be pissed off because he only sees himself, and you're nothing more than an accessory to his dreams. And I know this because you fucking fell in love with a guitar. And my brother has thousands of dollars saved up, but he's never given you the one thing that makes your heart sing. He doesn't see you. How can you take off your clothes for someone who doesn't. Fucking. See. You?"

I slowly shook my head, but I couldn't speak past my heart in my throat. It was easier when nobody saw me. Invisible people didn't feel vulnerable.

Isaac made me feel *everything*.

Finally, I cleared my throat and composed myself. "Beverly Whitmore ordered half a steer. I was looking for your dad."

Isaac tossed the rag aside. "I'll get it." He walked past me without making eye contact.

AFTER WORK, I returned the key and money bag, but I didn't linger in case Wesley was entertaining his mistress. On my way to my car, I saw Isaac in the pasture, working on a fence. He defiled my breast, so I should have climbed into the car and hightailed it out of there, but I was the moth, and he was the flame. So I trekked toward the pasture.

"Where's your dad?" I asked.

"He ran to town. Why? What do you need?" He tossed the wire cutter aside and glanced up at me while wiping his sweaty brow with his partially rolled-up sleeve that exposed his tattoos and muscly forearms.

"We're low on ones and fives for the register."

That was a tiny lie or at least a stretch, but I blurted out the first thing that came to me.

"Ya ever heard of a bank? They can exchange large bills for small bills."

"I don't take the money with me."

He gathered his tools and tossed them into a bucket. "Because you can't be trusted."

"Is that a question? It better be a question. And the answer is... Yes. Of course, I can be trusted. I'm way more trustworthy than you are."

"How do you figure?" He toted the bucket and a spool of steel wire toward the machine shed.

"Everyone trusted you not to write your name on my boob, but you couldn't control yourself."

Isaac looked over his shoulder, giving me a slow-growing smile. His teeth looked extra white because he was so tan, and he had dirt smudged along his scruffy face. I plucked a stem of hay and pulled off the seeds, scattering them with the wind as I tried to keep a straight face.

He redirected his gaze to the barn. "He doesn't deserve you," he mumbled.

I barely caught it, but I didn't think he meant for me to hear it.

"Would your dad write his name on my mom's boob?"

"I'm not sure. Why don't you ask him?" He opened the door to the barn.

"Don't you think you should apologize? You've had all day to contemplate your insane response to what I did to your *old* guitar case."

He dropped the bucket and the spool of wire before slowly turning toward me. "How old are you?"

I parked a hand on my hip. "Eighteen. Duh, you know that."

Pursing his lips to the side, he studied me. "That guitar case is maybe ten years old. So it looks like the excuse is mine, not yours. I just scribbled my name on your *old* tit. Why are you acting so *insane*?"

"Stop," I snorted, covering my mouth. "I'm serious. This isn't going to come off for a long time."

Isaac lifted his shirt and wiped his face, drawing my gaze to his tight abs.

"Well, maybe you'll just have to keep your tits covered until it comes off."

"What if Matt sees it?"

Isaac glanced at his watch. "What if some girl I like sees your name on the inside of my guitar case?"

I narrowed my eyes. "Who?"

"Sunday Morning, you're not the only girl who looks at me that way." He smirked, strutting past me to the door.

Again, I followed him as he headed to the horse barn. "I only look at you with pity because you're so obnoxious, and everyone knows it."

"You look at me like Matty's not getting the job done."

"What's that supp—" I caught it too late, but Isaac couldn't let anything slide.

"And just like that, you proved my point all by yourself." He filled a bucket with feed for his horse and carried it to the stall.

I watched him, letting my response die because I didn't want to talk about Matt or my boob, for that matter. I wanted to know why their father was cheating on their mother. It angered me and broke my heart at the same time.

"I'm sorry I wrote my name on your guitar case." In case God was still disappointed over the loss of my virginity, I thought showing Isaac kindness might get me back into His good graces.

He grunted while grabbing a broom to sweep the stall. I couldn't decipher the meaning behind his grunt.

"Are you going to apologize to me for writing on my boob?"

"No."

Maybe I wasn't supposed to apologize with any expectations—unconditional love and all that kind of godly behavior. But I wasn't God; I was human. And I expected something in return.

"Why?" I tried to act unaffected by his stubbornness.

"Because I'm not sorry."

My mouth fell open in a silent gasp. "In that case, I take back my apology." I pivoted and marched out the door and straight to my car. "Because I'm not sorry," I said in a mocking tone with my nose wrinkled. "Jerk."

"MATT'S ON THE PHONE!" Gabby yelled upstairs after I took a long bath.

Isaac's name wasn't leaving my skin anytime soon despite the nail polish remover I tried. It lightened it, but it didn't completely remove it.

"Hey!" I said, sitting on the edge of my bed, wrapped in a fluffy pink terry cloth robe and my hair swaddled in a towel.

My summer wasn't off to the best start, and I blamed all three of the Cory men.

"How's work?"

I hugged a knee to my chest. "Fine. How do you like the campus?"

"I love it so much. We're attending a game tomorrow. And I'm having dinner with the assistant coach. Sarah, this feels like a dream."

"That's awesome."

"I miss you."

I grinned. "Really?"

"Yes."

"Where's your mom?" I asked.

"She's at the pool."

"Have you talked to your dad?"

"My mom has. Why? Is everything okay?"

"Yep. It's fine. Since you called me, I'm just curious if all the Cory men are as considerate as you." I rolled my eyes. That sounded weird, even for me.

"My dad is. But I don't think Isaac is." Matt laughed.

"Isaac's a little considerate. He let me take his guitar home last night."

Oh my gosh! Am I defending Satan?

Why did I defend him? Isaac's behavior was indefensible, and I kept forgetting that I seriously disliked him.

"What did you have to do in exchange? Clean out the sheep stalls for the next week?"

"I don't know yet. I think he's waiting and plans on lording it over my head for the summer." I tried to return the same laugh as if Isaac was just being Isaac and not the guy who was coveting me and writing on my boob.

"You're probably right," Matt said with a long sigh followed by a long pause. "I miss you," he murmured.

"I miss you too," I replied on instinct. He hadn't been gone that long, so I wasn't drowning in my tears yet.

"I can't wait to get back and get my hands on you."

I wasn't sure his brother's name would be erased from my boob. But being the pleaser that I was, I replied, "Me too."

Our first encounter didn't involve removing my dress, so while Matt had felt my breast over my dress, he had yet to see me fully naked.

"Is everything okay? You seem quiet."

"I'm good. Are you good? What about your mom? Is she good?"

Matt chuckled. "We're fine. You're acting weird. Why are you acting so weird?"

"I'm not. I just have a lot on my mind."

"You mean what we did?"

I bit my thumbnail. "Yeah. And other things. Like, I want to go to Nashville. What do you think my parents would say if I told them I wanted to skip college for now and move to Nashville to sing even though I didn't get accepted to Vanderbilt?"

He laughed a little. "Well, I think they'd tell you what I overheard your mom telling my mom."

"What's that?"

"Your parents were relieved you didn't get accepted because they don't have the money to send you there."

I frowned.

"And I think your father will lose his mind if you go to Nashville."

"Well, I'm an adult. They don't have much say in the matter."

"We know you'll do exactly what they tell you to." He laughed again, and it irritated me more than it normally would have since Isaac pointed out Matt's lack of focus on my dreams. And I was tired of being such a pleaser to everyone except myself.

"Not this time," I said.

"Where are you going to sing?"

"I don't know. Wherever. I feel like I need to be where things are happening to stand a chance of being discovered."

"How will you support yourself if your parents refuse to do it?"

"Duh. I'll get a job during the day."

"You know I love you, and I think you're a great singer, but have you considered how incredibly rare it is for a no-name to show up in Nashville and actually make it big?"

"About as rare as it is for a rancher's son from Devil's Head, Missouri, to play in the big leagues."

"Sarah ..."

"Matt," I mocked him.

"Your parents are never going to approve of this."

"Well," I chuckled, "they were never going to approve of

what we did in your car, but we did it anyway. Do you regret it?"

"That's different."

"It's not. We made our own decisions no matter what anyone thought. And we did it because we had a passion that mattered more than anyone's opinion. That's how I feel about music. Writing, playing, singing it. How am I supposed to go to college when I have no idea what I could possibly want to do in life besides play my music?"

"That's not true. You thought about accounting."

"Matt, I had to think of something to get our guidance counselor off my back about planning my future. I don't want to be an accountant."

"That's why your parents suggested a community college. You can get prerequisites taken while you figure it out."

"Prerequisites for what? My parents suggested community college because I didn't get good grades like you."

"Sarah," Matt sighed. "Give it a year at a community college. You might decide music is more of a hobby."

"It's not a hobby. It's my dream. I want you to say that you think my dreams are important."

"Of course, I think your dreams are important."

"Then why are you trying to talk me out of following them?"

"I'm not. I'm only trying to help you set realistic expectations, so you won't be disappointed."

I gripped the phone tighter. "So you already think it's a foregone conclusion that I won't make it if I go to Nashville? And you want me to prepare to be disappointed? Wow. Thanks, Matt."

"Fine, Sarah. What do you want me to say? You're going

to be a big star? You're going to have sell-out concerts across the country? Then, sure, I'll say it. You're going to be the biggest star of our generation. No need to go to college. Happy?"

"You're an asshole."

Click.

Chapter Twelve

Eurythmics, "Would I Lie to You?"

THE FOLLOWING DAY, the farm stand was busy, and I didn't see Isaac or Wesley, not even when I returned to the house with the key and cash bag. A few of the other ranch workers were in the fields on horses and one was on a tractor near a grain bin.

After I closed the stand, I was itching to play Isaac's guitar again. Since he was still nowhere in sight, I figured chances were slim that he would look for it before I returned it. As I tiptoed up the stairs, I listened carefully for signs of anyone. I didn't need a repeat.

Securing the guitar in my arms, I hugged it with more passion than I'd hugged my *asshole* boyfriend. Then I skittered out of the house to my car. I peeled around the circle drive to make my escape but slammed on the brakes when Isaac stepped in front of my car.

My heart lurched into my throat as he eyed me for a few seconds before stepping to the side and opening the passenger's door.

"What are you doing? I nearly ran you over!"

"You are a thief." He pulled the guitar case from my back seat. "A delinquent, fucking criminal."

Isaac slammed the door and marched toward the house. I should have stepped on the gas and gotten my butt out of there, but I wanted—needed—to borrow the guitar again. I had songs to write. So I set the emergency brake, killed the engine, and chased after him. Really, I was only chasing the guitar.

"You know darn well you're not even going to use it tonight. You can't say that you covet me and then hog your guitar." I caught up to him just as he stepped inside the screened-in porch.

When I tried to grab the guitar case, Isaac glanced back at me with a wrinkled nose as if he didn't expect my level of determination. "Let. Go." He jerked it out of my grip. "You're way out of your league, little girl." He continued into the house and up the stairs.

"I'm not a little girl. I'm a woman. And I'm going to be something someday, and I'm giving you the chance to be part of it. You can tell all your friends that it was your guitar that I used to write my best songs."

Isaac deposited the guitar into his closet and shut the door, standing guard in front of it with his arms crossed over his chest.

I should have given up and walked away. The bear didn't need to be poked anymore, but I had a proverbial stick in my hand, and I couldn't resist.

"But like ... I know that won't happen because you don't have any friends."

Isaac's scowl morphed into something worse: a smile. His vengeful smirk was so confident that I nearly evaporated like a drip of water hitting a hot pan.

"Sunday Morning, *you're* my friend."

I shook my head a half dozen times. "I'm not *your* anything if you don't let me borrow your guitar."

"Well," Isaac pursed his lips, "you're my future sister-in-law. Right?"

Satan ruined everything good, which wasn't breaking news. After all, my dad had been preaching about sin and the devil since before I was born. Still, seeing evil in the flesh confirmed all the warnings were valid. Before Isaac came home, I spent most of my free time dreaming of Matt and music. One always led to the other. Matt and I wanted to play under bright lights with throngs of adoring fans—his baseball, mine music.

I blamed Isaac for ruining everything I saw in Matt.

"You're an awful brother."

His dark eyes widened. "What did I do? I love Matty."

"If you loved him, you wouldn't call him Matty. You wouldn't treat his good behavior like a flaw. You wouldn't get his girlfriend drunk and say inappropriate things to her. You wouldn't ruin his sex life. You wouldn't write your name on my boob. And you wouldn't smoke because it's gross." I clenched my jaw.

Evil danced in his eyes. "Let's back up. How did I ruin his sex life? I bought condoms." Isaac straightened his posture, as if he really needed to exude any more confidence. "And I didn't ask him to pay me back."

"That's"—I wrinkled my nose and shook my head—"not what I meant."

"Was the sex bad?" He narrowed his eyes, but it didn't erase the amusement on his face.

"I'm going home." I spun in the opposite direction. "Keep your stupid guitar, you selfish jerk." I jogged down the stairs.

"I'll talk to him," Isaac said, moseying down the stairs, knowing that he didn't have to catch me to make me stop. He just needed to say the right thing.

I halted at the front door and backtracked to the stairs, reaching the bottom at the same time as Isaac. "*Don't* say a word to him."

"So it *was* bad. What happened?" He rubbed his chin.

Despite not being raised to hate anyone or anything, I harbored intense hatred towards Isaac and everything about him.

Because he liked to be an instigator.

Because he was gatekeeping his guitar.

Because he smoked, and smoking was disgusting.

But mostly because I couldn't stop thinking about him in the most sinful ways.

And that made me feel like a terrible person, an awful girlfriend, and an all-around despicable human—like Isaac.

"Why do you hate me?" I asked.

Isaac's eyebrows drew together. "I don't. Why was the sex bad?"

Something hit me hard. I didn't see it coming, and I couldn't stop it. Tears burned my eyes, and emotions tingled like little pins pricking my skin, which made Isaac's grin die on the spot. I loved Matt, even though those three words started to feel generic when I thought of them. But I *wanted* to love everything about him even if we weren't going to be together much longer.

It broke my heart that something so intimate and special felt like one of the worst moments of my life. But the thing that broke my heart the most was Isaac seeing right through me.

"Did he hurt you?"

I jerked my head back and blotted the corners of my eyes. "You must love this." I laughed through my tangled emotions. "No. He didn't hurt me. Matt would never hurt me."

Isaac frowned. "I didn't mean it like that."

I turned, leaving the house. "If you say one word to him, I'm telling my father you wrote your name on my breast."

"So that's how this is going to go? Our friendship will be based on secrets and blackmailing each other?"

"We'll never be friends."

"Is it the smoking?"

I rolled my eyes even though my back was to him as I opened my car door.

"What if I don't say anything to Matty, you don't say anything to your dad, and I stop smoking?" He followed me to my car.

I scolded myself for thinking that he looked hot in his torn jeans, cowboy boots, and black threadbare shirt with dirt on it. But he did. Isaac looked like the inspiration for every sexy song I imagined singing from a stage surrounded by adoring fans.

"You're going to stop smoking for me? Why?" I laughed it off, sliding into my car.

Isaac positioned himself between me and my open door,

resting his hands on the top of my car. "I think you know why," he said.

I fidgeted with my car keys. "I love Matt," I murmured, unsure if I was saying it to Isaac or myself.

"You *think* you should love him. But you're going to let him go. It's the only way you'll be able to chase your dreams. And in another year, you'll both look back at your time together with fondness. However, neither one of you will regret not staying together."

At first, I thought he knew. I thought Matt said something to him, but that was unlikely. Isaac just had an eerie sense of the truth, so I scoffed. "So which is it? Will we be broken up, or will I be your sister-in-law?"

"You mean, will you be happy or miserable? I don't know, Sunday Morning. That's up to you."

WHEN I ARRIVED HOME, I didn't expect to see Wesley Cory's white truck in the driveway, which explained why I didn't see him at the house.

He wasn't there for me. It had nothing to do with the day I caught him in bed with the mysterious brunette. I told myself this over and over while I made my way into the house, whispering a quick prayer.

Eve did nothing to alleviate my fears when she shot me a panicked gaze as I stepped into the kitchen, where she, Mom, and Gabby were making dinner. Dad stood by the kitchen table with his hands in his front pockets, talking to Wesley.

"Hey," I said softly, ping-ponging my gaze between Eve and Wesley.

"There's my future daughter-in-law," Wesley said with a wink.

Yep. He knew I knew, and he was buttering me up. Wesley Cory had always been nice to me, but not *that* nice.

With a nervous smile, I looked to my parents and my sisters for help. Had he confessed his indiscretion in front of my sisters?

"One down, two to go," my dad said. "Now, if we can find faithful young men for my other girls, I'll be able to sleep better."

Faithful?

Wesley returned a hearty laugh before shaking my dad's hand. "I need to get home. Let me know if there's anything else I can do for you."

Eve pressed her lips together when I shifted my attention to her again.

As my dad walked Wesley outside, I slipped off my shoes and held them in one hand, my purse in the other. "What was Mr. Cory doing here?" I asked.

"The air conditioner has been acting up, so Wesley took a look at it. Your dad thinks it can be repaired, but Wesley insisted on buying a new one," Mom said with a simple shrug.

Gabby ignored her while retrieving the salad dressing from the fridge, but Eve nearly cut off her finger while slicing carrots for the salad.

"That's uh, nice of him." I tried to hide my nerves behind a smile.

"The Corys are good people," Mom said with a resolute nod.

Again, Eve eyed me with brown saucer eyes.

I jerked my head toward the stairs. "I'm going to wash up for dinner, then I'll help."

"Okay, dear." Mom smiled.

A few minutes later, Eve stepped into the upstairs bathroom while I was washing my hands. I grabbed the hand towel and turned to face her just as she closed the door.

"Oh my gosh, he knows. Right?"

Eve shook her head. "I don't know. Maybe. But now, I definitely don't think you should say anything to Matt or Mrs. Cory. I mean, it's not just the air conditioner. Before you got here, Dad told him we were a little short on rent *again*, and Wesley was like, don't even worry about it."

I opened my mouth to speak, but nothing came out.

"Just let it go." Eve rested her hands on my shoulders. "Pretend you didn't see anything. Marry Matt. Live happily ever after. The end."

The end?

That sounded awful.

That sounded like my dreams and life aspirations didn't exist.

That sounded like I would spend the rest of my life faking orgasms and praying for *it to end* quickly.

"The end," I echoed with a fake smile and lifeless gaze.

Chapter Thirteen

Eagles, "Heartache Tonight"

I LAUNCHED into Operation Avoid Isaac. He knew too much about Matt and me because I'd unintentionally over-shared. And what I didn't say, he figured out on his own. I was an open book with large bold print, and he read every word and the blank spaces between each line.

But the day before Matt came home, Isaac popped into the farm stand just as I was closing up. My body was as stiff as my smile when my gaze landed on the guitar case in his hand.

"I'll be at the rodeo tonight. I thought you might want to play my guitar since Matt's gone, and you probably don't have plans."

"Do you think I don't have friends? And why be nice now?" I cocked my head.

Isaac shrugged. "Fine. I'll take it back to the house." He turned.

"Wait!" I rolled my lips together. "I usually have plans. I'm a very popular person. But it just so happens that I don't have anything going on tonight. So ..."

"So nobody invited you to the rodeo?"

I laughed. "I've never been to the rodeo."

His lips parted as he peered at me with disbelief.

"Are you roping?" I asked.

After a few more seconds of nothing but a single blink, he slowly nodded.

"Don't look at me like that." I laughed.

"Like what?"

"Like I'm the preacher's daughter who has never been to a rodeo because my dad thinks there's too much smoking and drinking going on."

"You basically just confessed that you *are*, in fact, that person."

I stepped around the counter and tried to take the guitar from him, but he didn't willingly relinquish it.

"Come to the rodeo with me. I'm calf roping," he said.

"I don't think my father will approve."

"You're eighteen," he narrowed his eyes.

"Living at home."

"You have a car."

"He'll ask where I'm going."

"What's he going to do? Follow you?"

I chuckled. "You want me to lie."

"Did you tell him where you were and what you were doing when you fucked my brother?"

I flinched at his language. It felt like a one-way ticket to Hell.

"Well, Matt's not home to corroborate my lie. And if I ask Heather or one of my other friends to cover for me, they'll want to know why."

"Invite Heather. Let her be your partner in crime and your alibi."

I chewed on the idea, scraping my teeth along my bottom lip, eyes focused on the guitar. "I'll call her and tell her you invited us," I said.

Isaac beamed.

I peeled his fingers from the guitar case handle. "But I still want the guitar for the night. Two nights, actually."

He wet his lips. "A second night will cost you."

I hugged the guitar case. "Do you want to write your name somewhere else on my body?" I rolled my eyes.

Isaac's gaze surveyed said body. It made me feel dirty and exhilarated. I loved it and hated it in equal parts. I was ingrained with godly, moral behavior, but there was a streak of rebellion woven between those grins of purity that seemed to grow every day, especially on the days when I interacted with Isaac.

"Sunday Morning, I want to write my name on every inch of your body. But I don't think it would bode well for your relationship with my brother or the great union of the Cory and Jacobson families." Isaac turned and opened the door while gazing over his shoulder. "But I promise it would blow your fucking mind." He smirked. "The rodeo starts at seven."

That streak of rebellion? It divided and multiplied exponentially, poisoning my morality. Isaac dirtied everything. He dirtied me, turning white into gray.

I hugged the guitar tighter like it was Isaac, borderline wanting to hump it. My grin made my face hurt.

"WHERE ARE WE GOING?" Heather asked as I hopped into her car.

"The rodeo, duh," I said, eyeing her jeans, red cowboy boots, and straw cowboy hat.

"No duh," she said. "I meant, where do your parents think we're going?"

"Mini golf and the movies. What did you tell your parents?" I closed my door and fastened my seat belt.

She shrugged. "Nothing. I just told them we were going out. They don't give me the third degree like your parents do."

Heather was the youngest of three kids, so she basically raised herself. Her mom worked the night shift at the gas station, and her dad worked long hours at the tire plant just outside of Devil's Head.

She laughed. "And when I'm going out with Pastor Jacobson's daughter, they feel like I'm traveling with a guardian angel. Besides, we're adults. What are they going to do when we go to college in the fall?"

Or Nashville.

"True," I murmured. "But one of us isn't going away to college."

"Stop. You'll get in somewhere," Heather said as we pulled out of the driveway.

"I need to tell you something." I drummed my fingers on my legs. "I think Isaac's been flirting with me. Oh, and Mr. Cory is having an affair," I said quickly with one long breath.

I wasn't planning on spilling everything all at once, but the secrets were killing me. And Eve was *a* person I could confide in, but Heather was *the* person I needed. Nothing felt real until I shared it with her.

Heather didn't respond, not a blink or the slightest muscle twitch as she gazed at the road.

"If I had the money, I'd pack a bag, leave everyone a note, and move to Nashville now. When I got there, I'd find a cheap place to stay and a day job so I could get bar gigs at night. Then I wouldn't have to deal with any of this."

"S-Sarah," Heather coughed on her words. "What are you—" She shook her head. "W-when did this happen? Isaac? Mr. Cory? What the heck?"

I rubbed my hands over my face and mumbled, "I know. Don't be mad. I know you like him."

"Who cares about Isaac. Mr. Cory is having an affair?"

I nodded. "It's so unimaginable. Isaac has been letting me borrow one of his guitars. When I went to his room to get it, I heard something. And so I peeked my head around the corner to Wesley and Violet's bedroom, and some dark-haired woman was naked on top of him in bed. I totally died because the floor squeaked under my feet, so I hid in Isaac's closet until they left. Her voice sounded *so* familiar, but I couldn't place it. And I never saw her face. And then Isaac has been saying some really inappropriate things to me, which makes me think he likes me. And as if all of that isn't enough, I called Matt an asshole on the phone the other night and hung up on him because I don't think he cares about my dreams."

Heather shook her head a half dozen times. "I don't even know what to say. But I mean, are you going to tell Matt about his dad? And *how* inappropriate has Isaac been? Like, has he done something or just said things that make you think he likes you? Now I feel bad for kissing him if you like him."

"What? No. I don't like him. I mean, I don't ... it's just ... never mind. And I'm not telling Matt about his dad. Wesley owns my family's house, and he's overlooked my parents missing some rent payments. It would destroy everything if I were the one to tell on him."

Heather shook her head, speechless for a good minute or more.

"You can tell me if you like Isaac. Come on, Sarah; we've had a crush on him forever. Matt will totally *die* when he finds out, but you can't control your feelings."

"I wrote my name on the inside of his guitar case. It was so small you could barely see it. I still can't believe he saw it. So he marched into the farm stand, grabbed a Sharpie, and yanked the neck of my shirt down to write his name on my boob. *My boob!*" I unbuttoned my blouse enough to show Heather.

She nearly ran her car into the ditch, making a quick correction after refocusing on the road. "Oh my god, that's so ..."

"Deranged."

She shook her head. "Hot. That's so hot. And awful. And ..." Her face wrinkled. "Weird. Messed up. Sarah, your boyfriend's *brother* wrote his name on your boob!"

"I know. I was there." I buttoned my shirt.

"So *seriously*, do you like him?" Heather shot me another quick glance with disbelief etched into her brow.

"I like Matt."

"You can like more than one guy, but you shouldn't hog both Matt and Isaac. That's not fair."

I didn't want to laugh. It wasn't funny. But that's what

best friends did—they made you smile. Heather and I had a bond that felt stronger than family. Sometimes, I felt like we were the same person because we shared every secret and every experience.

"I don't want both guys. Right now, I'm mad at Matt, and I think Isaac is toying with me. But that doesn't matter anyway because I should love Matt, even though I'm mad at him. And the last person I should be with if I weren't with him is his brother. You know?"

"Should? Sarah, did you just hear yourself?"

"I know." I covered my face with my hands. "What is happening to me? And why can't I stop it?"

"Isaac's dreamy. Of course, you're attracted to him."

I grinned. "He is. But I don't *want* to be attracted to him. And if you ever tell anyone I said that, I'll deny it."

"Ugh! This is all too unreal. I can't believe Mr. Cory is having an affair," Heather quickly changed the topic.

I couldn't blame her. My head was all over the place, too, thinking about everything all at once.

"Violet is so nice," Heather said. "And she's pretty. And she does just as much around the ranch as he does. What kind of man does that to his wife and his family?"

I shook my head. "I don't know. I wonder the same thing."

As SOON AS we arrived at the rodeo, we found seats near the front. My jeans weren't as tight as the other girls. I wore a loose blouse, while other girls wore tank tops or halter tops. And I didn't own cowboy boots or a hat.

I had Keds and aviator sunglasses.

142

No makeup.

No hairspray.

No business being there.

Yet, I felt like an adult with endless possibilities and giddiness over my first rodeo. How I felt about seeing Isaac again—there were no words.

We watched barrel racing while eating popcorn and drinking Pepsi.

Then Heather grabbed my arm at the start of the next event. "Oh my god! There he is!" She pointed to a gate as the announcer introduced him. Isaac looked handsome in his gray and cream western shirt, blue jeans, and black cowboy hat. He adjusted his rope, holding a loop of it in his mouth for a second while he tugged at his gloves.

In the next breath, the gate beside him opened, followed by his gate. The calf sprinted through the dirt, and in a matter of seconds, Isaac had the calf lassoed around the neck. It was impressive. Heather cheered beside me while Isaac flew off his horse, ran toward the calf, and wrestled it while tying its legs. The calf struggled to get free.

I was horrified.

"What is he doing?" I stood. "He's hurting the baby cow!"

"Shh!" Heather pulled on my arm until I sat beside her again. "He's roping. And he's really good at it."

"That's cruel." I turned my head because I couldn't watch.

"Oh my gosh, Sarah. How did you not know what he meant by *calf* roping?"

"Roping is one thing. Wrestling it to the ground and tying its legs is just awful."

She giggled, covering her mouth. "It's the rodeo."

First sex and then the rodeo. Why did I hate such popular things?

Heather forced me to stay for the rest of the roping, but I didn't watch. I folded my hands, bowed my head, and prayed for the torture to end.

"Let's go." I stood, worming my way out of the stands and marching toward the parking lot.

"Hey, you came," Isaac called, wearing a huge grin while strutting toward us.

"Hey, Isaac. You were amaz—" Heather started to praise him.

But before she could step closer and stroke his animal-abusing ego, I grabbed his shirt and shoved him. "You are a cruel, heinous person, Isaac Cory. A brutal barbarian!" I punched his arm.

"Stop!" He grabbed my wrists. "What the hell?"

I tried to wriggle out of his hold, but it was futile.

"Um, you know the saying 'it's not my first rodeo'?" Heather asked Isaac. "Well, this *is* Sarah's first rodeo, and she's not a fan of roping."

I kicked his shin, and he released me. It wasn't just the baby cow; it was everything that had happened.

"Let's go, Heather." I grabbed her arm and pulled her against her will.

"Sarah, it's a sport." She laughed.

"You're taking me home." I yanked her arm a little harder as she resisted me

"I'll take her home." Isaac's boots scuffed along the gravel toward us.

"Uh ..." Heather looked at me with wide eyes.

"No. You're taking me. We're going now."

"Go, Heather. I've got this. I need to have a little chat

with my future sister-in-law." He hooked an arm around my waist.

"Are you sure?" She. Asked. HIM!

It was as if I didn't exist. Eighteen years of friendship and she abandoned me.

"No! Let go of me."

With a shrug and a wrinkled nose, Heather backed away from us. "Call me later."

"Heather!" I yelled as Isaac tossed me over his shoulder, *manhandling* me behind the stands, where nobody made any attempt to rescue me.

"Put me down!" I kicked.

"Stop it," Isaac said, swatting my butt.

Did he just spank me?

When we reached his truck and horse trailer, he set me on my feet. I pounded my fists against his chest as he backed me into the passenger's door while restraining me by holding my wrists and pressing them to my chest.

"Sunday Morning, I'm a little on edge because I need a fucking cigarette, but I quit. Now you're throwing a childish tantrum over a calf that's perfectly fine. Ya gotta cut me a little slack."

I hated his close proximity because as badly as I wanted to hurt him the way he hurt the baby cow, I felt intoxicated by his musky scent laced with leather and dirt. I never thought leather and dirt would smell good. But it did on Isaac—so did his calloused hands wrapped around my wrists, his gaze pointed at my mouth, and the heat of his body so close to mine.

My labored breaths slowed. "Why did you quit smoking?" I whispered.

"You know why."

I slowly shook my head.

"The problem is, I need something to occupy my lips if I can't have a cigarette between them." He lowered his head until his nose brushed my hair and his lips feathered across my forehead.

It paralyzed me with warring emotions and conflicting physical responses. Matt made me feel secure, but Isaac made the ground shake under my feet, leaving me unsure if I would fall or fly.

"I love Matt," I whispered while my eyes drifted shut. It was a terrible defense I clung to because the truth made me feel like a sinner. My head swam more than it had after that drink on Easter Sunday.

"I do too," Isaac murmured, dragging his lips down my cheek to the corner of my mouth. "So we should stop." He ghosted his lips over mine without kissing me.

My heart didn't merely race like someone startling me. It exploded.

I couldn't move—not my lips, not any other part of my body. I would not cheat on Matt. And I definitely wouldn't do it by kissing his brother. Still, I didn't want Isaac to stop whatever he was doing. *Of course*, we should have stopped. It was the smart thing to do, but I wasn't valedictorian. Was it fair to ask a girl with barely one toe into adulthood and a 3.2 GPA to make the smart decision?

My B-average mind went to work, sorting through my sins and trying to list my indiscretions in order from least to most offensive. Letting Isaac touch me like that was kind of wrong, but I wasn't married to Matt, so was it cheating in a biblical sense? (Of course, it was.) Then again, I had sex with Matt, and that wasn't right in God's eyes. And it had to be worse than letting Isaac's lips brush against mine. Right?

Bottom line: there was no denying that I'd been up to no good on more than one occasion. I just didn't know if I would feel more remorse for disappointing Matt or disobeying God. The effects of the former felt more immediate.

"I won't kiss you until you ask me to," Isaac whispered against my lips.

I was paralyzed, even though his hands were no longer gripping my wrists because they were undoing two buttons on my blouse. His lips trailed down my neck without kissing a single inch of my skin.

Neck.

Shoulder.

Chest.

And then his mouth hovered over the swell of my breast where his name hadn't completely faded.

Isaac was marking me again, only this time, it was invisible. But sometimes, the things we couldn't see made a deeper impact and the most permanent mark. It was an out-of-body experience. I couldn't control my reaction to him any more than I could control the weather.

When my senses returned, I pressed my hands to his chest and made him take a step back while shaking my head. "This is a terrible idea." I buttoned my shirt with shaky hands. "Your brother and our families are expecting a wedding in the future. I work for your parents. And your family owns the house that my family can't afford every month. But that's okay with your dad because he's willing to overlook a few missed rent payments from his pastor and future daughter-in-law." As much as it pained me, I lifted my gaze to his.

Isaac rubbed his lips together while tucking his fingers into his back pockets.

I cleared my throat. "I think you'll live longer if you go back to torturing baby animals and smoking and stay as far away from me as possible. Your dad will be less likely to threaten you with a shotgun."

He seemed to think about my words before the corner of his mouth twitched. "You're not a calf. I'm not chasing you with a rope. Just the opposite. I'm trying to free you. You're too big for this little town. You're a wanderer with dreams too vast to walk a straight line. I'm not trying to steal you from God or Matty. Although, if you're a Bible enthusiast, one of those two men loves you unconditionally, forgives all of your sins, and has given you the freedom to make your own decisions. The other one wants you barefoot and pregnant while he sprints after his own dreams. And for the record, that shotgun story is bullshit." He reached past me and opened my door.

Isaac's words, as far-fetched as they were, made my cheeks fill with heat. It was like a switch flipped. Isaac was right; I didn't know how to walk a straight line. And I knew I would never let it get out of control, the way I knew my heart wasn't ready to surrender to a life with Matt. But I couldn't deny the power and confidence I felt around Isaac because he wanted me, and I wanted a part of him, even though I didn't know what that was.

"What do you mean the shotgun story is BS?"

"Don't worry about it. Get in."

"If you didn't want me to worry about it, you shouldn't have said it."

He gave me a challenging expression with a hint of a grin. "Get in the fucking truck."

"Fine, Satan." I smirked, climbing into his *fucking* truck.

As hard as I tried, my confidence paled in comparison to

his. I was all talk while Isaac had real-life experience. That unavoidable fact was cemented into my brain as he adjusted himself.

"Fuck, Sunday Morning. You're making my dick hard by calling me Satan. I might have to say a few extra prayers at church this Sunday."

I fastened my seat belt, focusing on my hands instead of his crotch.

"I'll believe it when I see it," I said. It was a weak comeback. I had a lot of practice to do, but we had all summer.

We. Had. All. Summer.

He shut the door and drove me home. We didn't talk; instead, we listened to the radio, and I sang along. Isaac grinned, occasionally shooting me a sidelong glance, but I pretended not to see it.

"Don't pull into the driveway," I said as we approached my mailbox.

Isaac stopped the truck on the gravel road, just slightly off to the side, and shoved it into *Park*. "Are you playing my guitar tonight?"

"Yes." I unbuckled.

"Good. Lock your bedroom door and play it naked."

I swallowed hard, but that's all the reaction—the satisfaction—I gave him. "And why is that?" I laughed it off, reaching for the door handle.

"Because I want to think about something of mine pressed to your naked body, giving you pleasure."

Jesus ... Sorry, God. I mean gee whiz.

"Is that so? Well, you can think of *your* brother between my legs when he gets home tomorrow." I hopped out of the truck on said shaky legs, feigning confidence, shocked that those words came out of my mouth.

Isaac barked a laugh. "I said something of mine giving you pleasure. We know Matty's not doing that."

All the blood in my body surged up my neck and spread across my face as I slammed the door and marched toward my driveway.

Don't look back.

Don't look back.

Don't look—

I looked back.

He had his window rolled down, hat tipped low, but not low enough to hide his smile. "Sunday Morning, God will forgive you for what you're about to do."

Chapter Fourteen

Laura Branigan, "Show Me Heaven"

"You're home early," Mom said when I walked into the house, hoping to zoom up the stairs without questions.

I stepped into the living room, where Dad was using a TV tray as his desk, with the Bible open. He was furiously scribbling his sermon notes onto a sheet of paper.

"Mini golf took longer than expected, so we had to skip the movie," I lied.

I hated lying, although I was good at it. Not as good as my sisters, but still a worthy performance.

"You need to get registered for classes, or they'll all be filled. Why don't you see if Violet will let you do that first thing Monday morning before you start work," Dad suggested without looking up from his notes.

"Okay, sure. Isaac loaned me his guitar again, so I'm going to play for a while before everyone goes to bed." I jabbed my thumb over my shoulder and offered a toothy grin to my mom before jogging up the stairs.

"How was the movie?" Eve asked as I passed her and her friend, Erin.

"Good."

"See any cowboys?" Eve added, stopping me cold.

I whipped around. "My room. Now."

She smirked, following me and shutting the door behind them.

"Why did you say that?" I asked, eyes narrowed.

"Because Jody called. She rode with her dad to drop her brother and one of his friends off at the rodeo, and she said she saw you and Heather getting out of her car. Of course, I told her she must be lying because you don't go to the rodeo."

"I'm eighteen." I crossed my arms over my chest.

"Totally." Eve nodded slowly. "Is that what you told Mom and Dad?"

"It's what I'm telling you. In two years, you'll be eighteen too. So let's 'do unto others.' Okay?"

"You owe me." Eve opened the door.

"Are you blackmailing me?" The second the words left my mouth, I thought of Isaac suggesting I had blackmailed him.

"Call it what you want. I'm just saying you owe me." She and Erin headed toward the stairs.

I locked my door, leaning my back against it with my head tipped to the ceiling for a long sigh. After a few seconds, I closed my shades, took off my clothes, and sat on my bed with something that belonged to Isaac pressed to my naked body.

It was silly and ridiculous. And I was never going to tell anyone that I did it—and I liked it.

Saturday morning, my sisters and I helped my parents around the church grounds, mowing, watering flowers, and pulling weeds.

"So, seriously, how was the rodeo?" Eve asked as we tossed weeds into an empty five-gallon bucket and spread new mulch around the flowers by the sign at the parking lot entrance.

I glanced around to see if my mom or Gabby were in earshot. "Awful."

"What?" Eve sat back on her heels. "Are you serious? Why?"

"I'm serious." I rubbed my arm over my sweaty brow. "Matt's brother ropes. And while I thought I knew what that meant, I was totally wrong. On his horse, he chased a baby cow, lassoed its neck, and then jumped off his horse and hogtied it. The poor thing lay in the dirt, struggling and totally scared until they untied it. It was cruel and unnecessary, all in the name of entertainment."

"That's awful," Eve said.

I nodded.

"Did you talk to Isaac?"

I shrugged, keeping my gaze on the flowerbed. "Yeah, a little before I left."

"What do you think of him? He's so hot." Eve grinned, but she kept her head bowed as I glanced up. Her cheeks were already red from the heat, so I couldn't tell if she was blushing, but it wouldn't have surprised me. Isaac had that effect on women. He had many effects on them.

I shifted from my knees to my butt and leaned back on my hands, taking a break. "Matt and I don't plan to stay together when he goes to college this fall, but I'm afraid to tell Mom and Dad."

Eve's brown eyes shot wide open as her hands paused with weeds clenched into both fists. "Sarah, everyone thinks you two are getting married, not breaking up."

I stretched my legs out straight, lips twisted as I stared at my dirty old Reebok high-tops. "I know. But that's not what we want. Not now. I feel like, at some point, we stopped being together for the reasons we first started going together. And now we're still with each other just because everyone expects us to be together and get married. But sometimes I think, am I really going to marry my first love? It's a big world. What if we're together simply because there's been a lack of choice?"

Eve tossed the weeds into the bucket and pulled off her gloves. "Sure, you didn't graduate with two hundred other kids, and Devil's Head is small. But it doesn't matter what school you went to; Matt is a great catch. He's cute, smart, and so nice. He's respectful. And he's going to be a big deal someday. Everyone knows he'll get drafted. And even if, by some weird chance, he doesn't, he wants to go to law school. He's perfect. How can you possibly think you can do better?"

Better wasn't the right word.

"Because he's the only guy I've ever kissed. Mom and Dad like him so much that I think *they* want to marry him. He's going to Michigan in the fall, and I don't want a long distance relationship. Yet, it's a foregone conclusion in everyone's eyes that we're going to eventually get married, but I don't want to think about husbands or college because I want to move to Nashville." I sighed. "So, it doesn't matter that he's a good catch. Guys aren't a one-size-fits-all. And now that we're out of school, I don't know if he's right for me."

Eve shifted her eyes over my shoulder to our parents. "Whoa, that's a lot, Sarah," she murmured. "His family owns our house."

I closed my eyes with another long sigh. "I know."

"I'm not saying you should take one for the team, but ..." Eve wrinkled her nose, bringing her gaze back to me.

"No. It's not fair to ask me to *take one for the team*. Going on one date with someone you don't like because you're doing a friend a favor is taking one for the team. Giving up your dreams and marrying the wrong man is ludicrous."

"When are you going to tell everyone?"

I pinched the bridge of my nose. "I don't know. His parents will hate me. And ours will disown me, especially if we get evicted because Wesley and Violet hold a grudge."

"Is Matt onboard?"

I nodded, even though he also seemed to enjoy sex. And that was my fault.

My idea.

My really stupid idea.

LATER THAT AFTERNOON, Matt called while I played Isaac's guitar (with my clothes on).

"Hi," he said.

I tried to smile, but I couldn't, and I was glad he couldn't see me. We hadn't talked since I ended our last call with "you're an asshole." With a brave inhale, I acted like it didn't happen. "Hey. Are you home?" I asked.

"Yeah. We got home an hour ago, but I've been unpacking, and Dad needed me to help him and Isaac fix part of the fence. But I wanted to make sure we're okay. I know I upset you, and I didn't mean to."

"No. It's fine," I said, "I shouldn't have called you that. I'm sorry."

"I was a jerk. I'm the one who should be sorry. Listen, my parents are going out with the Kirks tonight. Card club at their house. So I was thinking we should grab dinner and go to a movie. And by movie, I mean we should come back to my house."

"With your brother?"

"Isaac spends most of his time in the barn, playing his guitar, drinking, and smoking. We'll have the house to ourselves. I *missed* you."

"Isaac loaned me his guitar again."

"Well, bring it back. Okay?"

"Matt, he'll know we're there and not at a movie."

He chuckled. "So? Who's he going to tell?"

"What if he comes back to the house while we're doing stuff?"

"I'll tell him not to."

I closed my eyes. Did I want Isaac to know I was messing around with his brother?

No. But kind of yes. I wanted to make Isaac jealous, but I didn't want to endure sex to achieve that result. And why did it matter? Was I going to cheat on my boyfriend just to have bad sex with another guy?

Of course not.

I didn't want to have sex with Isaac, but I wanted him to ghost his hands and lips along my skin. And I wanted him to say dirty things to me. Yes, I was going to Hell for thinking that.

"What time are you picking me up?" I asked.

"Five?"

"Okay."

"I can't wait."

Rolling my lips together, I hummed. After hanging up the phone, I played the lines I remembered from "Bette Davis Eyes."

I felt the rhythm.

The words.

And Isaac's arms around me.

At five, I was waiting outside with my bangs pulled into a barrette, white denim shorts that hit my knees, and a loose tee that said: "Jesus Loves Me."

I had a drawer full of Vacation Bible School shirts, and I secretly hoped Matt wouldn't feel as eager to remove my clothes if I wore a billboard reminding him that I was his pastor's daughter. And it made my parents proud to see me leave the house representing Jesus. There's no way they suspected Matt was planning on having sex *again* with their faithful daughter.

"Hey!" Matt smiled when I slid into his car with Isaac's guitar. He leaned over and kissed my cheek.

"Hi. You smell good." Matt always smelled good—not Drakkar Noir good, but Irish Spring good. "Where are we going to eat?" I asked.

"Pizza Hut?" he suggested, jockeying his El Camino in the opposite direction to pull out of our driveway.

I nodded. "Sounds good to me."

"How's it going with Isaac's guitar? Do you know any songs?"

I shrugged. "Yeah, I've figured out quite a bit."

"Consider yourself lucky that you're Pastor Jacobson's daughter."

"Why is that?" I glanced over at him.

"I'm pretty sure that's the only reason Isaac's being nice to you. He can be a jerk about his stuff. He's never been good at sharing."

"Lucky me." I gripped the side of the seat, feeling like my emotions were all over my face no matter how hard I tried to hide them.

We ended up eating at Pizza Hut with a group of school friends. Throughout the meal, Matt gave me bedroom eyes, which made me anxious.

Take one for the team.

We got to his house a little after seven.

"What time are your parents coming home?" I took his hand as he led me into the house.

"Between nine and ten. So ..." Matt glanced back at me, biting his lower lip.

So we needed to get to having sex.

Yay.

"Figured you'd be in the barn half drunk by now," Matt said to Isaac, who was in the kitchen.

"I'm half drunk but not in the barn yet. I'm making a sandwich," Isaac mumbled, keeping his head bowed as he spread mayo on the hoagie. "Then I'll get out of here so you can disappoint God."

"Shut up," Matt grumbled, shaking his head while we removed our shoes. "Ignore him. He's having nicotine withdrawal. Some girl he met won't kiss him until he quits smoking."

I set Isaac's guitar on the floor next to the stairs just as he glanced up at me and smirked.

With a fake smile, I cleared my throat. "Did this girl say that?" I asked.

Isaac screwed the mayo lid onto the jar. "Not in so many words. But she's mentioned my 'disgusting' habit on more than one occasion, so I've read between the lines because I'm smart."

"Maybe she just thinks you're disgusting and has no intention of kissing you even if you quit smoking." I returned a toothy grin.

Matt laughed. "That sounds more likely."

Isaac fought his grin while wrapping his sandwich in several paper towels. "Perhaps. However, when I touch her, she gets breathy and blushes from nose to toe. So I think it's only a matter of time before she's begging for it."

"It's so obvious why you're single." Matt rolled his eyes and headed up the stairs.

I didn't follow him quite yet because Isaac had me ensnared in his gaze as he walked toward me. At the last second, his gaze dropped to my shirt, and an enormous grin overtook his face as he leaned down to pick up the guitar case.

"Matty's going to bed with blue balls. He just doesn't know it yet." He snickered, sauntering toward the back door with four cans of beer dangling from a six-pack ring, the sandwich in one hand, and his guitar in the other.

When I reached the top of the stairs, Matt was sitting on the end of his bed. "Come here." He smiled.

I couldn't help but smile too. Matt was a good guy, and his joy rubbed off on everyone around him.

Except for his brother.

Joy and Isaac didn't belong in the same sentence. He was a lot of things, but joyous wasn't one of them.

"Shut the door," Matt said as I stepped into his room.

I closed it and padded my bare feet toward him, and that's when his gaze seemed to focus on my shirt for the first time that night. It elicited a frown, but I still stepped between his spread legs and rested my hands on his shoulders. I was fully prepared to have sex with him. I had endured worse. It wasn't so much that I was taking one for the team since there wasn't Team Sex, but I either needed to blow up everyone's world or bide my time for the summer. And biding my time meant sex.

Hookers did it. Surely, they didn't enjoy it. But at least they got paid for it. The fact that I kept equating my behavior to hookers wasn't a good sign.

"Sarah, how am I supposed to feel okay about doing this when you're wearing that shirt?"

I shrugged. "I assumed I'd take off the shirt. It's not like I'm going to ride you with it on, so the whole time you're reminded that Jesus loves me. He loves you, too, even if you're having premarital sex."

Matt looked disgusted. I remained nonchalant, acting like it wasn't planned or a big deal. When his shoulders sagged with disappointment, I caved and removed my shirt.

"Better?" I asked.

He shook his head and covered his mouth while bolting out of the room.

"Matt?" I plucked my shirt off the floor and followed him while threading my arms through it.

He slammed the bathroom door and hurled.

The door was locked, so I gently knocked. "Matt, are you okay? Open the door."

Again, he retched, and I wrinkled my nose with my hand

resting on the door like I wanted to rest it on his back and comfort him.

"S-Sarah ... I don't want you to see me like this," he said with a weak voice.

"Matt, everyone gets sick. It's fine. Open the door. Do you think it's food poisoning?"

"I don't—"

For a third time, he vomited.

"What can I get you? I can see if there's some ginger ale or 7UP. Want me to do that?"

"S-sure."

I jogged down the stairs and checked the fridge, but there was only a partial liter bottle of Squirt. When I poured it into the glass, it didn't even fizz, but I took it upstairs anyway.

"There was only Squirt, so that's what I have. Can you please unlock the door?"

"Just set it outside. Go home. I'm begging you."

"I don't have a car."

"Take mine."

"I'm not driving your car. If anything happened, your dad would be upset."

"Just ... Sarah ..." he released a noise that sounded like a mix between a sigh and a moan.

"I can call Heather or ask Isaac to take me home," I said with a heavy sigh.

The toilet flushed. "Do that," he mumbled. "I'm sorry."

"Don't be sorry. If it's food poisoning, I could be sick soon too."

"I hope not," he murmured, and it sounded like his voice was coming from under the door. He must have lain on the floor.

"Call me tomorrow," I said with a cringe.

Was it awful that I felt bad for Matt and relieved for myself in equal measure?

In the kitchen, I tried calling Heather, but no one answered. So I headed out to the barn, where I had played guitar with Isaac. I heard music as I opened the door. And once again, the creaking ladder to the loft announced my arrival.

"Out of condoms already?" he asked without looking up from the guitar. Isaac was perched on a haybale he'd covered with a stable blanket.

"Matt is sick. I don't know if it's food poisoning or what. I need a ride home. I don't want to drive his car. I called Heather, but no one answered at her house."

"And your parents?" Isaac glanced up at me.

I frowned. "I'd have to explain why I'm here when your parents are not."

"I can't take you home yet."

"Why not?"

He nodded to the empty cans of beer next to him.

"Well, when do you think you'll be sober enough to drive me home?"

Isaac chuckled, setting his guitar aside. "I'm being cut off early because you need a ride home?"

"Why do you make it sound like I'm asking you to make sacrifices for me? I'm never kissing you, so feel free to smoke. I'm never going back to the rodeo, so have fun abusing baby cows. And if you don't want to quit drinking yet, I'll walk home."

He looked at his watch. "Yeah, you should be able to make it home if you walk. What time is your curfew?"

I turned around and stepped toward the ladder. "Never mind."

"I'll stop drinking. Maybe I can teach you some new chords. Or I can teach you other things."

"What are you doing?" I murmured before turning around.

"You asked me for a ride home. I'm obliging."

I tucked my hair behind my ears and sighed while facing him. "Do you hate me, your brother, my family, God, or all of the above?"

Isaac scratched the back of his head. "Uh, none of the above. Why?"

"Because you're toying with me, *your brother's girlfriend*."

"I'm flirting with you."

"Why?"

"Sunday Morning," he grinned, "do I really have to explain flirting to you? If so, my brother has failed you more than I suspected."

"Why are you flirting with someone else's girlfriend?"

"Chemistry, I suppose. Combustion. Fermentation. Rusting. Photosynthesis. I'm not making a conscious decision to feel an attraction to you. I just do. And thinking I shouldn't feel a certain way or someone telling me that it's wrong doesn't change our chemistry."

"Our?" I lifted my eyebrows.

"Don't." Isaac stood, shaking his head. "Don't pretend that this is one-sided. You can be angry or feel guilty about it, and you can try to deny it, but that would only make you a liar."

"What if I told you I don't like sex?" I needed a good argument or deterrent, but the second that left my mouth, I knew it wasn't an argument; it was an embarrassing confession.

"I'd say you need better lingerie so Matt thinks he's having sex with his hot girlfriend instead of his pastor's daughter."

I glanced down at my shirt and grinned. "Nice try. I wasn't wearing this shirt when we had it. And I don't think it was his fault. I just think it's not my thing." I shrugged, owning my truth.

Isaac crooked a finger at me.

I shook my head.

He didn't stop.

I ignored all good sense and surrendered the three steps between us, swallowing hard as I stared at his gray T-shirt that hugged his chest and biceps.

"Do you want to touch me?" he whispered.

I shook my head.

A lie.

"Do you want me to touch you?"

Another headshake.

Another lie.

"*Can* I touch you?" he asked.

My pulse doubled because I could feel the heat from his body and smell his cologne. And I couldn't stop staring at his large, calloused hands and veiny, tattooed arms. Without a sane or coherent thought, I slowly nodded.

Isaac represented freedom. I didn't idolize him, but I wanted to shrug off other people's opinions the way he did. He was self-aware and had an enviable confidence. I wanted to focus on things like chemistry more than following a moral compass that confused me because not everyone needed to walk in the same direction.

"When I saw you in church on Easter Sunday," Isaac said, lifting my shirt over my head.

My heart ricocheted off the walls of my chest. This wasn't really happening. My thoughts swam in a dream state, a twisty, dizzying whirlpool.

"I knew I was fucked. Going straight to Hell." He dropped my shirt onto the floor. "But when you sang 'Bette Davis Eyes,' I knew I was going to wind up dead in a ditch either at the hands of your dad, mine, or my brother."

"Why?" I whispered in a shaky voice.

He unbuttoned my jean shorts, and my lips parted, each breath audible and ragged.

"I'm showing you why," he murmured, squatting to pull my shorts down my legs and remove my shoes with them.

When he stood, his gaze landed on my breast. It was red from a final scrub so Matt wouldn't see his brother's name on me. Isaac's gaze shifted to mine and he shot me a knowing grin. But I had no response because I was too drunk on the high I felt standing before him in nothing but my white bra and matching bikini underwear.

I didn't like sex, but I liked feeling sexy, and Isaac excelled at eliciting that from me. And I knew I needed to tell him we weren't having sex, but I wasn't ready to let go of that feeling.

"You are truly," Isaac pulled my hair away from my shoulders as he positioned himself behind me, "the most breathtaking woman I have ever seen." He kissed my shoulder and ghosted his fingertips down my arms until they were covered in goosebumps.

I closed my eyes and drew in a slow, shaky breath.

"Dare I say angelic?" He lifted my right arm, kissed my

palm, and rested it at the side of his neck. Then he feathered his hand down the inside of my arm to my breast.

As I tried to inhale, it caught in my chest. I couldn't breathe with his hands on me.

If it really was a dream, nothing but the sins of an unhinged imagination, then it couldn't be that wrong. Right? What man or woman was always pure in thought?

Isaac showed patience with his hand covering my breast, gently squeezing it while the pad of his thumb brushed across my flesh where his name had been. My fingernails scraped along his neck as my quickening pulse thrummed in my ears.

I was coming undone in the most thrilling, frightening way while his hands found my hips. Crouching behind me, he dragged his lips down my back and over the cotton material covering my backside. He slid his hands to the front of my legs, fingers gently curling into my inner thighs like his teeth teased my butt.

I was ...

Breathless.

Warm.

And my breasts felt fuller.

My muscles more tense.

And I felt wet.

I was aroused.

"Turn around," Isaac whispered, letting his lips hover over the hollow dip on the right side of my lower back before kissing it.

I can't do this.

Panic warred with desire. I couldn't have sex with him. Sex would ruin the way he made me feel. The pleasure would shift, and I didn't want to fake anything. I didn't want to feel any more guilt than I already felt for cheating on Matt.

Disappointing God.

Jeopardizing my family's living situation.

Isaac didn't push me to turn around. Instead, he guided my hand between my legs—the thin, wet cotton at my fingertips.

Again, he kissed my back, and then he rubbed his stubble-covered face along my skin, eliciting another sensation. I was drowning in pleasure, and I could no longer feel the line where his body stopped giving me pleasure, and mine began.

My fingers dipped beneath the damp fabric, and the slightest graze along my hypersensitive flesh made me weak in the knees.

I had never felt so aroused.

"If I were him, I'd put my mouth where your fingers are," Isaac whispered with his lips at my hipbone, teasing it with the tip of his tongue.

My legs squeezed together because his words made everything feel heightened. Blood whooshed until I could barely hear anything but my deafening pulse. I was a hair trigger, unimaginably aroused.

Then it happened. A million stars. I felt like every nerve in my body exploded at the same time.

"If I were him," Isaac hugged my waist, holding me to him and keeping my knees from buckling. "I'd be inside of you. We would be doing this together."

"Isaac ..." I panted. Waves of pleasure hijacked my entire body as my posture sagged, and I melted into him, lost in complete euphoria.

Isaac sat on his heels, bringing me to his lap when my knees collapsed inward. I was a rag doll in his embrace.

He buried his face in my hair, holding me tightly to him. "If only I were him."

Tears filled my eyes, but I didn't release them.

Oh, the guilt.

Why did everything I desired in life have to be wrong, sinful, or disappointing to others?

I wasn't sure. But I knew I didn't want to move. Isaac could have kept me wrapped in his arms forever. He made me feel so many things.

Coveted.

Beautiful.

Limitless.

Safe.

And seen.

Isaac didn't just see who I was; he saw everything I wanted to be.

"Let's practice the F chord and maybe a barred C chord," he murmured, his lips at my ear. "And then I'll get you home before my parents return." He released my waist.

I couldn't look at him while I dressed, but I managed a quick glance and smile when he handed me the guitar.

We played for an hour, and then he drove me home. I didn't say anything, and he seemed content listening to the radio with his window down and his arm resting on the door, fingers surfing in the breeze. When Laura Branigan's "Leave Me Breathless" played, I gazed out my window and softly sang every word, wondering if the lyrics resonated with him as they did with me.

I didn't have to ask him to stop before my driveway; he just knew.

My hand paused on the door handle as I stared at the

gravel road illuminated by his headlights. I had to say something, but I didn't know what.

"I'll see you at church tomorrow," he said.

My heart felt heavy. "Isaac," I whispered.

"Nothing happened," he said. "You can walk up the drive with your head up because nothing happened."

I stared at the floor and nodded. As soon as I opened the door, I hopped out and headed up the road. The gravel crunched beneath his tires when he pulled forward to make a U-turn.

Something happened.

I turned and ran toward his truck, smacking my hand on his window. He glanced up at me and stopped. Adrenaline took over, and I opened his door, grabbing the steering wheel and his shirt to step up and kiss him.

Isaac hesitated at first, but in the next breath, he tangled his fingers into my hair and kissed me with an open mouth. The kiss didn't end abruptly like a mistake; it ended slowly like neither one of us wanted it to end at all.

I bit my lower lip when we pulled apart just enough to look into his dark eyes. "It happened," I whispered.

A gorgeous grin stole his lips. "It happened," he echoed.

Isaac was right. I hopped down and headed toward my house with my chin held high *because* it happened.

Chapter Fifteen

Tina Turner, "What's Love Got to Do with It"

"We have to talk," I said, pulling Heather to the side of the church the second she stepped out of her parents' car. "I tried calling you a million times last night."

"Whoa! What's going on?" She fumbled her Bible onto the ground, so she pulled away from my grip to pick it up. "Sorry. My mom was talking on the phone to her sister like *forever*."

"It doesn't matter." I huffed. "Something big happened."

"With Mr. Cory?" She dusted off her Bible and followed me to the side of the church, where gates led to an old graveyard.

"With Isaac." I turned, surveying the area for anyone else.

"How big?" She inspected me with wide eyes.

I didn't hold back. I vomited every detail from the night

he took me home after the rodeo to the orgasm I had in the barn and the kiss goodnight at the end of my drive.

Heather didn't move.

And honestly, I was still in shock.

"Say something. I'm a terrible person, right? I'm going to Hell. Are you mad? Will Matt hate me? My parents will disown me. Just say it."

"Uh ..." Heather slowly shook her head. "I don't know what to say. I'm not mad. You're not a terrible person. You *could* go to Hell. We'll have to ask your dad. But Matt will hate you. Your parents won't disown you, but they might make you feel like a failure and a complete disgrace to them and God."

I wrung my hands together, face scrunched. "I'm not telling anyone. Not now. Maybe not ever."

Heather laughed. "So you're going to marry Matt and mess around with Isaac on the side."

"I'm not marrying Matt. I just need to get through the summer, and then we'll go our separate ways. Wesley and Violet can't get mad at my family if we mutually drift apart, right?"

Heather pressed her lips together and shook her head a half dozen times. "No. I mean, I don't know. Oh my gosh, why did you let it go that far? It's *his brother*! He got you off!"

I wrinkled my nose and bit my thumbnail. "I did it to myself."

Heather covered her mouth and snickered. "You're not that naive, are you?"

I didn't want to relinquish a smile, but I couldn't help it. "I'm not naive. I'm ..."

"In denial?"

I rolled my eyes. "Fine. I'm a little in denial, like on the edge of it, where accountability is optional. But Heather"—I pressed my lips together and took a moment—"I like him. I like how I feel when I'm with him. Music owns my heart. And when we play music in the barn, I feel like he's starting to own a little piece of my heart, too."

Heather's eyebrows jumped up her head. "You love him?"

"No, I'm not saying that." I wasn't sure what I was trying to say because Isaac made me feel something new and unfamiliar, something undefinable. "I'm just saying I like who I get to be when I'm with him."

She squinted. "And who is that?"

I lifted a shoulder. "Myself."

Something akin to realization stole her face. "This is awesome. Disastrous but awesome. Let's go." Heather giggled, grabbing my wrist and pulling me toward the back of the church. "Maybe we can sneak in and get our robes, and your dad will think we've been here all along."

"Fingers crossed," I said, opening the door.

We were in luck, my dad wasn't in his office, and several other choir members were retrieving their robes from the closet.

"Is Matt still sick?" Heather whispered as we took our seats in the choir.

I glanced at Matt's parents and Isaac while leaning into Heather. "Apparently. I called to check on him last night, and he was still pretty miserable. I think it's a stomach bug, not food poisoning, because I'm fine, and we ate the same thing."

Dad welcomed everyone and said a prayer, and then the choir led the congregation in several hymns. For the next forty-five minutes, I tuned out my dad's sermon and sneaked peeks at Isaac, who was looking at me the whole time with a mischievous grin.

"Those are some serious bedroom eyes," Heather whispered, nudging my leg.

I bit my lip and bowed my head, pretending to follow along in my Bible.

"We're in Leviticus, not Deuteronomy," Heather mumbled under her breath.

I flipped to Leviticus, barely registering my dad preaching about apologizing for not being enough and the importance of repentance. In hindsight, I probably should have listened better.

After church, I exited with my parents and sisters, and everyone scattered in the churchyard to chat, make afternoon plans, and catch up from the week.

I stayed nestled to my mom's side like the perfect duckling so Isaac didn't approach me. But that didn't stop his parents from finding us, which meant he was with them.

"Matthew is sick today. I'm sure Sarah mentioned it," Vi said.

Mom eyed me. "No. Actually, she didn't."

I cleared my throat, trying not to look at Isaac, but it was hard. "Yeah. We went to dinner, and then he wasn't feeling well."

"You were home kind of late for dinner," Dad said, casting a hard glance in my direction.

Again, I cleared my throat, clasping my hands at my back. "We left the movie early when his stomach was feeling funny."

"What movie did you see?" Vi asked, but she wasn't testing me. She had no reason to think I was lying.

I racked my brain to remember what movies were playing at the drive-in.

"Matty said you saw D.A.R.Y.L.," Isaac said.

I nodded enthusiastically. "Yes. We did. Well, we saw part of it."

Isaac rubbed his lips together to hide his smile when I looked at him.

"PG?" Dad asked.

I didn't know. "Yeah," I said. "It seemed PG. I mean, we're eighteen, so I guess nobody asked. But there wasn't any bad language or other things."

Other things like sex, which I'd had with Matt, and sexual things I had done with his brother. And just the thought of that made my stomach feel uneasy. Or maybe I was coming down with a stomach bug or just a severe case of guilt.

"Anyway," Vi said, "we don't have to come over for lunch."

"No. You should still come," Mom insisted.

I had no clue that my mom had invited the Corys for lunch. But then I thought about the roast in the crock pot and the extra pies on the counter, and it all made sense.

"I'll send leftovers home for Matt," Mom added.

"Then we'd love to. We need to go home first to get my cucumber salad out of the fridge, and I'll check on Matthew. We can be there in about forty-five minutes," Vi replied while tucking her purse under her arm.

I shifted my attention to Mr. Cory, but he was glancing over my dad's shoulder, so I turned to follow his gaze. Brenda Swensen peered in our direction, and that's when it registered that Wesley was looking at her, and she was looking at him.

Brenda Swensen and her long, dark, curly hair.

I held my breath while surveying everyone around us. Was I the only one seeing them? When my gaze snagged on Isaac's, he narrowed his eyes. I looked down, afraid to make eye contact with anyone.

Afraid someone would see what I was seeing.

Brenda Swensen was the mystery mistress.

That was the voice I couldn't quite place.

Brenda worked as a waitress at Cosmic Cafe. She was twenty-one. Her dad owned the local sanitation company, and her mom taught third grade. She had a brother who was a freshman at the high school.

Many people thought it was weird that she didn't go straight to college. She was smart, and her family had enough money to pay for her schooling.

"Want to go swimming at Laura's?" Heather asked, grabbing my shoulders from behind and startling me.

"Oh ..." I whipped around.

"We're having lunch with the Corys," my mom answered for me.

Heather eyed me, and then she shot her gaze to Isaac for a second and smirked.

"I'll call you after lunch," I said, taking her hand and pulling her toward the parking lot. "Don't look, but I know who was in bed with Mr. Cory."

Heather glanced around.

"I said don't look!" I let go of her hand and linked arms with her, plastering on a fake smile as we passed people milling around, making their way to the parking lot.

"Is she here? Who is she? Is she married too? Tell me!"

I felt sick to my stomach. She was twenty-one. Mr. Cory

was fifty-two. What was wrong with her? And him? He had a family. A reputation in the community.

Heather stopped me. "Sarah, who is it?"

My grimace felt permanent. I would never look at him the same way. It shouldn't have mattered who. Adultery was adultery. But the age difference made it exponentially worse.

"Brenda Swensen."

Heather blinked several times before shaking her head. "No way. She's twenty-one."

"It's her."

"No." She continued to shake her head.

I didn't blame her because I didn't want to believe it either. I wanted to be wrong. But I wasn't.

"You said you didn't see her face."

"I heard her voice. It was familiar. I just couldn't place it. But when I saw him looking at her, it all came together. The hair. The voice. It was her."

"Gross. No. Sarah, you have to be wrong."

"I'm not wrong. And they were looking at each other."

"So what? Maybe he forgot to leave a tip and seeing her reminded him, and maybe she was scowling at him for being cheap."

I frowned. "Stop. That's not it. I wish it were. I'm one hundred percent sure about this."

Heather's face mirrored mine. "What are you going to do?"

"Nothing."

"Nothing?" Her head jutted forward as her jaw unhinged.

"There's nothing I can do. I told you I can't be the one to expose his indiscretions. My family has too much to lose."

"But she's only twenty-one," Heather argued.

I shrugged. "An adult."

Heather rolled her eyes. "Barely."

"Legal."

She sighed. "We have to do *something*."

I shook my head. "*We* don't." I smiled at my family as they headed toward me. "I'll call you later," I said to Heather through my fake smile.

"Okay." She pivoted and gave my family a wave before heading toward her parents' car.

"Erin's coming to lunch," Mom said. "So you're riding with the Corys. They're going to their house first. Maybe you can check in on Matt too."

I nodded, but I wasn't focused on what she said because my gaze stuck to Mr. Cory walking his wife to their blue Cadillac Seville while turning his head one last time to look at Brenda Swensen. My attention shifted to Isaac as I headed toward their car. He did a good job of keeping a neutral face while opening the back door for me.

"Look at the nice boy I raised," Violet said.

Wesley eyed his son's chivalrous act and offered a half grin which made me think he wasn't as convinced.

"Thank you," I murmured, making eye contact with Isaac just as I slid into the back seat.

"Set this back there," Wesley said, handing me his suit jacket as Isaac sat behind him.

I set the folded jacket in the middle seat.

"I hope Matthew's feeling better," Violet said.

Wesley responded with a long spiel about his son needing to take better care of himself because the baseball team was counting on him.

Isaac and I didn't exchange a word. I stared out my window while thoughts of the torrid affair replayed on a long loop. I stiffened for a second when Isaac's hand touched my leg. He had it under his dad's jacket.

I inspected his parents before sliding my gaze to him, but he didn't look at me. He looked straight ahead, face neutral like a soldier at attention. I tucked my hand beneath the jacket too, and Isaac interlaced his fingers with mine. Heat spread along my skin. I liked how little my hand felt in his. The rough callouses. The warmth.

The allure of the forbidden.

Was that it?

Was that why Mr. Cory had an affair?

I knew most of the lessons from the Bible. And sin always seemed to accompany temptation.

When desire has conceived, it gives birth to sin.

Was I any different than Mr. Cory?

Sure, I wasn't married to Matt, but we were together. And I was holding his brother's hand in secrecy. Isaac had touched me intimately, and I had let him.

My thoughts were impure.

I was a sinner.

But ... we were all sinners. Right?

For everyone has sinned; we all fall short of God's glorious standard.

The Bible also said that through Christ Jesus, God freed us from the penalty of our sins.

Was I twisting God's words? Maybe.

But wasn't that basically what all religions did? Came up with their own interpretations of the Bible to suit their lives —to condemn those they wanted to condemn and condone the acts they valued?

Isaac released my hand when we pulled into their drive.

"Isaac, why don't you and Sarah check on your brother

while your father and I feed the cats and grab the salad," Violet suggested.

I didn't wait for Isaac to open my door. Instead, I high-tailed it toward their porch, deposited my shoes at the entry, and tiptoed up the stairs.

Matt's door was cracked open, and he was curled up in bed with his back to me. The floor creaked when I stepped into his room.

I hated creaky floors.

Matt rolled in my direction. "Sarah," he whispered. "Don't come too close."

I stopped halfway to the bed and opened my mouth to speak, but Isaac appeared behind me, spewing his less-than-sympathetic words first.

"Are you going to die?" he asked.

"I wish," Matt mumbled. He was pale, his voice weak, and his eyelids barely opened.

"We're going to Sarah's house for lunch. Do you need anything?" Isaac asked.

"No," Matt whispered.

"Feel better, okay?" I said to Matt.

He grunted, "I'm trying."

I frowned, wishing there was more that I could do, but Isaac pinched my dress at the back of my waist and gave it a little tug, so I turned and followed him out of the room, closing Matt's door behind me.

I stepped toward the stairs, but Isaac wrapped his hand around my wrist and pulled me into his room so quickly that I gasped.

"What are you—"

He hid us behind the door and kissed me with his hands cupping my head and his tongue sliding against mine. I grabbed his forearms to steady myself. When he released my mouth, it was only for a breath before he kissed me again.

I liked kissing my boyfriend's brother.

I liked his hands on my face.

I liked the confidence with which he kissed me.

I liked how my thoughts vanished, and that voice of common sense was silenced.

Again, he released my mouth, and he stared at me with those intense dark eyes while the pad of his thumb traced my bottom lip. He held my gaze as though it were his hostage as his hands unbuttoned the top of my blue sundress. Just three buttons.

Isaac dipped his head like he'd done at the rodeo and kissed the swell of my breast where his name had been.

I swallowed hard to suppress a moan.

Matt was in the other room—less than twenty feet away.

His parents were downstairs.

This is SO wrong ...

But I couldn't utter a single word in protest, not when he went a step further than he'd gone before, sliding the cup of my bra out of his way and sucking my nipple into his hot mouth.

Oh god ... I mean gosh ... darn ... FUCK!

It felt incredible.

If the rest of his family couldn't hear my heart thundering in my chest, then they were deaf. I brushed a hand along his head, curling my fingers, but his hair was too short. I couldn't pull him away, but I really didn't want to because it. Felt. Too. Good.

It felt good everywhere.

We were going to get caught. Isaac was taking his sweet

time, and I didn't want him to stop, but I also didn't want my life to implode that way.

As if he read my thoughts, Isaac adjusted my bra and buttoned my blouse. "You're blushing, Sunday Morning," he whispered.

I scowled at him. Was he *trying* to get me in trouble?

Isaac planted his face next to mine, lips at my ear. "I love seeing you flushed, breathless, and I imagine ... *wet*." He gathered the skirt of my dress in his hands and slid his middle finger along the crotch of my underwear on the outside.

Yes, I was wet there.

"Fuck ..." He groaned, dropping his forehead to my shoulder.

My knees trembled as the pad of his finger made tiny circles.

He needed to stop. Where was my voice? Why couldn't I tell him to stop?

After all, I didn't like sex. Did Isaac want to be with someone who liked everything except sex? Surely intercourse was his goal.

I bit my lips together to prevent myself from making noise, but my breaths quickened to the point that breathing through my nose made too much noise.

"Stop tempting me," he whispered.

His hand disappeared as quickly as he did. And I was left adjusting my dress and composing myself. I darted into the bathroom and splashed cold water on my cheeks.

When I made it down the stairs, Violet was putting on her heels at the door. "How's Matt? Do I need to check on him too?"

"Uh," I tucked my chin and slid on my flats, "no. He's really tired but still not feeling well."

"Then we'll let him rest. Come on, dear. Isaac and Wesley are already in the car."

"Okay," I nearly choked on that one word.

Satan had a hold on me, and I knew it was wrong, but I couldn't wait for the next close encounter.

The next thrill.

The next risk.

It was a glorious drug.

Chapter Sixteen

Philip Bailey & Phil Collins, "Easy Lover"

WITH MATT and Violet back from Michigan, it was nearly impossible to find time to sneak off with Isaac. Even when Matt was at baseball practice and Violet ran errands, Wesley had his eye on me. It had nothing to do with his sons and everything to do with a waitress.

I felt ninety-nine percent sure that he knew I knew.

However, there had to be a tiny part of him (at least one percent) that held a breath of reservation, a blink of doubt. Had he known with complete certainty, he would have confronted me.

I was *so* grateful for that doubt, and I did everything in my power to feed it. When I saw Wesley on the farm, I flashed him my best smile, told him my parents said to say "hi," and asked him questions I already knew the answers to, so he felt like a father figure to me as well.

"Hey," Matt snuck up behind me as I locked the farm stand door.

"You scared me." I dropped the money bag and fumbled the key. Then I shoved his chest while picking up the bag and key.

He laughed, walking backward in front of me as I made my way down their lane. He was wearing his dirty practice uniform and baseball hat. "My parents are going to the rodeo tonight to watch Isaac. They invited you, and my mom already talked to your mom, and she's fine with you going with us."

I frowned. "I don't like the rodeo."

Matt squinted. "You've never been."

Oh, that's right.

"I don't have to go to know that I won't like it. Heather's been to them, and she said it's animal cruelty."

Matt barked a laugh. "It's not animal cruelty. Isaac's really good. We'll grab snacks. And afterward, we'll meet up with some friends." He smirked. "Or at least that will be our story."

I needed to break up with my boyfriend so his brother could kiss my breast and touch me between my legs without making me feel guilty. Maybe I needed to come clean with Wesley so we could discuss the emotional and moral burdens of cheating—allies of sorts.

"Why do you care about watching him rope?"

"Isaac goes to my games when he can. Just because he's a jerk sometimes doesn't mean I'm not interested in his life. After all, he bought me condoms."

I returned a nod and a stiff smile. "That was so nice of him."

"What's your deal?" He took my hand and walked beside me.

"Nothing. There's no deal."

"Good. So I'll pick you up at six. I need to shower." He took the key and money bag, and kissed my cheek before sauntering toward the house when we reached my car.

As I reached for the door handle, the neighing of a horse caught my attention. It was Isaac walking his brown horse into the barn. I should have slid into my car and driven home, but I wasn't good at doing the right thing. So I made my way to the barn.

"I've been invited to the rodeo tonight," I said as Isaac emerged from the tack room and began brushing his horse.

"Oh yeah?" He shot me a quick glance and smiled.

"Yes," I said, resting my back against the stall. "What's his name?" I nodded to the horse.

"Sunday Morning," he said.

I giggled. "Shut up. I'm serious."

Isaac smirked. "Anakin."

"Anakin Skywalker?"

"Maybe." The corner of his mouth twitched.

"Matt loves Star Wars," I said.

"Who doesn't?" Isaac said.

"Can I brush him?"

Isaac paused for a moment before handing me the brush.

"I can't break up with him. Not yet," I said, making long strokes with the brush.

"I know." Isaac leaned his shoulder against the gate's rail.

"That means he's going to want to use one of those condoms you so kindly bought him."

"I know," he repeated.

I frowned. "And that's okay?"

"You're his girlfriend."

I couldn't help the sour expression that stole my face. "So what does that mean? You're sharing me?"

He grunted, crossing his arms over his chest. "What do you want me to say? You just said you can't break up with him. I'm not asking you to do it. So I guess you can interpret it however you'd like."

"I thought you'd be ..." I couldn't finish my thought. I knew better than to get emotionally attached to Isaac. Still, it irked me he wasn't even a little jealous at the thought of me having sex with another guy.

"I need to get away from all the Cory men." I tossed him the brush and strode out of the barn without another word.

Guess who I spotted the second we climbed into the stands at the rodeo?

Brenda Swensen.

I didn't know whether Wesley Cory's decision to bring his family to an open bench three rows below Brenda and her friends disgusted or impressed me. Brenda locked eyes with Wesley for a moment, and they exchanged subtle, secretive smiles. I knew those smiles all too well.

Her friends, however, didn't seem privy to anything, which, oddly enough, impressed me. I was good at keeping secrets, but not like a vault. I kept secrets from the necessary people, but not from everyone. Was Brenda having an affair with a fifty-two-year-old man without telling *anyone*? I couldn't imagine.

I did the math. Wesley was thirty-one with one child and a pregnant wife when Brenda was born.

"Your mom said this is your first rodeo. Are you excited?" Violet asked, sliding on her sunglasses since we faced the setting sun.

"I think so. As long as no animals are hurt."

Matt grabbed my hand and chuckled. "Sarah thinks roping calves is cruel."

"Oh, they're fine, sweetie. Don't worry about it," Violet tried to reassure me, but I knew what I'd seen.

"I love you," Matt whispered in my ear before kissing my cheek.

He said it all the time. And that should have been a good thing, but it wasn't. He said it so much that it felt less genuine, like the cashier at the grocery store who asked how I was doing. She didn't care. It was just something that people said.

We were going through the motions, but they felt emotionless because we had an expiration date. Matt knew it, but he seemed not to care. Did he think it was a good idea to go full throttle all summer and then just abruptly end?

Granted, I was partially to blame. After all, I encouraged the future split one minute, only to suggest having sex the next. But I never wanted it to mean more than sex.

Intercourse.

Throwing our virginities to the wind.

Gaining a little experience.

As we watched the events, I couldn't help but stare at Wesley and peek over my shoulder at Brenda. Then Violet nudged me, and I thought she was about to ask why I kept checking over my shoulder.

"There he is." She nodded toward Isaac on his horse behind the gate. "I have such handsome boys. I hope he finds a girl like you, Sarah."

I rolled my lips together and nodded several times.

The gates opened, and the calf didn't stand a chance. I focused on Violet's oldest—her *handsome* son—until he jumped off his horse and tied the calf.

Matt laughed as I tucked my chin and curled my shoulders inward while cringing. He wrapped his arm around me as if he could protect me. When I risked a glance up, Isaac was strutting back to his horse, adjusting his cowboy hat while peering up at me with an unreadable expression as Matt kissed the side of my head.

This time, I had no choice but to stay for the entire rodeo, but I didn't have to be an idle spectator, so I excused myself.

"Are there outhouses?" I asked, knowing that there were.

"Over there," Matt pointed. "Want me to come with you?"

"No. I've got it. I'm going to grab another Pepsi. Can I get you another one?"

He shook his head. "I'm good. Thanks." He scooted back to let me squeeze past him.

I meandered past the concession stand and made my way to the outhouses, but I wasn't sure I needed to pee bad enough to use the stink box.

As I passed the trucks and trailers and the loudspeaker faded a bit, I heard a familiar tune. Turning, I followed the sound, which led me to Isaac's truck. He was sitting in the passenger's seat with the door open and boots crossed in the open window while he strummed his guitar. I had never seen anything sexier.

He had a toothpick in his mouth, and I wondered if it was a replacement for his beloved cigarettes.

"Come here, gorgeous," he said with a hint of a Southern drawl that made me shiver.

Sometimes, I detected that same accent when Wesley talked, but I never noticed it with Matt or Violet.

"Can't." I crossed my arms. "It's going to take me a few days to forget about you being mean to that baby cow."

He grinned. "Is that so?"

"Yep."

He continued to play his song, but I didn't recognize it. "I heard Matt saying that you might go camping with Heather and a few other friends over the Fourth."

"Yeah. So?"

"So what if you didn't?" He stopped playing and eyed me with an unreadable expression.

"Why wouldn't I? It's the first time I've had permission to camp without parents chaperoning."

"It's four hours to Nashville. I'll be there for two nights."

Isaac brought me to life while everyone else tried to crush my dreams, slamming one door after another. He blew off the ceiling and gave me wings. I was still upset on behalf of that baby cow, but I couldn't fully suppress my grin as I took slow steps toward him, dragging my shoes in the dirt.

"What are you doing in Nashville?"

He sat up, pulling his feet from the window and setting his guitar on the floor. "Playing at a bar my buddy owns. Drinking too much beer. And watching fireworks."

"What buddy?" I tried to control my giddiness while I clasped my hands behind my back.

"A chief I served under as an MP. He retired last year, and he bought a bar with his brother." Isaac tossed his toothpick onto the ground and fished a pack of gum from his pocket.

I stood between his spread knees and rested my hands on them, gazing up at him. "What's an MP?"

He chuckled. "Military Police."

I twisted my lips. "So you arrested people?"

Again, he grinned. "I enforced the military laws."

"Hmm. Interesting. Tell me more about this bar. Are you asking me to sing with you?"

"Fuck, no." He unwrapped a stick of gum and shoved it into his mouth.

I frowned. "Then why bring it up?"

"Because I thought you'd like to watch some other people perform. You like to watch, right?"

Despite not being finished with my grumpiness towards him, I nodded.

He curled my hair behind my ear and ghosted his fingers along my jaw. "Come with me," he whispered.

I swallowed, fighting emotions that were unlike anything I had ever felt. "Um, where would I stay?"

"With me."

All the air left my lungs.

I longed to be an adult, carving out my own path and setting my own rules, but my conscience had been influenced by hundreds of sermons. Still, Isaac's "with me" felt like the day my dad took the training wheels off my bike, turning it into a "big girl bike." I faked it—feigning bravery until I realized I was doing it all by myself.

The road was mine.

The wind in my hair.

Hands gripped to the handlebars.

I knew there would be bumps, and I might fall a few times and scrape my elbows and knees, but it was worth it.

"Say it again," I said, stepping onto the running board

and removing his hat while he slid one hand along my backside.

"With me," he said before kissing me.

AFTER THE RODEO, Matt drove us to our favorite spot. It was torturous. The boy I'd loved and to whom I gave my virginity wanted to be intimate with me. But I still tasted Isaac on my lips and felt his hands on my body. Did it matter that with or without Isaac in the picture, I didn't want to be Matt's wife? Did it matter that we were going to be over soon?

Life didn't seem as simple as right and wrong. Truths and lies.

My relationship with Matt reached far beyond us. Did that make it okay to have sex with him so we'd stay together a little longer so our families didn't have any bad blood?

He put the car in *Park* and unbuckled, scooting toward the middle this time instead of walking around to my side. Maybe this meant we were just going to make out.

Even that felt forced and wrong.

But we did—we kissed.

He touched me on the outside of my clothes before pulling my T-shirt off. Again, we kissed, and he slid his hand inside my bra for the first time.

I choked on a suppressed sob.

Matt reared his head back and froze. "Sarah, w-what's wrong?"

I shook my head, holding my breath along with the emotions threatening to gush out with it. Then I wiped my eyes before the tears escaped. "N-nothing," I whispered.

"You're crying. That's not nothing."

I hugged my shirt to my chest. "This is so w-wrong."

Matt drew his brows together. "But we already ... I mean, do you regret what we did? I thought you wanted to? I thought you liked it."

"I did. I just ..." I shook my head again. "I'm sorry. I feel like we're going a million miles an hour, and I'm afraid it's too fast. You're going to college soon. I'm staying here. Our families are waiting around for us to get married, but they don't know we're breaking up. And I feel like it's too much. I can't do this." I shook my head and wiped my eyes. "There's so much pressure to make everyone happy, and we haven't had time to adjust to life outside of high school. And now we're having sex, and what if something happened and I got pregnant? And I know this is my fault. I brought it up. I thought we could do this without feeling like it had to mean something more. But ..."

Matt's expression softened, surrendered like he understood my concerns. "No. It wasn't just you. I wanted this too," he said, hugging me. "But you're right. A lot is happening all at once. I thought we could do this and enjoy our summer, like a really good farewell. But you're right. It will only make it harder, and it's not worth the risk." He sighed, releasing me and running his hands through his hair.

Isaac was wrong. Matt cared about me. He loved me. Maybe he didn't show it in grand ways, like buying me a guitar and taking me to Nashville, but I was the girl he fell in love with when we were just kids. And I think, had I not advocated for splitting up, he would have married me.

He loved me more than I loved him.

That. Broke. My. Heart.

I loved him, but not like that. Love couldn't be forced or faked. Not that kind of love.

It felt like an impossible choice—hurting my first love and risking my family's security or being honest. The truth felt more cruel than the lie. I wanted Matt to be the one with the wandering eye, finding someone else so I didn't feel like an awful person.

But he would never choose anyone but me as long as we were living in Devil's Head.

"Is it over?" he asked with a deep frown. "Should we stop now?"

I panicked. What if his dad stopped helping my parents?

"Hey," Matt grabbed my hand and squeezed it. "I'm not looking forward to telling my family either." He offered a small grin, obviously reading my mind. "I think they like you better than they like me."

I returned a nervous chuckle. "That's not true."

"So we don't tell anyone."

"For how long?"

He shrugged. "As long as we can get away with it. The rest of the summer. Thanksgiving. Christmas."

I chewed on the inside of my cheek.

"Why do you look so terrified?" he asked. "No one will find out. It's not like we won't see each other. I'm busy. You're working. No one will suspect anything. It will be fine."

I tried to nod and actually believe it. But everything wasn't going to be fine. There were too many secrets—the really bad kind that could break up families.

"So this is it?" Suddenly, my heart recalled all the reasons I fell in love with Matt. And while I *didn't* want to marry him or be his girlfriend any longer, the official decision to end things made my eyes burn with unexpected sadness.

"Don't. It's for the best." Again, he squeezed my hand, but that only made it worse.

So I hugged him as the dam broke, and I bled with empathy and guilt. Part of me wished Isaac would not have come home. That was the version of myself that aimed to please, the version that was a chameleon, fitting into whatever anyone needed me to be.

But Isaac did come home, and I got a glimpse of my true self, and I couldn't turn back.

Chapter Seventeen

Cyndi Lauper, "Girls Just Want to Have Fun"

"I NEED A HUGE FAVOR," I said to Heather the second she hopped into my car.

We were meeting a few friends for burgers and bowling two days after the rodeo.

"What?" she asked slowly with distrust in her eyes.

I wrinkled my nose. "I need you to let your parents think I'm camping with you and everyone else on the Fourth the way I'm letting my parents believe it."

"Uh, what do you mean? You're making it sound like you won't be camping with us."

"I won't. And please don't have a cow. I know we've been looking forward to this for weeks, but something has come up, and I can't pass up the opportunity," I said, backing onto her street.

"Just tell me. However, there's nothing that will make it

okay for you to miss this trip, short of death, but I'm totally listening."

"I'm going to Nashville."

"Not even!"

"Even."

"With who?" she gasped.

I pressed my lips together for a beat. "Isaac."

"Dude. No way. Why? How? Did he ask you? Are you in love with him? Tell me!"

I couldn't hide my excitement as I gripped the steering wheel to keep my whole body from shaking. "The other night, when I went with Matt and his parents to the rodeo, I headed to the bathroom to get another Pepsi, and Isaac was sitting in his truck playing his guitar. He called me 'gorgeous,' and it sounded so hot. And the next thing I knew, he was inviting me to Nashville over the Fourth. Some guy he knows from the Army has a bar there, and Isaac's going to perform. He said I'm not allowed to perform, but I'm going to change his mind."

"Dude ..." Heather shook her head. "That's crazy. What if your parents find out? What if Matt finds out? And why didn't you tell me this when we talked on the phone the other night? You only said that you and Matt weren't going to keep having sex. You totally skipped this very important bit of information."

I sighed, glancing in my rearview to switch lanes. "I wanted to tell you, but I didn't know if I was going to do it. And I didn't want you trying to persuade me one way or another. The decision has to be mine so that you don't feel responsible if anything happens and I get in trouble."

"Sarah, this is so wrong but so romantic. And I'm jealous!" She pinched my arm. "You're such a hog. You can't have all the good guys. If you don't want Matt, can I have him?"

"Well," I cringed and shrugged. "He's unofficially available."

Her eyes bugged out. "What?"

I nodded. "We parked in our spot to have sex, but I felt way too guilty, and the next thing I knew, we were breaking up."

"So he knows about Isaac?"

"No. Oh my gosh, totally not. We're not saying anything to anyone until we absolutely have to." I deflated. "I hate this. Why do my family and his have to be so intertwined? I just want to be friends with Matt. And I don't want our families to get upset. And I want my parents to have the money to buy their own place so that I don't feel like I have to marry Matt for some greater good."

"Why does it have to be Matt? Isaac is a Cory too. Maybe Mr. Cory would be fine with you just swapping sons."

"Stop," I snorted. "You know that's not how anyone will look at this. Whatever good graces Isaac has fallen into with his dad will be destroyed. Wesley will probably make him reenlist. And I'll be forced to marry Matt, pop out babies, and raise chickens."

Heather pulled down the visor to look into the mirror and apply her pink lipstick. "Whatever. I can't believe you're choosing a guy over your best friend. Are you going to have sex with him?"

I stiffened. It's not that I hadn't thought about it. After all, he said we'd be sharing a motel room. I even liked to think about Isaac in a sexual way. But actual intercourse would ruin everything because sex was a scam or an acquired taste. It made sense. All parents complained about the difficulties of parenting. Surely God wouldn't make procreation so easy. Making a human needed to be hard, like trigonometry, pull-ups, and brain surgery.

"I'd rather not," I mumbled.

"Sarah, Isaac is not taking you to Nashville to watch you give yourself an orgasm."

I blushed. "He's taking me to Nashville because he knows it's my dream."

She laughed. "Don't be that naive."

I pulled into the bowling alley parking lot. "If it were only about sex, I don't think he'd take me to Nashville *just* for that."

"I'm not saying he doesn't really like you. I'm just saying you can't risk so much without going into this with your eyes open. He's going to expect sex. And I bet he's good at it."

I snorted, shaking my head as I stopped the car and killed the engine. "There's nothing wrong with Matt. He's sexy. And hot. And a nice guy. It's me, not him."

"Duh. I'm not saying anything is wrong with Matt. He just doesn't have experience like Isaac does. Just imagine how much sex Isaac has had?" Heather smirked. "I bet he's totally done *all* kinds of sex."

"Stop!" I unbuckled and covered my red face.

We got out of the car and headed into the bowling alley. Heather looped her arm with mine as we laughed and stumbled like we were drunk.

"Did you ever think you'd do it with brothers?" she asked.

I couldn't stop giggling. "That sounds bad, like I'm doing it with both of them at the same time."

"A threesome." She gasped. "Would you ever do that?"

"No!" I released her arm and playfully shoved her just as we reached the entrance. "Listen. You can't tell anyone. I mean, *anyone* about any of this," I said, stopping before she opened the door.

"What am I supposed to say when everyone else asks where you are?"

"Tell them I got sick."

"Sarah," she frowned, "it's going to get out. Someone will say something, and it will get out to your parents because everyone will want to know if you're feeling better."

"Then tell them my dad changed his mind and didn't want me to go."

She sighed. "This won't end well."

I didn't think so, either, but not going to the place I wanted to go more than anywhere else felt like a bigger tragedy. Yes, I knew if or *when* I got caught, I might change my feelings about that.

"I've got your back," Heather said, opening the door for me.

"You're awesome."

"I know," she giggled. "Just don't get pregnant. You won't be able to hide that. And I don't think you'd get an abortion."

She was right. I wouldn't be able to hide it *because* I wouldn't be able to get an abortion. Even if God forgave me, my father would disown me.

However, it didn't matter. I wasn't having sex with Isaac.

Chapter Eighteen

AC/DC, "Highway to Hell"

THE NEXT MORNING, Isaac delivered baked goods and eggs to the farm stand just as I was getting everything ready to open it.

"My mom asked me to drop these off. She's under the weather," he said, sliding the two crates onto the counter before removing his hat. His hair was a little longer, and so were his whiskers. Isaac didn't look twenty-four. He looked thirty.

It was the first time I'd seen him since the rodeo, and it was weird. He wasn't under the influence and neither was I, yet part of me wondered if he remembered what happened. I'd been thinking about it nonstop. But what if Isaac offered to take girls to Nashville all the time?

"How are she and your dad?" I asked to avoid questioning him about his recollection of the rodeo.

Isaac scratched the back of his head and narrowed his eyes. "I just said she's not feeling well. My dad is fine. Why?"

I unloaded the baked goods without looking him in the eye. "No reason. I just meant, like ... you know ... are *they* good? Do they ever fight?" I should have talked about Nashville. Suggesting his parents might have a rocky marriage wasn't the best second choice.

When he didn't respond, I looked at his focused eyes and twisted lips.

"Forget it. Thanks for bringing this stuff."

"How are *your* parents?" he asked.

I returned a tight grin. "Fine."

"Do they ever fight? What about you and Matty? Do the two of you fight?"

With a nervous laugh, I turned my back and arranged the loaves of bread on the shelves. "Sometimes we fight about stupid stuff, but it never lasts. We always make up. And I used to think my parents never fought, but I discovered Grandma Jacobson took us for ice cream when my parents needed to fight. So I guess it's nice that they don't fight around me and my sisters. Now that we're older, they leave us home alone and take a drive when they need to fight. When they return, Dad does the best job of acting like nothing happened, but my mom is quiet for a day or so. I don't think they fight about anything big like ..." I shrugged. "No one is cheating on anyone."

I said it, and I immediately turned to catch his reaction. But he didn't have one. I didn't touch a single nerve. So either he had no clue his dad was cheating on his mom, or he was a pro at hiding his reaction.

"Like you're cheating on Matty?"

My heart plummeted into the pit of my stomach. No, I wasn't talking about me and Matty. It was easier to pretend that I was *not* cheating on him. We broke up, even if we weren't telling anyone. So I wasn't cheating on him—well, not anymore.

At least, that's how I imagined it. I didn't want to be a cheater. I wanted to be a strong woman who pursued her goals while being kind and considerate to those around me.

Kind to Matty, gently letting him go.

Considerate to my family, not jeopardizing their financial and living situations.

If I died, they would call me a martyr.

If I didn't die, I'd be a saint.

Realistically, I was going to Hell as a sinner.

I cleared my throat. "If you think I'm cheating on your brother, then why don't you tell him? If I knew some guy was cheating on one of my sisters or on one of my friends, I'd tell them." The second the words left my mouth, I felt a pang of guilt because I *did* know about someone cheating on someone I cared about, and I hadn't told her. Violet had always been kind to me, like a second mom. I should've told her.

"Define cheating," Isaac said.

We weren't that different. Isaac liked to push boundaries and twist the rules to fit his own moral compass. But didn't everyone do that to a certain extent?

"How do *you* define cheating?" I chickened out on giving him my answer because I was afraid to say it out loud.

"Sixty-nine."

I gawked at him. *The sex position?*

Isaac smirked.

"What about intercourse?" I blurted out the question on reflex.

"Don't say that." Isaac covered his mouth with his fist and laughed. "Only sex ed teachers say intercourse."

Heat crawled up my neck and consumed my entire face.

He shrugged. "I like to set the bar high."

The only thing that counted as cheating was sixty-nine? That was a ridiculously high bar.

"You're an idiot," I muttered.

He chuckled, unloading the cartons of eggs and stacking them by the register. "I'm only trying to ease your anxiety."

"Nice try, but I'm pretty sure you're the only person in the world with that definition of cheating. You're like the person who thinks calories don't count if you stand while eating."

He barked a laugh. "Who thinks that?"

I giggled. "My mom. She always skips dessert because it's not good for her waistline, but when she's making it, she's taste-testing every step of the way. And one time, I saw her eating the center of a cake and covering it up with frosting." As I grabbed two of the egg cartons, I peered at Isaac and his wolfish grin. "What?" I asked with a nervous laugh.

"I was just thinking I could eat your *center* and then cover it up with frosting, but I enjoy frosting, so I'd end up eating you twice."

Splat.

I dropped the cartons of eggs at my feet, and a few of the cracked ones oozed onto the concrete floor.

"Dang it!" I lifted my sundress to keep it from getting dirty as I crouched behind the counter to pick up the cartons and salvage as many eggs as possible.

The farm stand opened in twenty minutes. That wasn't how I wanted to start my day, and it was all Isaac's fault.

"Just go," I grumbled when he squatted next to me.

"I've got it," he said. "Just put the rest of the cartons on the shelf before you get yourself dirty."

The door chimed. It was just my luck; someone was early and didn't read the posted hours. I quickly stood and batted the hair away from my face.

"Good morning, Sarah," Mr. Cory said. "Have you seen Isaac?"

Isaac grabbed my ankle, and without ducking my chin, I lowered my gaze to him for a second.

He shook his head and pressed a finger to his lips.

"Uh, he, no. I mean, of course, he *was* here." My body jerked as Isaac's hand slid up my bare leg. So I cleared my throat. "He, uh, dropped off the uh..." I pinched my eyes shut for the briefest moment and swallowed hard. Then, my hand flew to my hip to stop his hand from pulling down my underwear.

Mr. Cory narrowed his eyes and shot his gaze to my arm. All I could do was freeze like a statue with a fake smile and my hand resting on my hip as if I had a little extra attitude with my boss.

"I don't know where he went," I squeaked as Isaac pulled my underwear down to my ankles and lifted one foot and then the other to remove them.

"When I find him," Mr. Cory nodded at me, "I'm going to have him run the stand today."

"W-what? Why?" I could barely speak because Isaac was kissing my inner thigh, just above my knee.

"Sweetheart," Wesley said. "You're burning up. You even have a little sweat on your brow. You must have the same thing that Vi has. Go home. Feel better." He pivoted, and the doorbell chimed again as he exited.

"Jesus Christ!" I gasped. It was the first time I had ever used the Lord's name in vain. "Isaac—" I couldn't breathe. I was scared out of my wits, embarrassed beyond words, and aroused at the same time. "Stop! Get up. We almost got—"

"Shh ..." Isaac was kneeling before me, sitting back on his heels. He rested one hand on the back of my knee while his other guided my hand to the top of my inner thigh. "You like to watch, and so do I," he murmured.

My tongue darted out to wet my lips as we peered at each other. "Isaac, we—"

"Show me," he tore his gaze from mine and stared at my hand.

This was *so* wrong.

Having sex with Matt in the middle of nowhere was wrong too, but touching myself while my boyfriend's older brother watched was really, *really* wrong.

"Give me my underwear," I said, taking a step back and cringing as I crushed an egg beneath my white huarache sandal. "Isaac," my plea sounded like a childish whine, but at that point, I wanted someone to save me from the situation.

"I'm not giving them back to you," he stood, "because you had no self-control, and now I'm stuck in this shed for the day."

"Control?" I gasped. "You removed my underwear while your dad was *right there!*" I jabbed my finger in the direction of the door. "Give them to me," I held out my hand.

I wore underwear all the time, and most of the time, I wore pantyhose with dresses, so my body was used to feeling covered. But the first of July was hot in southern Missouri, so I opted for shorts or long sundresses, but I still wore underwear. Without them, I felt naked, as if I wasn't wearing anything.

Everything felt exposed and a little breezy down there.

"No." He crossed his arms over his chest, eyes alight with the spirit of Satan.

"Where are they?" I stepped forward between the broken eggs and pulled at his arms to look at his hands.

"They're in my front pocket. You can slide your hand in there to get them. I'll be more patient than I was with you at Matty's game since my mom's not watching."

I glared at him. "You're a pervert."

Isaac glanced out the window to his left. I wasn't the only one who didn't want to get caught. He just hid his nerves better—but not completely. "Are you coming with me to Nashville on Friday?" He kept his focus on the window.

"We're not doing ... *it*."

"Going to Nashville?" He shot me a quick glance.

Sex was a three-letter word, not a four-letter word. Why did it feel so forbidden to say? In my head, I was a fearless rebel. I dreamed of breaking all the rules.

In reality, I was a good girl with the occasional sinfully brave moment. I was average in school, average at breaking rules, and average at being a good girl.

Averaged sucked.

It was forgettable and uninspiring.

"I'm not having *sex* with you." Okay, I went a little overboard with that emphasis.

Isaac lifted his eyebrows, rubbing his lips together to quell his amusement.

"Did I ask you to have sex with me?"

Dang it! I really wanted my underwear back. Confidence felt just out of reach with my lady bits airing out below.

"So you don't want to?" I tipped up my chin, but my voice still trembled.

Isaac unloaded the rest of the egg cartons. "Most days, it's all I want."

"You're messing with me." I removed my dirty shoe and hopped away from the mess, stepping into the bathroom to rinse it off in the sink.

"Sunday Morning, you could wrap me around your little finger if only you knew how to wield the power I'm giving you."

"Pfft." I slipped on my shoe and turned the corner as he cleaned up the egg mess with paper towels. "I don't believe you."

"Of course, you don't." He chuckled.

"I'm leaving. Give me my underwear."

"Nope." He tossed the paper towels into the garbage can and stood, again peering out the window to check for Wesley.

"Why?"

"I'll give them back to you in Nashville."

I balled my fists, and his attention shifted to my sides.

"Use your power."

His *power,* baloney, only made me angrier. As it was, I had to go home and not get paid for the day.

"Keep them, you perv." I pushed him out of my way and grabbed my purse from the shelf under the counter.

"Singing is performing," he said as I headed toward the door. "Performing is harnessing all of your power to be every-thing you are and everything you hope to be. Performing is finding courage in the face of fear. It's raw vulnerability." He grinned. "But it's the best fucking feeling in the world."

I didn't let on that his words gave me chills. Music was my love language. Isaac spoke my language in a world where my averageness made me feel invisible.

"What's your point?" I asked without turning toward him.

"You don't deserve to be on a stage until you're ready to harness that power, to take what's yours."

I opened the door and slammed it behind me, but I only got two steps before I turned and stomped back into the shed and straight to Isaac. He glanced over his shoulder as he stood with the freezer door open. When he started to turn, I pushed his back to keep him facing away from me. Pressing my chest to his back, I slid both hands into his front pockets, finding my underwear in one while my thumb grazed something else while searching his other pocket.

I was shaking, heart pounding. Yet, I mustered enough courage to lift onto my toes and whisper in his ear, "I'm going to sing with you on stage."

His lips twitched. "Have Heather drop you off in the church parking lot at six a.m."

Chapter Nineteen

The Cars, "Drive"

"It's okay to change your mind. If anything happens to you, your parents will have no idea. Do you really trust Isaac?" Heather lived on the edge more than I did, but she stepped up and gave me the mom talk on our way to the church. And I loved her for it. As much as we were each other's cheerleaders for taking chances and enjoying the beauty of being young, *naive*, reckless (and a little stupid), we loved each other like sisters.

I worried about her.

She worried about me.

"He was in the Army for six years. I think that makes him pretty trustworthy," I said despite my hands shaking.

"Does he have your phone number in case he needs to call your parents? Does he have condoms?"

"I said we're not—"

"Sarah Elaine Jacobson, stop lying to yourself. Whether you like sex or not, you know you're going to say yes to him. Don't. Get. Pregnant."

Chewing the heck out of my lower lip, shaky hands reaching for my seat belt, I nodded.

Heather pulled into the church parking lot at ten before six, and Isaac's truck was already there. Adrenaline surged through my body; it was almost too much to take. Maybe it was too reckless, too stupid.

Yet, it felt like a mistake that I would only regret *not* making.

The thousand-calorie slice of chocolate cake.

Missing curfew to hang out with my friends a little longer.

Spending a whole summer's worth of paychecks on the perfect leather jacket.

Kissing my boyfriend's brother.

"If he's the one, you'll look back on this and feel bad that you hurt Matt, but you'll never regret taking a chance on love," Heather said, putting her car into park.

"I love Matt because he was my first love. I love music because it's my endless love. Isaac is just a transition—a bridge to a new road."

"My song." Heather turned up the radio as Fleetwood Mac's "Landslide" played. It was her favorite song, and we sang it together whenever it came on the radio.

I laughed. "I can't stay and sing. Sorry." I opened the door as Isaac hopped out of his truck.

"Love you," Heather said. "Be careful. And have fun."

"Love you too. I'm bummed everything happened on the same weekend. Thanks for being the world's best friend and understanding." I hugged her and stepped out of the car.

"Sunday Morning," Isaac grinned, taking my backpack from me and waving to Heather as he led me to his truck.

"It's Friday Morning," I said.

"Every day is Sunday Morning in my world."

He's just a bridge. A bridge that could collapse.

Isaac tossed my bag into the back and opened my door for me. I watched Heather pull onto the road and disappear into the morning haze. This was it. No turning back.

"You're nervous," he said.

I shook my head.

He leaned his shoulder against his truck, not rushing me to climb into the seat. "The day I left for basic training, I couldn't stop shaking. Like the first time I performed in front of an audience. And the first time I roped at the rodeo."

I nodded slowly, lifting my gaze to his, knowing he'd see every ounce of doubt I felt.

"But that was nothing compared to you." He eyed me with an unreadable expression, lips twisted. "When you sang 'Bette Davis Eyes' while watching my hands on the guitar, I was scared out of my fucking mind."

"Why?" I furrowed my brow.

"You know why." He nodded toward the seat.

I didn't. I was *so* naive, and there didn't seem to be a way to expedite my way out of it. There wasn't a magic enlightenment pill. I was Silver Cord Sarah. Isaac wasn't trying to make me feel stupid. Just the opposite. He gave me more credit than I deserved.

He closed my door after I climbed into the truck, and we were off to Nashville.

We listened to music for several miles before I decided to make small talk. "Does your family know where you'll be this weekend?"

"Between my brother's girlfriend's legs? No."

"Stop!" I laughed. "I'm serious. We're not having sex. It's overrated, even if Matt and I are ..." I stared out my window, wishing that I could shed the guilt and leave it in Devil's Head.

"You and Matty are what?"

I couldn't look at him. Too many secrets burdened my conscience, and they all involved the Cory men.

"Our parents have high hopes for Matt and me. But he's going to Michigan, and I'm ..." I shook my head. "I don't know, but I'm not going to Michigan or marrying him. And I've known this longer than Matt. Honestly, I think he'd marry me tomorrow if I wanted to move to Michigan. And that totally sucks to not love someone the way they love you."

"But Matty won't give up his own dreams to marry you. So I think you're overestimating his love for you," Isaac said.

I shook my head. "I don't want him to give up anything for me. We're too young to make such life-changing sacrifices." I chuckled. "And we're cowards. We've kind of ended it, but neither one of us can bring ourselves to tell our parents because everyone else is *so* invested. Your dad practically owns my family. Maybe everyone will get used to us not being together in a literal sense, and maybe they'll—"

"Forget you two were dating and planning on getting married?" Isaac laughed. "Dream on."

I knew it was stupid. Matt probably did too. It was easier to ignore it and hope it went away than to suffer the consequences.

"So why have sex if it's all ending?" Isaac asked.

I shrugged, but I knew the answer. However, I didn't think Isaac would understand my thought process, my belief that Matt had earned the right to my virginity, or that I simply no longer wanted to keep it.

"Why are *you* cheating on your brother? And don't give me a scientific explanation."

"How am I cheating on him?"

"Loyalty. You're not showing family loyalty. At least I can say that I've known that Matt and I are ending, but you didn't know that until now."

"Oh, I knew it was over for you and Matty when I let you play my guitar."

I rolled my eyes. "Not the same thing."

He smirked, but after a few seconds, his expression softened into a more serious one. "I did something for my family, something big. And yet, Matty's always been the golden child. He has no interest in the ranch. He does very little to help out because he has baseball, or he can't risk getting injured or not getting good sleep. It feels like everything has been handed to him on a silver platter. And even though I know he didn't ask for this special treatment, I feel like he's not shown enough gratitude for it either. The least you can do when someone gives you everything is show a little gratitude. Right?"

I turned toward him, adjusting my seat belt. "What did you do?"

Isaac shook his head. "Can't say."

As I opened my mouth to prod him, I thought of the things *I* couldn't say. "So you're upset with Matt for letting you do whatever you did while he got everything on a silver platter?"

"No. Matty doesn't know what I did. So I'm holding a silent grudge, and those are the worst kind."

I frowned. "Are you saying I'm revenge? You just want him to have one less thing on his silver platter?"

"Baby," he laughed, "you don't belong to anyone. I could lasso you, but you'd break free. I'm not taking anything that's not given to me."

His short sentiment contained a lot. It was the first time anyone had ever called me "baby" in that way. I liked it coming from Isaac. And I felt a little more of that power he referenced in the farm shed. I was in control of us. He would only take what I was willing to give him.

The less he demanded, the more I *wanted* to give him. Isaac held me with open arms.

I turned up the radio, and we spent the next two and a half hours singing our hearts out with the windows down, my shoes off, one foot on the dash and the other outside the window. Nashville became an afterthought. Going anywhere with Isaac next to me and the radio blaring was *everything*.

He pulled over for fuel, and I ran into the gas station to use the bathroom. When I came out, he was waiting for me by the refrigerated section.

"Pepsi?" He opened the door and grabbed one.

"Yes."

He handed it to me and grabbed his Mountain Dew. "Hungry?"

I nodded. "Starving."

We found the stand of Hostess snacks. Isaac grabbed Ding Dongs, and I chose Twinkies. He also added a can of Pringles, Mentos, and a pack of lemon-lime Gator Gum. As we waited in line, he turned to face me, eyeing me with an unreadable expression.

"What?" I grinned, holding my pop and Twinkies.

"Nothing," he said as a smile crept up his face, and he dipped his head to kiss me.

He was *kissing me in public,* and my father did not approve of public displays of affection. It wasn't a long kiss, but a few people were staring at us, and it made me blush, so I dropped my chin to end the kiss. I kept my head down and strained my gaze to see if the bystanders were done staring. Isaac took my things and set them on the counter.

"I'll meet you outside," I mumbled, slithering out of the gas station.

Isaac, with his sexy Wrangler jeans, cowboy boots, white tee, and mischievous grin, strutted toward me as I stood at the back of his truck. "It's not locked."

"Just stretching my legs a little more."

"Well, you'd better get in the truck before I embarrass you again."

I shook my head. "I wasn't embarrassed."

"Liar."

"I'm not lying." I crossed my arms over my chest as he opened my door and set the bag on the floor.

"Are you sure?" he asked, shutting the door.

Before I could lie a second time, he took three strides, grabbed my face, and kissed me a lot harder than he did in the gas station.

Tongue.

A tiny moan.

Then he turned me without releasing my lips. My backside hit the bumper. He wedged one leg between mine, and his left hand slid down my neck and chest until he had my breast cupped, giving it a hard squeeze.

I knew with certainty that someone was going to report us for something like public indecency, and my parents would get a call from jail. When he released my mouth, I gasped.

"Do you like how I feel between your legs?" he asked with his lips at my ear.

My mouth dried up with panic.

Isaac didn't give me a fair chance to respond before he abandoned me. He climbed into the driver's side while I kept one hand on his truck to navigate my wobbly knees to my door.

Chapter Twenty

Stevie Nicks, "Talk to Me"

Isaac unlocked our motel room. It wasn't anything fancy, but I didn't care because we were in Nashville. He held the door, nodding for me to step inside.

This was happening.

"Two beds." I dumped my backpack on the end of the bed closest to the window. "I guess you understood me after all." I tried to hide my nerves with feigned confidence and flirty grins.

Truth?

I was disappointed there were two beds. Even if I didn't want to have sex, I wanted to sleep next to him.

Isaac set his bag and guitar on the other bed. "I play at nine, so we have time to get lunch and find you something to wear."

"What's wrong with my clothes?" I glanced down at my knee-length denim shorts and Keds.

"We're in Nashville. I'm playing at a bar, not a nursing home."

My jaw dropped. "W-what the heck? That's not nice."

Isaac lifted a single eyebrow, stepped into the bathroom, and pushed the door, but it didn't completely shut. He was peeing, which meant he just whipped it out. I could have stepped a little closer and peeked through the crack to see his penis.

"I only have a hundred dollars with me, so I can't buy anything too expensive," I said after he flushed the toilet.

"We'll work something out," he said, opening the door before fully zipping his jeans. I couldn't see anything, but I still averted my gaze.

"Uh, working things out feels like you're suggesting I give you something if I can't afford the clothes, and that makes me feel like a prostitute, so maybe not phrase it like that." I wrung my hands out in front of me.

I was *so* excited to be in Nashville with Isaac, but the reality of leaving my family—lying to them—and being away from home for three days with a hundred dollars in my purse and a man who scared me to death (in a good way) started to sink in.

He shut off the faucet and dried his hands. "I think you're missing my humor." Sitting on the end of his bed, he reached for my wrist and pulled me between his spread knees. "I'm going to rest my hands beside me." He released me and did just that. "And you're going to touch me wherever you want, however you want. It doesn't have to be sexual."

"Why?" I squinted.

"Because you're eighteen. And your nerves are palpable. We're in a big city. Your parents aren't here. And while I love playing with you and bantering with you, I don't take the responsibility I feel for your well-being lightly. So I need you to trust me implicitly. And I don't think you can do that if I make you tremble this much."

I shook my head, clenching my fists. "I'm not trembling."

He frowned, taking my hand and uncurling my fingers. My hand shook when he released it, so he guided it to his shoulder before returning his hand to the bed.

"Pretend I'm Matty if you have to."

"I don't want to think about him," I murmured, resting my other hand on the opposite shoulder. I ghosted both hands down his arms, letting my fingers trace the lines of his tattoos.

He shivered, and my gaze shot to his.

"Sorry," he said softly. "You *affect* me. Or maybe your touch *infects* me."

My gaze felt sluggish, like when he got me drunk. I skimmed back up his arms to his neck, then his face, fingers spread wide.

When the pads of my thumbs grazed his lips, he closed his eyes, and he drew in an unsteady breath.

"Are you shaking?" I whispered, feeling a tiny jolt of power.

Did I really have that *effect* on him?

"Why?" I asked, slipping my fingers into his hair.

"You know why," he said, opening his eyes.

That was it. That was the problem, the reason my nerves got the best of me. I didn't know *why* someone like Isaac would genuinely be interested in an eighteen-year-old who, despite her silver cords, didn't get into the college she wanted.

"Will you remove your shirt?" I asked.

"No. But you can remove it." He cocked his head to the side when I hesitated. "Wrap me around that little finger of yours."

I attempted to roll my eyes, but I couldn't peel my gaze away from him long enough to make it believable. With no sort of grace, I pulled his shirt up and over his head, dropping it to the floor.

Isaac let his hands fall back to his sides. There was no comparison, but that didn't stop me from seeing the six-year physical difference between him and Matt. Isaac was bigger and broader, and it did little to keep me from trembling.

I swallowed hard, and that's when I noticed Isaac doing the same thing as his Adam's apple bobbed.

Again, he closed his eyes when I pressed my hands to his bare chest. "For the next three days, I need to see you at all times." He opened his eyes. "If you need to pee, I want to know. If you need a snack, I want to know. If I can't see you, then you're not where I need you to be. Understood?"

"You'll be performing." I watched his abs tighten under my touch.

"I'll be watching you," he said.

Our gazes locked as I paused my hands.

He reclined onto the bed. "Keep touching. When I'm not on that stage, I want your hands on me, like you're blind and I'm your seeing-eye dog. Reach for me. Touch me. Feel me. Hold on to me."

I chuckled. "You make it sound like I'm going to get abducted." I rested my hands on his knees and slid my hands up his legs along the worn denim.

"Look at you, baby. Who *wouldn't* want to take you?" He laced his fingers behind his head.

"I think you just want a free massage." I crawled up his body and straddled his waist.

He lifted a brow before smiling. "I want absolutely anything you're willing to give me."

"Yeah?"

"Yeah."

Twisting my lips, I thought of what I would give him.

"Idle hands must mean you've gotten your fill of my body." He jackknifed to sitting.

I grabbed his arms to keep from falling backward as he shifted my center of gravity.

He stared at my lips, bringing his just inches from mine. "For the next three days, where will you be?"

"Near you."

He shook his head.

I grinned. "Touching you."

"Nothing can happen to you on my watch." He kissed the corner of my mouth.

ISAAC TOOK me to lunch and then shopping. I felt like the real deal—a grown woman exploring a new city with a man she had a crush on.

I practiced staying close to him, which wasn't hard because he usually had ahold of my hand. When he paid for my clothes or sifted through the racks for things he wanted me to try on, I stayed within inches of him and often had my fingers slid into one of his pockets or clasped to one of his belt loops.

Hours later, we returned with bags of clothes, boots, silver bangle bracelets, nail polish (which I rarely wore), and a gorgeous cream cowboy hat.

"What should I wear tonight?" I asked when we stepped into the motel room with my new wardrobe.

"The blue dress." He tossed his hat aside and collapsed onto the bed.

"Is it okay if I shower first, or do you want to?"

"Have at it," he mumbled.

I pulled the dress out of the bag, removed the tags, and carried it to the bathroom with my clean underwear and bra.

"What are you doing?" he asked, lifting onto his elbows.

"Um, taking a shower."

"With your dress?"

"Duh. Of course not."

"Then leave it out here."

"Because you want to see me naked?" I squinted.

"I've seen you naked."

"No. You've seen me in my underwear and bra."

"I've seen your tits."

I blushed. Isaac's bluntness was an adjustment for the girl who never missed church.

"You've seen one"—I cleared my throat—"nipple."

"I bet the other one looks really similar." He winked.

"You're a perv."

"You're the one who couldn't keep your hands off me earlier."

"Shut up!" I laughed.

"Go." He flopped back down onto the bed. "I'll see it later."

"In your dreams." I closed the bathroom door and locked it.

"Come on, Sunday Morning, where's the trust?"

I laughed.

After my shower, I emerged from the bathroom in my blue dress and a towel around my head. Isaac was asleep with his hands folded on his chest. I stole a moment to stare at him. He took gorgeous to a whole new level.

I combed out my hair and dried it a second time with the towel. I didn't have a hairdryer because I shared one with my sisters, and my family thought I was camping where I wouldn't need one anyway. Sitting next to the nightstand, facing Isaac's bed, I applied my dark purple nail polish. Just as I finished and capped the bottle, Isaac stirred, stretching his arms above his head and yawning.

"I'm done in the bathroom," I said.

He squinted, peeling open his eyes as he sat up. "Okay." He stood and leaned forward.

I didn't know if he was going to kiss me or what, but I held up my hands. "Don't touch me; my nails are wet."

He paused, gaze flitting between my face and hands, and he smirked. "Okay." Standing straight, he shrugged off his shirt.

"Two okays in a row. I think I like it when you talk less and obey more." I bit my lower lip to hide my grin.

Isaac unbuttoned his jeans. "Is that so?"

I tried not to stare at him. Instead, I inspected my shiny, wet nails. "Mm-hmm."

Don't react.

He removed his jeans. I still didn't look at him, but I had good peripheral vision. In nothing but his black briefs, he stood with his back to me, digging through his camouflage duffle bag. He pulled out clean briefs and a shirt, and then he set a strip of condoms next to them before pulling out a pair of jeans.

I had a minor heart attack.

We weren't having sex. I didn't like sex, and I was perfectly clear about that.

He turned, and it took everything I had to tear my gaze away from the condoms. Isaac's lips remained neutral, but I didn't miss the amusement and sheer confidence in his dark eyes. His gaze shifted behind him for a second as if he did not know what I was looking at.

"You're not using those on me," I said with a frog in my throat when he brought his attention back to me.

"They go on me, not you."

I shot him a sarcastic look, which I regretted instantly. It fed his need to push my boundaries as he leaned down again.

"Isaac—"

He kissed me, and I had no choice but to let him since I couldn't stop him with my hands. Well, I didn't *have* to kiss him back, but I did.

"Isaac ..." I sucked at piecing together a believable protest when he kissed his way down my neck. "My nails ..."

"Then don't touch me," he said, cupping the back of my neck as he guided me onto my back.

I was helpless while holding my hands away from him and the bed.

He unbuttoned the front of my dress so slowly that I thought my heart thrashing around in my chest might break a few ribs.

"W-what are you"—I was so breathy—"doing?"

"I'm going to make you come." He slid my bra up my chest, releasing one breast and then the other. When his gaze found mine, he smirked.

Yes, both nipples look similar.

My breath caught when he sucked my nipple into his mouth while his hand squeezed my other breast. With my arms out to the side to protect my nails, I had no choice but to arch my back and let him have his way with me. I squirmed a little more with every kiss, panting tiny breaths.

He stood, gazing through hooded eyes at my dress completely open and my breasts on full display. I couldn't read his expression, but he focused intently, as if the wheels were spinning. And that *thingy* in his briefs was huge and stiff-looking.

Grabbing the back of my knees, he guided my feet to the edge of the bed and skated his calloused hands along my legs to the waist of my underwear, bringing his gaze to mine, silently requesting permission.

Nope.

I couldn't let him take off my underwear in broad daylight and stare at my girly parts, spread wide for his inspection.

I rolled my head from side to side.

He twisted his lips, and then he wet them while bending down to kiss me again.

An all-consuming kiss with one hand on the mattress next to my head and his other hand on my hip, inching its way between my legs, fingertips teasing me over my underwear.

Why did I paint my nails? I felt bound to the bed unless I wanted to ruin the polish. Isaac knew what he was doing. And he did it *so* very well. He hooked two fingers into the crotch and pulled the cotton aside.

"Oh God ..." I jumped, breaking the kiss.

My mind reeled. I was using the Lord's name in vain,

but I couldn't focus on asking for forgiveness yet, so I added it to the long mental list of things I'd need to pray about later.

Isaac's lips twitched as his face hovered over mine, watching me lose my ever-loving mind. He took his time like his fingers needed the lay of the land, and every second was delicious torture.

He said nothing, content watching me react to his touch. When his fingers grazed my clit, it made my hips jerk, and my eyelids felt heavy.

"Fuck ... I've never seen anything so beautiful," he whispered, slowly pushing a finger inside me.

My breaths fell from my lips like they did twenty minutes into a cardio workout.

He pulled it out and nearly made me orgasm by rubbing my clit, but then he slid inside of me again, but this time, it was two fingers.

After I released a moan, his mouth crashed to mine like he was teetering on the edge of control. With his two fingers sliding in and out of me and the pad of his thumb rubbing my clit, I orgasmed. My heels dug into the mattress to lift my pelvis, grinding into his hand as my mouth fell open and my neck twisted to the side.

My blurry vision refocused, landing on my pretty nails, which survived without a smudge. Before I could formulate a coherent thought that didn't involve how shocked I was that my nails were safe, Isaac had my bra back in its place and was buttoning my dress.

The patience he showed while piecing me back together made my heart ache. I agreed to the trip to fulfill one of my dreams of visiting Nashville. Falling for my boyfriend's brother wasn't part of the plan.

Ex-boyfriend.

Pressing the heels of my hands to the mattress, I sat up as he finished the last button, and I stared at the strip of condoms on his bed by the bag. This time, he didn't need to follow my gaze to see what had ensnared my attention.

"I'm going to take a shower," he said, indirectly answering the question on my mind.

"If you want"—I dug my teeth into my lower lip for a few seconds—"I mean, it's not fair that—"

"Sarah, I'm not having sex with you because you feel obligated to return the favor. I'll sneak a cigarette later and call it good." The door clicked shut.

Chapter Twenty-one

Jackson Browne, "Somebody's Baby"

Nashville was more than my small-town heart could take. It exceeded all expectations. The raucous bars and vibrant nightlife blew my mind. Isaac didn't need a cigarette because the honky-tonks were filled with smoke, laughter, music, and dancing.

I felt so grown-up in my dress, boots, and new hat. Throngs of people filled the streets, wandering from place to place and gathering around the telephone poles to check out the stapled flyers to see where everyone was playing that weekend. Isaac kept a protective arm around me everywhere we went that night, popping in and out of little dive bars to listen to a few songs and grabbing a beer (soda for me) and a quick sandwich before landing at Leonard's Lounge in the rock block. I felt like a real aspiring musician alongside Isaac in his hat, boots, and guitar in hand.

"This doesn't feel real," I said when we entered the back of the bar.

"What's that?" He lowered his ear closer to my mouth.

I shook my head and mumbled, "Nothing," just as a tall guy with an orange mustache and thick biceps charged toward us.

Isaac released my hand and set his guitar on the floor before hugging the guy.

"How the hell are you?" he asked Isaac.

"Good, man. God, it's great to see you."

His friend released him and eyed me. "And who do we have here? Wife? Girlfriend?"

My eyes widened, looking to Isaac for help.

"My preacher's daughter. I kidnapped her. She sings in the choir but secretly loves songs about sex."

I fought my usual reaction, which was to turn ten different shades of red and avert my gaze. This was the start of my favorite dream.

I wasn't Sunday Morning.

I was the girl who planned on making my way onto the stage and showing the audience I was really the one they came to see. So I acted like that girl because she was more fun than the one who rarely missed curfew and knew every song in the hymnal.

"I'm Sarah. Isaac said I can sing while he plays the guitar," I said with my head held high. I followed Isaac's instruction by sliding my arm around him and tucking my fingers into his back pocket while holding out my right hand.

"I'm Lenny." He shook my hand and chuckled. "Sorry, sugar. Isaac misspoke. I can't let you onto my stage if I haven't heard you sing, even if you are sucking his dick."

I stiffened while fighting to keep my smile. That's what

229

adults did. Haha! He made a sex joke. So what. I had a sense of humor.

"I didn't tell her she could sing, but I am responsible for her. So when nine o'clock rolls around, and you kick the youngsters out, I need to let her stay perched in the front row."

"You're babysitting. Got it." Lenny winked. "I gotta get back out there. Y'all help yourself to food and drinks; it's on the house."

After Lenny disappeared through the doors, I faced Isaac with my hands on my hips. "So you just let him think I'm sucking your dick, and you're my babysitter?"

"Baby, he was my boss for four years, and he's letting me sing here for the next two nights. He can think whatever the hell he wants. You sucking my dick is optional, but it won't get you on that stage. Sorry, house rules."

I narrowed my eyes at him, but who was I kidding? Nashville was my Disneyland. Just walking through the throngs of people milling around that night was beyond my imagination.

"You're cute when you pout." He chuckled, taking his guitar out of its case and slipping the strap over his head. "Do you want something to eat or drink?"

"How about a beer?"

"You're not old enough to drink," he said, glancing up from his guitar to give me a quick grin. "I wouldn't feel right about letting my pastor's daughter drink a beer."

"What? Are you totally serious? After you fing—" I clamped my mouth shut.

Gah!

Why did I lose all bravery and momentum when it came to sex talk?

"Fingered you?" He strummed his guitar.

I was such a priss for thinking he sounded crude. If I was willing to let him do it, then I needed to grow up and use my words.

"Do you think I should write a song about fingering the preacher's daughter?" he asked.

I held my breath to keep from reacting as he waited for just that.

"Of course, I'd hide the meaning behind more poetic lyrics as all the good songwriters do." He continued to pluck the strings and adjust the sound.

"What are you going to sing? Are you any good?" I dismissed all other topics that involved his fingers inside of me, even if it was the best sexual experience of my life thus far.

"I'm going to do a little Jackson Browne and Tom Petty. Why? Do you have any requests?"

"I like Jackson Browne and Tom Petty. Which songs? We could sing together, so technically, it's not just me singing."

He chuckled. "You're relentless."

"Hypothetically, if I did what Lenny said, would you let me sing with you?"

"Did what Lenny said?" Isaac glanced up at me, eyes narrowed.

A few seconds later, the realization hit, and he shook his head. "Baby, don't ever suck a man's dick for anything except you having a good old hankering for it. Okay?"

"You didn't answer my question."

It was rare, but Isaac Cory blushed while keeping his gaze on his hands. "Let's find a seat for you."

"Is that a yes?"

"We'll continue this discussion at the motel." He returned his guitar to its case and took my hand.

"Why?" I followed him toward the saloon doors.

"Because you talk big when you know no one's going to immediately call your bluff. So later," he stopped just before pushing through the doors and turned toward me, "when we're alone in a room with two beds and a heavier dose of reality, we'll discuss your plans to get on stage."

I lifted my chin and made duck lips. "Fine."

There was no way I was sucking anyone's dick. I was only curious about the price of fame—window shopping of sorts.

Isaac couldn't find a table for me by the stage because most of the area was an open dance floor. So he sat me at the end of the bar with a Pepsi and instructions for Lenny to help keep an eye on me.

I watched with envy as Isaac took the stage, and everyone clapped. A group of women on the opposite side of the stage whistled and hooted at him. It was different than girls at school salivating over Matt because my boyfriend ignored the other girls.

Not Isaac; he shot a huge smile toward their table and winked.

Winked!

"So how long have you known, Isaac?" Lenny hollered from behind the bar.

"Um, I'm not sure. His brother and I graduated together. So our families have known each other for years." I dismissed Matt as someone I graduated with, and it fed the cancerous guilt in my gut. "What was Isaac like in the Army?"

Lenny laughed while filling a mug with beer. "Tough as nails. Smarter than everyone else combined. Loyal. Pretty much the perfect candidate for any position. I said he could go far if he wanted it to be his career, but he said the legacy of the family's ranch depended on him returning and taking things over someday. From what I gathered, their family must own a lot of land."

I nodded. "They basically own all the land in Devil's Head."

Isaac's voice drew my attention back to the stage as he started singing "Somebody's Baby." I loved that song. And I loved that when he sang it, he looked at me instead of the women on the other side of the stage trying so hard to get his attention with their boobs spilling out of their shirts and dresses.

For the next hour, I fell a little more in love with Isaac Cory, his rich voice, and flirty grin. Isaac was living my dream.

After the final song and a huge crowd of people applauding, he exited the stage and set his guitar case on the end of the bar before wedging himself between my legs on the bar stool. "You're such a distraction in this dress," he whispered in my ear before biting my earlobe.

I didn't know if it was his gravelly voice (a little worn from singing), his hands on my thighs, or his actual words, but it did something to me. And all I wanted was to kiss him.

That was a lie. I wanted to do so much more than kiss him.

But we were in a public place, so I settled for a kiss, the kind that felt a little too intimate for an audience.

"Any interest in seeing The White Animals play tonight?" Lenny asked.

I shoved Isaac's chest. "YES! Where? When? Are you serious?"

Isaac laughed. "It's past your bedtime."

I wrinkled my nose and playfully kicked his leg. "Shut up."

Lenny scribbled something on a white napkin and slid it to Isaac. "Tell that guy at the door that Lenny sent you."

"Thanks," Isaac said, pocketing the napkin. "Can I leave this with you?" He nodded to his guitar.

"I'll guard it with my life." He winked.

"Let's go, Sunday Morning." Isaac took my hand and pulled me toward the exit.

When we reached the venue, our connection to Lenny barely got us in the door, but I didn't care that we were as far from the stage as possible. Isaac rolled his eyes every time I tried to restrain my excitement. I loved every second of The White Animals' performance, especially when Isaac would let me have a few sips of his beer while he stood behind me with one hand around my waist, possessively pressed to my stomach. He dipped his head and nuzzled his face into my hair until his lips reached my neck.

Nothing about that night felt real, but *everything* about it felt right.

By three in the morning, we returned to the motel, and Isaac carried me inside because I was so tired and more intoxicated than he planned on letting me get.

"Let's have sex," I mumbled with a huge smile when he set me on my bed.

"You need to sleep." He removed my boots and my bracelets.

"Sleep is overrated," I said, unbuttoning my dress, even though my fingers and everything else felt a little too numb to be adept or nimble.

"I'm not having sex with you when you're drunk."

"I'm not drunk," I giggled. "I'm a little drunk. But I give you my consent."

He shook his head, pulling down the bedspread.

I shrugged off my dress, and he set it on the bags with my new clothes. By the time he faced me again, I had taken off my bra and was tossing my underwear onto the floor between the two beds.

"Jesus, Sarah, what are you doing?" He scratched his jaw and shook his head.

"I'm not a virgin."

"I'm aware, but we're still not doing this." Isaac gestured for me to lie back, and I did.

But when he tried to pull the covers over my naked body, I kicked them away.

He reared back so I didn't kick him. "Stop."

Again, I kicked my legs, so he grabbed my ankles. Everything was warm and soft. My vision was a little blurry; the air conditioner sounded more muffled. But his touch was sharp, and I liked it.

I dragged my teeth along my lower lip as the tense indecision in his face intensified.

"Touch yourself," he whispered, keeping a firm grip on my ankles.

Losing my inhibitions felt liberating like the dream day we were having would never end.

I slid my hand along my inner thigh, and Isaac's gaze followed it while mine remained affixed to his face and his tongue making a lazy swipe along his lips before he swallowed hard.

"Perv," I murmured with a smirk.

His attention flitted to my face for a moment while the corner of his mouth quirked into the hint of a smile.

I enjoyed touching myself, even if, according to my parents, it disappointed Jesus. I liked brushing my hair and rubbing lotion on my legs too. What was the big deal?

Isaac released one ankle at a time and crawled up the bed, settling on his stomach between my spread legs. He kissed my fingers as I slid them between my legs. His tongue stroked my flesh, and he sucked one of my fingers into his mouth and hummed.

My other hand rested on his head, and I spread my legs a little wider. The feeling left me speechless and breathless, so I knew it had to be a sin. I bargained with myself. If I could spend the next three days letting Isaac do that to me as much as possible, I would spend the rest of the summer on my knees, clutching a Bible, begging for forgiveness.

Isaac was so, *so* good at making me orgasm (better than me), so I removed my hand and clawed the bedsheet beneath me. What he did to me after our shopping trip was great, but this was mind-blowing.

My knees collapsed inward. "Isaac ..." I couldn't take it. I don't know if it was the alcohol or just my first time having oral sex, but I needed him to stop because it was almost too sensitive, but when he started to pull back, I realized I didn't want that either.

"N-not yet ... just ..." I curled my fingers and scratched at his head to keep him there as unrelenting waves of pleasure spread in all directions.

This is Heaven.

He chuckled before kissing my inner thigh. "Sleep, now. Okay?"

I murmured a lazy "Okay," and rolled to my side, curling up in a ball as he pulled the sheet over my body. I couldn't wait to tell Heather.

Chapter Twenty-Two

Loverboy, "Almost Paradise"

I PEELED OPEN my eyes and glanced at the clock: 11:08 a.m.

"Isaac?" I said in a weak voice.

The pillows and sheets of the other bed were tangled. He slept by himself. I felt a pang of disappointment. When I made it to my feet and winced from my headache, I used the bathroom and brushed my teeth. Then I slipped on the white T-shirt poking out from his duffle bag and peeked through the curtain.

Isaac was in his jeans and boots, no shirt, staring at the sky and smoking a cigarette. I opened the door, and he glanced over his shoulder, giving me a slow inspection.

"Morning," he said.

"Thought you quit."

He shrugged. "I did." He sucked on the cancer stick one

last time before tossing it onto the ground and extinguishing it with his boot. "There." He smiled. "I'm quitting again."

I frowned.

"Don't give me that look."

"What look?" I stepped aside to let him back into the room.

"The look my mom gives me when she sees me smoking."

"The look that says she doesn't want her son to die of cancer? How dare she love you like that." I closed the door.

He laughed, plucking another T-shirt from his bag and pulling it over his head. "Do you love me? Is that what you're trying to say?"

I wrinkled my nose. "No. I just think it's a disgusting habit."

"Well, good thing you're not the one doing it. And neither am I, now that I quit." He made his bed.

"I'm going to shower. What are we doing today?"

"It's a surprise." He started making my bed too.

"Well, what should I wear?" I fished out underwear and a bra from my backpack.

"Shorts and tennis shoes."

After my shower, I wrapped the towel around my body and opened the door. He was on the bed, watching TV. So I played it cool, despite my nerves trying to expose my wavering confidence, and I dropped my towel to the floor.

Without looking at him, I grabbed my clothes and set them on my bed as if I walked around naked in front of him all the time. But my curiosity got the best of me, so I glanced at Isaac.

He didn't even try to pretend that he wasn't looking at

me. I slowly stepped into my underwear, waiting for him to look at my face.

He didn't.

Wetting his lips, he kept his gaze on my breasts and adjusted himself in his jeans. It wasn't just a quick fix; he kind of rubbed himself with the heel of his hand. That took me out of my area of expertise. Well, *expertise* might have been an exaggeration.

I had a moment of: *Oh, yeah. You probably like to orgasm too.*

But I lost my nerve, so I made getting dressed a race against time while I turned my back to him so he wouldn't see me staring at him rubbing himself.

"So," I cleared my throat, "is it just the two of us today? Or will we see Lenny again?" I grabbed my comb and faced him while working through my tangles.

Isaac's hand had fallen to his side, and he regarded me for a few seconds as if to see if I saw him or if my striptease was on purpose. "I'll play at his bar tonight, but it's just the two of us today." Again, he eyed me, lips twisted, gaze intense as if he thought I'd confess my poorly executed seduction antics with a blush.

"Sounds great," I said, quickly turning toward the TV. "I wonder if Heather and everyone else are having a good time camping."

"Do you regret not going camping?"

"I mean, you brought like ... seven condoms. I said I wasn't having sex with you, so you planned on having it not once but seven times?" I turned with one hand on my hip.

Don't ask me where that came from. One minute, I was thinking about camping, and the next, I had a condom flashback.

To sum it up: I had sex on the brain—*bad*.

Isaac's eyebrows slid into peaks.

"Sorry," I shook my head. "I drank too much. My mind is all over the place. I need some food. Ignore me." I tossed the brush into my bag and loosely ran my fingers through my hair.

"Then let's feed you." Isaac jumped out of bed and grabbed his truck keys off the nightstand.

His failure to verbally acknowledge me going off the rails only made it worse. Did he regret bringing me? Who didn't want to take an inexperienced dreamer to Nashville, pay for everything, be responsible for her, and give her orgasms without receiving reciprocation only to get a lecture on planning for safe sex?

Good job, Sarah.

I couldn't even give myself the Be Like Jesus speech because He was a virgin who was too busy giving sight to the blind, healing the sick, and turning water into wine to keep an orgasm tally.

Slinging my purse over my shoulder, I slipped on my sunglasses as Isaac opened the door for me.

We backed out of the parking spot by our motel room, and he stopped before putting it into *Drive*. "We're either not having sex, or we're having it seven times."

I turned toward him, sliding my glasses down my nose to eye him over the frames. "What do you mean?"

He shoved it into *Drive* and hit the gas. "If we have it once, we'll blow through the other six in no time."

Oh my ~~God~~ gosh.

I blinked several times while he grinned, and then I pushed my sunglasses up my nose and faced forward.

I wanted to have sex with Isaac if for no other reason

than I needed to know if it was me or the curse of the first time. And after watching him rub himself through his jeans while he stared at me with glassy eyes, I was dying to watch him orgasm. *That* felt like the ultimate power.

It took us a while to navigate the holiday weekend traffic, but when he pulled into the parking lot, I squealed and covered my mouth. "Opryland!"

Isaac chuckled. "I take it you approve?"

I kept my hands fisted at my mouth, shaking with excitement. He pulled into a parking space, and I couldn't get out of my seat belt fast enough to slide across the bench seat and onto his lap.

"What are you—"

I cut him off with a kiss.

And another.

And another.

He laughed when I settled down a fraction.

"You're right. We'll use all seven," I declared.

"No." He rolled his eyes, grabbing my hips to move me off his lap.

When he hopped out, I grabbed my purse and made my way to his side as he locked the doors.

"So now you don't want to do it?"

He shut the door and slid on his sunglasses. Then he linked a single finger with mine and led me toward the entrance. "Stop using sex as currency. All right? We'll have it when you want to have it for no other reason than you *want* to have it."

I didn't know what to say as I lagged a few steps back.

He stopped to let me catch up. "Nope. You don't get to pout at Opryland."

I wrinkled my nose when he pressed his fingers to the corners of my mouth to make me smile. "Stop." I laughed.

"That's better." He linked his finger with mine again, and we continued toward the entrance.

We stood in line behind a man who looked close to my dad's age, or even older, and a girl who was either his daughter or his granddaughter. She seemed just as excited as me, beaming with a twinkle in her eye when she glanced in our direction. Then the guy put his arm around her, which was fine until his hand drifted to her butt, and he gave it a few playful taps before rubbing circles on it and ending with a little squeeze.

My eyes swelled into saucers, and I peered up at Isaac, who was watching the same thing. The guy pulled her in for a hug and then ducked his head to kiss her on the lips—with tongue.

I bit my lips together to keep from gasping. Isaac clenched his teeth like he was upset more than disgusted.

When we paid for our tickets and entered the amusement park, I faced him. "Thoughts?"

He shook his head while putting the change in his wallet, but he didn't look at me. "Let's go. What do you want to ride first?"

That was it.

Then it hit me. Maybe he knew about his dad and Brenda, but I couldn't ask him.

"That was gross." I couldn't keep my mouth shut.

He didn't respond as we stood in front of a map of the park.

"Do you think it's his wife? Girlfriend? Mistress? Not that I'm one to talk since I'm here with you, which makes me the worst kind of girlfriend."

"Then why'd you come?" he snapped.

I took a step away, eyeing him as I felt the sting of his words and the grit of his tone in my chest.

He continued to stare at the map for a few seconds before pinching the bridge of his nose and bowing his head with a long exhale. "I'm sorry," he whispered.

He knew. That was the only explanation for his outburst. That couple triggered him, and he took it out on me. And suddenly, I felt homesick.

My parents didn't know where I was.

My friends were camping, laughing, and not getting yelled at by hot-tempered men.

In a matter of seconds, my happy bubble burst, and I just wanted to go home.

Before my childish emotions escaped, I blotted the corners of my eyes and swallowed past the lump in my throat. But I wasn't a child. I was an adult dealing with a big dose of reality and the consequences of my decisions.

"Sarah—"

"Let's ride the Wabash Cannonball," I murmured, heading in the direction of the roller coaster.

"Sarah, I said I'm sorry." He followed me, reaching for my hand, but I pulled it away.

"Let's not do this." I stuck my hands in my pockets.

We spent the afternoon at the park, and after grabbing chicken fingers and fries, we headed to the motel to get ready for the show. I felt Isaac's gaze on me nonstop; even when he was driving, he kept glancing over at me.

"What do I have to do to make this right?" he asked, tossing his keys onto the nightstand when I entered the motel room.

Chewing on the inside of my cheek, I shrugged and

deflated. "I feel like I messed up. I shouldn't be here. I just ..." I shook my head and stared at the ceiling. "I've felt out of control since the day you sat in the back of the church on Easter Sunday. And while you make me feel like anything is possible when I'm with you, I also feel like I'm disappointing *everyone* else around me. I've spent too many years trying to please people. And when I do something that I know will *not* please anyone but me, I feel selfish, and the guilt is unbearable."

I looked at him and frowned. "When you snapped at me, I felt so—" I swallowed and tried to blink away the tears, but there were too many, so I quickly wiped them. "I felt so alone," I whispered. "I f-feel like I'm keeping too many secrets and c-carrying the weight of the w-world on my s-shoulders." I continued to bat away the tears, but they just kept coming.

"Baby," he whispered, cupping the back of my head and pulling me into his embrace. "I know lonely, and I know what it feels like to keep secrets and feel the weight of the world on your shoulders. It's the fucking worst. You are not alone. I had a moment, but I regretted it instantly. I'm *so* very sorry." He kissed the top of my head.

Then, he kissed my forehead, cheeks, and lips. I closed my eyes and melted into his embrace, savoring the slow kiss that felt more intimate than any other kiss we had shared. He lifted that weight from my shoulders, reminding me that it was okay to choose myself, even if it was only for three days. Isaac removed my shirt and kissed me again before shrugging off his. Our clothes piled onto the floor one at a time until we were naked on the bed, legs tangled, hands exploring, lips fused.

"I'm so undeserving of you," he whispered over my skin before kissing the inside of my wrist and up my arm.

His patience gave me chills and aroused me more than I thought possible. He touched me everywhere, only spending short amounts of time at my breasts or teasing his fingertips between my legs as if he was testing the waters.

"Isaac," I tried to guide his head between my legs without being too obvious.

When he kissed the skin along my hipbone to my navel, I could feel his lips curl into a grin. "What, baby?"

He knew exactly what he was doing to me.

Matt gave me ten seconds of foreplay; Isaac was giving me an eternity.

Finally, he went *there*.

"Isaac, *yesss* ..." I arched my back and thanked God (He probably plugged his ears). Then I rested my foot on his shoulder as he gripped the back of my knee and gave me a little slice of Heaven that, in the aftermath, would feel like Hell. This time, he brought me to the edge and stopped, crawling up my body, kissing me hard while his fingers teased me, sliding slowly in and out while the wet head of his erection rubbed against my leg.

I clawed at his back when he pulled away, and my neediness made him grin. He was beautiful from head to toe—marked in ink, tan and tone from long days on the ranch. I was shackled with panic and overcome with desire all at the same time. I wanted to have sex with Isaac more than anything, but I wanted to enjoy it.

I couldn't get Matt out of my head, wondering if it was a fluke, the first-time curse, or if I was broken.

Fitted with a condom, Isaac slid into bed next to me,

cupping my face while we kissed again. "Straddle me," he whispered.

I wasn't sure about being on top, but I did it anyway. The length of his erection rubbed between my legs.

"Show me how beautiful and sexy you are." He held his erection until the head of it slid inside of me, and then he guided my hands to my breasts.

Only Isaac could make me feel that safe and confident. Everything he did was to bring me pleasure as I sank completely onto him, and we began to move together. I got to see him lose himself inside of me, unraveling with need and intimate vulnerability.

It wasn't a race to the end; it was about the moment. Our connection. Everything felt different when I wasn't trying to lose something or give him something because I thought he'd earned it.

Isaac pistoned his pelvis. "Sarahhh ..." He grinned.

I couldn't believe he was trying to be funny during sex. But I also couldn't help but match his smile.

Then he sat up, and the humor faded, melting back into desire as we moved together slowly. I realized the thing I felt the most was my heart aching with love. Not the first kind of love with butterflies.

Not the kind that was earned over time, an extension of loyalty.

I loved Isaac in an all-consuming, jumping-off-the-cliff, be-damned-the-consequences sort of way.

"Baby," he whispered over my lips as I rocked my hips with his in a building rhythm. "I'm okay with dying right here—inside of you."

His hands tangled in my hair as I orgasmed, and then he kissed me while moving his hands to my hips, encouraging me to keep going. "Sarah." All his muscles seemed to tense at the same time, sweat beading on his skin, and the most painful yet beautiful expression stole his face.

It wasn't power; it was equality. I didn't feel like he was older, smarter, or more talented. It wasn't him, and it wasn't me. It was us.

I had sex with Matt. He had sex with me. And they were two very different experiences. With Isaac, *we* made love.

Wrapped in his arms, he laid us on the bed, my heart pounding against his. *That* was what I imagined musicians thought about when they wrote about sex and intimacy—and love.

Between labored breaths, he stroked my hair. "I'm sorry we feel like a lie. I'm sorry that this will hurt a lot of people we love. But, baby," he kissed the top of my head, "I wouldn't change what's happened. My feelings for you are too big; they don't leave any room for regret."

Chapter Twenty-Three

The J. Geils Band, "Love Stinks"

Isaac

I LOVED MATTY, but I saw the world through a different lens.

Not everything that was right was fair. And not everything that was fair was right.

Sarah Jacobson belonged to no one. No finders keepers—no dibs. I never asked her to love me, and she never asked me to love her.

Matty lived a charmed life, and I lived with the truth. I was good with the truth as long as no one judged me. I gave up my dreams so that Matty could have his—he just didn't know that.

"Are you sure it's not weird that I'm wearing the same dress?" Sarah finished buttoning her dress, hair wet from our shower together.

"Different night. Different crowd," I said. "I'm wearing the same jeans," I zipped them.

She rolled her eyes. "I feel like you're going to let me sing one song with you tonight."

I chuckled, sitting on the end of the bed to pull on my socks and boots. "You do, huh?"

She couldn't hide her grin, not that I would have wanted her to because that girl brought me to my knees with one look—wrapped around her finger or tucked in her back pocket.

It was that simple. She had me whether she wanted me or not. I never imagined my dream being as simplistic as watching someone else live theirs. Until her.

"Well, I did the thing. *Not* that I did it so you'd let me sing." She glanced up at me, balancing on one foot to pull on her boots while her cheeks turned pink. "I wanted to do it."

To be perfectly clear, I never would have asked her to put my dick in her mouth for any reason. But who was I to say no when she removed the towel from my waist after our shower and seemed eager to try something new?

"Lenny makes the rules, not me," I said.

"Oh," she twisted her lips and nodded several times. "I see. So, I sucked the wrong guy's ..."

I loved how her innocence tripped her up.

"The wrong guy's *dick?*"

She huffed and deflated.

"Sunday Morning, I'll never tell you what you have to do, but I'm sure as hell going to tell you what you're *not* going to do. And sucking another man's dick is at the top of the list."

"Same difference." She frowned.

"Not the same." I stood and adjusted my belt before

hooking my fingers into the pockets of her dress and pulling her to me.

She slid her hands around my waist and peered up at me with her mesmerizing blue eyes. "I don't want to go home tomorrow."

"What time do you have to be back?" I asked.

"By dinner. Heather said they were planning on returning around six. So just drop me off where you usually do, and we should be good."

"Well, that's not until tomorrow. Let's grab dinner. Hit the show. Fireworks. Bed."

She beamed. "I don't know what I'm looking forward to the most."

"Bed, baby. You're looking forward to getting in this bed with me and *not* sleeping for the whole night."

She giggled. "But I love fireworks."

"Get your ass in the truck."

I PLAYED FOR FORTY-FIVE MINUTES, watching Sarah at a table right next to the stage the whole time. It thrilled me to pretend that she was my favorite groupie, but I knew better. She was itching to wrap her hands around the microphone and sing her beautiful heart out.

Watching her jaw drop during my last song was almost too much. I sang "Love Stinks" and the crowd sang the chorus. By the end, Sarah lifted her hands in the air and sang along too.

"We have time for one more song," I announced, watching Sarah's shoulders fold inward, resigned to the idea that I wasn't going to give her a bigger glimpse at her dreams.

"If you'll indulge me, I'd like to bring a special guest on stage with me."

That look—the one she gave me—was bigger and better than anything in the whole fucking galaxy. With one single look, she simplified my existence and the meaning of my life to a singular purpose: spend every day working to earn *that* look from her.

And if I could do that, I'd die a happy man.

"When you hear her on the radio, and see her selling out venues, remember you got to see her *first* here tonight. Please welcome Sunday Morning."

She hesitated for a second and narrowed her eyes, but when the crowd broke into applause, she found her smile and joined me on stage.

I handed her the mic and leaned in to whisper, "Breathe, baby. You've got this."

She nervously smiled as I sat on the stool. The mic shook in her hands.

"Look at me," I mouthed.

She returned a tiny nod as I started playing, and then it was just the two of us in the barn loft, sharing the same passion.

When she sang the first line to "Bette Davis Eyes," the crowd went wild, and Sarah lit up the whole stage with her smile.

Matty gave her his letter jacket, her first kiss, his virginity, and he might even have given her his last name one day, but if he couldn't give her a chance at her dreams, he might as well have given her nothing.

The enthusiastic Fourth of July crowd gave her a standing ovation and deafening applause. And the second I lifted the guitar strap over my head, she threw her arms around my neck.

She rode that high for the rest of the night while we watched fireworks and made love until the sun rose the next morning.

Matty could have the fame and fortune. World titles and fancy cars. He could have six days and nights. I only wanted Sunday Morning.

I just wanted the girl.

Chapter Twenty-Four

Air Supply "All Out of Love"

Sarah

WE DIDN'T SAY much on the drive back to Devil's Head. My heart was filled with melancholy. How would things play out at home? Could we keep our relationship a secret until Matt went to school?

Then we could act like it just happened. (Which it did.)

We could say we didn't see it coming. (Because we didn't.)

Five weeks.

We just had to make it five more weeks until Matt left for college.

Isaac pulled into a truck stop just off the interstate ten miles from the exit to Devil's Head, parking in a spot far away from other vehicles.

"Come here," he said, removing his seat belt.

I did the same and slid across the seat, straddling his lap

with my arms around his neck. We shared one long kiss after another, each one making us hungrier for the next. When we stopped to catch our breaths, he pressed his forehead to mine.

"Let's tell them," he murmured. "Your family. My family. Let's just fucking tell them."

I lifted my head. "No. It's five weeks until Matt leaves. Nothing good will come from telling anyone now."

"Is it about the money? Your parents paying rent because—"

"No." I shook my head. "Well, yes, but that's not everything. I'm working for your parents this summer. I just don't want everything to fall apart at once. If we just wait until Matt leaves, he'll—"

"Baby, Matt going to school won't change how he'll feel about us. How would you react if, a couple of months from now, you found out Matt and Eve had been messing around all summer?"

I scrunched my nose. "She's sixteen."

"And he's eighteen. That's two years. There's six between us."

I shrugged. "I have you, so whatever." I lied because I couldn't process how something like that would make me feel, and I didn't want Isaac to be right.

"But what if you didn't have me?"

I frowned, which made him grin.

"Fine. I get it. Matt's not going to like it, but I'd rather he be upset with me in Michigan than upset with me here while I'm *working for your family*. I can use the rest of the summer to drop hints that Matt and I might not stay together. And you can start sitting in the front row at church, so my dad sees your commitment to God, and therefore increasing your chances of him finding you worthy of his daughter."

I knew that was never going to happen.

"And maybe you can spend more time teaching me to play the guitar, but not always in secret. Then Matt and your parents will get used to seeing us together, even if not really *together*."

He nodded slowly. "Okay. But *if* anyone finds out about this trip, I want you to let me handle it. I'll deal with my family and yours. Understood?"

"Why—"

Isaac framed my face in his big hands. "*Understood?*"

I returned a tiny nod.

"Good." He pecked at my lips. "Now that we have that straight," he unbuttoned my shorts, "I have one condom left."

IsAAc DROPPED me off fifteen yards from our driveway with one last kiss. Unfortunately, I had to leave my new clothes, boots, and hat with him so no one at my house would question where I got them. Despite leaving the tangible things behind, I grinned uncontrollably all the way to the front door because the memories we made in three days would stay with me forever.

"Sarah!" My mom ran toward me, hugging me so tightly I choked on my next breath. Dad and my sisters followed her to the front door, all hugging me. My mom, Eve, and Gabby wiped tears from their faces, but my dad blinked his away despite his red eyes.

My heart plummeted into the pit of my stomach. They

knew. But why were my sisters crying? I wanted to turn around and chase Isaac. Something wasn't right.

"Hey, um ..." I started to panic, but I didn't want them to see it, so I swallowed hard and plastered on a smile.

"Where have you been?" Mom pressed her palms to my face, releasing a sob.

My smile faded. The gravity of whatever had her in a fit of worry seemed bigger than my need to look happy.

"Uh, I've been camping with my friends. W-why?" My voice shook as I stuck with the lie because I didn't have the strength to share the truth.

Mom narrowed her eyes and reared her head back as she let go of me and cupped a hand at her mouth.

I looked at my dad and sisters. *Why* were Gabby and Eve crying?

"Go upstairs, girls," Dad said, eyeing them.

Without resistance, they obeyed, and they never obeyed that easily.

"*Where* have you been?" My dad's voice was thick with an emotion I didn't recognize. He seemed angry but hurt—scared but relieved.

He knew. But how? It didn't make sense. And if he knew, then why did he ask me as if he didn't know?

"W-what is going on?" I whispered past the lump in my throat, wide eyes ping-ponging between my parents.

Mom covered her face with both hands and cried.

"Sarah," Dad's voice cracked before he cleared his throat, "Heather and Joanna were in a car accident."

That was it. That was all I heard. The room spun, and his voice became a distant, mumbled echo. His mouth moved, hands making gestures before raking through his hair.

"Sarah?"

I heard him wrong. It was a weird dream.

"Sarah?" He grabbed my shoulders. "Did you hear what I said?"

My gaze made a slow shift from his moving lips to his narrowed eyes.

I shook my head. "W-what?" I could barely hear my own voice.

Did he hear me?

"Where have you been?" He moved his hands from my shoulders to my face like my mom had held me. "Sarah, did you hear me? Heather and Joanna were in a car accident." Dad's Adam's apple bobbed. "They didn't make it. Where have you been? We've been worried sick. Praying for your safe return. Nobody knew where you were. Your other friends thought you were home. We went to the police. Sarah Elaine Jacobson, talk to me!"

Everything burned like tiny bees stinging my skin, and my vision blurred behind my tears. I couldn't breathe. Where was the air? Why couldn't I find my next breath?

"H-Heath ... H-Heather ... no ... what ... NO!" I shook my head and backed away from him until I hit the door. "No ..." I continued to shake my head.

My parents stepped toward me.

"NO! Don't touch me. No. You're lying. That's n-not f-funny."

"Sweetie—"

Mom held out her arms and reached for me.

"STOP!" I batted at her hand. "W-why would you s-say that? Don't say t-that." I sobbed, wiping my nose with the back of my hand. "Don't. Ever. Say. That!" I grabbed my bag and ran upstairs.

"Sarah?" Eve called.

I slammed my door and locked it. Then I moved my desk in front of it, knocking the lamp on the floor and breaking the lightbulb. I choked on my emotions while backing away from the barricaded door. When I hit the opposite wall, I slid to my butt and hugged my knees to my chest.

"No no no no no no no ..." I whispered, pinching my eyes shut while my teeth chattered.

I hated my parents.

I hated Heather and Joanna for playing such a horrible joke on me.

But mostly, I hated God because my heart knew what my mind refused to believe. And no loving god would allow that to happen to my friends.

Chapter Twenty-Five

Kansas, "Dust in the Wind"

THE PHONE RANG NONSTOP, so I yanked the cord out of the wall. My family knocked at my door incessantly, so I put on my headphones and listened to music.

I sat in the same spot, staring at near darkness as the moon was barely a sliver that night. The bed was too far away. Moving felt impossible when breathing took everything I had left. So I eventually leaned to the side, resting on the floor in a ball, staring at black figures under my bed. They were boxes and boxes of pictures and yearbooks. Heather and Joanna were in those boxes.

Short spells of sleep gave me moments of reprieve between the endless tears. When the first morning light pierced through my shades, I winced while sitting up. My head felt heavy, and my eyes were painfully swollen. The desk was in front of my door, which meant it wasn't just a bad dream.

Heather and Joanna were gone, and I needed to pee.

I slid the desk just far enough to unlock my door and ease it partway open. My mom lifted her head from the pillow on the floor. She was in her robe, covered in an afghan.

"I can't talk," I whispered.

She stood with the blanket draped over her shoulders and hugged me.

No words.

No explanation.

She wrapped me in her arms, and it was the closest thing I could imagine to God's love. Only I knew my mom would never have let my friends die if she were as almighty as the deity my father praised every Sunday.

I pulled away and shuffled my feet to the bathroom. When I returned to my room, my mom was sitting on the edge of my bed, facing the window.

"We thought it was you," she whispered, "in the vehicle with Heather. And I died a little in that moment."

I sat on the opposite side of the bed so our backs were to each other. My emotions were too tangled to make sense of them.

Pain.

Denial.

Regret.

So much regret and remorse.

"Heather's funeral is tomorrow. Joanna's isn't until Thursday when her grandparents can be there."

I closed my eyes. It wasn't real.

"Where were you?" Her voice cracked.

I couldn't respond, so I lay on my side, my hands tucked under my cheek on the pillow.

My mom was everything a mom should have been, but I needed space for my thoughts and emotions—space for the truth to shape my new reality.

That's not what I got.

With two knocks at my bedroom door, Dad poked his head inside. "Matt's here, honey." He eyed the desk and slipped through the crack to move it back into place, using a piece of paper to sweep the broken lightbulb out of the way.

"Sarah," Matt whispered, sliding his hands into his pockets as he stepped into my room.

"We'll be downstairs," Mom said, taking my dad's hand and guiding him out of my room.

That was the first time Matt had been allowed in my bedroom.

"Where were you? Everyone thought you were ..."

Dead.

Everyone thought I was the one in the car with Heather.

My gaze affixed to the chipped corner of my nightstand. I couldn't look at him.

"Sarah?" He sat on the edge of my bed, resting his hand on my arm. "Talk to me."

"I can't talk about it," I whispered, releasing a tear with a heavy blink.

"Why? Our friends are dead, Sarah. And you—"

"I know!" I rolled onto my back and covered my eyes with the heels of my hands. "You have to leave. I don't want you here. I just want everyone t-to leave m-me alone." I sobbed.

"Sarah—" Matt touched my leg.

I jerked away. "Just. Go!" Emotion ripped through my

body in crashing waves, each one slamming into my heart as I held my breath to suppress my crying.

A few seconds later, the door clicked shut.

I'D NEVER THOUGHT about grief on a deep level, probably because I hadn't lost anyone close to me. It was like sex. I had this idea in my head from watching movies and reading books, but the reality didn't match. Or maybe it did for some people, just not me.

Anger suffocated all the sadness. My emotions were layered.

Anger.

Guilt.

Grief.

And whatever came after that.

Whatever *that* was felt unreachable, like chasing a mirage in the desert that would never quench my thirst for clarity and reason.

"Do you want me to curl your hair?" Eve asked as I stood in front of the bathroom mirror, staring at my lifeless reflection.

Black was my least favorite color, but Mom made sure my sisters and I always had one basic black dress to wear to funerals. Since my dad was the preacher at the only church in Devil's Head, we attended many of the funerals. But most of the time, we barely knew the deceased (predominantly elderly people).

Eve didn't wait for my answer. She plugged in the curling iron and brushed through my hair. "You can tell me," she said.

I glanced at her reflection, and she shrugged.

"Anything. You can tell me anything. I can keep a secret."

"I don't want you to have to keep my secret," I mumbled.

She began curling my hair. "Your friends died. Mom and Dad are so relieved you weren't in the car. I don't think you'll get in trouble."

"It's not about me. I just ..." I dropped my gaze to the sink. "I did something that will hurt a lot of other people, and I can't be the one to cause any more pain right now."

I commended Eve for not pushing me, but I saw it in her face, she wanted to help me.

Nobody could help me.

"We have to go," Mom called.

Eve added a few more curls, unplugged the curling iron, and hugged me when I turned toward her. "I'm sorry you lost your friends. It's not fair."

I nodded, choking on a suppressed sob.

We were the first ones at the church. My sisters divided up the funeral programs while Dad met with Heather's family in his office.

Mom walked me to the front of the church, third row back.

"Just sit here, Sarah." She handed me a few tissues. "Heather's mom asked me if I thought you'd want to say a few words. I know it's short notice, and you might not be up for it. But—"

"I'll do it."

I didn't want to. Breathing was hard. Speaking? Nearly impossible. Talking about Heather? Unimaginable.

However, when her aunt died of cancer, Heather read a poem and said nice things about her. I asked her how she did it without breaking down. She wasn't my aunt, yet I couldn't stop crying during the entire service.

Heather said she felt like it was the last time to say something about her aunt and have it matter. And she said she hoped when *she* died that the people who loved her the most would find the courage to say it *one last time*—make it matter.

"Are you sure?" Mom asked.

"I'm sure," I whispered.

"If you change your mind—"

"I won't." I stared at the closed casket and the picture of Heather next to it. She would have laughed at that photo. It was one of her senior pictures, the one she liked the least because the photographer asked her for a "soft smile," and it looked like a goofy smirk. But her mom loved that shot more than any other.

The church filled beyond capacity over the next hour. I'd been staring at the casket so long that the surrounding people went unnoticed until my mom and sisters filed in on one side of me. I tried to give my mom a reassuring smile that I was okay just as Matt and five other guys took a seat in the front row on the opposite side.

Pallbearers.

Matt gave me a quick glance, but he didn't try to smile. He looked hurt. I did that to him.

Someone touched my shoulder, drawing my attention in the opposite direction. Violet Cory sat next to me and gave me a big hug.

"I'm so sorry, Sarah. And I'm glad you're still with us. We were so worried. The whole town was worried."

I'm an awful human being.

Mr. Cory sat next to her. He gave me a sad smile. And on the other side of him, Isaac took a seat. When he glanced at me, my eyes burned with tears. I needed his arms around me more than anything.

He smoothed his hand down his black tie. I had never seen him in a suit, and after that day, I never wanted to see him in a suit again, just like my black dress. At the end of the week, it was going in the trash.

After Violet released me, I quickly reached for my tissues as Heather's family took their seats in front of us. I cast my gaze to my lap because I couldn't look at them.

My dad asked everyone to bow their heads in prayer. After a collective, solemn "Amen," he cited scripture. "Blessed are they that mourn, for they shall be comforted."

I lifted my gaze to the area behind my dad, where I'd sat next to Heather in the choir. She'd elbow me and grin. I'd tap my leg against hers and quietly snicker. My dad would shoot us an occasional glance and clear his throat to get our attention. That only made us giggle more as soon as he looked away.

Heather's mom sobbed as did mine and Violet Cory. I thought of the time Heather and I had to scrape wax from the wood floor below the candelabras as a punishment for putting Monopoly money in the offering plate. We didn't get in trouble often, but when we did, it was usually together.

We were inseparable.

"My daughter and Heather's best friend, Sarah, would like to say a few words," Dad said, bringing me back to a reality I wasn't ready to accept.

I stood and straightened my dress before sliding out of the pew past my mom and sisters.

Dad offered an encouraging smile as I stepped up to the lectern. I'd gazed at large crowds, especially on Easter and Christmas, but this was bigger. I had never seen so many people standing at the back because there wasn't enough seating space. I think nearly everyone from our graduating class was there.

I looked to my mom and sisters for reassurance, but they only gave me sniffles and tears. When I laid eyes on Matt, he dropped his gaze to his lap. Then I made the mistake of glancing at Heather's mom, and it felt like a knife in my chest.

Heather died. I lived.

She was able to speak at her aunt's funeral because Heather knew life would go on and she would be fine. I was drowning in a lie and suffocating from the guilt. I *didn't* know if I would be okay. And that uncertainty paralyzed my thoughts—until I looked at Isaac.

His lips moved. It was subtle, overlooked by everyone else, but I saw it.

"*I love you,*" he mouthed.

I pulled a tissue from the wad in my hand and wiped a few tears. Isaac declared his love to me at my best friend's funeral. I didn't know if it made me love him more or hate him forever because it squeezed more blood from my heart.

"I wanted to tell you how Heather and I met, but I don't remember. I also don't recall meeting my mom or dad. They've just always been there like Heather has always been there. According to our moms, we met in the nursery at Sunday school. We took our first steps together at a summer potluck behind this church. First words. First swimming lessons. First day of school. I shared more firsts with Heather than with my own sisters." I wiped a few tears, proud of myself for keeping it together.

"We braided each other's hair and finished each other's sentences. And when I broke my leg and couldn't go to the State Fair, she said she'd carry me." I laughed through my tears.

"I was too heavy; after all, we were only twelve. So Heather said she'd experience it for both of us and tell me all about it; and someday, if she couldn't go someplace, I would return the favor." I peered at the ceiling, looking for something—maybe strength.

"We planned our weddings when we were fifteen. She wanted to get married on a beach in Hawaii, and I wanted to get married at Graceland Wedding Chapel in Las Vegas, but I made her promise not to tell my dad."

The congregation laughed, and I knew Heather would be proud. She thought everyone should find a moment of laughter at funerals.

I eyed my dad, and he, too, had a smile on his face.

"Heather was always a little better at everything than I was, but she never made me feel less than her. She was the most inspir—" I choked on my words as everything blurred behind my tears. Wiping my eyes, I drew in a big breath and let it out slowly as the sanctuary filled with sniffles and soft sobs. "She was the most inspiring best friend anyone could have. And she was—" Again, I had to swallow past the lump in my throat as I pressed my lips together to fight for just a little more composure to finish. "She was m-mine," I whispered, tasting the salty tears on my lips.

"So it's okay that I don't remember the day we met," I stared at the casket, "because I don't want to imagine a time without her." My voice cracked along with my heart. "Heather, I'll carry you," I said softly, not caring if anyone else heard me. "I'll carry you w-with me. We'll l-live one life t-together. And I can't wait to t-tell you all about it." My knees shook, and the pain made me feel like I might pass out.

Everything hurt. All I wanted to do was find the nearest phone and call Heather to tell her about my nightmare and make her promise never to leave me. She'd laugh and tell me about some dream she had that was even more disturbing. That's what best friends did; they held hands and walked each other through life, sharing every moment of laughter and every single tear. Nashville with Isaac wasn't real because nothing was real until I told Heather.

Nothing would ever feel real again. I knew I'd spend the rest of my life stealing happy moments, and they would all come with an asterisk.

I took a step toward the stairs and saw Heather's mom collapsing to the side, falling apart in her husband's arms, and I couldn't take another step.

My gaze shot around the room as panic crushed my lungs. I couldn't breathe. My dad rested his hand on my shoulder, but I didn't need a reassuring hand. I knew he wanted me to pull it together and take a seat, but I. Couldn't. Move.

"Sarah," he leaned over and whispered in my ear as I buckled at the waist. "Sit by your mom, honey? Can you do that?"

I shook my head, and a sob ripped from my chest. Hundreds of people watched me, but I felt terrifyingly alone.

I can't catch my breath. I can't catch my breath ...

My mind screamed, but I couldn't speak.

Someone picked me up, and at first, I thought it must have been my dad. When I looked up, the blurry face before me was Isaac's. He carried me down the aisle by the windows and out the front of the church.

He carried me past the parking lot, across the road, and into the sunflower field. The giant stalks engulfed us like the corn mazes where the young kids in Devil's Head loved to play hide-and-seek. He walked and walked. I didn't know if he found the perfect spot or just tired of carrying me, but he lowered us to the ground with me cocooned between his bent knees and protective arms.

Isaac let me cry. He let me fall apart. And he didn't tell me I would be okay, we would be okay, or life would be okay. My best friend was gone.

Nothing would ever feel okay again.

"I should ... I sh-should ... I should have been ... in that c-car." I hadn't hyperventilated before, but that's what I imagined it felt like.

My heart raced. I felt lightheaded. And I couldn't catch my breath no matter how hard I tried.

"Shh. No, baby." He kissed my head. "You *could* have been in that car. But you weren't. And I'm so fucking sorry that you lost your friends. It wasn't your fault. And it wasn't their fault. It was life. And sometimes life can be cruel. But that's part of the deal. Death is part of the deal. No one knows how long they have. And it sucks that your friends didn't have more time, but nobody thinks you should have been in that car."

"I can't b-breathe ..." My chest puffed out in little staccatos as I clawed for a breath.

"Yes, you can." He pressed his hand to my cheek and rubbed his thumbs over my tears. "Purse your lips." He pursed his. "Slow it down. Slow each breath. There's plenty of air; just slow it down." He pressed his lips to my forehead. "I've got you." He took my hand and rested it flat against his chest. "Feel that? I've got you. Breathe with me."

Isaac wrapped me in his whole body while we sat in the middle of the sunflower field, dressed in black, with a lot of explaining to do.

Eventually, I found my breath, exhausted, like I could take an eternal nap. Isaac loosened his hold on me and stroked my hair while gently rocking us side to side.

"I have to go back. There's a burial. And I have to do it all over again in two days. And now I also have to explain why you carried me out of the church."

"You don't have to explain anything you don't want to explain. You don't have to bury anyone. You don't have to do it again on Thursday. And if you don't want to go home, I'll take you anywhere you want to go."

"Why would you do that for me?"

"You know why."

Because you love me.

I didn't want to run from the grief. Heather never would have done that. And I didn't want to leave my family. I loved them. And I wanted to make things right with Matt because by trying to chase my dreams while protecting him, I only hurt him.

"I have to go back."

Isaac regarded me, gauging my sincerity. Then he stood and helped me to my feet. We brushed the dirt off our backsides. Then I straightened his tie.

"You look handsome," I said, staring at his tie. The swelling caused my eyes to squint permanently. "But I never want to see you in a suit again. If I die first, wear jeans and your cowboy hat to my funeral."

"On one condition," he said, taking my hand and leading me out of the field.

"What's that?"

"You let me die first."

I stopped, tightening my grip on his hand so he would stop too. He turned, eyes narrowed.

"I can't lose you," I whispered.

His expression softened, and he brushed his knuckles along my cheek. "That's my line." He kissed me, and I released his hand to wrap my arms around his neck.

We were either the bad kind of right or the good kind of wrong. It was hard to distinguish the two. We had a reckless love and perfectly awful timing. We were impossible to describe, and that's why every time I tried to put us into words, it made no sense.

He released me and again took my hand, taking a step in front of me.

"Isaac?"

"Yeah?" He glanced over his shoulder.

"I love you too."

A slow smile slid up his face. "Then I'm a lucky son of a bitch."

Chapter Twenty-Six

The Beatles, "Let It Be"

WE RETURNED to the church just as Matt and the other pallbearers carried Heather's casket to the hearse. Isaac and I let go of each other at the same time. And I loved him even more for knowing it wasn't the right moment to take something suspicious (like carrying me out of the church) and turn it into an unquestionable declaration.

After all, Isaac spent six years serving and protecting. Was it a stretch to believe that he was the only one in the church who wasn't so lost in their own emotions to see me bleeding out?

My mom and sisters hurried toward us.

"Sarah," Mom hugged me. "I'm so sorry. I thought you'd be okay. I'm *so* sorry. No one should have asked you to speak."

I pulled away from her, peering at the casket as they

loaded it into the back of the hearse. It wasn't real. Her body wasn't in that shiny box. The cruelty and unfairness were too much, even if Isaac believed it was part of the deal.

I wanted to negotiate a new deal.

"I needed to speak," I murmured before forcing my gaze back to my mom.

Her expression bled with sympathy and remorse, and then she shifted her attention to Isaac. "Thank you for helping Sarah." She reached for his hand and squeezed it. "You've turned into a good man, Isaac."

He didn't help me; he saved me. But I was glad she thought he was a good man, even if I knew it would only be a matter of time before she changed her mind.

"Of course." Isaac shrugged it off.

However, Eve's gaze flitted between us. She was only two years younger than me. Eve dreamed of knights in shining armor, turning eighteen and feeling a new sense of freedom, and losing her virginity. Even if there had been nothing going on between Isaac and me, Eve's mind would have concocted something. So I played it safe and didn't make eye contact with her.

Isaac wasn't as astute. When my mom and Gabby turned to watch the hearse pull away, Isaac headed toward his family's car, but not before resting his hand on my lower back, then taking a half step and letting his fingers graze the palm of my hand.

Eve's gaze lifted from my hand to my face. But this time, I didn't look away. And I didn't say a word. She knew *that* was the secret I was asking her to keep. And she couldn't have looked more shocked.

We drove to the cemetery just outside of Devil's Head. It

seemed impossible that my body could leak any more tears, but there was something about that last goodbye.

That hole in the ground.

The short prayer and scripture.

"For everything there is a season ... a time to be born, and a time to die ... a time to weep, and a time to laugh; a time to mourn, and a time to dance."

I was *so* tired of crying, but the tears just kept coming, and my mom continued to hand me tissues that quickly disintegrated. Someone touched my shoulder, and I turned.

Wesley Cory handed me a crisp white, neatly folded hanky. It was the first time I'd made eye contact with him that day. A deep sadness lived in his eyes. That day, I hadn't once thought about his affair until he couldn't look at me. Surely, he had to know my mind wasn't on his indiscretions.

Matt leaned closer to his dad and started to whisper, "She doesn't want a hank—"

"Thank you," I said softly, accepting the hanky and pressing it to my eyes as I turned back toward Heather.

THE REST of the day passed in a slow blur. I felt like my brain was shutting down from overload. People talked to me at the luncheon, and I *think* I smiled and nodded, offered and accepted condolences. Basically, I did everything on autopilot, so there was little certainty.

No one questioned Isaac carrying me out of the church, not even Matt or my dad. I was the only one (except Eve) who thought of it as an intimate gesture only someone who loved me would do.

After we returned home, my family headed into the

house to change their clothes while I sat on the tree swing behind our house. I used to love swinging on it when we moved there five years earlier after living in a three-bedroom house in town.

"You were with Isaac," Eve said behind me.

I kept swinging.

"Sarah, he's your *boyfriend's brother*."

Still, I kept swinging, staring at the puffy white clouds.

"*Everyone* thinks you and Matt are getting married."

I couldn't remember who was the first person to jump to that conclusion; I just remember it wasn't actually Matt or me, but everyone accepted it as the truth. Eventually, we talked about life after high school, like marriage was a forgone conclusion. Maybe we should have said something earlier, like, "We're young. Who knows what the future holds."

I stopped pumping my legs, and as my swing came to a slow sway, Eve stepped in front of me, plucking my shoes from the ground. "Vi said that Isaac left town over the Fourth, and that's why he couldn't help look for you—because everyone was looking for you. But nobody considered that you might be with him. And why would they? He's your boyfriend's brother."

I stared at my feet and the tiny run in my pantyhose.

"If I'm wrong about Isaac," she continued, "then we know, at the very least, he's an admirable guy. If I'm right, then what he did today was the most romantic thing I have ever seen. You stood in front of everyone and told them about Heather offering to carry you and how you will carry her. Then Isaac literally stood up, ignoring what anyone thought, and he did that."

Had I not known better, I would have thought Heather

was whispering to Eve. Everything she said sounded just like Heather.

"Say something."

I lifted my gaze to hers and smiled. "It was the most romantic thing you've ever seen."

"Oh my god, Sarah!" She gasped. Eve wasn't as much of a pleaser. She used the Lord's name in vain without feeling guilty. "Where were you? You were with him. Where? You *have* to tell me. If you don't tell me, I'm telling Mom and Dad."

I frowned.

She rolled her eyes. "Okay, I won't tell them, but just tell me."

I pressed my lips together.

"Tell me!" She tossed my shoes aside and twisted my swing so when she let go I spun in fast circles.

"Stop." I tried to laugh, but my heart wasn't in it. I loved my sister, but I didn't want to have that conversation with her. I wanted to tell Heather.

But I couldn't.

I would never tell Heather anything ever again.

Eve's excitement faded when I failed to engage with her playfulness. "I'm sorry about Heather and Joanna, but I'm glad you were with Isaac. Otherwise, you'd be ..."

I nodded slowly.

As Eve gave up and took a few steps past me toward the house, I mumbled, "We went to Nashville."

"Are you serious? Did you—"

"That's it, Eve. That's all I have in me to give today. I need to be alone now. Okay?"

276

For the next two days, my parents continued to give me a reprieve from accountability, but I knew after Joanna's funeral that I wouldn't be able to keep my whereabouts a secret any longer. Matt called the house, but I didn't take his calls.

"Three funerals in one week is too much," Dad said during breakfast the morning of Joanna's funeral.

"It is," Mom murmured, giving him a sad smile while setting the pitcher of orange juice on the table.

"Are we going to Brenda's funeral too?" Eve asked.

My gaze shot up from my plate. "Brenda?"

Dad wiped his mouth and cleared his throat. "Brenda Swensen. She graduated three or four years before—"

"I know who she is. She died?"

Everyone else at the table stared at me.

"Yes, honey. Didn't you know she was the one who hit Heather and Joanna? They think she was intoxicated."

"What? No." I shook my head a half dozen times. "Nobody told me."

That was it. That was the look in Wesley Cory's eyes at Heather's funeral. He wasn't mourning her; he was mourning his mistress.

I thought I hated Brenda before the accident. After all, she was screwing a married man who was old enough to be her father—*in his wife's bed*. But I knew I hated her when I found out she killed my friends. And it also made me despise Wesley Cory.

"I hate her," I mumbled, dropping my chin and stabbing my fork into the pile of pancakes.

"Sarah Elaine Jacobson, we don't hate anyone because God doesn't hate people," Dad said.

"Am I God?" I shot him a scowl.

277

He drew in a controlled breath.

"That's what I thought. I'm not God. I'm human, and that means I'm capable of hating her even if God doesn't want me to hate her. I guess if He *really* didn't want me to hate her, He would have kept my friends safe. But He didn't." I shoved a huge bite of pancake into my mouth, even though I was no longer hungry. "That means I can hate her, and you don't get to tell me how I'm supposed to feel. I'm going to hate her." I rammed my fork into the plate like I was stabbing Brenda in the heart.

The plate cracked, startling my mom and sisters.

"Sarah!" Dad warned.

It was a rare moment because I was a people pleaser. But I was coming apart inside, and I no longer had it in me to please anyone.

"And while I'm at it," I stood, knocking my chair over, "I'm not overjoyed with God at the moment either."

I hate Him.

"Go to your room until I'm done with breakfast, then we're going to have a long talk, young lady," Dad said while setting his fork down with shaky hands like I'd trampled his last bit of control.

He was human, too, no matter how many times a day he talked to God.

I ran up the stairs and grabbed my wrinkled black dress, shoes, and car keys. Then I jogged down the stairs.

"Sarah!" Dad called.

I whipped around when I reached the front door. "I'm an adult now. You don't get to tell me what to do. I'll go where I want when I want. I'll say what I want. I'll think whatever I want. I'll have *sex* with whomever I want. And it will be between me and God. You're not the father who gets to judge me. Why don't you practice what you preach?" I flung open the door and stomped to my car.

When I started it and glanced at the house, everyone had gathered on the front porch.

I wasn't impervious to the guilt, but I was in a predicament with the Cory men because I caved to the fear of rocking the boat. The idea of living my life for anyone but myself no longer felt sustainable.

Chapter Twenty-Seven

Madonna, "Crazy for You"

WHEN I REACHED THE CORYS' lane, I slowed down to see if Matt's car was there. It wasn't, so I continued driving along the gravel road until there was a farm lane, and I parked my car there.

Shimmying through the fence, I trekked through the pasture to the horse barn. When I peeked my head inside, there was no one there; as I stepped backward to close the door, I bumped into someone and jumped around with my hand on my heart.

Isaac wiped his dirty, sweaty brow with his arm. "Hi."

"Hi," I replied while my shoulders relaxed. Just being in his presence lifted the weight of the world from them. "Are you going to ask me why I'm here when Joanna's funeral is this afternoon?"

He shook his head.

"Why not?"

"Because," he reached past me to open the barn door, "I'm just really fucking glad to see you. Do you *want* to tell me why you're here?" He lifted his T-shirt and wiped his whole face.

It was scorching, and so were his abs which distracted me for a few seconds.

"Brenda Swensen was the driver who hit Heather and Joanna. And they think she'd been drinking."

"Yeah," he said, giving me a shrug. "She died too."

There was no way that Isaac didn't know about the affair, not after his reaction to the couple in front of us at Opryland. We'd been dancing around the topic.

Right?

"And?"

Isaac squinted. "And what? She was drunk. She killed two people. And she paid the price."

"She didn't pay the price. She'll never pay the price. Brenda's dead. She's not here to suffer the consequences of what she did to my friends and your family."

"My family?"

He doesn't know?

I opened my mouth to speak, but I didn't know what to say.

"You mean Matt because they were his friends too?" Isaac asked.

Had I not had another funeral to attend or just stormed out of my house, I would have told him. Out of everyone, I wanted to be honest with Isaac because I believed what we had would last—maybe for a lifetime. His trust mattered the most.

"Yeah," I whispered. "They were Matt's friends too."

The lines of confusion on Isaac's face vanished. "I've wanted to call."

I nodded slowly. "Yeah, well, don't call now. I think I just ran away from home."

"What are you talking about?"

"I blew up at my dad and ran out. I have a dress for the funeral in my car that I parked at the tractor turnaround. Then I walked through the pasture." I lifted my foot. "And I got poop on my shoe."

"You're homeless?" He lifted a brow.

"Yes. Can I sleep in the barn?"

"You can sleep in my bed."

I gave him a dead stare before casting my gaze on the ground between us. "Can we just go back to Nashville?"

"I'll drive."

I reached for him because I loved him for saying that.

"I'm filthy," he said, taking a step backward and holding up his hands.

"I don't care." Again, I reached for him.

He took another step away. "You have to put on a dress in a few hours."

Everything was falling apart, including me. The only hands that could put me back together were his.

"I-saac ..." His name shattered as it fell from my quivering lips.

With his brow furrowed, he grabbed my face and kissed me. I curled my fingers into his shirt, tugging it, needing him to be as close to me as possible. If I could feel his heart beating against my chest, I thought mine would remember to keep beating too.

Everything ached bone-deep. The blank space Heather and Joanna left inside of me needed to be filled before I crumbled into something irreparably broken. It was a hundred degrees outside under a cloudless sky, but I hadn't seen light in days. My world was dark and suffocating.

I shoved Isaac's shirt up his sweaty chest, and he pulled it over his head and removed mine. As he walked me backward, we kissed, and he discarded my bra.

"Make it better," I whispered while his whiskery jaw brushed my neck. "Make everything better."

He closed the door as we stepped into the tack room, fighting for leverage to remove each other's clothes. The need felt unquenchable—a runaway passion so raw it brought tears to my eyes.

I loved Isaac more than anyone. He didn't earn it the way Matt earned my love. It wasn't bestowed by genetics. I didn't fall in love with Isaac. I found myself in love with him.

In him, I *found* myself.

"Oh *god* …" I tipped my head back and closed my eyes when he lifted me onto the bench and filled me. "I love you," I whispered as we moved together with my legs wrapped around his waist.

"You're my beautiful Sunday Morning," he said, kissing up my throat, dragging his tongue along my sweaty skin. "You're my every morning." He teased my earlobe. "And I thank God for you."

I kissed Isaac's bare shoulder as tears burned my eyes. Why did he have to remind me that I didn't hate God? Why did he have to be the better person? Despite the unimaginable tragedy and loss, I had Isaac. And when we were as close as physically possible, I could breathe.

I didn't feel hollow.

And even in the dark room, he helped me see the light.

"Isaac," I curled my fingers into his hard glutes, "thank ... you."

Thank you for taking it away.

Isaac rocked his pelvis into mine with purpose, slowly losing control with me. His calloused hands brushed along my cheeks before diving into my hair as he kissed me with an open mouth and a deep moan vibrating his chest.

My heart lost all control. Isaac didn't think I belonged to anyone, but he was so very wrong. I wanted to be his in every way possible.

No more coveting.

I wanted to be his world because he was mine.

For a moment, I felt nothing but waves of pleasure, and I didn't want it to end. Then he pulled out, and I was swimming in too much bliss, and the room was too dark to see what he was doing. But when he grunted and moaned deeply, I realized he had his hand around his erection, and he was coming on my stomach instead of inside of me.

Isaac dropped his forehead to my shoulder. We were drenched in sweat and my skin pulsed from head to toe.

Condoms.

I didn't once think about a condom. A million other emotions consumed my mind, preventing me from having a single responsible thought about a condom. But his withdrawal brought a little clarity—and a little panic.

"Isaac," I whispered, slowly unlocking my ankles from his waist.

He threaded his fingers through my sticky hair and kissed my cheek. "Yeah?"

"If I get pregnant, I won't—"

"I know," he murmured.

"You don't know." I teased the nape of his neck, resting my head against his. "I'm not Danielle. I won't get—"

"I. Know," he said, skating his hands along my legs to my hips. "I didn't ..." He sighed. "I would never ask you to do anything you didn't want to do." He unhooked my legs from his waist and stepped back. Then he turned on the light as I eased off the wood counter.

With an old rag, he wiped off my stomach. "For the record, I'm not trying to get you pregnant." After tossing the rag aside, he pulled on his briefs and jeans as I slipped on my shorts.

"My bra and our shirts are out there." I nodded toward the door.

"Did you hear me?" he asked, zipping his jeans.

I glanced up at him.

"I'm not that guy," he said.

I didn't want to accuse him of anything, but what happened, happened. He couldn't erase the past or blame me for needing to make my position clear.

"And I told you I'm not that girl, the one who gets an abortion." Pleasers, like myself, got lost in everyone else's expectations. But of all of my relationships, my one with God was the most complex, which was odd since He was the only one I believed loved me unconditionally—at least I thought that before the accident.

I wanted to be a good human, but I wasn't perfect. My values were personal, and I didn't want my dad or anyone else telling me what I should do or think. But it had been my experience that the people who cared for me held strong opinions about my life and my decisions.

But not Isaac.

He opened his mouth to speak just as the door to the barn creaked. I covered my breasts, and my heart exploded with panic. He held a finger to his lips and shut off the light before cracking open the tack room door, squeezing through, and closing it behind him.

I was being punished. God had it in for me.

"What are you doing?"

I held my breath. It was Matt's voice.

"Whatever I want. Why?" Isaac said.

"Dude, you have a girl in there?"

My bra.

"I do. Would you mind getting out of here and shutting the door behind you?"

"That's ..." Matt's voice paused. "Sarah has that shirt."

I closed my eyes, fighting the tears.

"Good for her. What's your point?"

Isaac didn't know it was over. The lie was out. Matt got me that shirt at the State Fair the previous year. He won it by playing a carnival game.

"Sarah?" Matt said with a tight voice.

"Dude, get the fuck out of here," Isaac said.

The tack room door rattled.

"Sarah!"

"Get *the fuck* out of here!"

"She's in there! Get out of my way. Sarah!"

There was a clanging noise, and one of the horses neighed.

"I swear to God, if she's in there, I'm going to kill you," Matt said.

"Get your hands off me," Isaac said. "Or you'll regret it."

I didn't even try to wipe my tears before I opened the

door, grabbing a horse blanket to wrap around my torso. Both men turned toward me. Isaac deflated as tears streamed down my face while I kept my gaze locked on Matt's.

He slowly shook his head, jaw set, eyes red. "What have you done?" he whispered.

I sobbed. It wasn't supposed to happen like this.

Matt swallowed hard as the muscles in his face twitched; his whole body shook. "Virgin to a whore."

I winced, turning my head like he'd slapped me.

"Matty," Isaac grabbed his neck, and Matt clawed at his hand.

"Isaac!" I yelled.

He ignored me as he walked Matt backward toward the door. "You don't get to talk to her that way. I won't allow it. Not today. Not ever. I love you, but I love her more. You and everyone else are done sucking the life out of her. You're done taking. Your privileges have been revoked. So go back to the house. Be the coddled child you've always been because you don't deserve someone you don't really see. Are we clear?" He released him.

Matt gasped, rubbing his throat. When he looked at me, I averted my gaze to the ground.

"When he knocks you up and leaves you for six years, and your parents kick you out, don't come crying to me," Matt said through gritted teeth before slamming the barn door behind him.

I continued to stare at the floor.

Numb.

Dazed.

"Look at me," Isaac said.

I didn't move.

"Look. At. Me."

With a shaky inhale, I peered up at him just as he pulled his shirt over his head. Then he took my bra and T-shirt and proceeded to dress me.

"I'll make my father buy me out. We'll pack up and go to Nashville, or anywhere you want to go."

I furrowed my brow. "What are you talking about? Buy you out of what?"

"The ranch." He closed the tack room and tucked his hands into his back pockets while facing me. "My dad did something. I helped him out. And in return, he gave me fifty percent of the land."

Fifty percent of the Corys' ranch added up to more than a fourth of the land in and around Devil's Head.

Brenda.

Isaac knew about Brenda, and Wesley gave him half the farm to keep his mouth shut.

"What did he do?" I asked.

"I can't say."

"Can't or won't?"

He shook his head. "Can't."

I frowned. "I already know. But I don't want to do this now. I need to figure out where to rinse off so I can get dressed for the funeral."

"I don't know what you think you know, but you're way off," he said.

"I'm not. But it doesn't matter. I have to go."

"It does matter," Isaac said as I brushed past him toward the door.

He grabbed my arm. "Sarah, whatever you think you know, you—"

"I know about the affair."

Isaac's grip on my arm tightened for a few seconds until I tugged it away from his hold. When I glanced back at him, his tan face began to lose its color.

"I'm sorry," I murmured. "But I'm tired of the secrets. They're destroying everyone."

Chapter Twenty-Eight

Aerosmith, "Dream On"

Isaac

SHE KNOCKED me on my ass.

I couldn't believe it. How did she know? And if she knew, who else knew?

When I entered the machine shed, Dad was sitting on an overturned bucket. He looked up at me and quickly wiped his eyes with his fists. I couldn't imagine why he was crying.

"What do you need?" he asked, clearing his throat and standing to busy himself with the equipment.

"Sarah Jacobson knows. How the hell does she know?"

"Knows what?"

"Don't be such an old, stupid fucker. You know damn well what I'm talking about."

"I know what you think she knows, but it's not that."

"Keep telling yourself that, but she said she knows about the affair. And you're running out of land to silence people.

290

And I don't think you can bribe her. She's better than you. And she's better than me."

With his back to me, he rested a hand on his hip and set his gaze on the ceiling. "You ever been in love?"

"Don't give me this. You didn't love Danielle Harvey."

"No, but your mom loved Clyde Jensen."

I squinted. "Who's Clyde Jensen?"

"The man your mother was engaged to when I met her."

"You said a mutual friend fixed you up."

"That's true. Your mom and Clyde had a big fight. And she decided to teach him a lesson by going on a date with me. Of course, I didn't know that, so I held nothing back. I liked her from the moment we were introduced. She tucked her chin and curled her hair behind her ear as she blushed when I told her how beautiful her eyes were."

I loved a girl with beautiful eyes.

He turned toward me. "She had every intention of going back to him, but after that night, I made her realize that she needed to rethink things. We were married a year later, and nine months later, you were born."

"What does this have to do with Danielle Harvey?"

"Five years later, Clyde contacted your mom. He was in St. Louis for the weekend, and he wanted to see your mom. Of course, I said no. And that prompted an argument over my not trusting her, so she went to St. Louis, leaving me to take care of you. The timing was awful because we'd been fighting. Not that it was an excuse, but it just ..." He shook his head. "The timing was awful for us."

When he didn't elaborate, I did the math and read between the lines, even if I hated the sum of my calculations and speculations. "Matty's not your son," I whispered.

My dad shifted his gaze to me, and I didn't want to feel

his pain. He didn't deserve my sympathy. Yet, I had a weak moment that stole some of the momentum I'd had when I entered the barn, ready to unload on him.

"Does Clyde know?"

"Yes." He rubbed his temples. "But he had a wife and two-year-old daughter at the time, so he wasn't interested in ruining his marriage."

"Why are you telling me this? Do you expect me to think that you deserved to have an affair too? And why wait thirteen years to even the score?"

"I wasn't planning on evening any score, but Clyde contacted her, asking to meet Matt. And I said no. She wasn't happy, and that made me not trust her. So I followed her to one of Matt's baseball practices, and Clyde was there, watching him practice from afar. She never introduced him to Matt, but she stood by his side the whole time. That sent me down a self-destructive path. And Danielle had worked for us for several summers, and she was always *attentive*. A girl with a crush on her boss." He deflated with a resigned sigh. "When she turned eighteen, I thought, why not?"

I furrowed my brow. "Does Mom know?"

He shook his head.

"How did Sarah find out?"

"She didn't."

I shook my head. It made no sense.

He didn't respond for a long moment. "Clyde was at Matt's graduation, lurking in the back of the gymnasium as if he had the right to be there. And he wore this fucking fatherly pride expression. Your mom invited him. And again, I lost it. Do you want to despise me more than you already do?" he asked.

"I don't understand what you're talking about. And I don't despise you."

"Well, you should." He clenched his jaw like Matt had done, fighting his emotions.

The last time my dad cried in front of me was when Danielle Harvey told him she was pregnant with his baby. Why was he crying again?

He swallowed hard. "The Friday before the Fourth, we had champagne and orange juice, but she had mostly champagne. We were celebrating while sitting on the tailgate of my truck in the middle of nowhere, watching the sunrise. She got an entry-level job at a news station in Houston. And I thought it was good timing because I wanted to move on as well. Put the past behind me once and for all. Forgive your mother.

"I asked her if she was okay to drive, and she swore she was fine. She only had three miles to drive on roads that were pretty dead, especially that early in the morning."

He looked at me, but I wasn't following anything.

"You think Sarah knows about Danielle Harvey," he said. "But she doesn't. She knows I was having an affair with Brenda Swensen." He broke down, pinching the bridge of his nose while he silently sobbed.

Jesus ...

"W-what?"

Brenda killed Heather and Joanna because she was drunk.

She was drunk because she was fucking my dad, and they were celebrating the end of their affair and the beginning of her minimum-wage job at a newsroom.

He was right; I despised him.

"You need to buy me out of my share of the land, or it's

all going up for sale," I said, harnessing every bit of control I could find because I wanted to end his miserable life.

"Whats's going on?" Mom asked as soon as I opened the front door.

I removed my boots, keeping my head bowed. "You'll have to elaborate."

"Matt ran into the house, very upset. I tried to ask him what was wrong, and he told me to ask you."

Lifting my head, I studied her. My parents were deeply flawed, and maybe I had every right to blame my indiscretions on them, but I was twenty-four. Blaming anyone else for my actions was cowardice.

"I took something he thought belonged to him. Don't worry about it. You have enough on your plate."

"What's that supposed to mean?"

I shook my head. "Nothing."

"Well I'm meeting Janet to help prepare food for after the service." She slid her purse onto her shoulder. "You and Matt will ride with your dad to Joanna's funeral."

"I didn't know Joanna." I stepped past her toward the stairs.

"But Sarah did, and someday she's going to be family. So, we need to be there for her."

I closed my eyes just before heading up the stairs.

When the front door clicked shut behind my mom, I knocked on Matt's door.

"Go away."

I grabbed the key from the ledge of molding above the door and poked it into the lock.

"Fuck off," Matt said, staring blankly at his ceiling, legs dangling off the end of the bed.

In the Army, they shared information on a need-to-know basis. As I gazed at my brother and grappled with recent revelations about my father, I made a decision. Matt deserved everything, and what he did with it was up to him.

I had no intention of telling my mom about Brenda Swensen or that I owned half the family's land because her husband impregnated a young woman. She started it. And I wanted to wash my hands of everything. I felt no loyalty to anyone.

"Once you're done tripping over your ego, you'll see that she was never going to marry you. And even if you and everyone else managed to guilt her into it, the marriage would not have lasted. And she said you two broke up. You can't suffocate someone's dreams without losing them. But more than all of that, it's time for you to grow up and deal with reality."

He clenched his jaw. "You mean that you're an asshole? And Sarah is a—"

"Careful," I warned.

Matt drew in a long breath and let it out just as slowly.

"Your reality is this," I said. "You have a bright future ahead of you if you choose to pack up your belongings and never look back. But you're going to struggle with it because what I'm about to tell you will hit you harder than finding out your ex-girlfriend likes another guy, even if that guy is me."

"There's nothing you could tell me that would feel worse than that," he mumbled.

"Mom was engaged to another man before she met Dad.

Nine months before you were born, she drove to St. Louis to visit her ex-fiancé."

Matt rolled his head toward me, brow furrowed as he slowly sat up.

"Your biological father's name is Clyde Jensen. And no, I haven't kept this from you. I just found this out today." I slid my hands into my pockets. "If you've had either of our parents on a pedestal, I suggest you take a few seconds, right now, to set them on the ground. Make them human. Open your mind to see their flaws, knowing that someday you will inevitably fuck something up, and you'll *beg* for understanding and forgiveness."

Matt didn't move, not a blink.

"But you won't get there today. So it's okay to be pissed off. It's okay to act out. It's okay to say things that might be hard to forgive. Six years ago, Dad let twelve year's worth of resentment turn into his own affair. He got Danielle Harvey pregnant."

Matt's head jerked back before he adamantly shook it.

"It's true. However, I drove her to get an abortion. I took the fall. And Dad signed over half of the land to me in exchange for being the fall guy and enlisting in the Army for a minimum of six years."

"You're lying." Matt continued to shake his head.

I returned a painful laugh. "I wish I were. Even now, I'm still struggling with my decision because no matter how much I stood to gain from the deal, no amount of money took away the resentment that I felt toward Dad for doing what he did. And I resented you for being the protected child. Then, when I returned, you had gone from the protected child to the perfect child. They support your dreams. And no one has ever asked me about mine. Do you really think it's my dream to take over the ranch? I had a fucking band in high school. Was it not obvious to everyone what I wanted to do with my life?"

Matt's eyes reddened, and I couldn't tell if he was drowning in anguish or fighting the urge to kill something —someone.

"Do you want the rest?" I asked.

He swallowed hard, quickly wiping his eyes.

"To be honest, I wish I knew none of this. Sometimes, ignorance *is* bliss. I can leave you with a shred of bliss, or I can go ahead and fuck up the rest of your world like what's been done to mine. Your choice."

Wiping his nose with the back of his hand, he looked away. "Did you have sex with her?"

Sarah.

My little brother rarely surprised me, but it was admirable that he asked about Sarah in the midst of everything I'd just told him. He gained back a little of my respect after I thought he didn't really care about her. He loved her enough to hide from the truth when it was right in front of him.

Her shirt and bra were on the ground in the barn, and she was in the tack room. She didn't tell him it wasn't what he thought, because it was exactly what he thought.

Yet, there he was, bleeding out, begging for me to tell him otherwise because, in his darkest moment, he needed her. But he needed to believe that she didn't cheat on him like everyone else in his life.

That was the first time I let myself feel actual guilt.

Not regret.

Not remorse.

I did something that hurt someone else, and I felt bad,

but regretting it wasn't an option because I loved the girl. And I believed I loved her more than he did because I loved all of her.

Her fears.

Her dreams.

Her insecurities.

Her everything.

Matt loved the version of her he made up in his head.

"Yes," I whispered.

His face scrunched while he choked on his emotions. "Go," he croaked.

"There's more—"

"I DON'T WANT TO KNOW!" He stabbed his fingers into his hair, panting out of control.

I stepped toward the door. "Get ready for the funeral. After today, you won't have to see me again. But for the next few hours, we'll pull our shit together and pay our respects."

Chapter Twenty-Nine

Marvin Hamlisch, "I'll Never Leave You"

Sarah

I COULD either love God or pretend that He had a plan for all of us, but I couldn't do both because His plans didn't feel like love.

While everyone filled the church for Joanna's funeral, I sat in the old cemetery, resting against a headstone.

Walter Arnold
Beloved husband and father
1902-1974

"*You should be inside,*" Heather said, taking a seat next to me. She wore the same stone-washed denim shorts and blue Gap pocket tee she had on the day she dropped me off at the church to go to Nashville with Isaac.

"Yeah, well, you should be alive," I said after a tiny grunt.

She picked a dandelion and plucked each little yellow petal. *"Tell me about Nashville."*

I smiled. "Isaac let me sing on stage, and I didn't want to leave. There's something really special about singing to a crowd of people. Music is so much more than notes and lyrics. It's an emotion, like when something moves you so deeply or gets you so excited that you can't just speak the words; you have to sing them because you don't want people to just hear the words. You want them to feel them. Music is what happens when your body and soul speak at the same time."

Heather leaned her head back against the headstone and closed her eyes while humming. *"I love that."*

"Me too," I whispered.

She stood.

"Where are you going?"

"Joanna's making popcorn for the funeral. You know how much I love popcorn." She nodded toward the church. *"Get going. I bet your family saved you a seat."*

"Don't go," I said, quickly standing and wiping off my wrinkled dress.

"I'm not going anywhere," she said, wistfully walking away and glancing over her shoulder with a sly grin. *"But you are."* She winked. *"You're going far. Carry me with you. Sing me all of your songs. Be with the man of our dreams. Just don't be afraid."* She turned back toward the gates and kept walking.

"Afraid of what?" I tried to reach her, but she remained effortlessly out of reach.

"Letting go."

"Letting go of what?"

"The hate ... the fear ... the need to please ..." She laughed, holding her hands out to the side like an angel. *"Let it all go."*

As quickly as she appeared, she vanished.

I combed my fingers through my sticky hair. After I left Isaac, I went to McDonald's for a drink and to use the bathroom to freshen up. Then I picked up a deodorant at the pharmacy. Still, I was a mess.

As I slipped into the church, my dad finished his opening prayer with a mumbled "Amen" from Joanna's friends and family. I hadn't been friends with her as long as I had with Heather, but ten years was still a long time, and my bravery was waning by that point. I just wanted to hide somewhere far away from these people who looked at me with pity as I padded my way to the row where my mom and sisters were sitting next to the Corys.

I don't know why I didn't expect to see Isaac, but he was there, and so was Matt. They sat together with their parents in the middle separating them. Everyone in Devil's Head excelled at brushing things under the rug and plastering on fake smiles when necessary. It was small-town protocol.

But my broom was broken, and I was fresh out of plaster.

Isaac sat on the end of the aisle, so instead of squeezing past everyone's knees to reach my mom and sisters, I wedged into the ten-inch space between him and the end of the bench. I didn't look at his parents or Matt, nor did I look at my mom and sisters.

When everyone scooted in to make room for me, Isaac didn't budge, not even as my dad eyed us while quoting scripture. Isaac held his space, which meant we were touching shoulder to toe. He didn't look at me, and I didn't look at him, but I felt him. And that was enough to hold it together.

Joanna's cousin sang a song, and our friend Kennedy recited a poem. I didn't sob as I did at Heather's funeral, but with every blink, I released tears. Isaac proved to be his father's son, whether he would have liked that label or not. He handed me a neatly folded hanky. As I blotted my tears, I slid my leg around the back of his. It wasn't holding hands, but it was a close second that was more discreet.

After the final prayer, I continued to look straight ahead at the stained-glass window while the casket and family were ushered out of the church. When our row stood, everyone filed toward the middle aisle, but I turned left, fleeing down the side aisle and squeezing past an older couple exiting the double doors. If Joanna and Heather were eating popcorn without me, I would not put myself through the burial. So I ran to my car, which was parked a ways down the road. As I drove past the steep drive up to the church, Eve came out of nowhere and smacked the back of my car with her hand.

I skidded to a stop, and she hopped in the passenger's seat, breathless.

When I opened my mouth to protest, she shook her head. "Just drive."

We had an hour, maybe two, before Mom, Dad, and Gabby would be home. I parked in front of the garage. Eve and I hadn't said a word since she got into the car. I didn't know what she expected from me, and it didn't matter. All that mattered was getting out of that stupid black dress that reeked of sweat and death.

Eve followed me into the garage like my shadow. I grabbed a pack of matches and a can of gasoline that Dad used for the lawnmower. Then I headed to the back of the house where we had a burn barrel.

"What are you doing?" Eve broke her silence.

I ignored her while unzipping my dress and kicking off my shoes. I threw them into the barrel and stared at Eve. After a silent exchange, Eve removed her dress and shoes and added them to the barrel. Then I poured gasoline on everything and tossed a lit match into the bin as we took a big step back when flames engulfed the contents. After a few minutes, Eve stood behind me and wrapped her arms around my waist, resting her chin on my shoulder. There was no way to hide the obvious: I would never be the same.

We stood idle, mesmerized by the fire— bereft with a heart wrapped in grief. Eve's empathy brought about a fresh round of tears. I rested my hands on hers and whispered, "Thank you."

We stood there until the flames died. I pulled out of Eve's embrace, walked into the house, and straight to the shower. But no matter how hard I scrubbed my skin with a bar of soap, I couldn't erase what had happened. There were too many layers of despair.

With a towel wrapped around my head, I wiped the steam from the mirror and gazed at the utter disappointment staring back at me. I escaped death. Did that make me lucky or a cheater? Would Heather have left that early in the morning? Would Joanna have lived had I been there and she would have sat in the back seat?

The answers to those questions didn't change reality, but they changed my self-worth. Did God punish my friends for covering for me? Did he spare my life so that I would suffer the most?

After another minute or two of self-loathing, I sulked toward my bedroom.

"Want to feel less awful for a little bit?" Eve said,

standing in her doorway. She was wearing a T-shirt and underwear and holding a bottle of tequila.

"I knew you were the bigger rebel," I said while padding my way toward her and taking the bottle as she shut her bedroom door behind us. "Where did you get this?" I removed the lid and took a swig, coughing the second it burned my throat.

"It's best if you don't know." She grabbed the bottle and tipped it at her lips, swallowing without a single cough before passing it back to me. "I'm still a virgin, which means you're still the bigger rebel."

"About that," I sat on her bed, folding my legs under me, "Don't give it to another virgin. It's not beautiful. It's awkward and awful."

Her eyebrows climbed up her head. "You had sex with Matt?"

I nodded.

"*And* Isaac."

After another big swig, I nodded again, already feeling the tequila hitting my brain. "It's funny how with most things in life, we learn from teachers or people who are far more experienced, but with sex," I laughed, "the Bible wants us to believe that men and women should just figure it out together for the first time." I waved my hand in the air as she took the bottle from me. "Nonsense." I fell back onto her bed next to her. "Find a guy who knows what he's doing. Who loves giving you orgasms." I closed my eyes as my head began to swim. "Isaac gives *the best* orgasms."

Eve giggled. "I'm pretty good too. I touch myself all the time, but I do it in the dark under my sheets so Jesus won't see me."

We laughed and drank until I was certain we'd confessed

all of our sins to each other, knowing neither would remember the next day.

"Sarah? Eve?" Mom called from downstairs.

Thunk!

I rolled off the bed and hit the floor, scrambling to stand as I lost the towel around my head and the one around my body. Eve giggled, covering her mouth. Then I snorted as I snatched a towel off the floor and wrapped it around my waist.

"Sarah." Eve pointed to my breasts, and I looked down.

"Oops ..." I giggled again, pulling the towel over my breasts and stumbling across the hall to my bedroom.

"Sarah?" Mom yelled again.

Quickly closing and locking the door, I turned, pausing as I faced my bed, where Isaac's guitar case lay with a folded note, my cream cowboy hat, boots, and the bag of clothes he bought me.

I looked around as though I thought he was hiding somewhere.

"Sarah?" Mom knocked on my door.

I scrambled to hide everything under my bed and shoved the note into my nightstand drawer.

"Open the door, Sarah."

I held my arms out, fingers stiff like a cat falling from a tree. "Be cool," I whispered to myself. If I could just stay cool, chilled, and calm, she wouldn't know I was drunk.

"Hey," I said, opening the door.

Mom grimaced. "Where are your clothes?"

The towel!

I dropped the towel in the process of hiding the guitar, and I forgot to cover up before opening the door.

Slapping a hand over my mouth, I laughed.

Mom stepped closer. "You've been drinking. You're drunk."

I shook my head, but I couldn't stop laughing.

"Go to bed right now. If your dad finds out, he's going to be livid. This week has been unbearable for him. You, out of all people, should know that. This is disrespectful to everyone. I don't know what has gotten into you lately, young lady, but this has got to stop."

"Welp, tell that to God. Maybe he should have thought about that before He let my friends die." I tipped my chin up, making duck lips as if I had a valid point instead of an acute case of too much tequila.

"Sarah Elaine Jacobson, *you* are alive. If that's not by the grace of God, then I don't know what is."

When the door closed behind her, I stepped back until the side of my bed hit my legs, and I fell onto the mattress, closed my eyes, and surrendered to the alcohol.

Chapter Thirty

The Clash, "Should I Stay or Should I Go"

At eleven thirty, I woke up to vomit.

At midnight, I woke to the sound of Eve vomiting.

At eight the next morning, I lifted my heavy head from my pillow when I heard my parents arguing. That was a first. They didn't argue with us in the house.

There had been a lot of firsts that week. Then I remembered the guitar, and I cringed as both my head and my stomach protested upon sitting up. I opened my drawer and retrieved the note.

> TAKE YOUR TIME. BE VULNERABLE. FEEL EVERY-
> THING. THEN FIND COURAGE IN THE FACE OF FEAR. I
> LOVE YOU, SUNDAY MORNING.
> —SATAN

I laughed through my tears as I set the note aside and opened the guitar case. Then I slowly cupped a hand over my mouth. It wasn't his guitar; it was a shiny new white guitar with a silver strap and "Sunday Morning" stitched into it. When I lifted it from the case, I uncovered an envelope. Inside, there was cash—a lot of cash.

Why did he give me a guitar *and* cash? It made no sense.

After throwing on a nightshirt, I sat on the bed and played my new guitar. It wasn't long before the arguing downstairs stopped, and Mom opened my door, peeking inside and eyeing my guitar.

I paused my fingers, staring at her for a few seconds while I returned the guitar to the case with the envelope of cash. "Are you fighting about me?"

Before she could answer, my dad stepped into my room, too, and closed the door.

"I should have died," I said, latching the case.

"Don't say that," Mom said.

"It would be easier for both of you."

"Why do you think that?" Dad asked.

When I lifted my gaze to him, he kept his emotions well-guarded, unlike the day I came home from Nashville.

"I'm a whore," I said.

Mom winced as Dad's jaw clenched.

"That's what you're going to think." I blew out a defeated breath. "And I don't even care. Not anymore. Trying to please you, Matt, his parents, and God ... it's all too much." I closed my tired, swollen eyes for a few seconds. "My faith has been tested, and I'm not passing the test."

"Sarah—" My dad started.

I shook my head. "You can't fix this. Not you. Not anyone. I can't pray my way out of this awful feeling that everything I've believed about God is wrong. Is He indiscriminate or calculated? Is everything part of a grand plan or by chance? Because I can't wrap my head around the idea that I'm here by God's grace, and Heather and Joanna are not. Good people die every day, and evil people live. The *only* way I can imagine forgiving God is if I can believe that He did nothing. That He *does* nothing but give us free will to live. To make mistakes, even if they cost us everything. But if you want me to believe He has a hand in it, then I'm out. I cannot worship that kind of god."

"I know you're hurting, but it's no excuse to—"

"To what, Dad? Act out? Question God? Drink? Have sex out of wedlock? Go to Nashville with my boyfriend's brother while my friends die in a car accident?"

Dad's expression hardened as Mom covered her mouth.

"I never signed up for classes at the community college. I'm not going to college. I'm going to sing songs. Songs about sex and love. And sometimes I might drink. And I'm going to have all the sex I want. And I'm eighteen, so you can't do anything about it." I felt strong.

I felt like an adult.

"Then get out. Pack up your belongings and get out of this house," Dad said with his hands fisted at his sides and the vein on his forehead pulsing.

"Peter, no." Mom stepped in front of him. "Sarah, take a shower. And—"

"No shower." Dad grabbed my mom's arm and yanked her out of the way.

I had never seen him treat her like that, so I internally recoiled.

"Get *out* of this house immediately!" He turned, dragging Mom behind him.

"Peter!" she protested. "That is our daughter. You're not acting rationally. Just take a minute." Her voice began to fade.

"If she's going to disobey God and me, then she can suffer the consequence," he said.

With shaky hands and tattered emotions, I shoved as much as I could into my backpack, quickly dressed, and carried my bag and guitar down the stairs.

"Sarah!" Mom chased me.

I reached for my car keys that I always had on the hook by the door. Then I remembered that I might have left them in the car after the funeral the previous day.

"Sarah! Stop." Mom followed me out the door.

But when I reached my car, the doors were locked, so I turned.

Mom grabbed me and wrapped me in her arms while Dad looked on from the front porch, dangling my keys from his finger.

"It's my car, Sarah. You're eighteen. You're an adult who has sex and disrespects God. Find your own transportation," he said.

"Just apologize. Just apologize. Please apologize, Sarah," Mom whispered in my ear while crying.

"Find courage in the face of fear."

"I love you," I said softly, pulling away from my mom.

She looked utterly crestfallen, red-eyed and sobbing. I turned and trekked down the driveway to the road.

It took me two hours to walk to the Corys'. In another life where God wasn't despicably cruel, randomly plucking innocent lives from the earth, I would have walked to the neighbor's and called Heather to come get me.

But I'd never call Heather again.

The sun left me parched. I'd sweated every ounce of water from my body in the July heat. By the time I reached their door, I had nothing to lose, so I rang the doorbell.

No one answered.

"Sarah?"

I turned as Wesley trotted toward me, pulling a dirty hanky out of his pocket and wiping his forehead. Sweat burned my eyes, which were red and swollen from the tears that accompanied the anguish of my two-hour journey.

"Is Isaac here?" I sniffled.

Wesley furrowed his brow and shook his head. "Darlin', he left last night. Matt is at baseball practice, and Vi went to town for groceries. Is everything fine?"

I nodded quickly, but my emotions and the heat got the best of me. "N-no." My bottom lip quivered as I lost it.

"Oh, no. Uh ..." He took my bag and guitar from me. "Come in the house," he said, opening the door.

I pressed the back of my hand to my snotty nose and headed into the house.

"What's with all the stuff?" He set my belongings in the entry before getting me a glass of water and a box of tissues. As I sat at the kitchen table, I fought to get control of myself.

"Thank you," I murmured, taking the water and tissues. "I can't go home. I'm no longer welcome."

Wesley pulled out a chair and sat down. "I find that hard to believe."

Blowing my nose, I nodded. "It's true." Pursing my lips, I tried to calm my breathing. "Where did Isaac go?"

"Dunno."

"Is he coming back?" I drank the water, gulping down the whole glass.

Wesley took the glass to the sink and refilled it. "I don't

know that either. But if I were to take an educated guess, I'd say no." He set the glass on the table and sat across from me again.

We stared at each other for a few seconds. I couldn't imagine Isaac not coming back for me.

"Her funeral is today," I said.

His Adam's apple bobbed as the lines along his brow and at the corners of his eyes deepened, and he averted his gaze. "Yes," he whispered.

"I'm glad she's dead."

He winced before offering the tiniest nod.

"Did you love her?"

He ran a finger along a scratch on the table. "I cared about her if that's what you mean."

When I didn't respond, he risked a glance at me.

I shook my head. "You do it for love, or you don't do it at all."

He hummed. "Are you speaking from experience?"

I shrugged, wadding the dirty tissue in my hand. "I don't know. I wasn't married when I cheated." I studied his reaction, having no idea if he knew anything for certain about my weekend with Isaac. There were so many unknowns.

Did Matt tell him about the barn?

Did Vi know about Brenda?

I hated the secrets.

"Cheating?" With a slight grin, he shook his head. "Sarah, you're right. You're not married. You're a young woman finding your footing in the world. Unless you're doing something with a married man, I don't think you qualify as a cheater."

"That wouldn't make me a cheater. It would make me a homewrecker."

"I suppose." He pursed his lips. "Not all affairs wreck homes."

"How can you say that?" I canted my head to the side.

"Because I have a wife and two sons."

"And a dead mistress." As soon as I said the words, I wanted to take them back.

Wesley's eyes reddened again as he swallowed hard.

"Why?" I whispered. "Why do that to your wife? Why risk it?"

He rubbed his temples. "It's not as simple as you think."

"I'm listening."

Wesley shook his head. "I appreciate your willingness to listen. You're a good person, Sarah. Don't ever let anyone tell you otherwise. But some things are personal, complicated, and far from what they seem on the surface." He rested his elbow on the table with his chin in his hand. "You don't deserve the burden of my life or the story of my marriage. I'm a flawed man who lost my way after something happened. It's not an excuse for anything that I've done. And the pain and—" He fisted his hand at his mouth and shook his head.

The tears fell, and his body trembled.

I wasn't expecting that level of reaction. Did Vi leave him? Was it all about Brenda?

"I'm sorry," he said with a strained voice. "I'm *so* sorry."

I reached across the table and grabbed his hand. "You don't owe me an apology."

He rubbed his eyes, and the pain in them said otherwise.

"Can I ask you for a favor?"

Wesley dug his hanky out of his pocket and wiped his eyes and nose. "Anything."

"I need a ride to a motel in town."

"You can stay here."

I shook my head and chuckled. "No. I can't."

After a few seconds, he nodded. "I'll get you a room."

"I have money. I just don't have a car."

"Sarah, you really should go home."

"I didn't run away." My heart ached as I reached for the hard truth. "My dad kicked me out because I'm a flawed human."

Chapter Thirty-One

Bonnie Tyler "Total Eclipse of the Heart"

ISAAC LEFT me two thousand dollars. It was a lot, but not enough to last forever since I had to pay for a motel room and food. I waited for days to hear from him. Wesley told me he'd let me know if Isaac called or returned home.

On Monday, Vi visited me.

When I saw her through the peephole, I took a big breath and found a smile as I opened the door.

"Sarah." Vi hugged me. "How are you holding up?"

"Fine," I murmured while releasing her.

I wasn't fine.

I was lost, angry, heartbroken, grieving, and scared.

She stepped into the room, surveying my minimal belongings, takeout bags scattered around, and my guitar on the bed. "I talked with your mom. She's worried sick. Wesley didn't think it was my place to tell her your whereabouts, but as a mother, I'm having trouble with it. I told her that you're safe."

"Have you heard from Isaac?"

She narrowed her eyes, adjusting her purse on her shoulder. "No. And Matthew won't talk to me or his dad, but I gather you've broken up. Is it because of Isaac?"

I cleared off my bed and sat on the edge as she leaned against the TV console. "Matt and I broke up because ..." I shrugged. Did it matter? "We just don't share the same dreams right now." I dropped my gaze. "And I love Isaac."

"What?"

On a slow inhale, I closed my eyes, and all I could see was him.

His knuckles brushing my cheek.

His adoring gaze sweeping along my body.

He made me feel like the sun because everything about him came to life when he looked at me. Indescribable adoration.

"It happened slowly at first, so slowly I didn't see it. Then it just happened all at once. Taking my breath away. And no matter how wrong this tiny voice in my head said it was, my heart wouldn't listen. It ignored every ounce of reason. I know I should feel regretful, but I don't." I looked up at the tears in her eyes. "Maybe I'm too young to handle a love that intense, but I'm not too young to feel it." I fought my own emotions. "It's all I feel," I whispered. "And I miss him. I miss him more than I miss my family. And I'm so scared that he's not coming back because ..."

Because your husband has ruined your family.

And I'm lost.

Jobless.

Hopeless.

Godless.

Oh ... and homeless and careless.

"Isaac is a complicated young man. He leaves when things get tough. But he always returns. I just"—she bit her lip for a few seconds—"I wouldn't wait around for him. Make things right with your family. Start college. Be the amazing woman I know you are."

I wasn't her definition of amazing. And I didn't want to do anything *but* wait for Isaac.

"You don't have any idea where he went?"

"He took his trailer and horse. So my best guess is he's rodeoing."

I chewed on my thumbnail.

"Sarah, how did you leave things with Matthew?"

I paused my chewing and stared at her.

"Sweetie, he won't talk to anyone. If he's not playing baseball, he's in his room with music blaring. I've been trying to do everything since Isaac left."

The farm stand.

"Sorry." I cleared my throat. "I don't have a car."

She frowned. "What if we helped you get something?"

"I don't think Matt will want me anywhere near him."

"I think you underestimate how much he loves you."

Be vulnerable. Feel everything.

"I think you underestimate how badly I hurt him."

Vi sat next to me and held my hand. "Did you mean to hurt him?"

"No. But I knew it would hurt him, and I did it anyway. Have you ever done that? Have you ever done something that you knew would hurt someone, but you chose to do it anyway?"

"Yes," she whispered.

I didn't expect that.

Vi squeezed my hand before standing. "By the grace of God, I am what I am." She opened the door to the motel room. "We'll drop a car off later, and you can come back to work when you're ready."

WITH EACH PASSING DAY, my anger toward Isaac grew.

I didn't want a guitar; I wanted him.

How could he abandon me after everything we shared in Nashville? After I lost my two closest friends?

A week after Violet and Wesley dropped off an old truck that had been parked in the machine shed, I found the courage to leave the motel and go back to work.

When I opened the door to the truck, my mom pulled into the parking spot next to me.

"Don't cry," I whispered to myself, taking a shaky breath.

She stepped out and gently closed her door. "Hi," she said with a much calmer demeanor than the broken-down woman I left over a week earlier.

"Hi." I gave her a sad smile as she walked around the car.

She stopped a few feet from me, and I took the last two steps and hugged her.

"Sarah," she whispered on a long exhale.

When I released her, she eyed the truck. "Vi said you were going back to work."

"Yeah."

She didn't beg me to come home, which meant Dad hadn't changed his mind. I could tell from the way she fiddled with her wedding band that she was there as a mother who needed to see her daughter. It was that simple.

"Do you need anything?" she asked, pressing her fingers to the corners of her eyes.

"I could use a few more things from my room."

"Of course. I can bring them to you, or you can come to the house during the day when your dad's at the church."

I stared at the truck keys, sliding the key ring over my finger. "I'll do that."

"He'll come around."

I wasn't so sure, but I returned a nod anyway.

"Your sisters are devastated."

"Tell them I'm fine."

She pressed a finger to my chin and lifted it. "But *are* you fine?"

No.

"I have a roof over my head, a vehicle, and a job." I smiled. "What more could I need?"

Heather ... Isaac ...

"Well, I have to get to the church before the kids show up." She glanced at her watch. "Your dad has a meeting Thursday night, so he'll be home late. Why don't you come home and have dinner with me and your sisters?"

"Yeah. We'll see."

She gave me one more hug and murmured, "I love you," before turning and tucking her chin to hide her tears.

It took me a few minutes to gather my emotions and tuck them away so I could function. When I let everything in at the same time, it was too much. I could carry a brick but not a whole house.

Matt's car was in the drive. God continued to test me, and I had to go inside to get the key and the money for the farm stand. My hand shook as I knocked on the door twice before opening it.

"Good morning," Vi said. "I have cookies and loaves of bread. Can you help me carry them?"

She handed me the money pouch, key, and two bags of baked goods.

"Oh, good, you can help Sarah carry these. I need to grab a quick shower," she said, glancing over my shoulder.

I turned toward Matt, and it felt like I was falling on my sword. His expression was dead, as if I was a complete stranger or a ghost he didn't see.

Vi handed him the other bags, but I didn't wait another second. I needed to get out of the house. He followed me up the lane to the farm stand. My nervous fingers fumbled the key, and I dropped it on the ground along with the money bag. When I bent down to pick them up, a loaf of bread fell out of the bag.

"Dang it," I whispered, tossing the bread back into the bag. As soon as I stood, the whole paper bag ripped open, depositing all the baked goods onto the ground. I dropped to my knees in defeat to gather everything. Matt took the key from my hand and unlocked the door. He stepped over the mess on the ground, set the sacks on the counter, and slid past me toward the house without a word.

"No," I said.

He stopped with his back to me.

"We've been through too much for there to be *nothing* left to say." I deserted the baked goods and stood as tall as I could under the weight of that brick house.

Matt turned.

"I don't want to give you a list of reasons; they'll only sound like weak excuses that won't change what has happened," I said.

He kept his stony expression firmly in place. "It's unforgivable, Sarah."

Pastor Jacobson's daughter would have had a lineup of Bible verses about forgiveness. But I felt abandoned by my pastor *and* God, so I didn't have a sermon to offer, no divine wisdom.

"You're probably right. But I wasn't in ..." I shook my head.

"In what?" He squinted. "In love with me? We broke up, and all of your feelings vanished?"

"No," I whispered. "But it's not like we used to be. With you, I felt less than. And I was tired of fighting for you and everyone else to acknowledge that my dreams mattered."

"I told you they did."

"No. You begrudgingly acknowledged them when we fought. That's my point. I was tired of fighting, tired of begging, tired of jumping up and down saying, 'Hey! Look! I have dreams too!' So, imagine how it felt when someone who shared my dreams looked at me like I was special and deserving. Like I was the only one in the room. Like everything I did made him smile." I wiped tears from my cheeks. "Matt, we were over."

"Anyone." He clenched his jaw. "Anyone but my brother."

"That's not how life works."

He grunted. "It is, actually. It's called self-control. You just close your knees, Sarah. It's that simple."

I tried not to react, but I couldn't help but flinch. "What do you want me to say?" I whispered.

"I want you to admit that you're a terrible person."

I swallowed. "I'm a terrible person."

"You should have been in that car with Heather and Joanna."

I blinked, and a fresh round of tears escaped. "I should have been in the car with them."

His face morphed with ugly pain, blue eyes streaked red. "Fuck you," he whispered, wiping his eyes. "Stop agreeing with me. Stop making me sound like a monster. I'm not the monster." His fingers curled into his hair, and he tugged at it.

I took a few more steps and rested my hand on his back. He jerked away.

"I should have told you. I tried to protect everyone except you, and I'm truly sorry for that."

Losing Matt, my friend, felt like its own death. I was *so* sorry for the pain I'd caused, but I didn't regret Isaac. And those two facts were hard to reconcile.

"I'm not coming back." He wiped his eyes and stared at me. "When I leave in August, I'm not coming back. I hate my parents. I hate this town. And ..."

"You hate me."

He leered over my shoulder with watery eyes. "I don't hate you. I actually love you. But I just don't want to see you again."

As Matt turned and headed towards the house, he gripped my heart and clenched it.

Tearing ... tearing ... tearing.

I did not hold back the tears. He stopped, angling his head a fraction toward his shoulder until his chin nearly touched it.

"But maybe someday," he said.

I closed my eyes, pressing my quivering lips together.

Someday. Maybe someday he'll forgive me.

Chapter Thirty-Two

Phil Collins, "Against All Odds"

MY CONFIDENCE WANED. Everything Isaac brought out of me started to dissolve with each passing day. Had he cheated on me and ended it, I would have felt less pain than the uncertainty of abandonment.

"Sarah!" Eve and Gabby barreled down the porch stairs when I arrived for dinner Thursday night.

"Oof!" I laughed as they hugged me at the same time.

"Please say you're staying," Gabby begged, taking my hand and pulling me toward the house as Eve grabbed my empty backpack that I needed to refill.

"I'm staying for dinner," I said.

"That's not what I mean." Gabby huffed.

"What's it like living in a motel?" Eve asked as we stepped into the house.

"Sometimes it's nice. But sometimes it's lonely."

"Sweetie, I'm so glad you made it." Mom wiped her hand on her pink apron before hugging me. "I made tuna noodle casserole, your favorite."

"With extra potato chips?"

She laughed, releasing me. "Of course."

I darted my gaze around the entry.

"He's working," Mom reassured me.

"Do you need help? If not, I'll go pack up more of my stuff."

Mom's smile faded. "Gabby's helping set the table. Do what you need."

"Okay." I headed up the stairs, and Eve followed me. "How much trouble did you get into for the tequila?" I asked, tossing the bag onto my bed.

"Enough." She wrinkled her nose. "I'm grounded for a month, and I have to clean the wax off the church floor under the candelabras."

I grinned, but it was bittersweet—a memory of Heather that I didn't want to forget, even if it was a reminder that she was gone.

"But Dad said if I show I'm trustworthy, I'll get your car."

I grunted while shaking my head. "Save all the money you can. You're going to need it when he kicks you out in a couple of years and gives that car to Gabby." I riffled through my closet.

"What makes you think I'll get kicked out?"

I laughed. "You're sixteen, and you had a stash of alcohol in your room. You've already said you can't wait to have sex. I was way more disciplined at your age."

"You mean obedient?" She plopped onto my bed.

"I suppose I do." I glanced over my shoulder, fighting the urge to react to her devilish grin.

"You look so sad." Her smile melted into a frown.

I hugged several shirts and two pairs of jeans. "He left me," I whispered.

"Isaac?"

I nodded.

"What do you mean? He broke up with you or left town?"

I set some old clothes on the bed along with the new ones from Isaac. "He bought me a new guitar. It's beautiful. And he left a note with cash." I wrinkled my nose. "A lot of cash. But that's it. No one knows where he went. It felt like a goodbye. A 'good luck,' but goodbye."

"Do you think he left you money because he knew Dad would kick you out?"

I shook my head. "That makes little sense. Nobody predicted that."

"Well, he has to show back up. Right?"

"I don't know." I tucked the folded clothes into my bag.

"What are you going to do? How long can you live in a motel?"

"I don't—" I choked, biting my lips together as tears burned my eyes.

"Sarah, he'll come back." Eve stood and hugged me.

I fell apart, fat tears falling down my face as my heart bled in her arms. "W-why did h-he leave m-me?" I cried.

"I don't know," she whispered. "But he has to come back. He loves you. He carried you out of a funeral. That's the ending to all the great love stories."

I laughed through my tears while releasing her and

wiping my eyes. "I don't know about that," I sniffled. "But he's a dream. And maybe that's all he is."

"Come on. Let's eat. Gabby and I made an apple pie."

"I like cherry," I said, following her.

"Apple is the only real pie. It's the American pie."

Eve made me smile, and I needed to feel something akin to joy again.

We sat down to dinner, and Mom said a prayer as we held hands. She asked God to heal the relationship between me and my father. I wasn't sure if she was talking to me or God.

"This looks amazing. Thanks, Mom," I scooped up a generous serving of casserole.

"I'm sure you're tired of McDonald's." She eyed me with a hint of disapproval as if I had much of a choice.

"Have you heard from any of my grandparents?" I asked, making small talk.

"Your dad's parents are planning a visit next month. And my mom has eye surgery next week, so your sisters and I are driving to Tulsa for a few days to help my dad take care of things."

"Tulsa's on the list," Gabby said.

"What list?" Mom asked after serving herself and setting the spoon on the edge of the casserole dish.

"The list I found on Sarah's floor when you made me vacuum her room."

Everyone looked at me, but I did not know what she was talking about.

Gabby sighed. "I set it on your desk." She pushed back in her chair. "I'll go get it."

"I think you should come to church this weekend," Mom mumbled, wiping her mouth.

"Because Dad can't yell at me in front of the congregation?"

"So he can see you're making an effort," she mumbled.

"What about him? Doesn't he have to make an effort?"

"I think it would have a more significant effect if he saw you taking the first step."

I didn't feel that forgiving yet.

"Here," Gabby said, setting the list on the table beside me before plopping back down in her chair.

It was a list of dates and locations in Isaac's handwriting.

Mom craned her neck to look at it. "That Tulsa address is for the fairgrounds."

Rodeos.

Violet was right. Isaac was traveling to rodeos, and he didn't abandon me. He left me with a list to find him and money to get there.

"It must have fallen out of the guitar case, and I didn't see it," I whispered.

"What?" Mom asked.

I shook my head. "Nothing."

"What is it? Whose handwriting is that? It's not yours," she prodded.

My gaze lifted to Eve's wide eyes and parted lips. Then I refocused on the dates. Springfield was in two days, and it was only a two-and-a-half-hour drive from Devil's Head.

With a shrug, I eyed my mom. "I won't be at church this weekend."

She stared at the note again and closed her eyes in realization. "Isaac," she whispered.

"I love him."

"Until you get pregnant or worse." Pain lined her face.

I slowly shook my head. "I'd still love him."

"Even if he breaks your heart?"

I folded the piece of paper. "Heartbreak is unavoidable if you let yourself fall in love."

Friday morning, I tracked down Wesley. He was feeding the sheep, sweat already dripping from his forehead as he glanced up at me.

"Hey," I smiled. "I have a big favor to ask." I wasn't happy with him, but he'd been nice to me, so I didn't have it in me to hate him completely.

"Anything." He tossed a bucket of feed into the bin.

On one hand, it was awful and gross that Brenda had a relationship with someone so much older than her. But when I looked at Wesley, it was easy to see what Isaac would look like one day—a handsome man with broad shoulders, a strong jaw, thick hair, and intense eyes. And he was kind, even if Violet might not have found his affair so kind.

"I love your son."

He glanced up at me again, brushing off his gloves and tugging at the fingers to remove them. "Need I ask which one?"

"The one that's going to be in Springfield at the rodeo tomorrow, and I want to go see him. But I don't have a car."

Wesley nodded several times. "I see. So you want to take the truck I loaned you to Springfield?"

"Yeah," I said softly, wrinkling my nose.

"When will you be back? You have work on Monday."

I thought about lying, but I couldn't handle any more lies. "I don't know when I'll be back."

He lifted an eyebrow and crossed his arms over his chest.

"So you want to borrow my truck for an undetermined amount of time while leaving my farm stand unattended, so you can chase after a boy and his horse?"

Biting my thumbnail, I nodded.

Maybe I should have told one more lie. Did it matter at that point?

"Do your parents know?"

"My mom does."

"And she's okay with it?"

"Mr. Cory, I'm eighteen. My parents kicked me out of the house. I think your permission is the only one I need since I do, in fact, *need* to borrow your truck."

After a few seconds, he stepped past me to the water spigot. "If anyone asks, I only gave you permission to use it until Sunday."

I grinned.

Chapter Thirty-Three

Journey, "Faithfully"

I MAPPED out my trip to Springfield and laid the highlighted map on the passenger's seat next to me with my guitar and two bags of clothes shoved onto the floor.

After I arrived in Springfield, I grabbed lunch at KFC and drove to the fairgrounds, where workers were setting up for the rodeo. I was four hours early, and Isaac's truck wasn't anywhere in sight, so I parked in a shady spot, ate my lunch, and spent the afternoon playing my guitar, scribbling lyrics into my notebook, and catching a nap.

Eventually, the parking lot filled in around me, and people funneled toward the gates. I put on the cowboy hat and boots Isaac bought me and got in line. The stands and crowd were five times the size of Devil's Head's rodeo.

Bright lights.

Music.

And not a familiar soul in sight.

I found a place to sit at the far end, way up in the stands, surrounded by loud fans drinking beer and having a good time. For the next hour, I nervously watched the events. What if I was wrong? What if Isaac accidentally left that list in his guitar case, and it wasn't for me? It wasn't a map of his planned travels? Maybe he wasn't going to every rodeo on the list. Maybe he wasn't going to any of them.

With a fake smile and a hand on my nervous stomach, I watched the first roper come out of the gate. Then the next ... and the next.

Until, he was there.

My heart exploded into tiny pieces of confetti, and I wanted to run into the arena and hug him. It was the first time I watched the whole thing, even when he tied the calf and headed back to his horse with a smile for the crowd while he adjusted his black cowboy hat.

"Excuse me. Pardon me. Oops. Sorry." I made my way out of the stands and ran toward the trucks and trailers. There were *so* many, and they all started to look the same.

"Nice job!"

I turned as a woman down one of the rows jogged toward a guy—toward Isaac—while he loaded his horse into the trailer. I inhaled, and it made my grin swell as I headed toward his truck. But then I stopped because the brunette threw her arms around his neck and he hugged her back, lifting her off the ground. That's when his gaze met mine, so I turned on my heel and walked away as fast as possible, hoping he didn't notice it was me. After all, I wore a hat, and the sun had begun to set, leaving that part of the fairgrounds rather dark.

"Sarah?"

He saw me, so I took off running, losing my hat. When I turned to grab it, he was gaining on me, so I abandoned the hat and trucked my way toward the nearest exit.

I was not his girl. I was just *a* girl like Danielle and probably a long list of others. My parents would be waiting to say, "I told you so," but I wasn't going home. I didn't know where I would go, but not home.

"Sarah, stop."

Oof! Ouch!

I tripped. *Stupid boots!*

Gravel pierced my hands and bruised my knees, dirtying my jeans.

"Are you okay? What are you doing?" Isaac asked, reaching for me with one hand while he held my hat in his other hand.

"Don't touch me!" I rolled onto my butt and kicked at the dirt to get away from him so I could stand and keep running. But my hands stung, and they were bleeding in a few places as I hugged them to my chest and fought the tears.

"She's my cousin. Well, second cousin. She lives here in Springfield," Isaac said, eyes wide and unblinking as if I were a spooked animal.

I swallowed past the sob in my throat because my hand hurt, and so did my pride.

He squatted in front of me, holding my hat between his spread knees. "Are you hurt?"

With a quivering lower lip, I nodded.

"Let me see."

I held out my hands, wincing from the pain.

"Baby," he squinted, "you have a piece of broken glass wedged into your palm."

I couldn't hold it back any longer. I released a sob. "It

hurts. And I left everything and everyone to be with you, and then I thought you were ..."

"I'm not cheating on you," he said, setting my hat on my head and lifting me into his arms. "Let's get you fixed up." Isaac carried me to his truck, where his cousin was waiting.

"Nicole, this is Sarah. She tripped. Can you grab the first aid kit under my seat?"

"Sure." Nicole retrieved the kit before moving so he could lift me into the passenger's seat.

I felt stupid for assuming he was cheating on me. Stupid for running. Stupid for tripping. And stupid because his cousin was meeting me for the first time when I was having a breakdown.

"This is going to hurt," Isaac said, pouring hydrogen peroxide onto my hands.

"Ouch!" I seethed.

"Sorry." He looked up at me for a second before removing the glass and gravel.

"Can I get you anything else?" Nicole asked.

"We're good. Thanks." Isaac looked back at her with a kind smile.

"Okay. Well, I'm meeting a few friends. Are you staying at the house again? You're both welcome."

"Not tonight," he murmured, returning his focus to my hands.

"Well, I'll see you in the morning when you pick up your horse," she said, resting her hand on his shoulder. "Nice to meet you, Sarah. Sorry about your hands."

I sniffled and murmured a tight "thanks" because every time Isaac removed something from my hand, it hurt. After he got the rocks and glass out of it, he applied an ointment and wrapped gauze around them. I looked like a boxer.

Then he looked up at me again. "Sunday Morning," he whispered, taking my face in his hands and wiping my tears before kissing me.

I was such a fool in love.

A young woman with so many painful lessons to learn.

But all that mattered was Isaac's lips were on mine.

He pulled back an inch and smiled. "Hi."

I laughed despite an extra round of unshed tears waiting to be released. "Hi."

"Let's drop Anakin off at my uncle's for the night, then get a motel room. Where are you parked? We'll get your bag and come back tomorrow for your car."

I eased out of the truck. "I don't have a car. Your dad loaned me the old gray truck."

"What happened to your car?" He wrapped his arm around my shoulders and walked with me toward the parking lot.

"My dad kicked me out of the house. And he took my car, *his* car." I fought to keep it together. I didn't need to tell him I walked for hours in the heat to his house.

"Why? Because of me?"

"Because I lost my cool and said everything I'd been feeling. And I said it all at once without sugarcoating anything. So I've been staying at a motel because I thought ..."

He stopped to face me. "You thought what?"

"It's so stupid. The list of rodeos must have fallen out, and I didn't see it. So I thought you just left. Then Gabby found it and showed it to me." I dropped my gaze, ashamed of how hurt I was over something he didn't do.

"You thought I left you with nothing but a guitar and some cash?"

Keeping my chin tucked, I nodded.

"Look at me."

I slowly lifted my gaze.

"You belong with me. Got it?"

"Say it again," I whispered with a grin.

"You belong," he ducked his head, lips brushing mine, "with me." He kissed me.

ISAAC SHOWERED while I gingerly used my fingers to undress and slip into an oversized T-shirt that I used as a swimsuit cover-up and pajamas.

"I'm still not okay with you tying up baby cows," I said when he emerged from the bathroom with a white towel around his waist and a few rivulets of water on his chest.

"But?" he said, digging through his bag for a pair of briefs.

"But what?"

He looked over his shoulder. "It sounded like there was a 'but' coming next. Like, *but* you love watching me rope. *But* the rodeo is growing on you. Or I'm growing on you."

"No buts." I bit back my grin as my legs dangled from the side of the bed.

He turned, adjusting his towel. I stared at his abs and the trail of hair that dipped beneath the towel.

"Why are you chewing on your lip?" he asked.

"Just thinking."

"About?"

I shrugged. "Just wondering if you have any condoms?" I risked a glance up at him as my cheeks filled with heat.

His dark eyes left me breathless every time he looked at me without saying anything.

I blinked first.

Isaac grinned and nodded. "Will I need one soon?"

Damn!

He was so sexy. I was way out of my league, but just like standing on that stage in Nashville, I faked every ounce of confidence.

Digging my teeth into my lower lip again, I nodded.

"Your move, baby." He stepped closer, his legs straddling my right knee.

My heart pounded; there was no way he didn't hear it.

"Wrap me around your little finger," he said, ghosting his knuckles along my cheek.

My eyes drifted shut for a breath before I tugged on his towel, and it fell to the floor. His erection bobbed right in front of me. With my bandaged hands at my sides, I leaned forward, eyes locked on his as I licked it.

He grinned, and so did I.

Isaac's patience with my inexperience was commendable.

"You know the rule," he said. "If you lick it, then it's yours."

I softly chuckled before taking the head into my mouth.

He closed his eyes, lips parted. After a few seconds of letting me toy with him like a cat with a ball of yarn for the first time, he brushed my hair away from my eyes. "Lift your arms."

I lifted them.

Isaac removed my shirt and tossed it aside; then he slowly removed my underwear. When he brought them to his nose, my whole body blushed, which made him grin. He set them on the bed with his bag and pulled out a condom.

As he tore it open and rolled it on, I cleared my throat. "I'm still not okay with you tying up baby cows."

He looked up from his erection as he finished rolling on the condom and gave me a lifted eyebrow.

I grinned. "*But* when you're on your horse, looking hotter than any guy I have ever seen, all I can think about is this."

Isaac's mouth twitched. "When I'm roping, it makes you want to have sex with me?"

"Very much so," I whispered, staring at his erection.

"Well, fuck, baby," he sat on the bed and grabbed my butt, pulling me between his legs. "I'm going to do nothing but rope and bury myself inside of you for the rest of my life." He sucked my nipple into his mouth.

I teased the tips of my fingers through his hair. It didn't take him long to get me so turned on that I pushed at his shoulders, making him lie back so I could straddle him, slowly letting him fill me.

"Sarahhh ..." He *sang*, before biting his lower lip to hide his grin while he gripped my hips and rocked into me.

"I love you," I whispered, ghosting my fingertips along the tattoos on his arms for a few seconds before closing my eyes.

I still told myself I hated sex, except with Isaac. Loving a man who made everything beautiful felt like the right path in the direction of happiness.

Chapter Thirty-Four

Prince and The Revolution, "Purple Rain"

Isaac

"SHE'S ASLEEP," I said in a quiet voice, sitting on the edge of the motel bed with the phone to my ear. The last time I talked with my mom, she told me to call in the evening so I could talk to Dad, but he had nothing to say. So we sat on the line in silence.

Sarah and I left the gray truck in Springfield at my uncle's place while we spent the rest of July and all of August traveling to rodeos. Sometimes, I had a place to leave Anakin for the night so we could get a motel, and other times we camped under the stars with him at the fairgrounds. It didn't matter where we were as long as I had her in my arms.

While she struggled with her faith, I never felt more blessed. Had my parents not made their mistakes, I would have headed for Nashville or L.A. after high school. I wouldn't have returned to sit in the back of the church on Easter to fall in love.

Rodeoing with Sarah in the stands made life exponentially brighter. Before the gate opened and Anakin took off after the calf, I always found my Sunday Morning in the stands. She'd blow me a kiss, but she never watched me tie-up the calf.

And for some reason, that made me love her more.

My girl was a lover, a dreamer, and a nurturer. The second we got to our motel or set up our tent, she called me her sexy cowboy and ripped off my clothes. After making love for hours, she played her guitar, wearing nothing but my cowboy hat.

"Now that Matt's settled at college, your mom and I are moving," Dad broke the silence. "So if you want to buy me out instead—"

"I don't." I rubbed my temples. "Just sell everything."

"I thought you loved this ranch as much as I did? It's been in our family for generations. I'd really love it if you'd buy me out and run it."

"Listen, if that ranch was ever my dream, it's not now." I glanced over my shoulder at Sarah's hair across my pillow, her soft lips parted and long lashes resting on her tan cheek. The bedsheet lay at her waist, and her dark red nipples begged me to tease them with my tongue. "Sarah wants to live in Nashville."

"But what do you want?"

I shook my head, rubbing the tension from my neck. "Don't you think it's a little late to be asking me this? But I suppose better late than never. So, if you really want to know, I want to spend the rest of my life with this woman. I want to watch her put her feet on my dash while jotting down lyrics to songs on fast food bags. I want to fall asleep to her playing the guitar. I want to get drunk on the outpouring of love from crowds of people when they hear her sing. And I want to die in her eyes while she smiles at me every time I look at her."

"Son ..."

"Don't do this. You don't have to. If you and Mom have worked through your *stuff* and Matty's happy, then I don't care to hold a grudge. I'm just tired of being part of it. I'm tired of the secrets. If you've come clean to everyone else, then please don't try to make things right with me. Just sell it all, give me what's mine, and let it go."

"What about forgiveness? If your mom can forgive me, can you? Do you think Matt can forgive me?"

"I'm not Matt. And for me, it's not about forgiveness; it's about acceptance. And that takes time. You have to give me time."

"Time," he echoed. "And Sarah's family?"

"She calls home when she knows her dad is at the church."

"I've talked to him. If she would just come home, I think he's ready to make amends, ready to give her another chance."

I chuckled. "Another chance at what? Being the daughter he wants her to be?"

"She's eighteen."

"Yeah, well, so was Danielle. At least Sarah's not getting knocked up by a married man."

"Babe," Sarah said with a raspy voice as she touched my back.

"I gotta go. Sell the land." I hung up the phone and lay beside her, pulling her into my arms.

"Who were you talking to?" She nuzzled her face in my neck.

"My dad."

"You were talking about Danielle?"

"Don't worry about it." I kissed her head.

"I'm not worried about it. I just want you to tell me why you were talking about her."

"Are you sure you want to talk?" I snaked my hand between her naked legs.

"Isaac, don't do that." She wiggled away from me and sat with her legs crossed and the sheet held over her chest. "Tell me."

I rolled to my back and folded my hands on my chest while staring at the ceiling. "We'll talk about this now and then never again. Okay?"

After a few seconds, she murmured, "Okay."

"I didn't get Danielle pregnant." I proceeded to tell her about the affairs, Matt's biological father, and how I acquired fifty-percent ownership in the ranch. Then I shut off the light and went to sleep.

THE NEXT MORNING, I went for a jog instead of reaching for a much-needed cigarette. By the time I returned, Sarah was dressed and packed.

"Where to next?" She grinned, eating a frosted toaster pastry on the bed.

I peeled off my shirt. "We're getting Anakin and heading home."

She stopped mid-chew as more crumbs fell onto the bed.

"I have to take care of a few things before we pack the rest of our belongings."

"Then where are we going?"

"Someplace you can sing your heart out every night." I stepped into the bathroom.

"Nashville?" Her voice jumped a full octave.

I grinned, turning on the shower.

"Are we going to *live* there?" she asked, standing in the doorway.

I tossed my shorts and briefs onto the floor and stepped into the shower. "If you want to."

"Isaac! Oh my gosh! I can't wait to tell Hea—"

I winced while washing my hair. Then I quickly soaped the rest of my body, rinsed, and dried off.

She was outside of our second-story room, resting her arms on the railing that overlooked the parking lot. I stepped into my jeans and opened the door.

Sarah sniffled, quickly wiping her eyes.

"Tell Eve. You said the two of you have gotten closer," I said.

"I want to tell Heather," she murmured in a weak voice. "I want to tell her how much I love you. I want to tell her I've been living my dream. I want to tell her about the bull that got loose at the last rodeo and scared everyone to death. I want to tell her about those tacos we had last week that were the best tacos I've ever had."

Pulling her back to my chest, I dipped my head and kissed her neck. "I think you just did."

"It's so unfair." She hugged my arms.

Chapter Thirty-Five

Whitney Houston, "Saving All My Love For You"

Sarah

MATT DIDN'T TELL ME.

I replayed our last exchange. What would I have said or done differently had I known about Violet's affair? Was I a terrible person?

My friends were dead. I destroyed my boyfriend when he was on the precipice of having his whole world turned upside down. What made me special?

Why did I get to ride off into the sunset and live out my dreams?

"You're awfully quiet," Isaac said as we reached the outskirts of Devil's Head.

"It's just ..." I shook my head.

"Just what?" He rested his hand on my leg.

I kept my gaze out the window. "This isn't how I imagined things going. I didn't think I'd have to choose between a man and my family. I didn't think I'd break Matt's heart. And I definitely didn't imagine my selfishness leading to the loss of lives."

"You weren't driving that car. Brenda was."

"No," I whispered, "I wasn't. But we would not have left our camping trip that early. I chose to go to Nashville with you. So ..." I bowed my head and closed my eyes for a moment. "I went from being a people-pleaser to not caring about anyone but myself."

"Stop."

"It's true."

Isaac pulled over along the side of the road and put the truck in *Park*. "Do you regret going to Nashville? Is this my fault too?"

"No. Yes." I shook my head a half dozen times. "It's not that simple."

"It is, Sarah. It's that simple. You can't live with regret over something that you can't change."

"Yes! I can." I opened the door and hopped out, walking along the side of the road with my head bowed and my hands on my hips.

Isaac followed me. "Just stop."

"What if this *is* my punishment?" I breathed faster, feeling on the verge of hyperventilating. "What if this is my lesson? Heather. Joanna. Matt. And now your dad is selling the land, which means my parents will have to move. How is this not my fault?" I stopped, pressing my hands to the side of my head. "I let you tempt me. I let you make me think nothing mattered more than what I wanted in life. If I just would have listened to my gut, everything wouldn't have fallen apart. They'd be alive. Matt would not hate me, and he wouldn't know about the affair. It's *all* my fault." I stared at Isaac with wide eyes drowning in tears as I covered my mouth with a sob.

He deflated, pinching the bridge of his nose as several cars sped by us. "You mean it's *my* fault. Just fucking say it." Blowing out a long breath, he looked at the sky for a brief moment. "Do you think I wanted to like my brother's girl-friend? The pastor's daughter? Do you think I did this for any other reason than I simply fell for you from the moment you smiled at me on Easter Sunday?" He shrugged. "Yeah. Maybe I'm selfish. Maybe after giving up everything for everyone else, I wanted something for myself. But fuck, baby"—his eyes reddened—"I want you." He pressed his hand to his chest, clawing at it. "I feel it so damn deep in my heart *nothing* else matters. And if that's selfish, then I'm guilty. If you need me to take the blame for everything that's happened, I'll bear the burden. I'll take everything as long as that includes you."

He took my face in his hands and wiped the pads of his thumbs along my wet cheeks. "I can't bring them back. But if you give me the chance, I'll make everything else right. Can you give me that chance?"

I couldn't hear my own thoughts around Isaac. My heart always beat too loudly, too quickly. With him so close to me, there weren't thoughts, only feelings. "Yes," I whispered.

※

"Go in the house. It's hot," Isaac said as I watched him put Anakin in the barn.

"I'll wait."

He grinned. "Matt is in Michigan. My dad is probably

on a horse somewhere or covered in grease fixing a tractor. And if my mom is inside, she'll be thrilled to see you."

I relinquished a tiny nod, retrieved my bags and guitar from the truck, and sulked toward the house. Why would Violet be thrilled to see me? I broke Matt's heart. Did falling in love with Isaac make up for that? After all, she did say she hoped he'd find a nice girl like me.

Maybe we'd bond over our commonality: we were cheaters.

But I wasn't supposed to know that. I promised Isaac we would never discuss it again, not with each other nor anyone else.

"Hey, young lady."

I turned just before reaching the front door.

Violet walked toward me in her overalls, boots, and a basket of eggs hooked over her arm. She set it down and hugged me.

"Hi." I stiffened as she hugged me.

She rested her hands on my shoulders, holding me at arm's length. "You need to go home. Your mom is beside herself, missing you something fierce."

I returned a sad smile.

"Your dad misses you too." She winked, releasing me and grabbing the basket.

I followed her into the house.

"I suppose Isaac told you we're moving to North Carolina."

"He did." I toed off my shoes and set my stuff by them.

"We're building a cabin in the mountains outside of Ashville." She sounded excited. "It would be a fresh start after years of running this ranch." She breathed a contented sigh while setting the basket on the counter and washing her hands. "Lord knows we *need* a fresh start."

"I'm sure you'll love it." I tried to infuse enthusiasm into my words.

It was awkward talking about them moving because they had to sell the land to give Isaac his half. And surely, she assumed I knew why Isaac owned half the land.

"What about you?" She dried her hands.

"We're ... I'm ..." I fumbled my words. "Nashville. I want to live in Nashville so I can sing."

Violet's smile was genuine, unlike mine. She seemed at peace with everything. Perhaps it was an act, and if so, it was a good one. "I know you'll be a star. And you'll only be a five-hour drive from us and even less to come back here to visit your parents." Violet retrieved a cutting board from the drawer and dumped a bowl of potatoes into the sink.

She made it all sound so normal like my friends didn't die, no one cheated on anyone, and my dad hadn't kicked me out of his house.

"Yeah," I murmured.

"Are you staying for dinner? I could invite your family over."

"No," I said quickly.

Violet paused, lifting her head.

I folded my hands behind me, pressing my lips together while cringing. "Sorry. I don't mean to sound ungrateful for the offer, but I don't think a group dinner should be my first face-to-face encounter with my parents in over six weeks."

"Of course. When are you heading home? Will you be staying for dinner?"

"Um ..."

Isaac opened the back door and removed his boots. The

second he peeked around the corner, Violet dropped the knife and headed straight to him for a hug. He had his bag over his shoulder and his guitar in his right hand.

"I missed you."

"You too," he said.

He had as much right (if not more) to be mad at his parents as I did to be mad at mine. Yet, he felt comfortable walking into his childhood home. He didn't hesitate to hug his mom.

Was he demonstrating his age and maturity, or was I an awful daughter who feared going home?

"Let's take our stuff upstairs," Isaac said, winking at me.

"Of course, you are welcome to stay in Matt's room, but I really hope you go home and let your family see you," Violet said, cutting the potatoes.

"We'll take the temperature of that water after dinner," Isaac said, nodding to my stuff. "For now, let's take our things upstairs." He set his bag and guitar in his room and turned just as I set my stuff down. "Matty's room." He nodded behind me.

I gawked as he carried my stuff to Matt's room.

"So much for being adults," I mumbled.

Isaac chuckled after depositing my stuff on the floor at the foot of the bed. "We won't be here long. No need to rock the boat."

"I'm drowning. I don't even see the boat." While I surveyed the room, an unexpected loneliness washed over me despite Isaac standing so close. I missed Matt because we were friends first, and I wanted to believe we would always be friends. But that seemed unlikely, and that hurt.

"He's fine," Isaac said, bringing my attention back to him. "He's doing what he loves."

"I didn't say anything."

"You didn't have to."

I managed a melancholy smile. "And what am I doing?" It was a rhetorical question.

Isaac pulled me to him, sliding his fingers into my back pockets. "You're doing what you love."

"Singing?"

"I was going to say me, but that works too."

I snorted, and it felt good because everything felt good with Isaac.

"Do you want to go see your parents now or after dinner?"

"I don't."

"You do, baby. You're just afraid." He pecked at my lips and bit my lower one, holding it hostage until I grinned and pulled away. "The question is, what are you afraid of?"

I looked to the side, glancing out the window at the oak tree. "I'm afraid they'll confirm all the awful things I already feel about myself."

"Then they're liars, and you're a liar because Sarah Sunday Morning is remarkable and kind. She's an extraordinary talent with great tits."

I shot my wide-eyed gaze to his.

He shrugged. "Just stating facts."

With a slight chuckle, I shook my head. "Take me home."

"Are you sure?"

"Yeah," I said. "It's time."

Chapter Thirty-Six

Gloria Gaynor, "I Will Survive"

"I NEED TO DO THIS ALONE." I rested my hand on Isaac's when he parked in our driveway.

"I won't stay, but I'm walking you to the door. I'm not dropping you off and slinking away like a coward," he said.

My nerves were shot, but Isaac made me feel a little less like the world was about to end.

As we walked to the door, he held my hand. I opened it slowly, and my mom poked her head around the corner from the kitchen.

"Sarah," she gasped, untying her apron while running toward me.

I stumbled backward a few steps when she hugged me. "Hey, Mom." As I gazed over her shoulder, my dad appeared in his dress slacks, white button-down shirt, and tie.

My bravery wavered while my mom released me. Then Isaac took my hand again.

Dad focused on our hands, brow furrowed. "Isaac, I need to talk to my daughter alone," he said.

"I'm aware. Before I go, you need to know that I love her. And as hard as it is for you to accept, she's alive because I convinced her to go to Nashville with me. I took care of her because nothing or no one is as precious to me as her. And while she's been grieving the loss of her friends, I've been thanking God every day for her life. And when we move to Tennessee, and my parents sell all of the land, I want you to know that I plan to ensure that your name is on this property as well as the house."

My dad's brow wrinkled in confusion, and my mouth hung open. Was he giving my parents the house and the lot out of his share?

"It's time for you to go, Isaac," my dad said with a stony expression, being a stubborn father more than a humble man of God.

"Call me later to come get you," Isaac said, pressing his palm to my cheek while kissing me.

I couldn't believe he was doing it right in front of my father. Isaac loved me without shame or fear. Everything he did was like nobody else had ever done. His love was almost too big for my young, foolish heart.

"She's staying here. No need to come get her," Dad said.

"My stuff is at Isaac's house."

"We'll get it later." Dad eyed Isaac instead of me.

But Isaac didn't flinch. After six years as an MP, it took a lot to make him cower. As he walked out the door, I felt naked. He'd been my home for six weeks, and in his arms is where I felt most secure. The house I stood in felt like a stranger's home. I barely knew the girl who used to live there.

"Where are Eve and Gabby?" I asked Mom because I wasn't as brave as Isaac. I still cowered under my father's scrutinizing gaze.

"They ran to the store to grab a few things for the rest of the soup," Mom said. "Are you okay?" She offered a hesitant smile. "Was Isaac good to you?"

I narrowed my eyes. Did she think he would hurt me? "Yes. We're in love. And we're moving to Nashville. And—"

"Sarah, let's go out back before you dig yourself into a hole again." Dad nodded toward the deck door. He didn't wait. It was just expected that I would follow—I would obey.

Mom squeezed my hand. "Just listen to him. Be patient. This has been terribly hard on him."

I returned a slight nod before heading to the deck.

"Have a seat." Dad pointed to the folding chair facing his.

I sat with my arms crossed over my chest, then I quickly unfolded them to appear open to his words, even though I knew I was going to be with Isaac no matter what.

"Does your mom need to get a pregnancy test from the pharmacy?"

My mouth opened to protest his implied accusations that Isaac was the guy who got girls pregnant and drove them to get abortions. I promised not to say anything about the truth, but it was hard because I wanted to defend him. So I returned a headshake.

"You're living in sin and throwing your life away."

Swallowing hard, I nodded. "You're right. It is my life."

He gazed off into the distance, the sun setting over acres of farmland. "It's not too late to do the right thing. You could still enroll in community college. Everyone in the choir misses you. And I want to forgive you."

I wanted to forgive him too, but he was making it impossible.

"I'm moving to Nashville with Isaac."

"How will you support yourself?"

I shrugged. "I'll be with Isaac. And I can get a job during the day so I can perform at night."

He rubbed his temples. "What happens when he finds someone else? Will you come crawling back to us?"

"What makes you think he's going to leave me?"

Dad grunted. "Don't be naive. I love you. I see all the things that make you a wonderful young woman, but that's not what he sees. And he's going to get bored and move on to the next young woman who's vulnerable and ..."

"Naive? Stupid? Gullible?" I laughed, shaking my head. "Wow. What's harder to believe? That a guy would want to be with me for the right reasons or that Isaac isn't a monster who preys on young women?"

"He smokes, drinks, and yes, gets young women pregnant."

"He quit smoking," I said, even though he occasionally sneaked one when he was really stressed.

"So he just still drinks and impregnates women."

I fisted my hands at my sides and gave him a fake smile. "I've been singing. And I love it. I'm happy."

"Heather and—" He pressed his lips together and closed his eyes for a few seconds.

"Heather and Joanna are gone, and I will live with that unimaginable reality for the rest of my life. But I'm alive, and they would want me to live. They would want me to follow

353

my dreams, fall in love, and do all the things they never got to do."

The muscles in his jaw flexed.

I stood. "That's the hardest part for you, isn't it? You can't figure out why I'm here. Why did God spare me despite my sinful trip with Isaac to Nashville? Well, I don't know either. And some days are easier than others, but I'm not wasting my chance, this gift, or blessing." I shrugged. "Maybe God likes Isaac. Maybe He made him just for me." I opened the door.

"If you leave—"

I turned and lost my resolve. My fists relaxed, as did my shoulders. With one blink, I released so many emotions that I'd been holding back. "If I leave, I want to believe that my family will come visit me and watch me do what I love. If I leave, I want to believe that I'm welcome home any time. If I leave, I know I'll never regret it because I'm not doing it for Isaac or anyone else. I'm doing it for me. God loves me unconditionally while allowing me to make my own decisions, even if they are mistakes. Can't you try to love me like He does?" I closed the door behind me.

WHEN MY SISTERS returned from the store, I told them over dinner about the stops Isaac and I made over six weeks away. My mom tried to restrain her smile as if she knew my dad wouldn't approve of her being happy for me.

"Are you getting married?" Gabby asked.

Eve shot me a smirk with wide eyes while Dad kept his gaze on the bowl of soup.

"Mom and Dad said Isaac needs to marry you before he

gets you pregnant." Gabby shrugged as if she didn't know that she was stirring up trouble. But she did. I could see the mischievous twinkle in her eyes.

"That's not exactly what we said," Mom corrected her.

"I don't want to get married. I'm too young."

"But you're going to live together?" Gabby's follow-up question stoked the tension.

I wanted to muzzle her.

"Yes," I said. "But you shouldn't be like me. You should find a nice boy who goes to church every week and wants to marry you before living with you." I shared a toothy grin with everyone at the table.

"You mean like Matt?" Gabby wiped a drop of soup from her chin. "I'd marry him."

"He's too old for you," Eve said.

"He's four years older than me. Isaac is six years older than Sarah." Gabby was too observant for her own good.

"Then you can marry him in four years," Eve said, earning matching scowls from Mom and Dad.

But I couldn't help but snort.

After dinner, I helped with dishes before calling Isaac's house.

"If you love your dad, you'll stay here tonight," Mom said as I dialed the number. She gave me a pleading look before joining my dad in the living room.

"Yes! Stay. Please!" Eve stood behind me, wrapping her arms around me so her lips were at my ear, and she whispered, "I have tequila."

I giggled. "Isaac's better than tequila."

"It's just one night. Stay and tell me all the ways he's better."

Violet answered the phone just as I twisted my head to look at Eve's hopeful smile.

"Hi. Is Isaac there?"

"He's in the shower, Sarah. I'll have him call you."

"It's fine. Just tell him I'm staying here, and I'll call him in the morning."

"That's wonderful to hear, sweetie. I'll tell him."

"Thanks, bye."

"Good night."

"Yay!" Eve clapped her hands. "Let's walk down to the creek."

"We'll get chewed up by mosquitoes," I said.

"Don't be such a baby." She pulled on my arm. "We're walking to the creek," she called to our parents.

"I'm going too!" Gabby barreled down the stairs.

"You can't. It's just me and Sarah," Eve said.

Gabby's lower lip pushed out as she tipped her chin down.

"You can come," I said, shoving my feet into my shoes.

Eve gave me an undecipherable look, so I grinned and shrugged. As we stepped outside, Gabby skipped ahead of us.

"How are we supposed to drink with her here?" Eve asked.

"Drink what? How were you going to sneak it out of the house?"

"It's not in the house. It's buried in a box by the creek," Eve said.

"Well, I didn't know."

"We can give her a sip," Eve said.

"No," I said. "She's fourteen."

"Almost fifteen," Eve countered. "One sip."

"She'll hold it over your head." I hopped onto a rock and then jumped off.

"Just the opposite. I'll hold it over hers." Eve laughed manically while looping her arm with mine.

When we arrived at the creek, Gabby picked up a rock and threw it into the water. "Are you getting your bottle of alcohol?"

Eve shot me a look.

Gabby glanced over her shoulder at us. "Sometimes I follow you and your friends."

"You're such a twerp. Have you told Mom or Dad?"

"Duh. Of course not," Gabby said.

Behind a fallen tree trunk, Eve dug up her box of alcohol and opened the lid, taking a big swig before passing it to me.

"Did you have sex with Isaac?" Gabby asked.

I choked on the tequila, spitting it out while Eve's hand flew to her mouth.

"What?" Gabby didn't crack a smile. "I'm not a baby. And Mom and Dad talked a lot about what they would do if you came home pregnant."

"Jeez, Gabbs ... you're such a little eavesdropping creep," Eve mumbled, taking another drink of tequila.

"What did they say they'd do?" I asked, stealing the bottle.

"They said they'd have to get rid of your desk to make room for a crib. Are you going to let me try that?" She eyed the bottle.

"No," I said.

"Just a sip," Eve said.

"Eve—" I started to protest.

Eve took the bottle, poured a tiny amount in the cap, and

handed it to Gabby. "It's going to burn your mouth, and you'll probably choke and spit it out."

Gabby wrinkled her nose. "Then why do you drink it?"

"Because if you drink enough of it, you feel really relaxed, like you don't have a care in the world. But we're not letting you drink enough to feel buzzed."

Keeping a sour expression, Gabby tipped the cap just enough to let the tequila touch her lips; then she licked them. "Yuck!"

We laughed.

"Gross!" She spat several times before returning to the creek to throw rocks into it.

"Are you pregnant?" Eve asked as we sat on the falling tree trunk.

"No." I laughed. "We use condoms."

"And it's good?" She smirked before tipping the bottle to her lips again.

"So good." A smile consumed my face.

"Does he go ... you know ..." she pointed between her legs. "Down there with his mouth?"

I closed my eyes and hummed with a nod. Then I replayed so many conversations I'd had with Heather about sex before I had it with Matt. I knew I would never stop missing Heather, but I had Eve, and she would be the person I called to share things—to make them feel real.

"How does it feel?"

I bit my lower lip.

"That good?"

I nodded.

"Do you have it a lot? Like every day? More than once a day?"

I laughed. Eve was so horny. *She* was the one our parents

needed to be concerned about getting pregnant. When I was her age, my focus wasn't nearly as much on sex.

"Tell me!" she giggled.

"It depends."

"On what?"

Again, I laughed. Eve was totally me.

"We have it a lot. Before we go to sleep, usually in the morning, too. Sometimes he wakes up in the middle of the night and ..." I blushed.

"And what?" Eve hung on my every word.

"And he puts his head ..." I pointed between my legs.

Eve's posture inflated along with her smile. "I'm *so* jealous. What about the shower? The truck. In public?"

"Stop!" I giggled.

"Just tell me."

"Yes. In the shower, but it's not easy. And yes, in the truck."

"Have you given him a blowjob?"

"Shh!" I covered her mouth with my hand.

The tequila was making her get louder.

"I heard that," Gabby said.

"We are done talking about me. How's Erin? Did you get all your school supplies?"

"Yes. I have a hundred number two pencils and a Trapper Keeper. Do you swallow it?"

"You're done." I snagged the bottle and cap from her. "Gabby, let's dip our toes in the water," I said, returning the bottle to the box and kicking dirt and brush over it.

"I've heard it tastes salty," Eve said with a giggle.

"Eve Marie Jacobson!" I pushed her off the tree trunk, and she rolled onto the ground laughing.

For the next hour, we splashed in the shallow water and

giggled, and for the first time in months, the world felt a little right again.

Hand-in-hand, we headed back to the house in the dark, knowing Mom and Dad wouldn't be happy with any of us, but we were in it together.

"We're going to miss you," Eve said, resting her head on my shoulder.

"So much," Gabby said, squeezing my hand a little tighter.

"I'll miss you too. But I'm not that far away. As long as Dad doesn't ban me from the house, I'll come back to visit."

"Maybe I can talk them into going to Nashville to watch you sing," Eve said.

I laughed. "Good luck with that. Can you see Dad listening to loud music that's not a hymn?"

We laughed together.

"When are you leaving?" Gabby asked.

"I don't know. I think as soon as we find a place to live."

A deep ache gripped my heart, yet my tummy felt a flutter of excitement. It was the good kind of fear.

My sisters fought over who was going to use the shower first. Eve was desperate to go to bed before Mom or Dad noticed that she was tipsy.

"Sarah, can you come in here for a second?" Mom asked just as I started up the stairs.

I sighed. Nothing they had to say would change my mind, even if they said I was never welcome home again

"Yeah?" I stepped into the living room, sitting on the arm of the sofa. My dad was sitting on the opposite end. He shoved notes into his Bible and closed it while my mom set her needlepoint aside and rocked in her chair.

"We don't approve of how you've chosen to behave with

a man six years older than you. And we don't want you to move to Nashville with him," she said.

I bowed my head and chewed on the inside of my cheek to hide my disappointment.

"But you're our daughter, and we love you no matter what choices you make. So if you insist on moving away, we hope you'll be smart about your choices. And we want you to know that you are always welcome here. If you ever need help, we are a call away. We hope Isaac will eventually do the right thing if you're going to stay together."

They hope he'll marry me.

I thought about Isaac telling me not to rock the boat. So instead of lecturing them on my dreams that didn't involve getting married right away and starting a family, I smiled and offered an easy nod. "Thank you."

Sometimes being a people-pleaser wasn't a bad thing. Perhaps a peaceful life existed somewhere in the middle.

I turned to head to my room but stopped after two steps. "I'm sorry," I said. "When I was in Nashville, and you did not know where I was, or if I was alive and safe, that must have been terrifying. I'm just ... really sorry."

Epilogue

Fleetwood Mac, "Landslide"

Ten Years Later

Isaac

"Mommy!" Heather pointed her tiny finger toward the television as I played the video from Sarah's first headlining concert in Kansas City.

We wouldn't let our three-year-old risk her hearing at concerts, so we hired a part-time nanny. But Heather loved watching the videos.

The tour bus cruised down the interstate toward Tulsa as my wife pulled Subway sandwiches from bags and set them on the table.

"That *is* your mommy," she said to Heather, grabbing her chubby hand and sucking her finger, which made Heather giggle.

"There's DADDY!" she screamed, seeing me appear on stage.

Sarah rolled her eyes.

I sang two songs with her: one I wrote called "My Favorite Sunday Morning," which she sang background, and one she wrote called "Into Sunflowers."

Heather was a daddy's girl, even if her mom was a famous musician and songwriter who was quickly becoming a household name.

"Let's have at least three more," I said as Sarah sat next to Heather's booster seat.

"Three more what?" she asked, focusing on unwrapping the sandwiches.

"Kids," I said, checking the lid on the blue sippy cup and then handing it to Heather.

Sarah shot me an unblinking expression, lips parted. "Uh ... are we moving from a part-time nanny to a full-time nanny?"

"Heck no. We've got this."

She chuckled. "*We?*"

"Yes. You'll work your butt off being the beloved Sunday Morning, and I'll take care of the kids."

"You're my manager," she said before taking a bite of her sandwich.

"I can do both."

She slowly chewed on more than just her sandwich, eyeing me the whole time as if I would break and say, "Just kidding!"

I wasn't kidding.

"Our parents will help. Our moms will *fight* over who gets to help."

She grinned, glancing up at the screen where we were singing together, each with a guitar in our hands. "I'll think about it," she murmured.

That was a yes, even if she wanted to pretend that she needed time to think.

Ten years earlier, I left Anakin with Sarah's sisters in a more tearful goodbye than I offered my parents. Then I bought us an old two-bedroom home in Nashville—a fixer-upper.

She wrote songs; I remodeled the bathroom and sanded the deck.

She made dinner, and I washed the dishes.

I was early to bed and early to rise.

She was up until the wee hours writing and ready to sleep until noon most days.

All I had to do was look at her, and she started removing her clothes. We made love the way we played music together —with an undying passion.

I took breaks from tending bar with Lenny to steal the stage, always singing Hall & Oates' "Sara Smile." But at home, I serenaded her with Sinatra's "Sunday."

I loved the memories we'd made.

After we finished our sandwiches, Sarah carried Heather to the back of the bus and read her a story before tucking her into bed while I took a shower.

"Sorry. I'm already done," I said with a grin when Sarah stepped into the bathroom.

She held a finger to her lips to silence me as she shut the door behind her.

"The bathroom on this tour bus wasn't built for two," I whispered.

She untied the bodice of her sundress and let it pool at

her feet while I dried my hair. My beautiful Sunday Morning slid her arms around my waist and gazed up at me in nothing but her skimpy underwear.

"And yet, we always seem to fit." She grinned.

I mirrored her smile. We fit perfectly. I knew it the day I saw her in church when the rest of the world thought she was going to marry my brother.

"Happy anniversary, baby," I said.

She bit her lower lip to suppress her giggle. We had two anniversaries: one from our first wedding at the Graceland Wedding Chapel (which her parents knew nothing about) and the other at her father's church.

"Speaking of babies," she whispered over my chest while kissing her way to my neck. "Let's make another one."

She didn't have to say it twice. I slipped my hand into the back of her underwear and kissed her.

Our love hurt a lot of people in the beginning, but I never felt an ounce of regret. Only gratitude.

Life had a way of working itself out.

THREE DAYS LATER, Sunday Morning took the stage for her second concert as the headliner.

Her parents had been at the Kansas City concert, but mine were front and center with me for the Tulsa concert— along with Matty and his wife.

Sarah sang her list with me joining her for our two songs, but she saved her only cover song for the last one. And I knew why she changed the order. The tears would be too overwhelming.

The lights dimmed with nothing more than a single spotlight on her, and the crowd delivered a chilling silence.

"It's been ten years to the day," she said into the mic before taking a breath to keep her composure, "since my best friend took her last breath." She strummed the guitar. "I promised to carry her with me forever." Her fingers continued caressing the strings. "I've held her through my failures, heartbreaks, successes, falling in love, getting married, and now I carry her in my daughter's name. While I love to play my own songs, I will always make an exception because this was Heather's favorite song. It's called 'Landslide.'"

I stepped as close to the stage as possible so she could see me and the Cadbury egg that I always unwrapped to make her smile instead of cry during Heather's song. But as I suspected, she didn't look at me that night while she sang.

She didn't look at anyone.

Sarah closed her eyes and played her guitar while singing "Landslide," letting all the tears fall down her face.

Holding the end of each line a little longer.

Letting every pause be a moment of reflection.

And when the crowd returned an applause that shook the whole venue, she opened her eyes, lower lip quivering as she fought for a shred of composure.

My dad touched my arm. When I glanced back, he handed me a clean, white hanky. I grinned, then I climbed onto the stage, took her guitar, and handed her the hanky.

She laughed through her tears while blotting her eyes. With my free hand, I laced my fingers with hers and led her off the stage.

One of the crew members took the guitar from me, and I faced her, seeing the pain in her eyes as raw as it was ten years earlier. I knew what she was thinking: *I don't deserve to be here.*

And as I did every year on the anniversary of the accident, I pressed my hands to her face and brushed my lips against hers while whispering, "But I'm really fucking glad you are."

The End

Acknowledgments

To four guys and a doodle, thank you for living this dream with me.

Thank you to my best friend and ride-or-die, Jyl, for being my Heather for over forty years.

Dad, thank you for teaching me that nostalgia is the best drug, especially when it's accompanied by great music.

Thank you to my favorite sidekick, Jenn, for everything. The list goes to infinity.

Thanks to my editing team—Leslie, Sarah, Monique, and Sian— for your hard work in meeting this deadline with me.

Georgana (my agent, publicist, and sounding board), thank you for flying to London for a cookbook and all the other awesome things you do.

These beautiful covers deserve special thanks to Jaime Burrow Photography for the gorgeous photo and to Boja99designs.

My readers, thank you for always taking a chance on my writing and being so generous with your time to share and review my stories. I adore you.

Also By
Jewel E. Ann

Standalone Novels

Idle Bloom

Undeniably You

Naked Love

Only Trick

Perfectly Adequate

Look The Part

When Life Happened

A Place Without You

Jersey Six

Scarlet Stone

Not What I Expected

For Lucy

What Lovers Do

Before Us

If This Is Love

Right Guy, Wrong Word

I Thought of You

Sunday Morning Series

Sunday Morning

The Apple Tree

Wildfire Series

From Air

From Nowhere

The Fisherman Series

The Naked Fisherman

The Lost Fisherman

Jack & Jill Series

End of Day

Middle of Knight

Dawn of Forever

One (*standalone*)

Out of Love (*standalone*)

Because of Her (*standalone*)

Holding You Series

Holding You

Releasing Me

Transcend Series

Transcend

Epoch

Fortuity (*standalone*)

About The Author

Jewel E. Ann is a *Wall Street Journal* and *USA Today* bestselling author. She's written over thirty novels, including LOOK THE PART, a contemporary romance, the JACK & JILL TRILOGY, a romantic suspense series; and BEFORE US, an emotional women's fiction story. With 10 years of flossing lectures under her belt, she took early retirement from her dental hygiene career to write mind-bending love stories. She's living her best life in Iowa with her husband, three boys, and a Goldendoodle.

Receive special offers and stay informed of new releases, sales, and exclusive stories:
www.jeweleann.com